How to Tame a Beast in Seven Days

Kerrelyn Sparks

St. Martin's Paperbacks

This is a work of fiction. All of the characters, organizations, and events portrayed in this novel are either products of the author's imagination or are used fictitiously.

HOW TO TAME A BEAST IN SEVEN DAYS

Copyright © 2017 by Kerrelyn Sparks.
Excerpt from *So I Married a Sorcerer* copyright © 2017 by Kerrelyn Sparks.

All rights reserved.

For information address St. Martin's Press, 175 Fifth Avenue, New York, NY 10010.

ISBN: 9781250108210

Our books may be purchased in bulk for promotional, educational, or business use. Please contact your local bookseller or the Macmillan Corporate and Premium Sales Department at 1-800-221-7945, ext. 5442, or by e-mail at MacmillanSpecialMarkets@macmillan.com.

Printed in the United States of America

St. Martin's Paperbacks edition / March 2017

St. Martin's Paperbacks are published by St. Martin's Press, 175 Fifth Avenue, New York, NY 10010.

10 9 8 7 6 5 4 3 2 1

To Michelle Grajkowski,
I'm grateful you're my agent
and honored that you're my friend.
You fought for this book.
Thank you, Warrior Princess.

AERTHLAN

Rupert's
Island

Great Western Ocean

Isle of Mist

Isle of Moon

Convent of the
Two Moons

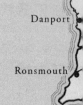

Danport

Ronsmouth

N

Prologue

❧

In another time on another world called Aerthlan, there are five kingdoms. Four of the kingdoms extend across a continent. There, the four kings thirst for war.

The fifth kingdom lies in the Great Western Ocean. It consists of two islands called Moon and Mist. There, the fishermen and traders rely on the two moons in the night sky to guide their boats safely home. Over time, the islanders began to pray to the twin moons, Luna and Lessa, and now they believe their goddesses are watching over them. The islanders and their queen live on the larger island of Moon. Only one person lives on the small Isle of Mist—the Seer.

The kings on the mainland refuse to bow to female gods. They worship the sun, a male god. They call their god the Light and their people the Enlightened. Anyone who denies their god is put to death.

Twice a year, the two moons align in the night sky. A child born on the night the moons embrace will be gifted with some sort of supernatural power. These children are called the Embraced. They are protected on the islands, but in danger on the mainland. The kings will not allow anyone to possess a power that they do not, so they dispatch assassins to kill the newly born Embraced. Parents who wish to save their child either lie about when the child was born or send the child secretly to the Isle of Moon where he or she will be safe.

And so our story begins on the Isle of Moon at the Convent of the Two Moons, where five young girls have been raised. They know nothing of their families. Nothing of their past. Nothing of the destiny in store for them.

They only know they are Embraced.

Chapter One

❧

Red as blood. Black as death.

The thoughts jumped into Luciana's mind the instant she spotted the red and black colored pebbles in her hand. Even the third pebble, marked with the number two, suddenly struck her as ominous. *Two deaths?* She quickly closed her fist around the Telling Stones to keep her companions from seeing them.

"Come now." Gwennore, who sat to her right, gave her a sympathetic smile. "It cannot be that bad."

"For sure," Brigitta agreed. "'Tis naught but a game. Remember last week when I picked the stone with the number seven, and ye said I would have seven suitors vying for my hand? 'Twas nonsense, but I still enjoyed the sound of it."

"Aye." Sorcha smirked. "Ye liked it better than the prophecy I gave yerself."

"That I would sprout seven whiskers on my chin?" Brigitta shuddered. "Thank the goddesses that hasn't happened."

"Neither have the seven suitors." Sorcha's eyes glinted with humor when Brigitta huffed and swatted at her arm.

"It doesn't matter," Maeve chimed in. "Why would any of us wish for seven suitors when we have one another?"

Gwennore patted Maeve on the knee. "Ye're only fifteen. In a year or so, ye could be changing yer mind."

"And there ye go again, treating me like a baby. I'll be sixteen in a few weeks, and then I'll be only one year younger than yerself." She lifted her chin. "Besides, I wouldn't care if I had a hundred suitors. I'm staying here at the convent with all of you till the end of my days."

"Aye," Sorcha muttered. "And we may reach the end of our days afore Luciana shows us the stones she has picked."

Luciana sighed, still reluctant to open her hand. Out of the forty pebbles contained in the wooden bowl, only one had been painted black. And only two red. She and her friends had painted most of the pebbles with pretty rainbow colors or simple numbers. Since the pebbles were supposed to tell their future, they'd been clever enough to stack the odds in their own favor.

"Why the worried face?" Gwennore asked. "Have any of our predictions e'er come true?"

"Yers have," Maeve reminded her. "One time I picked the pink, yellow, and number three stones. Then ye said I would find three pink seashells on a sunny day, and it happened the very next morn."

Gwennore snorted. "Because ye went to the beach to look for them. 'Tis the same as I have always said. We make our own futures."

"That's not always true." Sorcha frowned. "Did any of us ask to be left here as babes, rejected by our families?"

Luciana winced at the harsh reminder. Like the other girls, she'd been an infant when she'd been dropped off at the convent. According to Mother Ginessa, they were all orphans. But did that mean they had no family at all?

Gwennore's white-blond hair, lavender-blue eyes, and slightly pointed ears could only mean that she possessed

some elfin blood. Did she have family in the elfin kingdom of Woodwyn? Sorcha had fiery red hair like the fierce
warriors from Norveshka. And Brigitta looked similar to
the people from the coastal kingdom of Tourin.

Luciana suspected they had been abandoned because
they were Embraced. But whether they had family or not,
they still had each other, so at a young age they had declared themselves sisters. They were their own family, and
the one prophecy they had all agreed upon was that the
Convent of the Two Moons would always be their home.

Each day, there was an hour before dinner that the nuns
had set aside for quiet meditation. Luciana and her sisters
had tried when they were young, but whenever they had
formed a circle on the floor in their room, attempting to
meditate, invariably someone made a funny face and the
others started giggling. It didn't take long before pillows
started flying and the air was thick with goose feathers.

Luciana, the oldest and eight years old at the time, was
told that she and her sisters should invent a quiet game that
would leave their room neat and tidy and not disturb the
nuns, who were meditating nearby.

Since the convent was located on the Isle of Moon, there
were several beaches close by. Early one morn, the girls
had accompanied a few nuns to the nearest beach, where
they had dug for clams. And while they had worked, the
nuns had talked about the latest prophecy from the Seer.
He had predicted more wars on the mainland. More death
and destruction.

Not surprising, Luciana had thought. In her eight years
of life, she had never heard of peace on the mainland. Fortunately, the four mainland kingdoms were so busy fighting one another that the island kingdom was mostly
forgotten. And the two islands, Moon and Mist, never
fought each other. What would be the point? There was
only one inhabitant on the small Isle of Mist—the Seer.

And that was when the idea had struck. Why not invent a game where she and her younger sisters could pretend to be Seers? After collecting forty pebbles, they had decorated them with colors or numbers. Since most of the nuns spent their days in the workroom translating and illustrating books, there was always a supply of colored paints on hand.

The nuns had given them an old wooden bowl from the kitchen. After the paint had dried, the girls deposited the pebbles in the bowl, then draped a cloth on top. To play the game, each girl would reach into the bowl, grab a few Telling Stones, and then her future would be told.

And now, eleven years later, Luciana clutched three of the stones in her hand as a chill shuddered down her spine. Why would three harmless pebbles unnerve her? Prophecy was not her gift. Or curse, as she was more apt to put it.

"Hurry," Sorcha told her. "I want to have my turn afore the dinner bell rings."

"O Great Seer"—Brigitta repeated the line they spoke before each prediction—"reveal to us the secrets of the Telling Stones."

Luciana opened her hand to show the pebbles. Two of her companions frowned. The other two winced.

Like the others, Maeve quickly adopted a hopeful expression. "Perhaps the black stone refers to yer lovely black hair."

"I think 'tis sadly obvious what the stones foretell," Luciana began, her words causing apprehension to steal over her sisters' faces. She affected a bright, cheery smile. "The number two means that in two weeks I will meet a tall and handsome stranger."

"Of course!" Brigitta clapped her hands.

Luciana pointed at the red stone. *Not blood.* "He will have red . . ."

"Freckles?" Sorcha wrinkled her nose. "Like me self?"

"Hair. Beautiful hair like yers." Luciana motioned to the black stone. "And he will have a black . . ." *Heart?* She shoved that thought aside as she set the stones on the floor. "A black horse."

"Excellent!" Gwennore nodded. "Whose turn is next?"

"Mine." Sorcha slipped her hand under the cloth. The pebbles clattered against one another as she rummaged through them. When she withdrew her hand, fisted tightly around some stones, the wind picked up outside.

Maeve closed her eyes briefly. "A storm is brewing over the Great Western Ocean and headed our way."

This was one prediction that Luciana felt sure would come to pass, for Maeve was somehow connected to the sea. "We should close the shutters."

"But first ye must tell my fortune," Sorcha insisted, opening her hand to reveal four pebbles. "O Great Seer, reveal to us the secrets of the Telling Stones."

Yellow, green, one, and three.

"In one year ye will meet a tall and handsome stranger," Luciana began.

Maeve groaned. "Why do ye always have us meet tall and handsome strangers?"

"Would ye prefer a short and ugly one?" Gwennore asked.

Maeve huffed. "Why must we meet a man at all?"

"Because I'm not keen on marrying a squirrel," Sorcha muttered.

"We're not marrying," Maeve argued. "We're staying here forever as sisters."

"I know," Luciana admitted. "I just like to pretend we'll experience exciting adventures and true love."

Sorcha lifted her hand with the four pebbles. "And?"

"He'll have blond hair and green eyes," Luciana said.

Sorcha nodded. "Very good. And the number three?"

Luciana bit her lip, considering. "He'll have three . . ."

"Teeth," Gwennore said, her eyes twinkling with mischief.

Sorcha glared at her, while everyone else grinned.

"He'll give yerself a necklace of three precious stones to demonstrate his love and devotion," Luciana finished.

Sorcha smiled. "Ye always give the best predict—" A blast of wind shot through the windows, whisking the cloth off the bowl of Telling Stones. Drops of rain blew in and splattered onto the wooden floor.

"I'll get the shutters." Luciana scrambled to her feet.

"I'll help ye." Sorcha dropped her pebbles back into the bowl as she stood.

When Luciana unlatched the door, a gust of wind whisked it open. Sorcha helped her pull it shut as they stepped onto the covered portico that bordered the eastern side of the courtyard. The wind whipped at their braided hair and tangled their long skirts about their legs.

Luciana stepped into the courtyard to peer up at the thick gray clouds. Even though there should be a few hours of sunlight left, the sky was rapidly growing dark. A fat drop of rain plopped onto her cheek, then suddenly the clouds released a deluge.

"Hurry!" She jumped back beneath the portico while Sorcha ran to the window on the right side of the door.

A clap of thunder sounded in the distance as Luciana rushed to the window on the left. She caught a glimpse of her sisters inside, lighting candles and drying the floor.

The bell outside the convent clanged wildly, distracting her from her task. At first she assumed the noise was caused by the wind, but then a male voice shouted beyond the thick wooden gate. A visitor, now? Perhaps he was a poor traveler who sought refuge from the storm.

Two nuns scurried across the stone-paved courtyard to meet the stranger, their cream-colored woolen gowns soaked by the time they reached the grated lookout hole in the gate. Luciana couldn't make out their words over the howling of the wind. When the nuns opened the gate, a man tromped into the large courtyard, leading a horse.

He was a tall man with a large floppy hat pulled low against the storm. With the dim light and heavy rain, Luciana couldn't see him well, but he moved like an older man who carried a heavy weight on his broad shoulders. While he tethered his horse to the nearby post, a covered wagon slowly rolled through the gate.

After closing the gate, the two nuns rushed down the portico on the western side of the courtyard till they reached the last door that led to the office of Mother Ginessa, the leader of the convent.

This was strange, Luciana thought. The merchants who came to collect finished books usually did so in the morning, and they would never come in the rain, when the water could destroy the beautifully copied and illustrated books that the sisters were famous for. Their books, transcribed in all four mainland languages, were considered treasures throughout the known world, and the money earned kept the convent well maintained and the nuns well fed and clothed.

Two men descended from the driver's bench of the covered wagon, and the man with the floppy hat talked to them as they circled to the back of the wagon.

A flurry of movement brought Luciana's attention back to Mother Ginessa's room. The two nuns had exited and were dashing south, apparently headed for the kitchens that lay beyond the chapel and graveyard.

Mother Ginessa left her room and hurried down the portico to where the man was waiting. He removed his hat in greeting, and to Luciana's surprise, Mother Ginessa curtsied. Not a merchant then. The man must be a noble.

A flash of lightning lit up the sky, allowing Luciana a better look at the man. He was dressed all in black.

Black. A clap of thunder broke overhead, and the wind blasted more rain at Luciana. She turned her back. *Think nothing of it,* she admonished herself. Many men wore black.

She closed the shutters, then held them still with one hand while she turned the sharp hook into place to latch them shut. It was normally an easy task, but the wind was rattling the shutters so badly that she rammed the hook down with too much force and pricked her thumb.

With a wince, she stepped back and looked at the blossoming dot of blood. *Red.*

A sudden noise made her spin around. Her heart stilled as she realized what the two men had just removed from the wagon and dropped onto the courtyard. A black coffin.

Red as blood. Black as death.

"Come on!" Sorcha unlatched the door to their room, and the wind whipped it open with enough force that it banged against the inner wall.

Luciana followed her inside, and together they pushed the door shut and shot the bolt. The room was darker now with the shutters closed. The light of four candlesticks cast flickering shadows on the whitewashed walls.

"Whew." Sorcha brushed damp red curls back from her face, and Brigitta handed her and Luciana towels.

Luciana dried her face, then winced at the splotches of blood she'd left on the cream-colored linen.

"Ye're injured?" Gwennore asked.

"Only a prick of my thumb." Luciana pressed the towel against the small puncture.

A crack of lightning sounded outside, followed quickly by the rumble of thunder.

Sorcha patted her hair dry. "I wonder if the visitors will be joining us for dinner."

The three girls who had remained inside stared at her.

"Visitors?" Gwennore asked. "Who are they?"

Sorcha shrugged. "I haven't seen them afore. There was a man in charge and two servants."

Maeve frowned. "He'd better not be one of yer tall and handsome strangers."

"He's a nobleman," Luciana said. "Mother Ginessa curtsied to himself."

The other girls gaped. Usually, only book merchants came to the convent.

"The servants were driving a covered wagon," Sorcha continued, then dropped her voice to a dramatic whisper. "And ye won't believe what was inside. A coffin!"

The other girls gasped just as a booming crack of thunder sounded overhead.

"May Luna and Lessa protect us." Brigitta lifted her hands to her chest, thumbs pressed against forefingers to form two circles, a gesture of supplication to the twin moon goddesses.

As the other girls made the sign of the moons, Luciana peered at her injured thumb. The bleeding had stopped, thank the goddesses, but her nerves were becoming increasingly tense. The arrival of a coffin did not bode well. It had been three years since one of the nuns had died. Three years of peace from her accursed gift.

A pounding on the door made them all spin around.

"Open the door, please," the voice outside called. "This is Sister Fallyn."

Sorcha pulled back the bolt, then unlatched the door, carefully jumping back as the wind slammed the door open.

Sister Fallyn's gown of cream-colored wool was soaked and smelled like a wet sheep.

"Please come in from the rain," Brigitta urged her.

The young nun shook her head. "I must not tarry. I'm to take Luciana to Mother Ginessa's office."

Luciana's breath caught. The nobleman was there.

Sister Fallyn looked her over and clucked her tongue. "Heavenly goddesses, yer hair is a wild and tangled mess. Ye should braid it again afore ye meet—" She winced.

"Meet . . . ?" Luciana gripped the bloodstained towel as a sense of foreboding pressed down on her. Something was about to happen, something she wasn't sure she wanted.

Sister Fallyn peered over her shoulder at Mother Ginessa's office and mumbled to herself, "Perhaps she should know afore, so it won't come as such a shock . . ."

Luciana stepped back. Thunder rumbled overhead, making the air around her feel charged with tension. The skin on the back of her neck tingled.

Sister Fallyn turned to face her. "Aye, 'tis best to tell ye now. The man who just arrived is yer father. And he's come to take ye away."

Luciana gasped. The towel fell from her hands and fluttered to the floor. *A father?* She looked at her sisters, and her heart clenched at the sight of their stunned expressions. They must have heard the same thing she had. Even so, she didn't want to believe it. "Nay. I don't have a father."

"That's right!" Maeve latched on to Luciana's right arm. "She's an orphan. We all are. Mother Ginessa said so."

Brigitta took hold of Luciana's left arm. "She's not going away. Her home is with us."

Sister Fallyn sighed. "I know how close ye are to one another, but there is no help for it. Luciana's father has the right to take her with himself."

Luciana swallowed hard. "How can I have a father?"

With a grimace, Sorcha muttered under her breath, "Mother Ginessa lied to us."

The other girls gasped, and Sister Fallyn quickly raised her hands. "Don't judge her harshly. She was only doing what Luciana's father asked her to do. He wanted Luciana to be raised as an orphan, so she wouldn't wait her whole life for a reunion that would ne'er happen."

Luciana stiffened as if she'd been slapped on the face. "Ye mean he didn't plan to e'er come back for me self?"

Sister Fallyn winced. "I'm only making matters worse. Come along, so ye can hear what yer father has to say."

And just like that, with a few words from her father, everything would be resolved? All these years her father had been alive. *Nineteen* years. How could nineteen years of being unwanted suddenly disappear as if they'd never happened? Anger swelled inside her. "Why should I see him? He abandoned me."

"That's right." Maeve tightened her grip on Luciana's arm. "She's staying with us."

"He's yer father." Sister Fallyn motioned impatiently with her hand. "Come now. Show some respect. Don't leave himself waiting."

Respect? Luciana's anger twisted in her gut. How could she respect a father who had never planned to return for her? She should reject him, just as he had rejected her. He should feel the pain—

A twinge of shame pricked at her. Since when did she knowingly try to inflict pain on anyone? She'd been raised better than that. Even though it was not her parents who had raised her. "Is my mother alive, too?"

Sister Fallyn sighed. "I don't know. Ye'll have to ask yer father."

"She's not seeing him," Brigitta cried. "She's not leaving us."

Luciana's eyes filled with tears. How could she not remain with her sisters, as much as she loved them? But if she refused to see her father, he might leave and never come back. She might lose her only chance to meet him.

"Are ye not curious about himself?" Gwennore asked.

She *was* curious. But what would she say to a father she'd never known? *Why did ye not want me?* Was it because she was Embraced? Had he sent her here to protect her? But why make her believe she was an orphan? He could have come to visit her. He could still have been a father to her. But he had completely rejected her.

And why did he suddenly want to take her away? This was the only way of life she'd ever known. Her sisters were her family.

"Are the rest of us orphans?" Sorcha demanded. "Or was that a lie, too?"

Sister Fallyn turned pale as she hesitated. "I don't know. But I do know this—if Mother Ginessa lied to us, then she had a very good reason for doing so."

"Perhaps she was protecting us," Gwennore suggested. "Because we're Embraced."

Sorcha huffed. "I don't care what the excuse might be, I don't like being lied to!"

Luciana took a deep breath, her decision made. "I would know the truth." *No matter how much it hurts.*

As she stepped toward the door, Maeve and Brigitta reluctantly released their grip on her arms. She stopped at the door and looked back at her adopted sisters.

Sorcha still looked angry. Gwennore attempted to smile, while Brigitta sniffed. Maeve looked so young and lost with the tears streaming down her face that Luciana thought her heart would break in two. As the oldest, she'd been the one to dry Maeve's tears when she'd scraped a knee or hold her in the middle of the night when she'd had a bad dream.

"Chee-ana," Maeve whispered, using the shortened version she'd called Luciana when she'd been too young to manage her full name.

"I'll come back," she assured them. Somehow, she would convince her father not to take her with him. She needed to stay with the only family she'd ever known.

Chapter Two

❧

As Sister Fallyn scurried across the courtyard, Luciana followed at a slower pace, heedless of the heavy drops of rain pelting her head and shoulders. No doubt she would look like a drowned rat by the time she met her father.

Did it matter what he thought of her? A rebellious streak in her wanted to answer no, but she knew herself better than that. Whether it was her natural demeanor or a result of growing up dependent on the generosity of nuns, she didn't know, but she had always been the sort of child who was eager to please. She simply hated to disappoint.

The wind seemed to mock them, shoving them back a step for every four they took. She turned her face away from the stinging rain and slowed to a stop when she spotted the two servants carrying the coffin into the chapel.

A streak of lightning lit up the sky so brightly she squeezed her eyes shut. When she opened them, a movement and flash of color drew her attention to the graveyard. Through the sheet of rain, she detected a woman wandering among the gravestones, her head covered with a sheer black veil. Her gown looked expensive—a rich red brocade.

Thunder cracked overhead just as Luciana was struck

with a sudden realization. Even though the woman looked as solid as Sister Fallyn, her skirt was not moving with the wind. Her red gown and black veil were dry. *Red as blood. Black as death.*

The inhabitant of the coffin had not remained inside.

Luciana sucked in a long breath. Her gift was still with her.

"Luciana!" Sister Fallyn cried out. "Why on Aerthlan are ye standing there in the rain?"

She glanced at the nun, who had reached the shelter of the portico, then looked back at the woman in red. The ghost must have heard Sister Fallyn, for she had turned toward them. She lifted her veil to uncover her face.

Luciana gasped.

It was her face. Automatically, she lifted her hands to form the sign of the twin moons. May the goddesses protect her. How could this spirit look exactly like her? Was this some sort of premonition that she would soon be dead?

But no, the ghost seemed real.

"Hurry!" Sister Fallyn yelled once more, and Luciana lifted her rain-soaked skirts to run toward her.

The nun shook her head disapprovingly. "Heavens, ye look like ye took a swim in the ocean."

"I—I'm fine." Luciana glanced back at the graveyard. Her look-alike ghost was gone, thank the goddesses.

Sister Fallyn knocked on Mother Ginessa's door, then opened it slightly. "I've brought herself."

Luciana's heart pounded so loudly she couldn't hear Mother Ginessa's response.

Sister Fallyn opened the door. "Go inside now."

This was it. Luciana brushed back wet tendrils of hair that had become plastered to her cheeks and hooked them behind her ears. Steeling her nerves, she stepped inside.

The room was dark, lit only by a candle on Mother Ginessa's desk and the low fire in the stone hearth that illuminated the bottom half of a large man. His shoulders and face were still in shadow, but Luciana heard his quick intake of breath.

She attempted a curtsy. She'd never had a reason to do one before, so her execution was a bit wobbly.

"Luciana," a deep male voice whispered.

She stilled. He knew her name? Had he always known it, or had Mother Ginessa told it to him a few minutes ago?

"Amazing," he said. "You look just like your sister."

Sister? Was that the ghost? Luciana shivered.

"By the goddesses, child, ye're soaked through." Mother Ginessa drew her closer to the hearth. "And yer hands are like ice. We cannot have ye catching a cold."

"I'll build up the fire." The man turned toward the hearth and added a log.

Mother Ginessa wrapped a woolen shawl around Luciana's shoulders, then used the edge to pat her face dry.

Luciana's gaze met Mother Ginessa's. *Why did ye ne'er tell me?* she asked with her eyes.

Mother Ginessa pressed her warm hands against Luciana's cold cheeks. "'Twill be all right. Now sit yerself by the fire. I have some wine warming on the brazier."

Luciana perched on a leather-covered footstool, her gaze venturing to the man nearby. He was leaning over, using a poker to coax the fire into a brighter blaze. The flames illuminated his face. A long straight nose, wrinkles around his eyes as if he'd spent too much time squinting into a bright sun, a trimmed beard with more gray in it than black. His hair, almost entirely gray, was tied with a strip of leather at the nape of his neck.

He continued to jab at the fire as if he knew she needed time to adjust to his presence. She attempted to feel some sort of connection . . . but he was a stranger.

He settled in an armchair across from her and leaned forward, his elbows propped on his knees. His eyes were a sharp blue, as if age had not diminished his sight or intelligence. "Please allow me to introduce myself. I am your father, Lucas Vintello, from the kingdom of Eberon, where I hold the title of the Duke of Vindalyn."

Luciana stiffened so suddenly she nearly slid off the narrow footstool where the leather had been made slick by her wet gown. She righted herself before he could grab her. He was a duke? Lucas? Had she been named after him?

He lowered his hand once he saw she was steady. "No doubt, my arrival has come as a great shock." He gripped his hands together so tightly his knuckles turned white.

He was nervous, too, she thought, and that realization made her feel more at ease. She lifted her gaze to meet his eyes. They were glimmering with unshed tears.

"Luciana," he said softly. "I want you to know that I have always kept you in my heart. I've prayed for you every day, and I am so . . . *happy* to see you again."

Her heart swelled with a longing that threatened to push aside her resentment. But not quite all of it. For why would a loving father abandon a child?

"Mother Ginessa has been telling me how well you've done with your studies," he continued, glancing toward the nun who was busily filling two goblets. "She says you're proficient in all four of the mainland languages. And I know how well you can write and draw."

"Aye, that he does," Mother Ginessa agreed as she handed him and Luciana each a goblet of warmed wine. "Remember how surprised ye were when someone purchased the first book ye transcribed and illustrated?"

Luciana curled her hands around the warm goblet as she gave the duke a questioning look. She'd completed her first book two years ago. As a practice exercise, it had clearly been inferior to the works produced by the more experienced nuns at the convent.

He nodded, beaming proudly. "I have everything you've

done. Even the drawings you did as a child. Mother Ginessa sent them, along with reports on how you were faring." His smile faded. "Of course, I had to keep them secret."

Why? What was wrong with her? Luciana took a gulp of wine and nearly choked. It was much stronger than the watered-down wine she and her sisters usually drank.

"Are you all right?" the duke asked.

"Aye." She set the goblet on the stone floor with a clunk. "Nay, I am not," she corrected herself and lifted her chin to face him. "I don't understand why I am a secret. Why did ye send me self here as a wee babe? If ye truly care, why did ye ne'er come back for me?"

"Luciana," Mother Ginessa fussed. "Ye shouldn't—"

The duke lifted a hand to silence the nun as he shot her an irritated look. "Why does she have an accent? She's of noble blood, yet she speaks like an islander."

Luciana winced. Her first time to open her mouth and she was a disappointment. *Why should ye care?* a rebellious streak in her mind hissed. *Ye don't plan to leave with himself.*

Mother Ginessa huffed with exasperation. "She was raised here. Of course she speaks like an islander. Would ye prefer that she'd grown up standing out as different, without e'er knowing a reason why?"

With a sigh, the duke set his goblet on a nearby table. "You make a valid point, but I didn't anticipate this problem. I assumed she would speak like an Eberoni, since the islands and Eberon share the same language. She'll have to lose the accent within a fortnight. Can she do that?"

Mother Ginessa nodded slowly. "Aye, I believe so. She's very bright—"

"And I'm right here," Luciana added, growing increasingly annoyed that she was being discussed like a codfish at the local market. "Yer Grace—"

"You should call me Father."

She opened her mouth but couldn't bring herself to say it. "I appreciate ye remembering me self after nineteen years, but I see no reason to be changing. I speak like an islander because this is my home. I have no wish to leave."

"Luci—" Mother Ginessa began but hushed when the duke lifted a hand.

"I can understand why you're somewhat . . . distrustful, since it must look like I abandoned you. But I never forgot you, Luciana. Not for a moment." His eyes flared with emotion as he pressed a fist to his damp coat. "Giving you up was like having part of my heart ripped from my chest."

He seemed so sincere, Luciana blinked back tears. "Then why? Why did ye want rid of me?"

"My dear child." He clasped her hands in his own. "I never wanted rid of you. Even when your mother begged me to send you here, it was the hardest thing I've ever done."

"My mother? Is she alive?"

A pained look swept across his face. He released her hands and with haunted eyes turned to gaze at the fire.

You killed her.

The soft voice carried across the room like the wisp of a breeze.

Luciana looked sharply across the room. There, beyond Mother Ginessa's desk, stood the look-alike ghost.

The woman in red stared back, her mouth twisting into a knowing smirk. "So you can hear me, too."

Luciana glanced at Mother Ginessa and the duke. Neither of them seemed aware of the new presence in the room.

"Don't pretend you can't see or hear me." The ghost moved closer, her steps gliding silently over the wooden floor. "You obviously have the same gift I had." She shrugged. "Hardly surprising, given the fact we're twins."

Luciana swallowed hard. No wonder they looked identical. But how could she have shared a womb with another soul and not know it? Wouldn't she have felt a terrible loss as an infant? Perhaps that was why she'd bonded so fiercely with Brigitta, who was only six months younger than herself. And why she felt so close to all her adopted sisters. She'd needed to fill a void.

Her sister chuckled. "You didn't know, did you? That there were two of us."

Two. Luciana remembered the third Telling Stone.

"I was the firstborn," the ghost continued. "I was the one Papa wanted to keep. While you . . ." Her nose wrinkled with disgust. "You were sent to this wretched rat hole. Just punishment, I would say, for killing our mother."

Not knowing how to react, Luciana simply grew still. After being raised in a convent that valued peace and harmony, she was not accustomed to being on the receiving end of such cruel words. Could it be true that she was somehow to blame for her mother's death?

She didn't know what to believe, but one thing was certain. She couldn't converse with her dead sister without revealing her gift. Mother Ginessa knew about it, but Luciana wasn't sure how much the duke knew. Besides, what could she tell him? *I just met my sister and she hates me?*

She leaned toward the duke, who was still gazing forlornly at the fire, apparently lost in painful memories. "Ye mentioned afore that I look just like my sister?"

He covered his mouth to suppress a sob. "Poor Tatiana."

Luciana glanced at her sister. Even their names sounded alike. "What happened to herself?"

Tatiana snorted. "I died, obviously. Not too sharp, are you?"

With his shoulders sagging, the duke wiped tears from his face. "Poor, beautiful Tatiana. To have died so young."

"You see?" Tatiana moved closer. "See how he grieves for me? I'm the one he cares for."

Mother Ginessa crossed her arms. "It seems very chilly all of a—" She blinked, then cut a questioning look at Luciana, who nodded very slightly. With a wary glance around the room, the nun made the sign of the two moons.

"How did my sister die?" Luciana asked the duke.

"Struck down by a plague," he grumbled. "The king demanded we go to his palace in Ebton. On the journey there, we stayed at an inn in the port of Ronsmouth. Tatiana and I both became ill, though she was suffering much more than I. Keeping our identities a secret, I hired a vessel to bring us to the Isle of Moon. I'd learned from my correspondence with Mother Ginessa that you have a gifted healer here in the convent."

"Aye." Mother Ginessa nodded. "That we do."

Another tear rolled down his cheek. "We were too late. My poor Tatiana died on the voyage."

Luciana felt a surge of sympathy for him. He obviously loved his daughter. "I'm so sorry for yer loss."

He gave her a sad smile and patted her hand.

"You should feel sorry for *me*!" Tatiana stomped a foot, but it made no noise. "It's terribly unfair. I was so looking forward to showing off my new gowns at court."

"I'm sorry you didn't get to meet her," the duke told Luciana. "You would have loved her."

Luciana glanced at her sister's pouting face, then decided to change the subject. "Can ye tell me about my mother? What was she like?"

His eyes took on a faraway look. "She was the world to me. It was an arranged marriage, of course, ordered by the king, but Ariana was so clever, so lovely, so kind and pure of heart, I couldn't help but fall madly in love with her."

Luciana smiled.

"There." He pointed at her, his eyes glistening with

tears. "She smiled just like that. And she had beautiful black hair and sea-green eyes. You and Tatiana resemble her greatly, although you both have blue eyes like me."

"I obviously inherited the greater share of their intelligence," Tatiana boasted.

Luciana ignored her sister and asked, "Can ye tell me what happened to my mother?"

He shut his eyes briefly. "She died. Two days after birthing you and Tatiana. You and your sister were born on the night the moons embrace, but of course we didn't want anyone to know that. Even though Ariana suffered greatly, she held on for two more days, so we could convince everyone that you were born at a later date. Her last request was that I send you away—"

"Why?" Luciana winced at the sound of her sister's snickering.

"My dear child." He took her hands in his. "We did our best to conceal the time of your birth, but there was no way to hide the fact that there were two of you."

"Twin girls are considered a blessing here on the island," Mother Ginessa explained, "but I'm afraid it is quite different on the mainland."

"Twins are considered an abomination, caused by the twin moons. Female twins are even worse, for they represent the goddesses themselves." The duke squeezed Luciana's hands. "The only way to keep you both alive was to separate you. We could never let anyone know that you're twins."

"So ye sent me self here to protect me?" Luciana sighed. "But why let me think ye were dead? Could ye not have come to visit?"

"Repeated visits here would have aroused the suspicions of the king's spies. I couldn't risk them finding out about you, not when it would mean your death."

She winced. "Is it truly that dangerous?"

"I'm afraid so," he replied. "In your studies, have you learned about the religion of the Eberoni?"

Luciana nodded. "They worship the sun god called the Light, so they are called the Enlightened. The head of the church is the Eberoni king."

"Exactly. So anyone who refuses to follow the king's religion is considered a blasphemer and put to death."

Luciana sat back. "He would kill someone for worshipping the goddesses? Why? Luna and Lessa are helpful. They guide the men home from the sea."

Mother Ginessa raised her hands to make the sign of the moons. "The Eberoni fail to understand the loving care the goddesses bestow upon us."

The duke snorted. "It has nothing to do with love or understanding. It's about power. As long as the king is the head of the church, he alone can decide who has offended his god and deserves death."

Luciana regarded the duke curiously. "Then ye do not follow his religion?"

"I do, actually." A corner of his mouth lifted with a wry look. "As does everyone in Eberon who values his head. You will have to, also, when you return with me."

Luciana stiffened. "Ye expect me to change my beliefs?"

"I won't tell you what to believe, but for your own safety you have to at least pretend to be Enlightened."

"Nay." She shook her head. "I cannot go. I would have to give up my beliefs, my home, and even my sisters."

He tilted his head. "Sisters?"

"Aye. I have four sisters here." Luciana's eyes misted with tears. "I belong with them. We made a vow that we would remain together forever."

The duke watched her sadly. "You . . . truly have no wish to come home with me?"

"My home is here. I cannot leave my faith. Or my sisters. I am the oldest. They need me self."

He rubbed his brow, frowning. "And what if I need you?"

Tatiana snorted. "Why would Papa need you? You're as coarse as a peasant, and your accent is simply horrid."

Luciana sighed. "I don't want ye to think I'm ungrateful for yer visit. I hope ye'll come back often."

He leaned toward her, watching her closely. "Have you been happy here? That is what I prayed for every day."

She blinked back tears. "Aye. I've been very happy."

Mother Ginessa rested a hand on Luciana's shoulder. "Luciana and her sisters have been a delight to us who ne'er hoped to have children of our own."

Luciana smiled up at the nun. "We've been blessed to have a loving home."

The duke exhaled slowly as he leaned back in his chair. "All right, then. I will leave you here."

Luciana grinned. "Thank you!"

Mother Ginessa stepped back, clearly stunned. "Bu—but, Yer Grace. Ye told me earlier that ye need her—"

"No. She's happy here. And safe." He rose to his feet. "I stand by my decision. When the ground dries, we'll bury Tatiana, then I'll be on my way."

Luciana stood, growing increasingly concerned by the frantic look on Mother Ginessa's face. "What is wrong?"

The duke took hold of her shoulders and gazed at her with tears in his eyes. "Luciana, live a long and happy life for me. That is all I can ask."

"Ye'll come see me self again, aye?" Her heart dropped when he lowered his hands and looked away. Was she going to be rejected once again?

Mother Ginessa paced across her office, then turned with a defiant look. "Nay. I will not have this. Ye will tell yer daughter—"

"She *is* my daughter," he ground out. "That means the decision is mine."

"Nay, the decision is hers!" Mother Ginessa pointed at Luciana. "This is not the mainland where the men order the women about. Yer daughter is well educated and perfectly capable of making a decision for herself."

"I cannot ask her to do this for me!"

Mother Ginessa snorted. "Ye felt fine with it less than an hour ago."

"I was wrong!" He grimaced, clenching his fists. "I thought I could do it, but I dare not. I've lost one daughter. I cannot risk losing the other."

"Why would ye lose me?" Luciana asked, but he shook his head, refusing to answer.

Mother Ginessa scoffed. "Clearly ye don't understand the way yer daughter has been raised. Here, in the Kingdom of Moon and Mist, a queen is our ruler. Women run the fish market while their husbands are away fishing. Women manage the shops while their men are away on their trading ships. Ye will tell yer daughter everything she needs to know, and then *she* will make the decision—"

"I will not endanger her," he insisted.

"Then ye endanger yerself!" the nun yelled. "If ye go back without her, ye'll be executed."

Luciana gasped.

The duke gritted his teeth. "You overstep yourself, madam."

Mother Ginessa merely shrugged. "My convent, my rules."

"My daughter, my decision."

"Nay." Luciana lifted her chin. "Ye will tell me. I have the right to know."

He sighed. "You're so much like your sister." His mouth lifted with a wry smile. "Every bit as stubborn."

"Stubborn? Ha!" Tatiana turned her back.

Luciana sat on the footstool. "Tell me everything."

With a groan, he settled back in the armchair. "All right, then. What do you know of Eberon?"

"Of the four mainland kingdoms, it is the closest to the islands," Luciana began. "'Tis named after two major rivers—the Ebe River in the north and the Ron River to the south. The capital is Ebton, which lies on the Ebe—"

"Very good," he interrupted. "And the history?"

"Seventy years ago, the nobles rose up in rebellion against a tyrant king. The leader was the Earl of Benwick. He became king and founded the royal House of Benwick."

The duke nodded. "Then the king rewarded those who had helped him by giving them tracts of land. His greatest ally, Allesandro Vintello, became the Duke of Vindalyn. He received a large amount of land far to the south."

"He was yer ancestor?" Luciana asked.

The duke smiled. "Yours, too. The land was considered too dry and too far away from the royal court in Ebton. Nobles usually prefer to be closer. But Allesandro was a wise man. He planted vineyards and olive trees. After years of hard work, Vindalyn became famous for its wine and olive oil. The castle of Vindemar on the Southern Sea is one of the strongest fortresses in the kingdom. Now Vindalyn is the richest and safest duchy in Eberon."

Luciana glanced at her goblet. The wine they drank at the convent came from Vindalyn. All these years she'd been drinking it without knowing it came from her father's land.

"Unfortunately," the duke continued, "the House of Benwick has now become as corrupt as the tyrant they once usurped. What do you know of the current king?"

"King Frederic," she replied. "He has ruled for almost thirty years. He has one son—his heir, Prince Tedric."

"Exactly." The duke gave her a wry look. "But no doubt your books have refrained from mentioning how cruel and ruthless Frederic is. He detests the nobles who own so much land and the allegiance of a great many vassals. So he has devised several methods for stealing the land back. One way is to deny a noble permission to marry. If there is no legitimate heir to inherit, the land reverts to the Crown."

Luciana blinked. "Is that why ye didn't marry again?"

The duke nodded. "He doesn't want me to have a male heir. Frederic has craved my land for years."

Luciana bit her lip. With Tatiana gone, she was next in line to inherit.

"Another way the king steals land is by ordering a nobleman to fulfill a task for him. If the nobleman fails, he is declared a traitor to the Crown, and he and his entire family are executed. With no heirs left alive, the land goes to the king."

Luciana winced. The king was definitely a tyrant.

The duke leaned forward, resting his elbows on his knees. "A month ago, the king decreed that Tatiana must marry his nephew, Lord Leofric of Benwick, the current Lord Protector of the Realm."

"Ugh." Tatiana shuddered. "The Beast of Benwick. It's enough to make me grateful I died."

"I was ordered to deliver her to court," the duke said.

"Would ye not be excused if ye explain that yer daughter has died?" Luciana asked.

"There are no excuses for disobeying a royal command. Frederic is eager to label me a traitor and seize my land." The duke sighed. "Then all my people would come under his power and be subjected to his harsh rule."

And ye'll be executed, Luciana thought. But the duke hadn't mentioned that. He seemed more concerned about the welfare of the people who depended on him. And he'd planned to return home without letting her know about the danger he was in. He did love her. He loved her so much he was willing to face execution in order to keep her safe.

There, she thought as a pang reverberated in her chest. There was the kind of love she'd always craved in her heart. And there was the connection, the resemblance. She loved her sisters with the same kind of love he was showing for her.

Her heart swelled. This was the man she wanted as her father. And he needed her.

Tears filled her eyes. "That's why ye need me self to go with you. So ye can deliver a daughter to the royal court as ye were ordered."

He nodded. "I still have two months before the deadline runs out. Unfortunately I cannot present you at court as Luciana. Once the king realizes you're a twin . . ."

She would be killed. A chill stole down Luciana's spine. "Then I must pretend to be my sister?"

He regarded her sadly. "I'm afraid so."

Tatiana scoffed. "What a ridiculous notion! No one would ever believe that you're me."

"And if the pretense is discovered, we would both be executed for deceiving the king," her father added.

Luciana swallowed hard. This was too much. How could she possibly do this? She started when her sister suddenly burst into laughter.

"I just realized!" Tatiana slapped her leg noiselessly as she continued to laugh. "Oh, this is too rich. Now *you* will have to marry the Beast of Benwick!"

Luciana gasped. A surge of panic bubbled up her throat. How could she marry a man who was referred to as a beast? Without thinking, her hands formed the sign of the moons.

Her father winced. "That gesture alone will get you killed."

She flattened her hands against her chest. Her heart was thudding beneath her palms.

"I can see how frightened you are." Her father patted her shoulder. "Fear not, child. I will not ask this of you. The king doesn't know of your existence here. As long as you stay here, you will be safe."

How could she remain, knowing her life here would cost her father his life? "I . . . I cannot stay here."

"Think, Luciana." Her father grabbed her hands. "If the king ever learns that we tricked him, we will die. One slip of your accent, one sign of the moons, one mistake, and you will die. You must remain here where it is safe."

She blinked back tears, but they threatened to overflow. How could she say good-bye to her sisters? And if she left, she would have to give up more than her home, her sisters, and her beliefs. She would lose her identity.

But how could she send her father back alone when it would mean his execution? How could she live with herself then? "I will go with you."

"Luciana." Her father's eyes glimmered with tears.

She squeezed his hands. "Together, we will succeed." Or together, they would die.

Two deaths. The Telling Stones mocked her.

Red as blood. Black as death.

Chapter Three

❧

Of all the enemies of Eberon, it was the damned elves that didn't make any sense.

As Lord Protector of the Realm, Leofric of Benwick was accustomed to fighting the three kingdoms that bordered on Eberon. To the northeast, the coastal kingdom of Tourin was easy to understand. The country was full of greedy thieves and pirates. Whether they invaded by land or sea, their aim was always the same: stealing precious metals and jewels.

To the northwest, the mountainous terrain of Norveshka extended far into the frozen north. When Norveshki warriors swept across the border, they stole livestock. Or worse.

Then to the east lay the elfin kingdom of Woodwyn. When the elves attacked, they came with no warning and left with nothing. Leo shook his head. No sense at all. As far as he could tell, the big-eared buggers simply liked to kill.

He was standing on top of a hill, surveying the Woodwyn border. Behind him, the army was making camp for the night. Next to him, a beacon tower rose from the crest of the hill. Over the years, the former Lord Protectors had

developed an early warning system to stay informed of
any incursions along the border. A long line of beacon
towers had been erected, stretching across the thousand-
mile border that began at the Great Western Ocean, then
extended eastward past Tourin and Norveshka, then turned
southward along Woodwyn to finally end at the Southern Sea.

Leo had allowed the army to halt its march early today,
for he knew his men were still tired from a battle with the
elves two days ago. Leo and his troops had inflicted some
damage on the elfin army before they'd retreated across
the border. After leaving some soldiers there to keep watch,
he'd taken the rest of the army north, traveling close to the
Woodwyn border to keep an eye on the elves.

The border was marked with a stone wall. Only waist-
high, it was easily breached. It was the forest on the other
side that served as more of a deterrent. Thick and impen-
etrable, dark and deadly, it was the inspiration for many a
late-night horror tale around a campfire. Eberoni mothers
used threats of the elfin forest to make sure their young
ones behaved.

On this side of the border, the Eberoni had cleared
away the trees to make farm- and pastureland. The process
had taken a few centuries, but now the effect was startling.
No trees, just rolling green farmland, then *bam!* A solid
wall of forest.

"Hey!" a voice called behind him.

Leo glanced back to see Nevis charging up the hill.

"See anything?" Nevis yelled.

"No." Leo shifted his gaze back to the forest. No one
ever saw the elves until they crossed the wall.

Nevis caught up with him and eyed the border. "Do you
think they're there? I can't see anything but trees."

Leo gave his friend a wry look. "That's a common problem with forests. You have to wonder about them, though. What do they eat?"

"The trees?"

"No, the elves. If they never clear any of their land, how do they grow crops or raise cattle? What do they eat?"

Nevis shrugged. "Never thought about it. When one of them comes at me, swinging his sword, I'm more worried about *my* next meal than his."

Leo eyed his friend's wide girth. "It wouldn't hurt you to miss a meal."

With a huff, Nevis thumped his stomach with a fist. "This is solid muscle."

Leo snorted. "They're eating something."

"Maybe they live on acorns like a bunch of squirrels. Could explain their pointy ears." Nevis gave the forest a wary look, then raised his voice. "No offense!"

"They can't hear us. We're too far away."

"How can you be sure?" Nevis asked. "They might have super hearing with those big-assed ears. *No offense!*" He lowered his voice. "Maybe we should back away. Some of them can shoot arrows really far."

"I think we're safe for now." Leo smiled at his friend. Nevis had been watching out for him ever since their first battle at the age of fourteen. When Leo had been named Lord Protector seven years ago at the young age of nineteen, it had been obvious that the king hoped the job would cause his death.

King Frederic had successfully gotten rid of his younger brother, Cedric, by making him Lord Protector. Cedric had died at the age of thirty-five, leaving behind a wife and Leo, his son. When Cedric finally fell in battle, Frederic had quickly enacted a plot to kill Cedric's son.

Leo had been eight years old when the assassins had arrived on the family estate. He'd survived. His mother hadn't. His father's best friend, General Harden, had charged in and killed the assassins. A few minutes too late for his mother. Then the king had acted innocent, claiming to have no knowledge of the affair.

Leo had lived in a daze for a while, traveling and training with the army. General Harden was named the new Lord Protector, which was the king's way of wishing him dead. With Leo under the general's protection, the king was forced to delay any plans to murder his nephew.

The general's son, Nevis, a few months older than Leo, was assigned as his sparring partner. Soon, the two became best friends, with Nevis declaring he would always be there to watch Leo's back.

Now, years later, Leo glanced at his friend. Beneath the shaggy brown hair that fringed Nevis's brow, there was a jagged scar that ran from his brow to his left temple. Nevis usually kept it covered, so Leo wouldn't be reminded that he'd been the cause. Not that Leo could ever forget. He curled his hands into fists, and the leather of his gloves stretched tight against his knuckles.

Nevis shifted his weight. "I came here to warn you. You were so busy looking east, I figured you hadn't noticed . . ."

Leo turned his head sharply to the west. Across the horizon, there was a dark strip. A storm.

Instantly his body grew tense. His nerves hummed with the familiar mixture of dread and anticipation. Dread for the pain that would come. Anticipation for the power.

Nevis gave him a worried look. "Hopefully, there won't be any lightning."

"Hopefully, there will."

"Dammit," Nevis muttered. "Do you enjoy courting death?"

"Of course not. But it's been four months since the last lightning storm. My power is seriously depleted." Leo glanced down at his gloved hands. "I could probably touch someone now."

"Good. You could live a normal life for a change."

"I am not normal. I never will be."

"You've never tried!" A gust of wind blew Nevis's hair back from his brow, revealing the jagged scar.

Leo gritted his teeth. "There is no escape from it. I've tried hiding in houses, castles, even dungeons. It never works. When the lightning comes, it always finds me. It burns down houses and destroys buildings to get to me."

"How about a cave? That might work."

"Enough!" Leo clenched his fists, then slowly released them. "I am what I am." *A monster.* "At least my power scares everyone so much that no one has tried to kill me for being Embraced. Others are not so fortunate."

"It has caused you too much pain."

"And it's kept me alive. There have been many times in battle when my power saved my ass. Yours, too."

"I know," Nevis grumbled. "I'm grateful for that. But it pisses me off that you keep taking in all that power so you can protect people, and do they ever thank you? No! They run away from you and call you names."

Leo arched a brow. "So I should let them die? It is my job to protect the people of Eberon."

"At what cost? Each time the lightning finds you, you take in more power than before. More power than you can handle. One day it'll be too much, and you'll—"

"Burst into a ball of fire," Leo interrupted him. "I've heard it before. Maybe I should consider myself lucky. Doesn't everyone want to go out in a blaze of glory?"

"You think it a jest?"

"I think it a theory. You have no proof—"

"So I'm supposed to wait till you explode so I can say I told you so?" Nevis gave him an incredulous look, then with a resigned sigh, he shook his head. "Dammit, Leo. I'm just trying to keep you alive."

"I know." Leo didn't want to admit that deep inside, he suspected Nevis's theory was correct. But there was nothing he could do. Whenever there was lightning, it sought him out. It burned its way through wood, clawed its way through stone to find him. Since there was no escape, all he could do was accept it. And use the power to protect his people.

He dragged his gloved fingers through his hair. Already, he could feel his scalp itching as the storm approached. His curly red hair would eventually stand out, the strands crackling with energy as if they were calling the lightning to him.

Nevis sighed. "I don't know which will kill you first— the lightning or the king. You're going to be in big trouble, you know. Disregarding his orders. Again."

Leo shrugged. He'd decided it was more important to protect the country than go to court to meet his latest betrothed. The last woman his uncle had chosen for him had run away to Tourin, preferring the life of a poor refugee rather than marriage to the Beast of Benwick. "Why should I bother to please the king? He's wanted me dead for years, and nothing will change his mind."

"He's a royal pain in the ass," Nevis mumbled. "No offense."

"None taken."

Nevis sniffed the air. "I smell dinner. I'll see you later." He dashed down the hill toward the commissary.

Leo smiled. Nevis never missed a meal. Nevis's father, General Harden, was almost finished setting up camp. After losing both his parents at the age of eight, Leo considered the general a second father. A harsh father, since the general had always known Leo would have to excel as a soldier if he wanted to survive. The general had pushed him and Nevis so hard that by the age of nine, they were calling him General Hard-Ass in private.

The years had been rough on the general, too. He walked with a limp, thanks to an ax that had badly gashed one leg in battle. A jagged red scar ran the length of his face, bisecting an eyebrow and puckering the skin of his cheek before disappearing into his thick gray beard.

Once, at the cocky age of thirteen, Leo had boasted that they could track a foe at night if the general would only remove his helmet, for his shiny, bald head glowed in the moonlight. Most soldiers were afraid to touch Leo, but General Hard-Ass had not hesitated to box his ears.

Good times, Leo thought, then shifted his gaze to the ever-growing dark strip at the horizon. Already, the wind from the west was picking up. He could see the flags flapping briskly from the tops of tents where the army had set up camp. Above him, the clouds were filling up the sky, hiding the sun and making the fields appear a darker, more emerald green.

He would need to be alone when the lightning came. Over the years, he'd learned that many times when the lightning struck him, it splintered, shooting off jagged shards in all directions. It was how Nevis had received his scar. Most who came too close were killed.

Those deaths had been attributed to him. The Beast.

The hair on the back of his neck rose, and his scalp tingled. There would be lightning with this storm. He could already feel it, the sizzle of energy in the air. Damn, he was a monster. He knew the power would cause him pain, but as much as he hated it, he also craved it.

The blast of a horn drew his attention, and he spotted a small band of armed soldiers on horseback entering the camp. They were dressed in the uniforms of the royal guard, and the lead soldier was carrying the royal banner. The entourage for an envoy from the king.

With a groan, Leo started toward his tent. On the way, a large black-and-white-spotted dog loped up to him.

"Brody!" Leo smiled at the dog, and he could swear that the dog grinned back. His face was mostly white, except for a black nose and a black patch of fur around his left eye. His legs were caked with mud and his fur still damp. "You had to travel through the rain? Did you tag along with the royal envoy?"

When the dog nodded, Leo continued, "Go wash up and get dressed. I want to hear your news."

The dog trotted off to Nevis's tent. Everyone assumed he was Nevis's pet, but in truth, Nevis merely kept Brody's clothes for him, so the dog had a private place to change back to human form.

As a dog shifter, Brody was Leo's best spy. In canine form, he could join other dogs in any castle keep in the country. Then, while he pretended to be napping, he heard all sorts of secret agreements and negotiations.

Leo reached his tent at the same time as the envoy and his entourage. Their clothes were all wet, and the sodden feathers in their caps drooped. The envoy dismounted and bowed just as General Harden arrived. Leo invited them both inside and found his squire busily polishing his sword. Edmund already had the inside of the tent in order. Two candles burned brightly on his desk.

"Good work, Ed." Leo stepped behind his desk and faced the envoy. "You have news?"

"Greetings from His Most Royal Majesty, King Frederic the Great," the envoy began in a high-pitched, whiny voice. "May the Light shine upon his magnificence forever."

Leo bit his lip to keep from laughing. Behind the envoy, the general was making a rude gesture. "The news?"

With a grand bow, the envoy handed Leo a rolled piece of parchment, sealed with a glob of wax imprinted with the royal insignia. "His Royal Majesty has gifted you with a few words of his glorious wisdom. Surely you are blessed."

Leo broke the seal and unrolled the parchment.

Dear nephew,

You bastard. Your failure to come to Ebton has been noted and added to your list of transgressions. Luckily for you, your betrothed is also late to make an appearance. Your new orders: Go directly to Vindalyn. Find the damned duke and his daughter and escort them to the royal palace in Ebton. You have two months. Failure means death.

And with a grand flourish, Frederic had taken up the bottom half of the page with his signature.

Leo set the parchment on his desk and dipped a quill into a bottle of ink. In the small margin at the bottom of the page, he wrote:

Dear Uncle,

Your order has been noted and added to your list of commandments. See you in two months. By the way, I'm harder to kill than my father. Assassins will not succeed. Failure means death.

There was only room enough left to sign a simple *Leo*.

He rummaged through the drawers of his desk till he found his insignia ring. He didn't normally wear it since he had to wear thick gloves. By then the ink had dried, so he rolled the parchment back up, drizzled some candle wax on the seam, and stamped it with his ring.

"Here." He handed the message back to the envoy, then turned to his squire. "Edmund, take them to the commissary so they can have a meal before they leave."

"You expect us to leave today?" The envoy's voice grew even more highly pitched and whiny. "But, my lord, the—"

"Today," Leo interrupted. "His Most Royal Majesty deserves an answer as soon as possible, don't you think?"

"But the storm . . ."

"You would let a little rain dampen your loyalty to the king? I would hate for my uncle to hear about that."

The envoy's eyes widened with panic. "Have no fear, my lord! I will deliver this message with the utmost speed and diligence."

"Glad to hear it." Leo smiled. "You may go." *And take your damned spies with you.*

"Yes, my lord." The envoy backed toward the tent entrance, bowing repeatedly. On the way out, he bumped into Nevis and Brody, who were coming in.

"This way, sir." Stifling a grin, Edmund led him away.

General Harden chuckled as he poured a cup of wine.

"Looks like you've frightened another envoy." Nevis headed toward his father. "Pour me a cup, too."

"Me, as well," Brody added. "I'm famished."

"Here." Leo handed him the plate of food Edmund had left on his desk. "It's a long journey from Ebton."

"Thanks." Brody took a big bite from the loaf of bread.

"Tired as a dog?" Nevis smirked as he handed Brody a cup of wine.

Brody snorted. "I'm in better shape than you are."

Nevis thumped his stomach. "This is muscle!"

The general nodded as he handed his son a cup of wine. "I've always believed a little added weight keeps a soldier better seated on his horse during battle."

"Exactly!" Nevis agreed and downed his drink.

Leo smiled. Of course they both believed that. They both had the same square-shaped bodies. Brody, on the other hand, was tall and slim. His pale face contrasted sharply with his long black hair. He had the same blue eyes he had in dog form, but the black patch of fur around his left eye was now a dark freckle on the outside corner of his eye.

Nevis handed Leo a cup of wine. "So what news did the envoy bring? Are you in trouble?"

"A little." Leo took a sip. "I'm not the only one who's taking my time. The duke and his daughter haven't arrived yet, either."

"Maybe she ran away like the last lady you were supposed to marry." When his father cleared his throat, Nevis added, "No offense."

"I doubt the Duke of Vindalyn would run away, not when it would mean losing all his land and wealth." Leo sat behind his desk. "We have new orders. Now we're to go to Vindalyn and escort the duke and his daughter to court."

General Harden drank some wine. "We can break camp at dawn. Or later, if the storm hasn't passed."

All three men gave Leo a worried look.

"I went through the storm on the way here," Brody said quietly. "There was lightning."

Leo nodded. "I'll get away from camp before it starts. We don't want any of the tents catching fire." His jaw tightened as the three men continued to watch him with wary expressions. "I'll be fine. What news do you have, Brody?"

Brody gulped some wine, then began, "I heard the king talking to his chief counsel. The duke and his daughter actually began the journey to Ebton. But when they arrived in Ronsmouth, there was an outbreak of plague."

"Plague?" General Harden asked.

Leo winced, then motioned for Brody to continue.

"That's when the news gets sketchy. There are rumors that the duke and daughter died. Other rumors that they boarded a ship. No one seems to know what happened."

Leo narrowed his eyes, considering. "So the king suspects they're alive and have sailed back to Vindalyn."

"Any news about the plague?" General Harden asked.

Brody shook his head. "None at all."

"That's strange," Nevis muttered.

Strange, indeed, Leo thought. Ronsmouth, at the mouth of the Ron River, was the busiest port in all of Eberon. If a plague had occurred there, it would have spread. "Brody, go to Ronsmouth to investigate. You can travel with us part of the way since we'll be headed south."

"Aye, my lord." Brody bit into a chunk of cheese.

Nevis smirked. "Don't bring back any fleas."

Brody continued to eat, but responded with a rude gesture.

"You suspect something?" the general asked.

Leo drummed his fingers on the desk. "We know why Uncle Fred wants me to marry the heiress of Vindalyn. He's wanted that land for years, and once the girl marries me and her father passes away, it becomes mine. Then the king only has to wait for me to die for it to become his. But what if he's decided he doesn't want to wait?"

Nevis nodded. "If he kills the duke and daughter, then the land automatically becomes his."

Leo leaned back in his chair. "What if the king never planned for the wedding to actually happen? It could be a ruse to force the duke and his daughter out of Vindalyn."

"I see what you mean." The general rubbed his beard. "The fortress at Vindemar is rumored to be impregnable. The easiest way for the king to attack the duke and his daughter is to lure them out."

"Then kill them on the way to court," Nevis added.

Leo nodded. "They could be in grave danger."

Brody set the empty plate on the desk. "Hardly anyone at court has ever seen the daughter, but according to the gossip I heard, she is truly beautiful."

Leo stilled for a moment, then realized the three men were eyeing him with speculation. He finished his wine and set the cup down with a clunk. "We march toward Vindalyn at dawn, and Brody—"

A bell clanged outside, and he jumped to his feet.

"The beacon alarm." Nevis rushed toward the tent entrance just as a soldier arrived.

"Report," Leo ordered.

"The beacon to the north has been lit," the soldier said. "Three puffs of smoke."

That meant the original beacon was three towers to the north. The border with Norveshka. Leo fisted his hands.

"What color was the smoke?" the general asked.

The soldier winced. "Red."

Leo sucked in a breath. The Norveshki warriors were using their worst weapon. "Nevis, gather your best men. We ride north. Now."

Nevis dashed from the tent.

"What about Vindalyn?" General Harden asked.

"You will go." Leo buckled on his sword belt. "Take the army. We'll catch up with you after we're done."

"I'll ready your horse." Brody dashed from the tent.

Leo slung a full quiver of arrows onto his back and grabbed his bow.

"Good luck, son," General Harden said.

He would need it. The Norveshki had some terrible creatures at their command. Leo strode from the tent.

Nevis and his troop were readying their horses. Brody led Leo's black horse to him. Fearless, Leo called him, for he was the only horse who didn't balk at Leo's power. Even so, he had to be covered from head to tail with black quilted material to keep from being fried.

Leo mounted his horse. "Let's go kill some dragons."

Chapter Four

As Leo and his companions rode north, the rain began, and the rolling green landscape gave way to increasingly taller hills. Their horses went at full gallop, eating up the miles before the rain could turn the dirt road into a sea of mud.

By the time they passed the second beacon, the rain was pounding on them. Their uniforms were drenched, their hair plastered to their heads. The hills had become mountains, and flocks of sheep huddled in the narrow glens where a few trees could give them shelter.

Thunder clapped overhead, and Leo spotted the first flash of lightning to the west. *Good.* He was going to need all the power he could get. Normal people didn't stand a chance against the winged creatures that breathed fire. People like his father.

Leo had heard the story many times over a campfire. His father's last battle had been against the Norveshki. Cedric had plowed through a dozen of their fierce warriors, but when a dragon had attacked, all his bravery and expertise had been in vain.

Another flash of lightning, this one a little closer. Leo would need to break off from the group soon. As they neared the village, a mountain loomed to the right, topped with craggy cliffs and a beacon tower. It was Mount Baedan, which the village was named after. He spotted a cliff that overlooked the village. That was the perfect place.

"My lord." Nevis drew his attention to a horseman charging toward them. A scout.

Leo and his companions slowed to a stop. "Report," he said, loud enough to be heard over the pouring rain.

The scout bowed his head, causing a puddle of rain to slosh off the brim of his cap onto his chest. "Four dragons from Norveshka have attacked the village of Mount Baedan."

"No warriors?" Leo asked.

"None, my lord. Just the dragons. They swooped into the valley and set the village ablaze to force the people from their homes. While the villagers ran to a nearby cave, two of the dragons captured two small children and flew away."

Leo stiffened, his hands tightening on the reins, as the men around him cursed under their breaths. Ten years ago, the dragons had started snatching sheep. Now they were nabbing small children.

He glanced westward, hoping to see another flash of lightning streak across the sky. He needed the power now.

"The rain put out the fires," the scout continued. "The villagers are starting to leave the cave. A group of men rode out, hoping to rescue the two children."

Leo swallowed hard as bile rose up his throat. The rescue attempt would be in vain. Men on horseback could not cross the mountains as fast as a dragon could fly.

Thunder cracked overhead so loud, the men flinched.

"Ride on to the village," Leo shouted at them. "The last two dragons could still be close by. I'll take care of them. You protect the people." He turned his horse and started up the slope of Mount Baedan.

Higher and higher his horse climbed, but eventually the path became too muddy. Leo dismounted and patted the horse, the quilted material now drenched through.

"Go join the others." He gave the horse a slap on the rump, and it started down the mountain.

Leo abandoned the muddy path that snaked back and forth up the mountainside. Instead, he scrambled straight up the rocky slope. He was halfway up when a bolt of lightning shot from the sky and struck the ground thirty yards away, blasting a boulder into bits.

Yes! The lightning had found him and was zeroing in. Energy from the blast rolled toward him, seeking him out in waves he couldn't see, but could feel. His skin tingled. His hair, which had been plastered to his head, now crackled as it lifted into the air.

Thunder boomed overhead, sending another wave of energy toward him. It slithered under his damp clothes, giving him a slight shock. Then an increase in power. And speed. He charged up the mountainside faster than any human could go.

Anticipation swelled inside him as he reached the first set of cliffs. Another lightning bolt ripped through the sky, this one hitting only fifteen yards away. It blasted through the rocks, causing the cliff to crumble away. As the ledge beneath his feet trembled, he ran and leaped.

He landed on the next cliff six feet away as thunder cracked and the first cliff tumbled down the mountainside. More energy surged into him, and he scrambled higher up the mountain. Faster. In a race against the next strike.

He reached the highest cliff. Nearby on the mountain summit, the beacon tower stood, deserted in the storm, its flame long smothered by the rain. The village lay nestled in the valley far below. He spotted houses built of stone with their thatched roofs burned away. The chapel of Enlightenment partially destroyed. The village lookout tower stood as high as the chapel bell tower and was manned by a lone villager. No doubt, he was keeping an eye out for the last two dragons.

Nevis and his troop arrived, and the villagers poured from their homes to welcome them. Leo winced at the sight of small children running about. *Dammit, Nevis, get them back into the cave.*

A rumbling noise echoed through the valley, sounding much like thunder, but Leo knew better. It was the beating of dragon wings. The last two dragons had waited for the people to reappear.

Leo ripped off his gloves and threw them down, along with his bow and quiver. Then he drew his sword and pointed it to the sky. "*Now!*"

Lightning broke through the dark clouds, racing toward him. He widened his stance and braced for impact. It struck his sword, fracturing so that a dozen smaller streaks shot off in a circle around him.

The major portion of the lightning sizzled down his sword, eager to reach his flesh. It hit his bare hand and jolted him so hard he fell to his knees and dropped the sword. The dozen fractured shards rebounded, drawn to him like a magnet. They pounded into him, jerking him back and forth. Thunder cracked over him so loud his ears rang.

Power surged through him, so fierce and scorching he thought his skin would melt, his guts would boil, and his head burst like a kernel of corn dropped into a fire. Pain and power, power and pain, he could no longer tell the difference. He only knew he wanted it, wanted to drink it in, soak it up, and claim it all.

The fiery torture eased to a warm, buzzing sensation, and he found himself on all fours, gasping for air. How many times had he endured this? And it still hurt like hell. He rested back on his knees and splayed his hands in front of him. Sparks skittered around his fingers like a host of fireflies.

Good, but not enough. The Beast wanted more.

He grabbed his sword and hefted himself to his feet. "More, dammit!" He lifted his sword in the air.

Lightning struck again, driving him to his knees and knocking the sword from his grip. He cried out as both pain and power ripped through him. Nevis was right. Someday he would explode.

Thunder cracked around him as if he'd become the center of the storm. His ears grew numb, only hearing the buzz of energy pulsing around him. This time, when he examined his hands, streaks shot out a few yards. Not enough to kill a dragon.

He fumbled for his sword once again. Nevis's question reverberated in his head, bouncing off the inside of his skull. *Do you enjoy courting death?* Over the years, he'd found he could take in more power each time, but what was the limit? How would he know when it was too much?

He stumbled to his feet and slowly lifted the sword. When he had the weapon only waist-high, the lightning streaked toward him. Like a desperate lover, it pounced, not even waiting till he was fully cocked. It struck hard, flinging him through the air into the wall behind him. His head cracked against stone, and he crumpled into a heap.

Rain splattered on his face, keeping him conscious. The pain was merely the price he paid for the ability to protect his people. The pain would be fleeting.

The power he could keep for months.

He rose to his feet. If he were normal, he'd have suffered a concussion and some broken bones. Hell, if he were normal, he'd be dead. But instead, he swelled with strength and power. Tiny streaks of lightning swirled around him so fast, he appeared to glow.

He strode to the edge of the cliff to see what was happening. The dragons were flying low, probably to avoid the lightning. They swooped down at the screaming villagers, herding them away from the cave. Making them easy to prey upon.

With the superfast speed he now possessed, Leo pulled a length of coiled rope from his sword belt and tied one end loosely to a tree deeply rooted in the rock wall of the cliff. The other end, he tied to one of his metal arrows. He grabbed his metal bow, nocked the arrow, and imbued them with some of his energy. Now, when he shot the arrow, it would fly faster and farther.

He aimed for the lookout tower and let the arrow fly. It whistled through the air and struck the top wooden beam of the tower, embedded deep. Continuing at his fast speed, Leo tightened the rope, tossed his bow and quiver over his shoulder, sheathed his sword, then looped the sword belt over the rope. He ran to the cliff's edge and pushed off.

Hanging on to the belt, he careened down the length of the rope. Just before crashing into the tower, he swung his legs up and over the top beam and landed on the top platform. The lone villager gaped at him.

"Go!" he shouted. With lightning sizzling around him like a golden nimbus, he didn't need to speak twice.

The villager scrambled down the ladder, yelling that the Beast had arrived.

After dropping his sword belt on the platform, Leo quickly readied another arrow and pivoted, searching for the dragons. Even though it was possible for him to simply shoot a lightning bolt from his hand, he'd learned from experience that raw power didn't always go exactly where he wanted it to go. Since there was a chance of hitting innocent bystanders or setting their homes on fire, he preferred to use a metal arrow imbued with his power so he could control the force and trajectory.

There, through a steady sheet of rain, a pair of red,

glowing eyes was glaring at him. The dragon was perched on the bell tower of the chapel. It sat up, expanding its chest, a sure sign it was about to breathe fire.

Leo released enough energy to make sparks pop and crackle around the metal arrow. When he shot it, the arrow would fly with enough speed and power that it would actually pierce the dragon's scaly skin and release an electric shock wave through the creature's body.

He aimed for the dragon's chest, but just as he let the arrow fly, the dragon pushed off, flying straight at him. Fire erupted from the dragon's mouth, forcing him to drop flat onto the platform. Flames shot over him, missing him by a few inches. Meanwhile, the arrow hit the dragon's hip.

Sparks spread from the arrow, jerking the dragon around in midair. It shrieked, then shot up into the sky and turned north toward Norveshka. Leo notched an arrow to shoot again, but screams below made him look down.

The second dragon had grabbed a child.

"Nevis!" Leo shouted. "Catch it!"

Nevis spurred his horse and galloped after the dragon. It was gaining altitude, now higher than the rooftops of the houses.

Leo sent a surge of energy into his bow and arrow and aimed, trying to keep a safe distance from the child. The arrow zipped through the air. Direct hit to the dragon's tail. Sparks exploded around the wound, racing up the dragon's body, and it jolted, bellowing in pain and dropping the child. A dress flapped in the wind. It was a little girl.

Nevis charged onward as she tumbled from the sky. Villagers screamed, then let loose a round of cheers as Nevis managed to catch her.

The dragon flew away, filling the sky with an angry roar.

Leo lowered his bow and arrow and watched through the rain as the villagers crowded around Nevis. The little girl was safely deposited in the arms of her crying mother. Nevis glanced back at Leo and gave him a thumbs-up before being dragged off his horse by a swarm of happy villagers.

With a cheer, the villagers led Nevis and his men into the cave. Boys led the horses, including Leo's horse, to the stables. Women dashed into their homes to gather cups and jugs of beer and wine. A few men rushed into a nearby pen to slaughter a lamb. Leo wasn't sure if the village was celebrating the rescue of one child or drowning their sorrows for the two who were lost, but clearly they intended to partake of food and drink. And even more clearly, it was a celebration he could not attend.

He glanced at his hands. Sparks still shimmered around his fingers. One false move, and lightning would streak from his fingertips, possibly killing someone. He'd been in such a hurry he'd left his gloves on the cliff. With a sigh, he picked up his sword belt, then buckled it on.

The rain was still pelting him, so he climbed down the ladder to a second platform just below. Drops of rain leaked between the wooden planks overhead, and the wind blew more rain at him, but it was an improvement. He sat in the driest corner and rested his back against a wooden pillar. For a short while, because he had released so much energy, he would feel all right. But soon the pain would start again.

He spotted two men rolling a cask toward the cave. The villagers must have run out of beer. Sounds of laughter emanated from the cave. Soon he could smell the scent of a lamb roasting over a fire. His stomach grumbled. A quick search of his pockets came up empty.

With a sigh, he leaned his head against the pillar. Alone again. It was always this way. He was too damned dangerous to be near anyone. Even Nevis had learned to stay away from him when he had this much power.

He closed his eyes as a memory flitted across his mind. The first time lightning had found him, he'd been only five years old. One strike had sent him flying, and he'd crumpled onto the ground, twitching uncontrollably. His nanny had run to him. Calling out to him, she'd touched his face. Then a surge of energy had shot through her, and she'd collapsed beside him dead.

His first victim. Someone he'd dearly loved.

"I didn't mean to . . ." Leo whispered, the sound whisked away with the wind. "Forgive me."

Since then, everyone had known to keep their distance. And if a stranger didn't know, he soon learned when he heard the new name Leo had been given.

Never touch the Beast.

Never let the Beast touch you.

The rain continued to fall. The energy inside him spread throughout his body, expanding, rebelling against the narrow confines of his human shell, demanding to be released and used. *Not now.* He had to keep as much power as possible so it would be available whenever he needed it.

The sun lowered in the sky, and the wind became more chilled against his wet clothes. He welcomed the cold. It made it easier to deal with the energy boiling inside him, threatening to escape like steam from a kettle.

The strains of a pipe and fiddle came from the cave. The people were dancing, their music accentuating the thudding rhythm in his head. The energy kept expanding, pushing against the inner walls of his skull, pushing so hard he expected to hear the sound of bone cracking. He squeezed his eyes shut, gritting his teeth against the pain.

Sometimes he thought this was the worst part about his gift. The headaches would torture him until either he released some power or it managed to escape on its own.

"My lord?" a female voice spoke below.

He opened his eyes. On the ground by the ladder, a

young woman stood, a tray of food and drink in her hands. She smiled up at him with rosy, dimpled cheeks. The rain had dampened her blouse enough to leave it clinging to her breasts. Lovely breasts.

Damn. Leo groaned. There was always one. Every village seemed to have one young woman who believed her beauty could somehow magically protect her from a monster. Somehow, they would be special enough to tame the Beast.

They were always wrong.

"Leave," he called down to the young woman.

She bobbed a quick curtsy. "We thought you might be hungry, my lord. And thirsty." She shifted her weight to jut out one hip. "I've heard some frightening tales about you, but you seem very handsome to me."

"Leave the food if you wish, but go!" He motioned toward the cave, and a streak of lightning shot from his fingertips and blasted a hole into the ground.

With a shriek, the young woman dropped the tray and dashed back to the cave.

Leo heaved a sigh. No doubt she would tell everyone in the cave that the Beast had tried to kill her. The release of power had been accidental, but that was precisely why he was so damned dangerous. When he was too full of power, like he was now, he couldn't always control it.

At least the pain in his head had lessened. The woman had not been harmed, and the rain had doused the small fire caused by the blast.

He descended the ladder and brought the tray back up to the platform. The roasted meat, though a little wet, was still tasty. He glanced toward the cave, where the party was still raging. How the hell was he supposed to marry?

A sudden thought made him drop the lamb chop back onto the tray. That was why the king had betrothed him to the heiress of Vindalyn. If Frederic failed to kill her before the wedding, he could always count on Leo to do the deed for him.

For how could any woman survive marriage to the Beast? With a groan, he closed his eyes. Brody's voice echoed in his sore head. *She is truly beautiful.*

She was truly doomed.

Chapter Five

❧

The twin moons gleamed in the night sky, and Luciana sent a silent prayer to Luna and Lessa, beseeching the goddesses to watch over her sisters. The storm had long passed on to the mainland, leaving in its wake a calm sea.

She knew she should be at the front of the ship, looking forward to her new life. But her heart had drawn her aft, where she could gaze in the direction of the Isle of Moon. She'd left home that morning, but already she missed her sisters something fierce.

When she'd first broken the news that she was leaving, they'd reacted angrily and had refused to talk to her for a few hours. Then Maeve had started crying, and soon they were all hugging and crying. Ever faithful, her sisters had vowed to help her prepare for her new life.

Over the following days, her father taught her to speak like an Eberoni. Her sisters learned, too, so they could help her practice. Several of the nuns had come from Eberon, so they were enlisted to assist. One sister, a former noblewoman, had been to court, so she taught Luciana how to do the court dances and dress in Tatiana's gowns.

When the ground had dried enough, they buried Tatiana. Luciana had wept, not so much for her sister, since

Tatiana's ghost spent each day tormenting her. No, she had wept for her father, who was grieving deeply.

Luciana shuddered whenever she thought about the headstone that marked her sister's grave. It had been engraved with the name LUCIANA.

She was now Tatiana. Tatiana Vintello, the Lady of Vindalyn. On the morrow, they would arrive at the castle of Vindemar on the coast of the Southern Sea.

But her heart remained with her sisters. They had wanted to write to each other, but her father had warned them that too much correspondence would look suspicious. Every three months, he bought books from the convent and paid for them by sending cases of wine. That was how he'd communicated with Mother Ginessa over the years, and it was the safest way for Luciana to keep in touch with her sisters. But three months seemed like an eternity to them, so they devised a secret plan that would allow them to exchange letters soon after Luciana's arrival.

Now, twelve days later, she was on board a ship, wondering if she would ever see her sisters again. Grief tore at her, and the words of the Song of Mourning filled her mind. Women on the Isle of Moon sang it whenever they lost their men at sea, but it seemed fitting since she'd lost those who were dearest to her heart.

Facing the Isle of Moon, she sang softly. "My true love lies in the ocean blue. My true love sleeps in the sea. Whenever the moons shine over you, please remember me."

"Keep singing like an islander, and they'll kill you for sure," a soft voice said behind her.

Luciana spun around to find Tatiana smirking at her. She glanced around quickly to make sure they were alone, then whispered, "What are you doing here?"

With a shrug, Tatiana glided up to the railing. "Did you expect me to stay where I was buried?"

"Well, yes, actually."

"How could I spend eternity at that boring place? All they ever talk about are books. And all that praying—" Tatiana shuddered. "They don't even have any men there!"

"It's called a convent."

Tatiana scoffed. "More like hell. Wait till you see all the guards at Vindemar. Sometimes, in the heat of summer, they practice wrestling without their shirts."

"Why haven't you tried passing into the Realm of the Heavens? You could be at peace—"

"Boring!" Tatiana interrupted. "Besides, I can't watch you fail if I don't tag along. Do me a favor, will you, and wear my blue brocade gown to your execution? The blue matches the color of our eyes, and I'd like everyone to remember me looking my prettiest."

Luciana gripped the railing. "Why are ye so eager for me self to fail?"

"Because it's not fair! You get to sleep in my bed and wear my gowns—"

"And for that, ye want me to die?" Luciana gave her an incredulous look. "Do ye even know how petty ye sound?"

"Sound?" Tatiana stomped a foot silently. "I can't make a sound at all! I'm dead! And you're alive. Why shouldn't that make me angry?"

Luciana took a deep breath. She was letting her frustration cause her speech to slip, something she couldn't afford to do once they landed at Vindalyn. Even now, it would be bad for any of the ship's crew to hear her accent or wonder why she was talking to an empty space.

She lowered her voice to a whisper. "No one wanted you to die. Don't you realize that if I fail, our father will, too? Do you want to see him executed alongside me?"

Tatiana frowned.

"You could help me so much. For our father's sake."

"What can I do? I'm dead. My only consolation is I no

longer have to marry the Beast." She slanted a sly smile at Luciana. "Now you have the honor of being his bride."

A chill skittered down Luciana's spine. "Why is he called the Beast?"

"He's a monster." Tatiana leaned close and whispered, "I heard he killed his nanny and his mother."

Luciana gasped.

"They say he's murdered hundreds. Thousands, even." Tatiana's eyes gleamed. "All he has to do is touch them and *poof!* They're dead. You'll be lucky if you live through the wedding night."

"That can't be true." How could someone's touch kill?

"I heard he's Embraced, but no one can kill him for it because he kills them first. That's his gift. He fries people with his touch." Tatiana waggled her fingers in her sister's face. "*Sizzle.*"

Luciana flinched and made the sign of the moons.

Tatiana snorted. "Won't that get you killed?"

"If I fail, Father fails. Remember that."

"Are you still practicing?" Lucas Vintello asked.

Luciana whirled around to find her father approaching. He must have heard her whispering. "Good evening, Father."

He stopped beside her and gave her a kiss on the cheek. "Did you study the list I gave you?"

"Yes." That morning, he'd given her a long list of the servants who worked at Vindemar. "There are so many. I'm afraid I'll call someone by the wrong name." She slanted a look at Tatiana to let her know this was something she could help with, but she shrugged and looked away.

"I wouldn't fret over it. Tatiana rarely called a servant by name." Her father leaned an elbow on the railing. "I heard you helped in the galley this evening."

Luciana nodded. "There are twenty mouths on board and only one cook. I thought he needed some help."

"I'm sure he appreciated it, but unfortunately, it confirmed a serious problem I've been worried about." He shook his head. "No one will believe you are Tatiana."

Tatiana scoffed. "Told you so."

"But I've practiced so hard," Luciana protested. "And my speech is near perfect. You said so yourself—"

"I know how hard you've worked. But the problem is you're too kind." When she blinked in surprise, he gave her a wry smile. "Don't misunderstand. I love how kindhearted you are, but I fear it will put you in danger."

"Too stupid to live," Tatiana muttered.

Luciana groaned inwardly. In order to survive, she would have to spend the rest of her life being obnoxious?

Her father turned to face the ocean. "It's all my fault. After your mother died and I lost you, all I had left was Tatiana. And she cried for days after the two of you were separated. I felt so guilty that I did everything I could to make her happy. Too late, I realized that I'd made a dreadful mistake. My poor Tatiana. She'd become . . ."

"What?" Tatiana leaned closer. "Endearing? Adorable?"

Father sighed. "Demanding and selfish."

"*What?*" Tatiana shrieked.

Luciana winced. "I'm sure she wasn't that bad."

"I'm afraid so." Father tapped his fist against the railing. "Whenever I tried to remedy the situation and impose restrictions, she would throw a fit. Break things or refuse to eat until she got her way."

With a huff, Tatiana crossed her arms.

"I don't really need to know—" Luciana began.

"She was thoroughly spoiled, I'm sorry to say," Father continued. "Not to mention, vain and lazy. I could never get her to study. She was barely literate."

Tatiana sniffed. "Why is he being so mean?"

"Father, please," Luciana urged him. "We shouldn't speak ill of the dead."

"But you need to understand how different you are," he insisted. "You're naturally kind to people, but Tatiana was arrogant and rude. None of the servants liked—"

"*Enough!*" Tatiana screeched.

"Stop!" Luciana grabbed her father's arm. "Don't say another word. Not now."

He gave her a confused look, then slowly, his eyes widened with horror. "You have the same gift. You can see her?" When she nodded, he grimaced. "And she's here?"

Luciana glanced to the side, but her sister had vanished. "She just left."

With a groan, he dragged his hands down his face. "The Light help me, what have I done?" He turned toward her quickly. "When you see her again, will you tell her how sorry I am, how much I love her?"

"Of course. I-I should have told you about my gift."

He waved that aside. "I should have realized it before. And it's good that you've learned to keep it a secret. You must continue that on the mainland. No one can ever know you're Embraced. Understand?" After she nodded, he added, "How long have you been seeing her?"

"Since the day I met you."

He smiled. "So the two of you have been reunited! You must be thrilled."

Luciana shifted her weight.

His smile faded. "What's wrong? Is she all right?"

"She's a bit . . . miffed. About being dead and all."

"Poor child. She never could handle disappointment very well." He winced. "I can't believe we're having this conversation. So is she directing her anger at you?"

"A little." Luciana smiled. "You know her so well, but you still love her. I like that."

He gave her a wry look. "You were trying to spare her feelings, weren't you? Even after she's been mean to you."

Luciana shrugged. "She's been through a great deal."

"You're a treasure." He wrapped an arm around her shoulders and pulled her close. "As much as I hate putting you in danger, I'm glad it is you who will be going to court. You're clever and cautious. Much better equipped to survive than your sister ever could have been."

Luciana's heart squeezed in her chest. She loved his compliments, but still, she couldn't help but worry. "You said no one would believe I'm Tatiana."

He nodded. "Your kind heart. I don't want you to lose that, so I've come up with a story."

He held her by the shoulders. "You were dying from the plague, so I took you to the convent for the good sisters to take care of you. While you were near death, you deeply regretted your past sins, so with help from the sisters and many hours of reflection, you were able to reach a higher level of spiritual understanding. And now that the Light has seen fit to restore your good health, you wish to spend the rest of your days spreading kindness and goodwill."

Luciana bit her lip. "Will people believe it?"

"When they see how nice you've become, they'll fall on their knees and praise the Light for his mercy."

She supposed it would work. What servant would complain about being treated well? "I guess I'll have to attend mass for the Light?"

"Yes. And you'll need to go to confession beforehand. Remember the priests are spies for the king, so never confess anything the king could use against you."

"Then what should I say?"

He chuckled. "Tatiana's favorites were *I slept past noon* or *I looked at myself in the mirror for an hour.*"

"Those might have been true."

He snorted. "Probably so." He kissed her brow. "Thank you for doing this. I know you'll do well."

Luciana smiled. She was glad she could help her father. And with his new story to explain her change of heart, she could now feel free to be herself. She might even enjoy some exciting new adventures.

The problem was the Beast. How could she survive him?

After rejoining the army, Leo had headed south toward the Duchy of Vindalyn. Tonight, they had set up camp by the Ron River. He was in his tent, finishing supper. He preferred to eat with his gloves off, which meant that for everyone's safety, he had to dine alone.

Alone again. He extended his right hand toward his goblet and willed it to move toward him. As if it were drawn to a magnet, the metal cup slid right into his grasp.

He took a long drink. The wine helped with the headaches. And the nightmares. Like the one that replayed the death of his nanny or the one where he saw his mother murdered by the king's assassins.

"Permission to enter?" Nevis called from outside.

"Come in." Leo tugged on his gloves as Nevis pulled aside the flap and entered with the dog shifter. Edmund rushed in and gathered Leo's empty dishes on a tray.

"Bring another tray for Brody," Leo said to his squire, and Edmund hurried off.

Nevis shot Brody a wry look. "You wouldn't be so hungry if you didn't spend all your time as a dog."

Brody scoffed. "What's your excuse for overeating?"

"This is muscle!" Nevis thumped his chest.

"Enough." Leo passed a goblet to the dog shifter. "What did you learn in Ronsmouth?"

"No plague." Brody took a sip. "I found the inn where the duke stayed and overheard a meeting in the alley. The innkeeper was complaining to a guy in a hooded cloak that three of his customers had died and it was destroying his business. He was mad about having to poison so much of his food just to target the duke and the daughter."

Leo sucked in a breath. "So it was attempted murder."

"Real murder for the three who died," Brody said wryly. "The innkeeper demanded more money. The cloaked man said he'd take care of it, then he slit the guy's throat."

"Whoa," Nevis breathed.

No honor among criminals, Leo thought. "And then?"

Brody took another drink. "I followed the cloaked guy, and he met another hooded man close to the docks. The second man reported that the duke and his daughter had fled by ship. Both still alive. So the first man told him to send three assassins to Vindemar to kill the duke and daughter before you arrive."

"Bastards," Nevis grumbled.

Leo tapped his fingers on the desk as he considered what to do. "The army will reach Vindemar in two days. I want you to go ahead of us. Nevis, I'll give you a letter to pass on to the duke, warning him of the danger. You will guard the duke. Brody, you will guard the daughter."

Brody nodded. "Aye, my lord."

Leo sat back in his chair. "Since the assassins are supposed to finish before I arrive, we'll keep my presence a secret. General Harden can say I've been delayed a few days. That will force the assassins to move quickly."

"We'll leave at dawn. I just have one question." Nevis smirked at Brody. "Did you bring back any fleas?"

"No. I just drooled all over your clothes."

"Brody," Leo said quietly.

"What now?"

"Keep her safe." Leo was beginning to feel protective of a woman he'd never met. Maybe because she was a pawn like him. And the king wanted them both dead. It was a sad thing to have in common.

She is truly beautiful. She'd be lucky to live till the wedding day. And even luckier if she survived as his bride.

Chapter Six

❦

Big, Luciana thought. That one word best described her new life. The first time she'd spotted the fortress of Vindemar from the sea, she'd been amazed by how big it was.

The promontory it sat upon was wide and flat on top. On three sides, it was surrounded by water. Waves crashed against the cliffs, leaving white foam to drizzle down the cracks and crannies. The northern side of the fortress was connected to the mainland, separated by a dry moat. A high curtain wall of gray stone circled the perimeter of the promontory, interspersed with tall, round towers. A flag in the blue and white colors of Vindalyn topped each tower and flapped in the constant breeze from the sea. Inside the walls, there was a big pasture for sheep and goats, in case the fortress was ever besieged.

The stables were big, as were the guard barracks, kitchens, and gardens. Even the chapel was big. The castle keep was huge, three stories high, built in a square around a courtyard. A round tower marked each corner, and the top was lined with battlements. In the northeast corner of the stone-paved courtyard, a deep well provided water.

Beneath the castle, the wine cellars were as large as caverns. Long, dark catacombs housed the bones of those who had died at Vindemar for the past sixty years.

Luciana and her father had arrived the day before, and so far, so good. No one seemed to doubt her identity.

She'd supped with her father in the Great Hall at the high table set on a dais at one end. The only mishap that had occurred was when a servant had placed a platter of food on the table in front of her, and she'd said, "Thank you." The poor servant had been so shocked, he'd tripped and fallen off the dais, landing facedown in a soup tureen another servant was carrying. Everyone had been too busy laughing to even question the Lady of Vindalyn's sudden attack of manners.

She'd also made a new friend at dinner. A shaggy black-and-white dog had crept up onto the dais to sit by her feet. She'd thought him adorable with his cute grin, striking blue eyes, and black patch over his left eye. That's when she'd decided to name him Pirate. She'd slipped him a pork chop under the table, and ever since then he'd followed her around. He'd even curled up outside her bedchamber door last night to sleep.

An envoy from the Lord Protector had arrived shortly before dinner, and he'd been invited to sup with them. After eating heartily, the envoy, Captain Harden, had requested a private meeting with the Duke of Vindalyn. Her father didn't tell her what was discussed, but he'd immediately posted a guard outside her bedchamber door. And he'd warned her that the Lord Protector and his army were on their way.

Now it was the next day, and she woke in her sister's bedchamber. Just like everything else at Vindemar, the room was big. Well furnished, also, with a round table and two upholstered armchairs in front of a wide fireplace.

She sat up in bed and peered at the large windows.

Good goddesses, the sun was already high in the sky. It must be nearly noon. She'd been too nervous to sleep her last night at the convent or on the boat journey, so her state of exhaustion had finally caught up with her.

"So, did you enjoy my bed?" Tatiana grumbled.

Luciana shifted her gaze to the foot of the bed where her sister's ghost was hovering. "It's very comfortable. I've never slept so late in my life."

Tatiana scoffed. "Well, that's the first smart thing I've seen you do. You should always sleep late if you want to convince everyone you're me."

Luciana smiled. Perhaps her sister was going to start being helpful. "Did you sleep well, too?"

Tatiana sighed. "I don't seem to need sleep anymore. But I do miss my pretty bed." She reached out to touch the embroidered blue brocade coverlet, but her hand passed through it. "I hate it when that happens!"

"I'm sorry. Wait just a minute, and I'll be right back." Luciana hurried to the adjoining dressing room to relieve herself, then brought back a gray linen gown to change into. "I told Father you've forgiven him—"

"That's not true! I'm still angry."

"And he still loves you." Luciana dropped the gown on the bed.

Tatiana huffed. "You picked the ugliest gown I own. I haven't worn that in years. You might as well make a public proclamation that you're not me."

"Then help me," Luciana said as she quickly braided her hair. "Tell me what you used to do every day. Did you sew your pretty gowns? Work in the rose garden?"

"That's what servants are for." Tatiana rolled her eyes. "You're such a peasant."

"Then tell me, please."

"All right." Tatiana smirked. "I would start every day with a long bath. And my maid, Gabriella, would add things to the water. Rose petals. Lavender. I liked to mix it up, always something different every day to make it exciting."

Luciana groaned to herself. "And then?"

"I had to wait for my hair to dry and for Gabriella to arrange it. And then I had to choose which gown to—"

The door flew open and Gabriella ran inside. "My lady! The army has been spotted. The Lord Protector will be here within the hour!"

Luciana gasped. Her betrothed was arriving today?

"The Beast is coming!" Tatiana's eyes widened as she regarded her sister. "Oh, your days are numbered now."

A wave of light-headedness struck Luciana. *Goddesses help me!* Her knees gave out and she plopped onto the bed.

"I've ordered some hot water for your bath." Gabriella dashed into the dressing room. "You'll need to wear one of your finest gowns. Maybe the emerald-green velvet."

"Good choice!" Tatiana floated behind her.

While servants rushed about readying her bath, Luciana attempted to calm her racing heart. Perhaps it wouldn't be as bad as she feared. After all, the Telling Stones had predicted she would meet a tall and handsome stranger in two weeks, and now that she thought about it, she realized that this was the fourteenth day. *But that is only a game*, she chided herself. This was real life, and there were real reasons why her betrothed was called a Beast.

But hadn't she always dreamed of meeting a tall and handsome man who would be her true love?

As she bathed in rose-scented water, her thoughts waffled back and forth from excited anticipation to outright terror. The more Gabriella fussed over her, the more tense she became.

The maid had just helped her into the green velvet gown when her guard banged on the bedchamber door. "They're here! You can see the army from the battlements."

"We have to go!" Luciana couldn't bear the suspense any longer. Was her betrothed a tall and handsome stranger or a horrid beast? She flung open the door.

"But your hair," Gabriella objected. "It's still damp."

"It can dry in the sun." Luciana lifted her heavy skirts and ran down the hall, followed by her maid and guard. She wondered briefly what had happened to her new canine friend, Pirate. Maybe he'd gone in search of food.

She exited the keep and ran across the sheep pasture to the outer wall. The castle guards were in full uniform, blue and white. Some were lined up in front of the gatehouse, while others stood along the outer wall.

Quickly, she mounted the stairs to the wall walk. She didn't want to disturb the guards who were on duty, so she stood off to the side, a distance from the main gate.

Beside her, Gabriella gasped.

Stunned, Luciana made the sign of the moons, then she quickly fisted her hands. The entire horizon to the north was taken up by the army. She hadn't realized the Eberoni army was so huge. But then, it would have to be, wouldn't it, if the country was always at war with its neighbors?

The sun gleamed off countless shields. Long poles were topped with banners bearing the Eberoni royal insignia. The royal colors, red and black, flapped in the breeze that constantly blew in from the sea.

Red and black. Luciana took a deep breath as she recalled the colored stones she'd picked two weeks ago.

Her guard wandered over to the other guardsmen, who were all gossiping about the size of the army.

"I need to make sure your gown is ready for tonight," Gabriella said and ran back down the stairs.

There was a blast from several horns, then a group of horsemen broke off from the army and rode toward the main gate. The sun gleamed off their silver helmets and chest armor. They came to a stop in front of the draw-bridge.

"Impressive, aren't they?" Tatiana whispered, and Luciana started. She hadn't realized her sister had followed her there.

The castle guard marched out in a double row and positioned themselves on the drawbridge.

"There's Alberto!" Tatiana pointed at the captain of the guard in front. "Isn't he the most handsome man ever?"

Luciana was too distraught to answer. She clenched her fists as the lead horseman dismounted. Was this the man she would have to marry? Was he the Beast?

The Duke of Vindalyn strode across the drawbridge.

"Papa looks grand, don't you think?" Tatiana asked.

He did, but Luciana held her breath as the lead horseman removed his helmet and greeted her father.

She gasped.

Tatiana broke into laughter. "No wonder they call him the Beast. Look at him!"

Luciana struggled to breathe. The man was bald with a gray beard and a hideous scar running down his face. She looked away. How could she marry him? A breeze whipped her hair in front of her face, and she pulled it back.

And then she saw him.

Far to the left, under the shade of a tree, a man sat on a horse. A black horse. He wore a black cloak, the hood drawn forward to cast his face in shadow. She couldn't see his eyes, but she could feel him looking at her.

The skin at the back of her neck tingled. Time seemed to slow to a halt as she stared at him. And he stared back.

"What are you looking at?" Tatiana asked.

The envoy, Captain Harden, and another man approached the cloaked man on the black horse. They seemed to be talking to him, but as far as Luciana could tell he was still focused on her.

Suddenly he stiffened and ran a gloved hand over his head, causing his hood to fall back.

Luciana gasped. Red hair. Black horse. *Red and black*.

"Oh, I see him," Tatiana said. "He's a handsome one, all right. Much better than the Beast you have to marry."

Luciana's heart sank. Why couldn't this man be her betrothed?

Since the fortress of Vindemar lay on the Southern Sea, it enjoyed warmer weather than Leo was accustomed to. He and his army had crossed the duchy's northern border the day before, and it had taken all day and half of this morning to reach Vindemar. After traversing miles of well-tended vineyards, olive groves, and prosperous villages, Leo could see why his uncle craved this land.

Leo had never met Lucas Vintello before, but he grew more impressed with him the more he saw of the duke's domain. The man took excellent care of his land and people. And he was wise enough to remain here instead of frequenting the royal court where constant intrigue and inconstant loyalties could easily cause a nobleman to lose his head before the age of thirty.

When the army reached Vindemar and made camp, Leo put General Harden in charge and retired to his tent. There he removed his uniform and put on black breeches, a white shirt, and a hooded black cloak. He rode off alone, seeking a place where he could observe the proceedings unnoticed.

As he neared the castle, his heart began to pound. This could be his future home. And his future wife was nearby. She'd invaded his thoughts more and more over the last few days. Was she as beautiful as the rumors claimed? Would she be able to accept him as a husband?

He'd grown tired of referring to her as his betrothed or the duke's daughter, so a few nights ago, he'd dug through the letters from his uncle, searching for her name. He'd found it.

Tatiana.

As he neared the coast, a breeze brushed his face with the scent of sea and salt. He spotted an oak tree, growing at an angle caused by the constant wind from the sea. He reined his horse underneath.

From there, he studied the fortress. Surrounded on three sides by water, it was well prepared for a naval attack. The walls were thick, and the wide towers were topped with trebuchets. The fortress's true weakness lay on the northern side where it was attached to the mainland.

Leo surveyed the dry moat, drawbridge, and gatehouse, mentally marking where he would make improvements. On top of the gatehouse, some guardsmen in blue-and-white uniforms were posted, and he winced at their lax behavior. The men were gossiping and pointing at the army like an excited group of children at a fair. Even though the castle was in no danger at the moment, there was no excuse for failing to attend one's duties. Leo made a mental note to dismiss the current captain of the guard and have General Harden give the soldiers some serious training.

He moved his gaze back along the curtain wall, then stopped. His heart stilled.

A young woman had come into view. Her long black hair was loose and fluttered in the breeze. He couldn't see her face well, but he knew she must be beautiful.

His hand tightened on the reins. Was she Tatiana?

He had to know. Now.

His eyes narrowed, searching for clues. She was clearly a noblewoman. Her green gown was rich and elaborate. Her lack of headdress was unusual, but he liked seeing her long black hair stirring in the breeze.

A series of images jumped into his mind. Her hair spread across a white pillow in bed. Her hair sweeping against his chest as she leaned over him. Her hair wrapped around his fist as he pulled her down for a kiss.

Not possible. He shoved the images away.

A guard and maid were accompanying her, although the guard quickly abandoned her to go talk to his friends. Leo winced. The man was neglecting his duty.

Her maid left, and she was alone. Vulnerable. He scanned her surroundings, assessing the danger. If an assassin was standing on the battlements atop the keep, he could shoot an arrow at her. Or one of the guards on the wall walk could approach her and stab her with a knife.

The horns blasted behind him, and Leo twisted in his saddle to watch General Harden and his entourage start their ride toward the gatehouse. A dozen of the castle guard marched out to position themselves on the drawbridge.

He returned his gaze to the woman. She was watching the general arrive. Alone and unprotected. Dammit to hell.

Suddenly she stiffened, and he caught his breath, wondering if she'd been hit by a weapon he couldn't see. He followed her line of sight and saw that General Harden had removed his helmet and was greeting the duke.

She looked away, and a breeze swept her hair across her face. With a graceful gesture, she brushed her hair back, then she stilled.

She'd spotted him. She was looking straight at him with an intensity that took his breath away. Time seemed to stop, and he no longer heard the sounds of his army or the call of seagulls. He no longer felt the heat of the sun or the breeze from the sea.

How long he stared at her, how long she stared back, he didn't know. Didn't care. For in those few seconds that stretched into an eternity, he felt like an essential truth was being imprinted on his soul, a truth that would remain as eternal as the sea and sky.

She was meant for him.

She was the one he wanted.

A second truth struck him hard, like a hammer shattering his soul into the jagged fragments of a broken mirror. And in those fragments, he saw his own reflection. Multiple images of himself. The Beast.

No matter how much he wanted this woman, no matter how much he felt she was destined for him, he could never touch her. His heart squeezed painfully in his chest. How cruel of fate to reveal her to him only to keep her beyond his reach.

You knew it was impossible before you came here, he reminded himself. *Why do you let it torment you now?* But back then he hadn't seen her yet. Hadn't felt her eyes upon him.

Now he knew she was real.

"Leo!"

Brody's shout drew his attention. The dog shifter and Nevis were standing right next to him. Damn, he hadn't even heard their approach.

"You're alive," Nevis muttered.

"Of course I'm alive," Leo replied.

"We said *my lord* six times," Brody grumbled. "We were beginning to think you were asleep on your horse."

"Or in a trance," Nevis added.

Leo ignored that and motioned with his head toward the woman. "Is she the Lady of Vindalyn?"

"Where?" Nevis looked toward the fortress wall. "Oh. Aye. That's her."

Yes! Leo smiled to himself. *Tatiana*. He'd known it was her.

Nevis snorted. "He *is* in a trance."

"Sod off," Leo replied, although he was too relieved to be angry. His betrothed was also the woman he wanted.

"I think she's looking at us," Brody said.

Me, she's looking at me.

"The rumor about her beauty was true," Brody added.

"I hope some of the rumors are false," Nevis grumbled.

Leo slanted a quick glance at him. "Why?"

"It's nothing," Brody said, shooting Nevis a pointed look. "The castle is full of servants who gossip for entertainment. It would be foolish to believe it all."

Nevis scoffed. "You just think she's perfect because she gave you a pork chop and rubs your ears."

"It's more than that," Brody protested.

"What?" Nevis smirked. "Did she rub your belly?"

Leo gritted his teeth.

"I'm not the only one she's been kind to," Brody explained. "She's kind to all the servants."

"She's all the servants talk about," Nevis said.

"*Why?*" Leo growled, his jaw still clenched.

Brody heaved a sigh. "I'm sure it's nothing, but there's a rumor that she has changed a bit."

"More than a bit." Nevis glanced at the woman on the wall. "She wasn't always kind. They say she was vain and rude before she and her father left for court. But during their travels, she came close to dying."

Leo nodded. "She was nearly poisoned to death."

"Aye," Nevis agreed. "Although her father believed it was a plague until I told him otherwise. Anyway, her brush with death made a huge impact on her, and she decided to change her ways."

"For the better," Brody added. "Her inner beauty now matches her outer beauty."

Leo eyed the dog shifter. He seemed more than a bit smitten with her. Somehow the woman had managed to earn his loyalty in only one day. Maybe she had rubbed his belly.

"And there's more—" Nevis began.

"I don't think it's true," Brody interrupted him.

"He still needs to hear it." Nevis gave Leo a sympathetic look. "It's rumored that she has a lover."

Leo jolted back in his saddle. *No.* He ran a gloved hand over his hair, accidentally knocking off his hood. *No.* She was *his* betrothed.

He looked at her, and for some reason, she appeared equally stunned. She stared at him, her eyes wide, her face pale. Would she do that if she loved someone else?

"I heard she's having an affair with one of the guards," Nevis said.

"I don't believe it," Brody insisted. "I haven't seen her meet anyone or make any attempts to arrange a meeting. Look at her. My lord, she has eyes only for you."

True, Leo thought, as he watched her. She couldn't take her eyes off him. *She will be mine.*

Suddenly she turned and walked away.

He winced. She wasn't his yet.

Caw, caw. The seagulls mocked him. "Any leads on who the assassins could be?"

"Aye," Nevis replied. "In the last two weeks, three new guardsmen were hired. I think they're the assassins."

Brody shook his head. "I think one of them is a priest. A few days ago, two new priests arrived."

"*Two* priests?" Leo asked.

"Aye," Brody replied. "There's an elderly priest here who wanted to retire, so he requested a replacement, and the king sent two. An older man and a younger one, who looks too athletic to be a priest, if you ask me."

Leo nodded. "The five newcomers are our best suspects. But we need to watch everyone. The king could have planted someone here long ago or recently bribed someone to switch loyalties. Nevis, I want you and your father to work with the guardsmen. While you're training them, watch them like a hawk. Use as many of our soldiers as you need and rotate them, so the guards don't realize they're being watched. We want the assassins to make their move, so we can catch them."

"Aye, sir," Nevis replied with a quick nod.

"Brody will continue to watch over the Lady of Vindalyn." Leo glanced up at the empty space where she had been standing. "Keep her safe."

"Aye, my lord." Brody inclined his head. "What about the priests?"

"I'll go to the chapel soon to check on them." Leo flexed his gloved hands. He agreed with Brody that the young priest seemed suspicious. The king already used his priests as spies. Why not use them as assassins, too?

Chapter Seven

Luciana rushed back to her bedchamber. It had been a shock to see the handsome, redheaded man on the black horse, especially when he seemed to match her prediction so well. But the Telling Stones were only a game. The gorgeous man could never change the truth.

She had to marry the Beast.

Images of her betrothed swirled in her mind. Bald head. Gray beard. Jagged red scar. A touch that would kill her?

Panic seized her, squeezing the air out of her lungs. *Luna and Lessa, help me!* She slammed her bedchamber door shut. Would anyone hear her if she screamed?

But all she could manage was a strangled whimper. She struggled to breathe as the room started to spin around her. How could she marry that old man? She fell to her knees, her mind flooded with more images of the Beast.

"Are you all right?" Tatiana eyed her curiously.

"Cannot . . . breathe."

Tatiana knelt beside her. "I have to admit the Beast was a bit horrid looking. And older than I expected. But look at it this way. He could be great in bed! You know experience counts for something. And you could always keep the bedchamber dark so you don't have to look—"

"Not helping," Luciana gasped.

"Oh. Well, maybe you won't have to bed him. Since his touch kills people, he might decide to leave you alone."

Luciana moaned. Her survival was dependent on the mercy of a Beast?

"You had better pull yourself together," Tatiana warned her. "If you fail at this, you'll die, and Papa will die with you."

Luciana was so surprised, she stopped gulping air. "Now ye want me to succeed?"

"I want Papa to live." With a shrug, Tatiana rose to her feet. "That doesn't mean I'm going to help you."

Luciana took a slow, deep breath. Her sister was right about one thing. She had to be strong. There was no point in lamenting over her fate. She would have to marry the Beast. And the gorgeous man with the red hair and black horse would be relegated to her dreams.

Her life wouldn't be that bad, she assured herself. She would keep herself and her father alive. She and her sisters had devised a way to correspond with each other, so she would have their letters to look forward to. And she had a beautiful man to dream about. If she kept him secretly in her heart, no one could take him away from her. As her dream man, he could be perfect. He would think she was beautiful and strong. He would believe in her.

Feeling much better, she stood and looked around the large room. Tatiana was hovering by the bedside table, attempting to touch a stack of notes. She hissed each time her hand passed through them.

"What are those?" Luciana approached her.

With a frown, Tatiana crossed her arms. "Why should I tell you? What could you possibly know about true love?"

"You have a secret admirer?"

Tatiana scoffed. "My life is far more dramatic than that.

If you must know, I've been having a glorious love affair. With Alberto, the captain of the guard."

Luciana tried not to let any shock register on her face. After all, she was already harboring a secret dream man in her heart, so she was in no position to judge. Her father had included the captain of the guard's name on his long list, so she attempted to recall it. "Captain Booger?"

"It's Bougaire!" Tatiana stomped a foot silently. "No one ever says his name correctly. My poor Alberto. It's tragic enough that I can never touch him again. Now I can't even hold his letters."

"I could read them to you," Luciana offered.

"No! They're mine."

Luciana gathered them up and headed toward the hearth.

"Wait!" Tatiana followed her. "What are you doing?"

"I have to marry a Beast whose touch could kill me. It is far too dangerous for me to keep love letters from another man."

"We—we could hide them," Tatiana suggested.

"It's safer to be rid of them." Luciana dumped the notes in front of the fireplace.

"You can't burn them!"

As Luciana picked up a lit candlestick from the nearby table, a terrible thought occurred to her. "Did you write letters to Captain Booger?"

"It's Bougaire!" Tatiana huffed. "And yes, of course I did. I love him."

Luciana's heart sank. "You're going to get me killed."

"No!" Tatiana looked aghast. "Alberto would never use them against me. He loves me!"

With a sigh, Luciana sat in front of the empty hearth, then set the candlestick on the floor beside her.

"No," Tatiana wailed.

"I have to." Luciana held a letter over the flame, then tossed the burning note into the fireplace.

"My poor Alberto," Tatiana whispered. "How will he live without me?"

Luciana picked up another note, then hesitated when she saw a tear roll down her sister's cheek. "I'm sorry. I can't afford to make the Beast angry. He could kill Father. With that huge army, he could even destroy Vindemar."

"Fine!" Tatiana waved a hand in the air. "Burn them! It doesn't matter. Alberto's love for me will never die."

"That's good." Luciana lit the rest of the notes and tossed them into the fireplace.

There was a knock on the door, then Gabriella walked in with a tray of food. As Luciana returned the candlestick to the table, she noticed her guard was back at the door. And Tatiana had disappeared.

Her maid set the tray on the table, then drew a note from her pocket. "A letter from His Grace. I'll be back for the tray in a little while."

"Thank you." As the maid left, Luciana broke the wax seal with her father's insignia and unfolded the letter.

My beloved daughter, the note began, and Luciana smiled at the way her father avoided calling her by the wrong name.

I will be conferring with General Harden for the next few hours. There will be a banquet tonight and a celebratory mass tomorrow morning that you will need to attend. Please be sure to go to confession today.

All my love, Father.

Luciana sighed, then read the note again. Who was this General Harden? Captain Harden's father, perhaps? Whoever he was, she would probably meet him at the banquet.

The thought of going to confession made her groan. So far, she'd avoided having anything to do with the priests who worshipped the Light. As she ate her soup, she recalled the lines her father had taught her to say. And his warning that she not confess anything serious.

With a sigh, she rose to her feet. There was no point in putting this off. She strode to the door of her bedchamber and found her guard standing outside.

"I'm going to the chapel," she informed him.

He bowed. "I will accompany you, my lady."

She started down the hall and wondered again what had happened to her new friend, Pirate. She slanted a look at her guard. If he was going to be her shadow, she might as well be friendly with him. "What is your name?"

He blushed. "Jensen, my lady."

"Thank you for watching over me."

They started down the stairs, but when they reached the landing, she spotted Captain Bougaire coming up the stairs.

He glared at her, then said, "Jensen, go have your meal. I'll take over."

"Aye, Captain." Jensen dashed down the stairs and out the door.

Luciana started down the stairs, intending to ignore the captain, but he grabbed her arm and pulled her across the landing into a corner.

She gasped. "What are you doing?"

"What have *you* been doing?" he snarled. "Why aren't you answering my letters?"

Luciana pulled her arm from his grip. This was the man her sister loved? Alberto's dark eyes were angry, and his lips curled in a way that made her shudder. She jumped when he slammed his hands on the wall on either side of her.

"I've written to you four times," he growled. "Twice I asked you to meet me in our secret place, and twice you left me there waiting."

She steeled her nerves and looked him in the eye. "It is not safe for us to meet. My betrothed has arrived—"

"No, he hasn't. He was delayed a few days."

"What?" Luciana's head spun. "The man who greeted my father is not my betrothed?"

"That was General Harden." Alberto chuckled. "You thought you'd have to marry that old man?"

Luciana let out a deep breath. *Oh, thank the goddesses!*

Alberto suddenly grasped her by the shoulders. "The Beast will be here in a few days. We have to elope!"

She gasped. "Unhand me self. Someone could see—"

"Tomorrow night!" His grip tightened. "Meet me—"

"I'm not going anywhere with you."

"*What?*" His fingers dug painfully into her skin. "Don't back out on me now. I love you. You know that."

She gritted her teeth. "I am betrothed to another."

"You love me! You—Ack!" His face contorted with pain, and he jumped back, releasing her.

Pirate growled, his jaws clamped onto Alberto's leg.

"Get off me!" Alberto yelled.

Luciana slipped by them. "Don't ever touch me again."

"*What?*" Alberto shook his leg, but Pirate held on.

"It's over!" Luciana ran down the stairs, out the door, and into the courtyard.

She took a few deep breaths to calm herself. The man had unnerved her to the point that her accent had slipped. Thankfully, he hadn't seemed to notice.

With a shudder, she started toward the western gate. She would probably have bruises on her arms. What had Tatiana seen in that man?

In front of the chapel, she heard a bark behind her. She turned to find Pirate loping toward her.

With a laugh, she knelt down and held out her arms. "My hero!" When he trotted up to her, she gave him a hug, then rubbed his ears. "Good boy. Thank you."

Pirate sat in front of her, grinning.

"Poor thing." She cupped his sweet face in her hands. "I bet that ugly oaf tasted awful." When Pirate whimpered, she laughed and gave him another hug. "Now you wait out here. I have to go inside for confession."

He gave her a forlorn look.

"I know." She eyed the chapel. "I'd rather stay out here with you, but this is something I have to do."

She opened the door and stepped inside. The entrance was dark with stone walls and a smooth stone floor. Candles flickered on a wide table, surrounded by vases filled with sunflowers. The scent of roses hovered in the cool air.

Through a wide, open doorway, she saw rows of wooden pews, lit by the sun streaming through long windows. At the end of the chapel, a few steps ascended to an altar. A large gleaming orb sat on the altar, and an even larger circle of gold was hanging from the high ceiling.

To the side of the altar, she spotted a man in a hooded black robe moving in the dark shadow of an alcove.

"Excuse me, Father?"

He stopped with a jerk, his back turned toward her.

Pirate woofed softly behind her, and she spun around. "What are you doing?" she whispered. "I don't think dogs are allowed in here."

He crouched low to the ground and slunk underneath one of the pews.

"Pirate, come out of there." She leaned over to look at him. He didn't appear inclined to move. With a sigh, she straightened, then caught a glimpse of the hooded priest slipping into a confessional booth.

You can do this, she assured herself, then strode down the aisle. She opened the door of the booth next to the priest and let herself inside.

It was not quite as dark as she had thought it would be, for there was a small opening at the top of the booth to let in some light. She settled on the wooden chair and glanced toward the metal grate. The man was turned away from her, his face completely hidden by his dark hood.

Was he one of the king's spies? She would have to be careful and convince the priest she was one of the Enlightened. And not let her accent slip again.

With her best Eberoni accent, she recited the first line. "Greetings, Father. May the Light shine upon you always."

Damn, damn, damn!

Leo gritted his teeth. Of all the stupid situations to get himself into. And everything had gone so well up to this point. He'd accompanied Nevis and Brody into the fortress. Brody had shown him the location of Lady Tatiana's bedchamber before dashing off to the catacombs to shift back into a dog. Then Leo and Nevis had proceeded to the Great Hall, where the midday meal was being served. Leo had remained hidden upstairs on a curtained balcony at the far end of the hall. He assumed it was a gallery for musicians, but with no musicians there, it afforded him the perfect place to study all the people below. When he spotted the three priests busily eating, he hurried to the chapel to search their rooms for the sort of weapons an assassin might have.

Just before he could reach the door that led to their rooms, a female voice had called out to him. Luckily, a dog named Pirate had distracted her. It had only taken a second to realize who Pirate was and who she had to be. And like a fool, he had turned to look at her.

Tatiana. So close. And even more beautiful than he'd imagined.

How long did she intend to pray in the chapel? He couldn't afford to be trapped in the priests' rooms until she left, not when the priests could return at any moment. A quick look around gave no sign of another exit. Before she could finish fussing at Brody, he slipped inside a confessional booth. It hadn't occurred to him that she would enter the next booth. *Shit!*

When was the last time he'd confessed? Ten years ago? Twelve? He'd seen no reason to tell anything to the king's spies. But apparently, others still went through the ritual. Perhaps they feared the priests would report them if they didn't. These days, a bad report from a priest could get a person killed.

She cleared her throat as if she thought he might not be aware of her presence. How could he not be aware? Her voice was soft with the tiniest hint of a lilt. Charming. Her scent of rose petals wafted through the grate. Sweet. He could hear every rustle of her skirt as she settled on a chair. Feminine. If he dared to turn his head, he would see her. Beautiful.

He clenched his gloved hands. *Dammit.*

"Greetings, Father," she said softly. "May the Light shine upon you always."

What was the proper response? He cleared his throat. "Blessed be the Light."

"Blessed be the Light that can illuminate my sins," she answered.

He winced. Did she actually have something to confess? Like consorting with one man while she was betrothed to another? He turned his head slightly so he could see her through the grate. She was staring straight ahead, biting her lower lip. Her skin was pale and luminous. Her profile sweet and delicate. Small nose, pink cheeks, and a soft curve to her jaw. She looked so young. And innocent.

"First, if you don't mind," she began shyly, "I would like to give thanks to the Light for restoring my health."

He leaned closer to the grate, trying to see any lingering signs of her close brush with death, but her cheeks were pink and full, her eyes unmarked by shadow. "I heard you were quite ill."

Her blush deepened and she lowered her head. Her loose black hair swept forward like a silk curtain, hiding her face. So close. He rested a gloved hand against the grate, imagining how soft her hair would be. How soft her skin would be.

"The Light was merciful. I am much better."

"Beautiful," he whispered, then turned away quickly when she glanced sharply toward the grate.

"Excuse me?"

"The . . . the Light is beautiful in his mercy." He winced and pulled the hood forward to better hide his face. "Did you have something you needed to confess?"

She hesitated, then answered, "I'm afraid so."

His jaw clenched. If he had to hear about her lover—

"May the Light shine upon my transgressions for the world to see. I—I took a long bath."

He blinked. "That's it?"

"Well, it was a really long bath."

He snorted. "You should be ashamed." He certainly was, for he was starting to imagine her naked body immersed in warm, sudsy water.

She sighed. "I'm afraid I lounged in the tub for hours. And I used far more soap than was necessary. I must have lathered up my entire body three times. It was terribly wasteful."

He groaned silently as more visions flitted through his mind. Long, shapely legs extending into the air with soap sluicing down her skin, headed for her sleek thighs. Rounded breasts, slick and glistening, peeking above the water with soapy bubbles clinging to her nipples.

"And I sent my poor maid out in the heat to gather rose petals to scent the water."

No wonder she smelled so good. He shifted his weight

on the hard chair. His breeches were getting too damned tight.

"And she had to keep heating more water over the fire, because the bathwater would cool down, and I like it hot."

"Enough!" He rubbed his brow. "No more, please."

"Oh. I'm so sorry, Father. I won't take such a long bath again."

Not unless I'm there to watch. Leo pinched the bridge of his nose. Didn't a husband have the right to watch? And if she liked it hot . . . *Get ahold of yourself.* "If that is all, you may go."

She hesitated, then peered at him through the grate. "What about my penance?"

"What about it? Come back when you've done something you actually regret." *Like killing your own nanny.*

She bit her lip and was quiet for a moment.

Oh, shit. She had done something.

"I'm not sure if I should talk about it," she said.

He grimaced. *No, dammit. I don't want to hear about your lover.* Although it was safer for her if he was the one who heard it. If she confessed it to an actual priest, she could be in serious—

"You have probably heard that I'm betrothed."

He cut a quick look at her. She was looking down at her lap. "Yes, I have." He eased closer for a better view. She was gripping her hands together.

"He'll be here in a few days. I-I know I must marry him. It's the king's command." She looked up at him, and he quickly moved back into the shadows. "And I would never disobey. But I—" She lifted her clenched hands to her chest. "I'm afraid . . . of my betrothed."

Leo inhaled sharply as if her words had stabbed him through the heart.

Her eyes glimmered with tears. "I've heard some horrible things about him."

He pressed back into the corner. "You shouldn't believe everything you hear."

"Is it true? Does his touch kill people?"

Yes. Leo's heart wrenched. "He will not harm you."

She leaned closer, her hand resting on the grate. "Do you know him?"

Leo swallowed hard. "Yes. You need not fear him. He will not harm you."

A tear rolled down her cheek. "Oh, thank you, Father. You made me feel much better."

You nearly killed me. "You may go. May the Light shine upon you always."

"And you. Thank you, Father." She left the booth and soon he could hear her talking sweetly to Brody. Telling him what a good dog he was. How cute he was. How brave he was. *Dammit.* No wonder the dog shifter was smitten.

The chapel door shut with a thud, and Leo emerged from the booth. No one in sight. He slipped through the door to the priests' private rooms.

Chapter Eight

❦

You need not fear him. He will not harm you. Luciana repeated those lines to herself as she hurried back to her bedchamber. Her heart grew lighter; her step acquired an extra bounce. Who would have thought that a priest of the Light could make her feel so much better?

Back in her room, she paced about. Was she supposed to do nothing until the banquet that evening? She stopped with a jerk. Of course, the banquet!

She rushed to the dressing room to take off the green velvet gown.

"What on Aerthlan are you doing?" Tatiana asked.

"Oh, you're back." Luciana selected a simple cream-colored linen gown and slipped it over her head.

"Do you have a strange aversion to pretty things?" Tatiana asked with an incredulous look. "That's the second ugliest gown I own. I never wear it. It fits like a sack."

"I have the utmost respect for your lovely gowns." Luciana tied a brown leather cord around her waist. "That's why I'm wearing this. I'm going to work in the kitchens."

"What?"

"There's a banquet tonight. I'm sure they could use

some help." Luciana returned the green velvet gown to its shelf and smoothed it out.

"Don't go to the kitchens."

Luciana turned toward her sister. Tatiana seemed paler than usual, and her form was wavering, a sure sign of distress. "What's wrong?"

Tatiana wrung her hands. "Don't go to the kitchens."

"Why not?"

Tatiana hesitated, then crossed her arms. "Just don't. Are you trying to ruin my reputation?"

"Yes." Luciana smiled at the horrified look on her sister's face. "This is the new me, or rather, the new you. You see, after your brush with death, you had an epiphany."

Tatiana huffed. "I have never had a seizure."

"Not epilepsy." Luciana braided her hair in a simple ponytail. "The head cook is named Yulissa, right?"

"Don't go." Tatiana flickered, then disappeared.

Luciana wondered what was upsetting her sister as she left the bedchamber. Jensen hadn't returned yet, but Pirate was waiting outside her door. He followed her down the stairs and out the door into the courtyard.

"We're going to the kitchens," she told the dog as they passed through the south gate. "Maybe I can find something yummy for you."

Pirate woofed a reply and grinned at her.

"Be a good boy and wait right here," she told him at the entrance to the large stone building.

She peeked inside and saw a dozen servants bustling about. The head cook, Yulissa, was shouting out orders as she rolled out some pie dough. The scullery maid was washing dishes, while other servants were chopping fruits and vegetables. A pig was roasting in the huge fireplace and large pots of soup were boiling. In the oven, bread was baking.

Luciana lingered at the entrance, letting the delicious aromas sweep over her.

"We're going to need more carrots," one servant said.

"And more onions and cabbage," said another.

"Good afternoon," Luciana greeted them with her best Eberoni accent. She smiled as everyone spun around to gape at her. "Is there anything I can do to help?"

Their jaws dropped even farther.

Luciana noticed a pile of wet, recently washed dishes next to the sink. "Shall I dry these for you?" She grabbed a clean linen towel.

"N-no," the scullery maid stammered. "That is much too hard for your ladyship."

Luciana grinned as she dried a pewter plate. "Not hard at all." She dried a second plate and stacked it on top of the first. "So how have you all been?"

The servants stared at her, then at one another.

"My dear child." Yulissa smiled tremulously, her eyes soft with emotion. "It is good to see you again."

"I think it's been ten years," one servant whispered.

"Aye," another agreed. "Ever since the . . . accident." She gave Yulissa a sad look.

Accident? Luciana picked up a goblet to dry.

"I have such fond memories of your ladyship and my sweet Christopher." Yulissa blinked as tears glimmered in her eyes. "The two of you would help me roll out the dough for pies and biscuits. And then I would give you a few biscuits fresh from the oven. You were such good friends."

One of the servants clucked her tongue. "Poor Christopher. He was such a darling boy."

"Aye, taken from me so young." A tear ran down Yulissa's face and she wiped it with her apron.

"Tatiana!" a young voice cried out.

Luciana gasped and dropped the goblet. It landed with a clatter on top of the other dishes.

"Oh, my!" The scullery maid lunged forward to keep the dishes from cascading off the table.

Another servant gave Luciana a sympathetic look. "I'm afraid this work is too difficult for you."

"No, I'm fine." Luciana waved a dismissive hand. "It's quite easy, really." It was seeing the charred face of a child ghost that had been difficult. Christopher had popped out of nowhere, giving her quite a shock. The poor boy had obviously died in a fire. His hair and skin were burned away on the right side of his head, and he was grinning at her with half a mouth.

"Tatiana! You came to see me, right?" he asked.

He looked so hopeful, she couldn't bear to ignore him. "I'll fetch the vegetables you need." She grabbed a basket from the table next to the door and hurried outside, hoping the young ghost would follow.

Pirate trotted alongside her to the nearby garden. Thankfully there was no one else there. She knelt down by the row of carrots and took the hand trowel from the basket. Pirate sat beside her.

"You have a dog?" Christopher grinned. "I didn't know you have a dog!" He tried to pet Pirate, but his hand passed right through him.

Pirate jumped up and whirled around in a circle.

He was sensing something, Luciana thought, and patted the dog on the head. "It's all right. Just stay here, and if anyone sees me talking, they'll think I'm talking to you."

Pirate tilted his head with an inquisitive look.

"Oh, that's a great idea!" Christopher knelt on the other side of her. "Now we can talk all we want."

She took a deep breath and reminded herself not to cringe. He was a child. Frozen in time at the age of eight or nine. She turned to smile at him. "How have you been, Christopher?"

"I'm great, now that you're here. I kept hoping you

would come to visit. I knew you could see me 'cause you looked right at me during the funeral. Then you screamed." He hung his head. "I guess I look kind of scary now."

"I'm so sorry that you suffered."

He shrugged. "It was my fault. Mama warned me so many times not to play close to the fire."

The poor boy must have been lonesome all these years. Luciana dug around a carrot.

Christopher giggled when Pirate moved right through him, sniffing the ground. "I like your dog."

"So do I." She rubbed Pirate's ears, but he looked at her and made a whimpering noise. "You know, Christopher, if you passed on to the Realm of the Heavens, you could return to your normal handsome appearance."

He laughed. "I was never handsome. And I like to stay close to my mom." His face grew sad. "I just wish I could talk to her."

"Is there anyone else you can talk to?"

He stuck out what was left of his bottom lip. "I tried to talk to you a few times, but you ignored me."

Luciana winced. "I'm sorry. I'll do better from now on. I promise."

He smiled briefly before making a face. "There are a bunch of ghosts in the catacombs, but whenever I go there, they chase me away and say I'm too horrid to look at."

She ripped a carrot from the ground. "That's terrible."

"They call me Crispin."

She winced.

Pirate collapsed on the ground with a mournful whine. She gave him another pat on the head. The poor dog looked so confused.

Christopher jumped to his feet. "If I get too lonely, I go see your mother. She's—"

With a gasp, Luciana dropped the trowel. "My *mother*?"

Christopher nodded. "She's always nice to me."

Her mother's spirit had remained here? Luciana's heart thudded in her chest. "Wh-where is she?"

Christopher pointed at the southwestern tower of the outer wall. "That's her favorite place. She loved it so much, she had a room made for her there. It's where she gave birth to you, you know."

Luciana gazed at the tower as tears crowded her eyes. "Thank you for telling me, Christopher."

"She told me she came from a village along the coast. She likes to look out the tower window at the sea. I guess she gets homesick."

"I can understand that."

"Do you want to hear everything that's happened with the servants?" Christopher asked.

"Yes. Please." Luciana dug up more carrots, onions, and cabbages while the boy talked and talked. He was actually a valuable source of information, she realized. By the time he was done, she felt like she really knew the servants.

She took the basket of vegetables back to the kitchen and promised to come see Christopher again. Then she ran across the sheep pasture to the tower. Pirate loped along beside her.

Up the spiral stairs she climbed, with Pirate following close behind. The first landing had an open area and a door that led to a privy. She climbed some more and reached a second landing. Slowly she opened the door, and Pirate slipped inside just ahead of her.

The room was furnished with a bed, a table, and two chairs. There was a fireplace and two windows, one that overlooked the outer curtain wall of the fortress and a second one with a view of the Southern Sea.

In front of the second window, a form materialized. A woman with long black hair and a red dress, gazing out at the sea.

Luciana's heart pounded in her ears. The woman was young, but then her mother had died young. "Mo—" She groaned when the woman turned to face her. She should have known who it was by the red dress.

Her sister glowered at her. "What are you doing here?"

"I was hoping to see my mother. You should have told me she was here."

Tatiana scoffed. "Why would she want to meet you? You're the one who killed her."

"Don't even try that," Luciana warned her. " 'Tis not true!"

"It is! My nanny told me Mama was fine after I was born. It was you who wore her out. But I could never talk about it because you were a big secret."

Luciana snorted. No doubt the nanny had been trying to appease a frightened child by passing the blame on to someone else. Someone like her, who had been absent and unable to defend herself. "I'll ask Mother about it."

"You don't need to talk to her!" Tatiana gave her a scathing look. "You came to see her like that? Your hands and gown are filthy."

"I was working in the garden . . . with Christopher."

With a gasp, Tatiana turned toward the window. "I don't want to hear about it."

"He misses you." Luciana approached her sister. "You were the best of friends ten years ago."

Tatiana shrugged. "I know better than to befriend a servant now."

"I heard you used to help in the kitchens. Did you stop because of Christopher?"

Tatiana grimaced. "It was too awful. I saw the fire. I could hear him screaming."

"He was your friend. He could still be your friend."

"Don't tell me what to do!" Tatiana's eyes shimmered with tears. "It hurts too much to see him like that."

"Mother sees him. And she's kind to him."

"Why are you pestering me? If I see him, he'll know I'm dead. Then he'll know you're a fake. Do you want that?"

"Who is he going to tell?"

Tatiana stepped back, wringing her hands. Then she glanced to the side. "Mama!"

Luciana whirled around to see a beautiful black-haired woman, dressed in white, hovering in the doorway. The woman looked at both of them, her eyes widening in shock and then focusing on Tatiana with horror.

"Mama!" Tatiana dashed toward her and both of them vanished.

"Wait!" Luciana lunged toward the door, but they were gone. Her hand was touching nothing but air. "Mother?"

Her eyes filled with tears. Why had her mother run away? Was it the shock of realizing one of her daughters was dead?

A whimpering noise drew her attention, and she turned to see the dog, Pirate, approaching her slowly. She'd forgotten he was here, but she could swear he actually looked concerned for her.

"She'll come back," Luciana said softly as she wrapped her arms around herself. *My mother will want to see me.* Unless Tatiana was right and she was to blame for her mother's death.

Nay, it can't be true. She shook her head, then recalled Tatiana's words about the man she was to marry. *I heard he killed his nanny and his mother.*

She might be the perfect match for the Beast after all.

Chapter Nine

"Are you sure I should wear this?" Luciana was sitting in her dressing room, gazing down at herself in dismay. The blue brocade gown was beautiful, but the neckline was much lower than she'd ever worn before. She was afraid if she so much as sneezed, her nipples would pop out.

Gabriella gave her a quizzical look. "You always loved this gown before."

"I still do!" Luciana forced a smile. "I just came so close to dying that I fear any sort of illness now. I would hate to catch a cold."

"Oh." Gabriella's expression turned sympathetic. "I'm sure you'll be all right, my lady. The Great Hall is likely to be hot tonight with so many guests." A knock at the door sent her rushing toward the bedchamber door. "I'll get it!"

Luciana's father was outside, dressed in dark-blue breeches and waistcoat. His white shirt had lace at the sleeves, and his head was topped with a blue velvet cap. Like Luciana, he was dressed in the blue and white colors of Vindalyn.

He smiled as she approached. "You look lovely, my dear."

"Thank you." There was no help for it, she'd have to go to the Great Hall with half her chest exposed.

Her bedchamber was one floor up on the west side of the square-shaped keep, while the Great Hall was one floor up on the south side. As they walked down the hallway, her father signaled the guards to follow at a distance.

The floor was paved with black and white tiles, set in a checkered pattern. On the left side, open archways allowed a view of the courtyard below. She could see some of her father's vassals, all dressed in their finest and making their way to the Great Hall for the banquet.

As she and her father passed the staircase, she recalled how Captain Bougaire had assaulted her on the landing. Did her father know about Tatiana's affair?

He cleared his throat. "When I received notice that the army was drawing near, I made arrangements for this banquet, thinking you would be meeting your betrothed for the first time. But I'm afraid he's been delayed."

"That's all right."

The duke glanced back at the guards, then whispered, "I heard you worked in the kitchen garden this afternoon."

"I didn't do that much."

"I understand you wish to be helpful, but from now on you must be more careful. You'll need to attend mass tomorrow morning, but after that I want you to return straight to your bedchamber."

She could see the worry in his eyes. "What's wrong?"

He patted her hand. "We can't discuss it here. Just stay by my side during the banquet."

She bit her lip, wondering what had happened. Did someone suspect she was an imposter? Or perhaps Captain Bougaire was causing trouble?

The duke sighed. "Father Grendel came to me a little while ago, complaining that you never came for confession."

"But I did. I went today."

"Really? Perhaps he forgot. Father Grendel's memory has gotten worse in the past year. That's why he's retiring."

Luciana thought back to her confession with the priest. It had been hard to see much of him, what with the dim lighting and the hood he was wearing, but she'd gotten the distinct impression that he was young. His voice had been strong. Deep and very . . . male. "I don't think the priest who took my confession was old."

Her father stopped with a jerk. "He was young?"

"I believe so."

The duke's eyes widened with alarm. "Don't go to the chapel again without me and our guards."

"What is going on?"

Her father resumed walking with her. "I'll explain later when we're alone. And you'll be getting a second guard tomorrow afternoon from the Lord Protector's army. The general insisted."

She winced. Why would the general want her guarded with one of his own soldiers? A likely answer popped into her mind. The Lord Protector might suspect she was planning to run away rather than marry him. He might even hear from the priest that she'd confessed to being afraid of him.

She groaned inwardly. She shouldn't have confided in the priest. But she'd felt compelled to say something honest. He hadn't seemed to buy her long-bath story. *Come back when you've done something you actually regret.*

But he had made her feel better. His words of assurance had buoyed her spirits, much like the handsome, redheaded man who had watched her so intently that morning.

When they entered the Great Hall, she was astonished by how many people were there. The castle guards were in full uniform, blue and white, while a few high-ranking officers from the Eberoni army were there, dressed in the royal red and black. Her father introduced her to General Harden, who didn't seem nearly as horrid now that she knew he wasn't her betrothed.

The duke led her through the crowd, and she smiled and greeted people with her best accent. When it came to her father's vassals, these were people she was supposed to know. Thankfully, her father was extremely helpful.

"Tatiana, dear," he would say, "you remember Baron Suffield, don't you?"

"Yes, of course," Luciana would reply with a curtsy. "So good to see you again."

And then they would move on to the next guest.

When the three priests approached, the duke greeted them by name. The two older priests were Fathers Grendel and Owen. The young one was Father Rune. She said a few words, her smile freezing when she saw the young priest ogling her breasts.

His gaze lifted to her face, and he sniffed with his long hawk-like nose. "My lady. How kind of you to grace us with . . . so much of your presence."

Luciana stiffened as a mixture of embarrassment and alarm swept through her. Her father's arm tensed beneath her hand, and she turned toward him. "I fear our good guests have gone hungry long enough."

"Quite so, my dear." He motioned to the servants to begin bringing in the food, then led her onto the dais, where they would dine at the head table with their special guest, General Harden.

The general sat to her father's left, while Luciana took her seat to his right. Her heart pounded, and as her gaze drifted over the Great Hall, all she could see was a blur of bright colors. All she heard was a hum of noise. For her mind was still focused on the sound of the young priest's voice. It had been nasal and high-pitched. Rude and sneering.

He was not the man who had taken her confession. None of the priests sounded like him. Her hands gripped the arms of her chair. She could come to only one conclusion.

The man who had listened to her was not a priest.

So who was he?

At the far end of the Great Hall, Leo was upstairs in the musicians' gallery. Once again, there were no musicians, so the balcony was dark and empty. With his hooded black cape and his body partially concealed behind a heavy curtain, he had remained unnoticed by the crowd below.

The banquet was a dangerous event for the duke and his daughter. With so many people milling about, it would not be difficult for an assassin to attempt something with a knife. His gaze scanned all the castle guards, searching for any signs of a hidden weapon. A few of his highest-ranking officers were below, and since they knew about the danger, they were watching everyone carefully. They also knew he was keeping his presence a secret for a few days in order to spur the assassins into action.

His breath caught when Tatiana came in, escorted by her father. Her cheeks were rosy with color, though he was quick to note that her blush did not extend down her lovely neck to the creamy white mounds so sweetly displayed. His groin tightened. God, she was beautiful. How would he resist touching her?

And why was he feeling so damned possessive? He didn't even know her yet, but each time a male guest lowered his gaze to her breasts, he wanted to rearrange the man's face.

A quick look around confirmed that her gown didn't expose any more than the ones worn by other women in attendance. But the other women could strip naked and his eyes would still gravitate back to Tatiana. What was it about her that drew him in?

Yes, she was beautiful. And if rumors were correct, she might also be vain and selfish.

He didn't believe it. After leaving the chapel that afternoon, he'd spotted her working in the kitchen garden. Would a selfish woman help the servants? And she hadn't bothered to protect her head from the sun or her hands from the dirt. Her confession about taking a long bath made her appear vain, but his gut told him she'd made it up. No doubt she'd been warned that the priests were spies for the king. As far as he could tell, the only time she'd been sincere was when she'd admitted her fear of her betrothed.

He sighed. How was he going to court her if he couldn't touch her? He was a warrior, not a poet, so he doubted he could win her heart with words.

Fool, he chided himself. No noble expected to find love in his marriage, not when the king was the one who mandated whom you would wed. So why did he worry about winning her heart? Why did he care so damned much?

As a warrior, he was accustomed to analyzing battle plans, not emotions. Even so, he made an attempt to put labels on what he was feeling.

Lust. That was the easiest to discern. She was a beautiful woman. Lovely face, gorgeous body. A glint in her eye and a lift of her chin that spelled intelligence and courage. Of course he desired her. He could lose his right nut and still lust for her. Hell, he could be on his deathbed, and she'd still make him hard. He shifted his weight. His damned breeches were getting too tight. He'd better stop thinking about lust. What else was he feeling?

Possessiveness. He didn't want to share her. Something about her filled him with greed. And lust. *Move on.*

Protectiveness. The king wanted her dead, so his protective instincts were in full swing. Along with lust. *Get a grip.*

Kinship. The king wanted both him and her dead, so he felt a connection to her. And a great deal of lust.

Dammit. Wasn't there more to him than lust? He might be a Beast, but he still had a soul. He delved deeper into his heart till he reached an inner core of truth.

The Beast needed to be loved.

Hungry men could dream of food, thirsty men might dream of wine, but his soul was shriveling from a different kind of starvation. How many years had it been since he'd touched someone? Since someone had touched him?

His soul was starving.

Dammit to hell. The truth made him feel pathetic. From the age of five, he'd lived as the Beast. Feared and reviled. Everyone believed he was so powerful, but deep inside he was plagued by a desperate weakness. He needed someone who could love him in spite of what he was.

Her words came back to taunt him. *I'm afraid . . . of my betrothed.*

"You should be afraid," he whispered.

"Of what?" Nevis asked, and Leo whirled around to see him entering the gallery.

"Dammit," Leo growled. "Don't sneak up on me." This was the second time today his friend had caught him unaware.

"Would you rather I make a lot of noise to draw everyone's attention?" Nevis asked wryly as he approached the balcony railing.

"Stay behind the curtain," Leo warned him. "Do you have news?"

"The duke gave me permission to bunk in the barracks with the castle guards, so that should help me figure out who the assassins are. The captain of the guard was rude about my moving in. Acted like an ass."

"I want him dismissed."

Nevis's eyes widened. "You . . . know about him?"

"I know his men are poorly trained. What else is there to know?"

Nevis winced. "Well, he appears to be the source of the rumors about the Lady of Vindalyn."

Leo stiffened. "He's the one spouting garbage about her?" He scanned the people below. "Where is he?"

"That's him." Nevis pointed a finger around the edge of the curtain. "Captain Bougaire."

Leo eyed the man in full uniform with an abundance of medals and ribbons pinned to his barrel-shaped chest. The man definitely had an inflated idea of his own importance. And he kept glaring at Tatiana. "He doesn't like her?"

Nevis snorted. "He claims to love her."

Leo tensed. "He . . ."

"Yes. He's the one having an affair with—"

"Alleged affair," Leo cut in.

Nevis sighed. "According to the other soldiers, he openly boasts about his . . . conquest. He's so obnoxious about it, they call him Captain Booger."

"I prefer bastard."

"Works for me." Nevis nodded. "My father had a long talk with the duke. Convinced him of the danger he's in. The duke has agreed to let us provide guards for him and his daughter."

"Good." Leo continued to watch Tatiana and her father to make sure no one pulled a knife or sword on them.

"Where's Brody?" Nevis asked.

Leo gestured toward the hearth where a group of dogs sprawled on the cool stone. No fire would be lit tonight since the room was already warm. "He's blending in."

Nevis snorted. "And picking up fleas, no doubt. What about the priests? Did you check their rooms?"

"Yes. Two of the priests enjoy comfort. Expensive wine,

fine furnishings, silk underclothes." Leo spotted the three priests, who were approaching the duke and Tatiana.

"Those are probably the two older ones," Nevis said. "They look like they've been eating well for years."

"The third room was like a prison cell—narrow cot, rough blanket, no pillow." Leo narrowed his eyes on the young priest, who resembled a black crow with his dark hair and long beak-like nose. "Under the cot, there was a whip with seven leather cords knotted with barbs. Stained with blood."

"Damn." Nevis grimaced. "He whips people?"

"That was my first thought. Then I discovered some of his undershirts had bloodstains on the back." Leo scowled at the young priest, who was smirking at Tatiana. "He's doing it to himself."

"Sick bastard."

"The shirts were too narrow for the older priests. I think—" Something about Tatiana's face made Leo pause. She was disturbed by something the young priest had said.

"You think the younger one, Father Rune, is an assassin," Nevis finished for him.

"Aye, and fanatical enough to believe he's following the will of the Light." Leo watched Tatiana and her father ascend the steps to the dais. General Harden joined them.

"The dinner's starting." Nevis headed for the stairs. "Maybe we can sit in a back corner without being seen."

Leo didn't move as he observed Brody trot over to the dais and scramble up to be next to Tatiana. She leaned over, cupping his face in her hands, and dammit to hell, his big snout was about two inches away from her breasts!

"Shit," Leo muttered. He could practically see Brody drooling from here.

"Come on." Nevis motioned impatiently. "I'm hungry."

"I need to remain hidden."

"Fine. I'll bring two plates up here."

"No. I have a mission for you."

"What?" With an annoyed huff, Nevis approached the balcony railing. "Why don't we eat first?" He leaned over the railing to look at the food. "Damn, it looks good."

Leo eased back into the shadows. "Are you trying to announce our presence?"

"No one sees us," Nevis insisted as he looked over the room. "Well, maybe a few have noticed me, but so what? I'm just one more of your officers here tonight in uniform. They'll think I'm working on security detail. If I brought food up here, no one would think twice about it."

With a groan, Leo dragged a hand through his hair, accidentally knocking his hood off. "We have more important matters to attend to. Right now, the castle guards are either here or on duty. That means the barracks will be empty. You should take this opportunity to search their rooms for hidden weapons or correspondence."

"But what about—"

"The duke and his daughter will be safe for now. The general and some of my best officers are here, so we can leave. While you're checking the barracks, I'll examine Lady Tatiana's room to see how secure it is. Come to my tent in two hours to report. And bring Brody with you."

"But the banquet—"

"We can eat at the camp." Leo gave him a wry look. "You don't appear to be starving."

Nevis thumped his stomach. "This is muscle!"

Leo snorted. "Go." As his friend grumbled and tromped down the stairs, Leo glanced toward the dais once more. *Damn.* His heart lurched. Tatiana had spotted him. Quickly, he scanned the room. Everyone else was focused on their food. But Tatiana was clearly watching him, her hand frozen with a spoon lifted halfway to her mouth.

He inclined his head.

Her eyes widened, and a pea tumbled from the spoon and landed in the tight valley between her breasts. With a gasp, she dropped the spoon and lifted a napkin to cover herself. She glanced at him again, her face blushing.

Yes. He had an effect on her. Just as she had an effect on him. He slowly smiled.

She glanced furtively around the room, but everyone was too busy eating and conversing with one another to notice her dilemma. Slowly, she eased a hand beneath the napkin to retrieve the pea. Then, her cheeks still flushed a rosy pink, she slipped the pea into her mouth.

Holy shit, he'd never seen anything so damned arousing. His groin swelled. She lowered her napkin to her lap, once again revealing the upper curves of her lovely breasts. Dammit, he was growing hard, and as far as he could tell, she didn't have a clue what she was doing to him.

She would be the death of him. With a wince, he realized the opposite was far more likely. *Dammit.* He pulled up his hood and headed down the stairs.

Chapter Ten

❧

Luciana hardly tasted any of her food, for her mind was racing with one alarming thought after another.

First, an imposter had listened to her confession.

Second, she was supposed to receive a message from her sisters at dawn tomorrow. It was going to be difficult with her guard following her every move, but she was determined to go through with it. Nothing would keep her from communicating with her sisters!

Third, her mother was somewhere in the castle. Luciana desperately wanted to meet her, but how could she manage to talk to her mother without her guard overhearing her? She certainly couldn't risk anyone finding out that she possessed a supernatural power that only one of the Embraced could have. And tomorrow afternoon, she would acquire an additional guard from the Lord Protector's army. She didn't know why, but she assumed her betrothed was afraid she'd attempt an escape.

Fourth, she feared Captain Bougaire would do something disastrous. The way he kept glaring at her was unnerving.

Fifth, her betrothed would arrive in a few days. The

Lord Protector, otherwise known as the Beast of Benwick, whose touch could kill.

And last, but not least, she'd seen *him* again. The handsome, redheaded man who so perfectly matched the prediction from the Telling Stones. He'd been at the far end of the Great Hall in the musicians' gallery.

Captain Harden had first drawn her attention when he'd leaned over the railing. But he'd soon disappeared down the stairs. She supposed most of the people in the hall could only see the area close to railing, but in her position on the dais, she was facing the gallery and able to see farther into the shadows. And that was how she'd spotted the hooded man who was talking to the captain. When he'd pushed back his hood, and she'd realized it was *him*, her heart had leaped in her chest.

Even now, her cheeks grew warm just thinking about him. And when she thought about the accident with the pea, she wanted to crawl under the table. By the goddesses, he must think she was hopeless!

He, on the other hand, had appeared more gorgeous than ever. Standing in the shadows, he'd looked dark and mysterious. As far as she could tell, his hair was cut a little shorter than most men's, just above his collar, and it curled around his ears in a slightly disheveled manner as if he'd given up on taming it. That gave him a boyish look she found endearing.

But there was nothing boyish about the rest of him. His black cape couldn't hide the fact that he had long legs and broad shoulders. His mouth, wide and sensuous, had smiled at her as if he had the power to melt her from across the room. And his eyes—that hungry look in them had taken her breath away.

Apparently, he hadn't been hungry for food, for he'd left without eating. The banquet had seemed terribly dull after that. Somehow, she'd managed to make it through four courses. Now she was pushing roast duck around her plate.

"Are you enjoying your dinner?" her father asked.

"Yes, but I was full after the last course. Do you mind if I turn in a bit early?"

He smiled. "Go ahead. Everyone believes you're still recovering from a terrible illness." He leaned toward her and whispered, "You did well. I'll see you in the morning for mass."

She stepped down from the dais, and Jensen escorted her back to her bedchamber. Tomorrow evening she would have two guards, so tonight was her best chance for sneaking back to the tower room to meet her mother.

"You may return to the festivities, if you like," she told Jensen once he delivered her to her door.

"I dare not leave you unprotected, my lady."

He wasn't going to leave his post outside her door, Luciana realized, and she couldn't think of a likely excuse for going to the tower. "I-I'll see you in the morning." She closed the door with a silent groan.

It was just as well, she thought as she trudged to the dressing room to remove the blue brocade gown. She needed to retire to bed early tonight, for tomorrow at dawn the message from her sisters would arrive. She wasn't quite sure how, but Maeve had assured her that it would happen.

Two hours had passed, and Leo was in his tent, finishing his dinner, when Nevis called out.

"Come in." Leo tugged on his gloves as his friend pulled aside the flap and strolled inside. Edmund rushed in to gather Leo's empty dishes on a tray.

Nevis poured himself a goblet of wine. "Brody's in my tent getting dressed."

"Good. He'll be hungry. Edmund, go to the commissary and bring him back a tray of food."

"Aye, my lord." Edmund left with Leo's dinner tray.

Nevis snorted. "You weren't worried about me going hungry. You always act like Brody's half starved."

"A bite or two passed to him under a table doesn't constitute a meal. He usually is hungry."

"Then he shouldn't spend all his time as a dog." Nevis took a drink. "What's with him, anyway? Does he hate wearing pants? Does he prefer sleeping on the ground?"

"You make him sleep on the ground?"

"I gave him a pallet," Nevis muttered. "You would think he'd rather sleep on a cot like a human being."

Leo sipped some wine. "I guess he didn't tell you."

"Tell me what?"

Leo shrugged. "I thought he might have said something since you share a tent."

"Like what? It's a little hard to have a conversation with him when he's a dog all the time. So help me, if he gets fleas on my blanket one more—"

"He can't help it," Leo interrupted. "He was cursed. By a witch."

"To have fleas?"

"No! To be the way he is."

Nevis gazed around the tent with a confused expression. "He was cursed? That's why he shifts into a dog?"

"No. He was born a shifter. He's Embraced. Turning into a dog is his gift."

"You call that a gift?" Nevis scoffed. "I'd rather change into something awesome. Like a wolf. Or a bear."

"Brody can wander into any castle in the country. Try doing that as a bear. Being a dog makes him trustworthy."

"Man's best friend," Nevis muttered. "I think he actually likes getting his belly rubbed."

Leo sat back in his chair. "You do that?"

"No!" Nevis grabbed the goblet and gulped down more

wine. "But I've seen other soldiers do it. They think he's actually a dog. So what's the deal with the curse?"

"It forces him to remain a dog. He can only retain his human form for a total of two hours each day."

"Damn," Nevis breathed. "Poor guy."

Leo nodded. "He's tracked down some witches to try to undo the curse, but they all tell him it can be repealed only by the one who cursed him."

"I see." Nevis set the goblet down and paced across the tent and back. "Then we need to find that damned wi—" He paused when Brody walked into the tent. "That damned wretch of a cook and tell him the roast beef was too tough!"

"Roast beef?" Brody asked. "Sounds good. I'm starving."

"Right." Nevis quickly poured another goblet of wine. "Here you go, old pal."

Brody accepted it with a wary look. "Thanks."

Edmund walked in with a tray loaded with food.

"Put it here." Nevis motioned to the desk, then pulled a camp chair up close. "Have a seat, buddy."

Brody eyed Nevis suspiciously for a moment, then sat and forked some roast beef into his mouth. "Doesn't seem too tough to me." He kept eating.

Nevis watched, then shook his head. "I think we'll need more wine."

Edmund gave Leo a questioning look, and when Leo nodded, he rushed from the tent.

Brody glanced up with his mouth full. "What's going on?"

"Nothing." Nevis sipped some wine. "We're glad to have you back. Right, Leo?"

"Right." Leo cleared his throat to keep from grinning.

Brody's eyes narrowed as he looked them over. "I think I brought some fleas into our tent."

Nevis's fist tightened around the stem of his goblet till his knuckles turned white. "No . . . problem."

"And I chewed on your favorite boots."

"You—" Nevis gritted his teeth. "You have good taste."

Brody dropped his fork with a clatter and shot an irritated look at Leo. "You told him, didn't you?"

Leo shrugged. "He can keep a secret."

"And I'll help you find that damned witch," Nevis declared.

"It's not that easy." Brody gave them a tired smile as he picked up his fork. "But I appreciate the offer."

"I just have one question." Nevis leaned forward. "Did you really chew my favorite boots?"

"No. They stink."

"They do not." Nevis huffed. "So, are you saying my boots aren't good enough for you?"

"Enough," Leo said. "Did you find anything in the barracks?"

"Some weapons," Nevis replied, "but you have to expect that with soldiers." With a wince, he removed a folded paper from his vest and dropped it on Leo's desk. "This was in Captain Bougaire's room. A letter from the Lady of Vindalyn."

Leo's hands clenched. *Dammit.* "You were supposed to find information about the assassins, not . . ." *Proof she's having an affair.* He didn't want to believe it. Didn't want her to love anyone else. Not when he needed her.

"She doesn't care for him," Brody said softly. "I'm certain of it."

Leo took a deep breath. Why was Brody so quick to defend her? "I don't think her bedchamber is secure enough."

"Really?" Brody ate more roast beef. "Her guard and I have been watching the door."

"Yes, but did you know there's a second door that leads to her maid's room and another hallway? And two large windows that are easily accessible from outside. Are the duke's chambers similar?"

"His rooms are on the east wing next to the library," Nevis answered. "There are several entrances, but I'll make sure each one has two guards. And I'll ask the duke if he wants his daughter moved to another location. Where do you suggest?"

Leo refilled his goblet. "One of the towers would be best."

"Did you find anything on the priests?" Brody asked.

Leo repeated what he'd told Nevis earlier. "I think Father Rune is one of the assassins. What have you learned?"

Brody paused, then gulped down some wine. "I'm still trying to figure it out."

"Figure what?" Leo asked.

Brody shrugged, then took another long drink.

Leo narrowed his eyes.

"I knew it," Nevis muttered. "She had a secret meeting with her lover." He glanced at Leo. "No offense."

"She did not!" Brody slammed his empty goblet down. "She doesn't even like him. She was cringing when he accosted her on the stairs."

"He *what*?" Leo jumped to his feet.

"Nothing happened," Brody insisted. "And it was clear she wanted nothing to do with him."

Leo sat back down. Then she wasn't having an affair?

"But what about this love letter?" Nevis pointed at the paper on the desk. "It's from the Lady of Vindalyn."

Brody hesitated, then mumbled, "Then it's one more strange thing that doesn't make sense."

"What's not making sense?" Leo asked.

Brody shrugged and quickly finished his dinner.

Leo tapped a finger on the desk. His spy wasn't telling him everything. "Nevis, take his tray back."

"Huh?" Nevis looked confused.

Leo gave him a pointed look. "Take his tray. I'll see you tomorrow. Tell Edmund I won't need him again tonight."

"Oh." Nevis picked up the tray, slanting a wary glance at Brody. "All right. Good night." He wandered from the tent.

With a grimace, Brody refilled his goblet.

Leo frowned at him. "What are you not telling me?"

"I'd rather not say—I mean, she seems to be keeping it a secret, so I thought I should honor—"

"So you're loyal to her now? Do I need to remind you that you work for me?"

Brody flashed him an annoyed look.

Leo tensed. "Are you . . . attracted to her?"

"No!" Brody closed his eyes briefly. "Yes, but not the way you think. She has a kind heart that reminds me of my younger sister."

Leo exhaled with relief. "I didn't know you had a sister."

"I haven't seen my family in years." Brody gazed sadly across the tent, seemingly lost in thought.

"So you feel a need to protect Lady Tatiana."

Brody visibly shook himself. "I'm following orders. You told me to protect her."

"Not from *me*! I would never harm her." Leo winced. "On purpose." *Dammit.* He was the most likely person to cause her harm.

"I know that." Brody gave him a wry look. "I actually think she'll be good for you."

"Then talk."

"Fine. But I'm warning you. It's . . . strange."

"She's *my* betrothed. I'll decide what's strange."

Brody ran a finger around the rim of his goblet. "At first I feared she might be insane."

"What?"

"Then I thought she might be a witch. But she's too kindhearted to be a bad witch."

"What?"

"Then I realized it must be a gift. A secret gift."

Leo leaned forward. "What, dammit? Spit it out!"

"Fine! She . . . talks to people who aren't there."

"Aren't where?"

"Here. As in . . . dead."

Leo blinked. "She's talking to dead people? Are you sure? I mean, perhaps she was talking to you. Or herself. Sometimes I talk to myself. That's not strange."

"This was strange. As far as I could tell, she was talking to a boy who died in a kitchen fire ten years ago."

"Damn."

"And then she ran up to a tower room and talked to someone else who wasn't there." Brody ran a hand through his shaggy black hair. "I could only hear half of the conversation, but she seemed eager to talk to her mother."

Leo grimaced. "Lady Tatiana's mother is dead."

"Exactly."

Leo shook his head. "This is crazy."

Brody scoffed. "I'm stuck as a dog for most of my life. You shoot lightning from your freaking fingers. We're not exactly in a position to judge what's crazy."

"We can't help it. We're Embra—" With a quick intake of air, Leo sat back. "Holy shit. She's Embraced."

Chapter Eleven

❧

The next morning, Luciana woke before sunrise and quickly dressed in the simplest clothes she could find—a gray linen dress, black leather slippers, and a black leather cord tied around her waist.

When she opened the bedchamber door, her guard, Jensen, bowed. "My lady, did you have need of anything?"

"No, thank you." She frowned at the dark circles under his eyes. "Jensen, did you not get any sleep at all?"

"I'm fine," he assured her.

"I think you should go rest." She started down the dimly lit hallway, but he followed her. "There's no need for you to come. I'm only going to watch the sunrise."

"I dare not leave you unaccompanied, my lady."

She groaned inwardly. How could she find the message from Maeve when he was watching her every move? A soft woof drew her attention. "Pirate!"

The dog sat in front of her and lifted a paw.

She shook his paw. "Would you like to see the sunrise with me?" she asked, and he woofed in response.

"Good boy." She rubbed him behind the ears.

She went down the stairs and out the door into the courtyard, followed by Jensen and Pirate. The sky overhead was still dark, but a few torches lent enough light for her to pass through the eastern gate. She hurried to the outer stone wall on the eastern edge of the promontory.

After climbing a narrow stone staircase, she arrived on the wall walk overlooking the coastline to the east. The two moons had moved west, the larger Luna reaching the horizon first and casting a silver glow over the sea.

Below her, she could barely make out the beach. Maeve had told her to watch the eastern beach at sunrise, so she could only trust that her youngest sister knew what she was doing.

Next to Luciana, Pirate was sitting and watching her curiously. Jensen glanced over the curtain wall and, after seeing no danger below, marched down the wall walk, surveying the keep and inner bailey.

She kept her back to him and focused on the eastern horizon. After a few minutes, a soft, golden glow inched into view. "May the Light shine upon us always," she said loud enough for the guard to hear, then in her mind she sent a prayer to the goddesses to watch over her sisters.

"Amen," she said softly, and since no one was watching except Pirate, she made the sign of the two moons.

The sun rose slowly, painting the sea and sky with colors of pink and gold. She held up a hand to shade her eyes and focused on the sea just below.

Now she could see the different colors of the sea: the darker blue of the deep and the bright turquoise close to the shore. The waves rolled in, crashing and foaming over large boulders that dotted the shallow turquoise water.

Softly, she sang the Song of Mourning as if the words could somehow bring her the message from her sisters. "My true love lies in the ocean blue. My true love sleeps in the sea. Whenever the moons shine over you, please remember me. Please remember me."

Suddenly a seal leaped from the sea and landed on a

large, flat boulder. The sea around the rock churned as more seals gathered around it. The first seal barked, and more seals skidded up onto the boulder. They waddled into a tight group, their wet skin glistening in the sun.

Next to Luciana, Pirate rose onto his hind legs to peer over the wall. When more seals barked, he barked in reply.

She laughed. "Are you trying to talk to them?"

All the seals slipped back into the water. And there alone on the boulder was a glass bottle, the kind the nuns used to hold their different colors of paint.

"That's it," she whispered. Maeve had done it! She'd used the seals to deliver a message.

With a small squeal of excitement, Luciana hugged the dog. "I'm so happy!"

Pirate gave her a confused look, but she just laughed and headed down the stairs. The dog and Jensen followed her as she ran past the keep and toward the main gate.

At the gatehouse, another guard tried to stop her. "My lady, it's not safe for you to leave the fortress."

"I'm only going to the beach." She motioned to Jensen and Pirate. "I won't be alone." Before the gatekeeper could object, she dashed across the drawbridge, then headed for the path that led to the shore.

She hurried down the path as quickly as she dared, worried that at any moment a wave would crash over the boulder and wash away the bottle. Pirate ran ahead of her and scampered along the beach, sniffing here and there.

"Why are you doing this?" Jensen asked behind her.

"Why not?" She reached the sand and looked about. Far to the east, the waves had blasted a cave into the rocky cliff. "I think there's someone there!" She pointed.

"I'll investigate," Jensen replied. "Stay here."

"Of course." The minute the guard took off running

down the beach, she kicked off her shoes and walked into the water. She winced, surprised by how cold the water was.

Pirate splashed into the water to get in front of her, then attempted to herd her ashore.

"You're not stopping me." She gathered up her skirt around her knees and waded deeper, headed for the boulder. The waves receded, sucking her feet with them, and she skidded a bit before regaining her balance.

She hitched her skirt up higher as the water reached her thighs. Almost there. She winced as the cold water reached her private parts, then lunged forward to grab onto the boulder.

The bottle was a few inches out of reach. Pirate barked at her. He was up to his neck in water.

"Stay there!" she warned him. Letting go of her skirt, she felt around the rock till she found an indentation she could slip a foot into. She heaved herself up till she could grab the bottle.

"Got it!" She jumped back into the sea just as the waves receded. The undertow whisked her off her feet and she went under. She struggled to get back onto her feet, but it was difficult with her skirt in the way.

Finally, she managed to stand. The wind was chilly against her wet hair and clothes. Taking deep breaths, she thanked the goddesses that she'd grown up on the Isle of Moon where she'd learned to swim at a young age. The water was only waist-high, but the undertow was strong. She glanced at the bottle held tightly in her fist. It was sealed with a tight cork, and inside was a rolled-up note.

She let the next wave push her closer ashore. Pirate grabbed her skirt with his teeth and pulled her toward the beach. She splashed through ankle-high water till she reached the dry, warm sand.

"My lady!" Jensen ran toward her. "What are you doing?"

"I'm fine." She waved at him with one hand while holding the bottle behind her back with the other. "I felt like having an early-morning swim. So invigorating!"

"Are you all right?" He stepped toward her, but jumped back when Pirate shook himself, sending droplets of water in all directions.

"I'm perfectly fine." She motioned for him to turn around. "Could I have some privacy, please? I need to wring out my skirt."

"Aye, my lady." He turned his back.

She plopped down on the sand, wrenched the cork out of the bottle, then fished out the note. Pirate made a whimpering noise as he sat next to her, his head cocked with an inquisitive look.

She put a finger to her lips to signal silence, then unfolded the note. It was signed at the bottom by her sisters. With a grin, she hugged the paper to her chest, then held it up where she could read it.

Our dear sister, Luciana,

We pray every day that you are safe and doing well. We miss you something terrible. Our room seems empty without you. Our meals seem lonely without you.

We tried playing the Telling Stones last night, but no one gives predictions as good as yours. We were talking about your last prediction, and we wondered if it had come true. You said in two weeks you would meet a tall and handsome stranger who had red hair and a black horse. Did it happen? Did you meet him?

To bring you good luck, we have put your Telling Stones in the bottle.

Luciana peered at the bottle, and sure enough, there were three pebbles in the bottom. The number two, red, and black. With a sigh, she pressed the bottle against her chest. She had indeed met a tall and handsome stranger with red hair and a black horse.

"Are you done, my lady?" Jensen asked.

"Not quite," she replied, then went back to the letter.

We cannot wait to hear from you! Maeve says on the third day after today at dawn, you are to place a note in this bottle and put it in the same place that you found it.

Please write! And know that you always have our love. Brigitta. Sorcha. Gwennore. Maeve.

Luciana wiped a tear from her cheek. "I love you, too."

Jensen stiffened. "My lady?"

"I was talking to the dog."

Pirate snorted and flopped onto his belly, a forlorn look on his face.

Quickly, she inserted the note back into the bottle and corked it. Then she squeezed some water from her skirts, deposited the bottle in a deep pocket, and slipped on her shoes. "I'm ready to go."

Back in her bedchamber, she built up the fire in the hearth, then quickly removed her wet clothes and put on a robe. It was dangerous to keep the correspondence from her sisters, but she couldn't bring herself to burn it. The bottle and pebbles were harmless, she figured, since they wouldn't mean anything to anyone but her. After inspecting the room, she found a slight opening in the upholstery of one of the chairs and slipped the note inside.

When Gabriella came in with her breakfast tray, she gasped at the sight of wet clothes in front of the hearth. Luciana was equally shocked, for her maid had come in through the dressing room.

"How did you do that?" Luciana wandered toward the dressing room door, which was still open.

"There's a servants' door," Gabriella replied as she set the tray on the table. "My room is on the other side. I thought you knew that."

"Oh, of course." Luciana waved a dismissive hand. Now that she was looking for it, she could make out the lines of a door hidden in the wooden paneling. "And your room has another way out?"

"Yes, a servants' corridor." Gabriella gathered up the wet clothes. "I'll take these to the laundry room, then come back to help you dress for mass."

"Thank you." Luciana watched as Gabriella pushed a hidden latch in the paneling and a door swung open. As the maid left, she smiled to herself. This was a way she could leave without being followed by her guard.

Mass wasn't as bad as she had feared. A new guard escorted her to the chapel and back, since Jensen was finally getting some rest. Afterward, she did as her father had requested and spent the rest of the day in her bedchamber.

That afternoon, a new guard from the Lord Protector's army arrived. Unfortunately, he knew about the second exit through Gabriella's room. He spent his time marching from one exit to the other.

Dinner in the Great Hall was uneventful. Luciana kept glancing at the musicians' gallery, hoping to see her dream man, but he never put in an appearance. Disappointed, she retired to her room early.

As Gabriella helped her change into her nightgown, she told her, "I won't need you for the rest of the evening."

"Really?" Gabriella's eyes lit up. "The servants are having a party tonight with all the food and wine that was left over from last night's banquet."

"Then you must go and enjoy yourself."

"Thank you!" Gabriella rushed through her small room and out the door.

Quickly, Luciana pulled on a black gown and dark cloak. In her bedchamber, she plumped up a line of pillows and pulled the coverlet over them. Now if a guard or Gabriella checked on her, they would think she was asleep.

A twinge of guilt pricked her. It was not like her to

deceive people, but how could she explain her need to go to the southwestern tower? And she certainly couldn't risk anyone hearing her reunion with her mother. Besides, if the guards were here to keep her from escaping her betrothed, there was no need for that. In order to keep her father alive, she would go ahead and marry the Lord Protector. Even if he was a Beast.

This one small act of rebellion would not cause anyone any harm. She slipped through Gabriella's room and peeked out the door. The hallway was empty! The guard from the Lord Protector's army must be by the other door. She dashed down the servants' corridor before he could return, then scurried down the stairs.

In the courtyard, she stayed in the shadows, her dark gown and cloak keeping her hidden. There was quite a bit of traffic going back and forth through the south gate as servants brought food from the kitchens to the hall where they were having their party. She followed a group out and no guards stopped her.

It was a dark night, with clouds hiding most of the twin moons. She dashed across the sheep pasture, then climbed the stairs in the southwestern tower till she arrived at her mother's favorite room.

"Hello," she whispered as she shut the door. The small bedchamber was dim with a little starlight shining through the two windows. "It's me. Luciana."

There was no one there. Yet.

"Report," Leo told Nevis and Brody that evening in his tent.

"Nothing happened," Nevis said as he poured himself a goblet of wine. "It was a quiet day."

Leo drummed his gloved fingers on his desk. What was taking the assassins so long to make their move? He'd only arrived here yesterday, but already he was getting damned tired of lurking about the camp when he should be in the castle, attempting to court Tatiana.

He glanced at Brody. "Anything to report?"

The dog shifter looked up from the meal he was wolfing down. "She . . . stayed in her room most of the day."

"And when she wasn't in her room?"

Brody slanted a wary glance at Nevis, then downed his goblet of wine.

Leo sat back in his chair. Had she talked to more dead people today? "Nevis, you may go."

"Huh?" Nevis looked them over, then lifted his chin. "Why should I? Do you think I can't be trusted?"

"I trust you when it concerns me," Leo told him. "But this is about Lady Tatiana."

"She's going to be your wife. I would protect her just like I do you." Nevis thumped his chest. "With my life!"

Leo gave his old friend a wry smile. "All right. But there are some strange things going on you might find hard to believe. And you'll need to keep it secret."

"Of course." Nevis stepped closer. "What is it?"

"We believe she's Embraced," Leo said softly. "And her gift is the ability to see and talk to the dead."

Nevis stiffened. "Damn. That is strange."

Brody sighed. "It's about to get stranger."

"How do you get stranger than that?" Nevis asked.

Brody refilled his goblet. "She received a secret letter at dawn."

"From her lover?" Nevis asked.

"No!" Brody shouted, then gritted his teeth. "She's not having an affair."

Nevis scoffed. "Of course she is. I found that note she wrote to Captain—"

"Forget the note." Leo folded his arms on the desk and leaned toward Brody. "How did she receive this letter?"

Brody sipped some wine. "It was on a rock offshore.

She had to wade into the sea to get it. I tried to stop her. The undertow was strong and swept her off her feet—"

"Is she all right?" Leo asked.

Brody nodded. "And she was delighted with the letter."

"It must be from her lover," Nevis grumbled.

"No." Brody shot him an annoyed look. "If the letter was from Captain Booger, why would he leave it in the sea where it was dangerous for her to retrieve it? He could leave it anywhere in the castle."

"That's true." Leo frowned. "Unless he's one of the assassins and he's trying to kill her."

Brody shook his head. "I don't think he left it there. He was nowhere in sight."

"Then who left it?" Leo asked.

Brody hesitated, then looked away. "I don't know."

Leo narrowed his eyes. "You do."

Brody made a noise of frustration. "It was . . . seals."

"*What?*" Leo and Nevis both asked.

Brody shrugged. "I told you it was strange."

"Seals?" Leo ran a gloved hand through his hair. "Some creatures from the sea brought her a message? How?"

"It was in a bottle. With a few colored pebbles." Brody shifted in his chair. "And there's more."

"What?" Leo muttered. "A walrus?"

"She made the sign of the moons."

Leo sat back. *Holy shit.* "That could get her killed."

"Did anyone see her?" Nevis asked.

Brody shook his head. "She was careful."

"Not careful enough." Leo tapped a finger on the table. "Why would she pray to the goddesses? That only happens on the islands."

"According to the gossip I heard, that's where she was nursed back to health. After she and her father became ill in Ronsmouth, he took her to a convent on the Isle of Moon. They have a nun there who's a renowned healer."

Nevis nodded. "I heard the same thing."

"So she switched her faith to their goddesses?" Leo asked. "She couldn't have been there a fortnight."

Brody shrugged. "But if she nearly died, and the nuns saved her, she might believe it was their goddesses who made it happen."

"I suppose." Leo didn't actually care which gods she prayed to. He just didn't want her endangering herself in the process. He sat up when something occurred to him. "The message could have come from the Isle of Moon."

Brody's eyes widened. "Perhaps."

"But who would send it?" Nevis asked.

"A nun from the convent?" Brody suggested.

Leo tilted his head, considering. "Would a nun use seals as a messenger service?"

Brody frowned. "You're thinking a witch sent it?"

Leo sighed. "I don't know what to think." But one thing was clear. His betrothed was much more interesting than he had ever imagined she could be. Beautiful and intriguing. He couldn't wait to discover more about her.

Luciana woke with a start and gazed around the dark room. She'd waited so long she'd fallen asleep on the bed.

She rushed to the tower window that overlooked the Southern Sea. The twin moons were still above the western horizon. Dawn was an hour or so away.

Disappointment needled her as she made her way down the spiral staircase. She'd waited for hours, and her mother's spirit had never appeared. Or perhaps her mother had come, but she'd slept right through it.

At the base of the tower she found Pirate, curled up and waiting. "How did you know I was here?" She rubbed his ears. He'd probably tracked her with his excellent sense of smell. "Come on, let's go."

They ran across the meadow. A heavenly scent emanated

from the kitchens. The daily bread was being baked. As they entered the ground floor of the keep, she spotted a huge pillar candle that had been burning all night long. On the table surrounding it were smaller candlesticks. She lit one, then climbed the stairs.

As they walked along the upstairs hallway, her steps sounded loud on the black-and-white tiled floor. Even Pirate's claws made little clicking noises. At this time of night, the castle seemed deserted. They reached the smaller hall that led to her bedchamber.

It was dark. Pirate crouched low and growled. She eased forward, holding out her candle, but Pirate jumped in front to stop her. Why was her door open? She glanced down and gasped.

Jensen was on the floor in a crumpled heap.

Pirate gave him a quick sniff, then slipped through the open door.

"Jensen?" Luciana knelt beside him. Her heart thudded in her ears. Was he dead? She didn't see any blood.

She shook him and he moaned. *Oh, thank the goddesses!*

"What's happening?" Tatiana asked, and with a yelp, Luciana nearly dropped the candle on her guard.

"Ye scared me self to death." Luciana pressed a hand to her pounding heart.

Jensen moaned again.

"It looks like someone knocked him out," Tatiana whispered.

"I wonder what happened to the guard from the Lord Protector?" Luciana asked.

"Oh, I saw him," Tatiana replied with a smirk. "He's outside Gabriella's door, snoring away. He's going to be in big trouble."

Luciana's gaze shifted to the open door. Was Pirate all right? "Go inside and see if anyone's there."

"Me?" Tatiana scoffed. "Are you trying to get me killed? Oh. Right. Just a minute." She slipped inside.

With a groan, Jensen sat up. His eyes widened with alarm. "My lady. Are you all right?"

"Yes. But someone's been in my room." She helped him to his feet.

Tatiana filtered through the wall. "There's no one there, but the dog. He's—"

"Stay behind me." Jensen drew his sword and pushed the door wider open.

Luciana followed close behind, holding the candle aloft so they could see. When they neared the bed, she gasped.

Her pillows were still lined up under the coverlet to look like she was asleep. But a sword had been plunged right through them.

"By the Light," Tatiana whispered. "Somebody wants you dead."

Chapter Twelve

꩜

"Is she all right?" Leo demanded. It was an hour before dawn, and Nevis had woken him with alarming news.

"She's shaken, but otherwise fine," Nevis replied.

"What the hell has happened?" General Harden threw on a cloak as he rushed out of his tent and headed their way.

Nevis quickly repeated the news while Leo paced in front of his tent, eyeing the fortress in the distance. It was still dark, so he could only make out a few torches on the curtain wall. "Where is she now?"

"Her guard took her to her father," Nevis explained. "She's now heavily guarded in the duke's private rooms."

Leo continued to pace. "And our guard? Where the hell was he?"

Nevis winced. "He fell asleep outside the maid's door."

Leo halted with a jerk and clenched his gloved hands. "See to his punishment. And where was Brody? How did an assassin get past him?"

"Brody wasn't anywhere near her bedchamber," Nevis said. "He spent the night guarding the southwestern tower. Somehow she sneaked out of her room to go there."

"Why?"

Nevis shrugged. "Hell if I know, but it saved her life. The assassin stabbed her bed in the dark, believing a line of pillows was her body."

She'd sneaked out without her guards knowing? Leo groaned inwardly. "Was she meeting someone?"

Nevis shook his head. "Brody said she was alone the entire time she was in the tower."

By the Light, what was she up to? The woman was too intriguing for her own good. Leo resumed his pacing. "And no one saw the assassin?"

Nevis sighed. "The guard caught only a glimpse of him before he was knocked out. He was masked and moving extremely fast. Brody was able to detect the man's scent, so he should be able to identify him."

"Where's Brody now?" the general asked.

"He's outside the duke's private rooms," Nevis said. "If the assassin comes near, he'll recognize him."

Leo continued to pace, too tense to remain still. "Tell the duke to move his daughter to a tower and install guards at every entrance. Two at her chamber door. Station the guards inside the tower, where no one can see them. Only a select few should know her new location. Make sure to include some of our guards. Meanwhile, the duke will spread the word that she is back in her old rooms, where she is in bed, seriously wounded and not expected to live."

The general nodded. "A good plan. If the assassins think they've succeeded, they won't make a second attempt."

"What about Brody?" Nevis asked. "Shall I take him through the barracks to track down the assassin?"

"Wait a few hours. I want the assassin to believe he got away with it, so he'll relax his guard. And I want to be there when Brody finds him." Leo tugged at his gloves. "For now, have Brody guard the tower. And tell the duke to double the guard around himself. The assassins will target him next. Go now. Keep me informed."

"Aye." General Harden gave him a reassuring smile. "Don't worry. We'll keep them safe." He strode toward the fortress with Nevis at his side.

Leo watched them go. His plan had worked. Too damned well. The assassins had tried to complete their mission before the Beast could arrive. But dammit, they might have succeeded tonight if Tatiana had been in her bed where she belonged.

Shit! He could have lost her. He tilted his head back, dragging his gloved hands through his hair. To hell with the plan. He couldn't hide here in the camp any longer. Tatiana was his betrothed. He should be with her, guarding her himself.

No one would dare mess with the Beast.

Luciana was back in her mother's room in the tower. Under normal circumstances, she would have rejoiced that her father had moved her here. Now she had a much greater chance of meeting her mother.

But circumstances were far from normal. Someone had tried to kill her, and according to her father, the assassin was following orders from the king.

The king wants me dead. The words repeated in her mind as she paced back and forth in the dark room. Father had insisted she stay hidden here for a few days.

Only a little moonlight came through the two windows. The candlestick on the bedside table cast a flickering glow against the walls, making shadows loom and fall as if they were reaching out to grab her.

She shuddered. Her imagination was getting out of hand. But why shouldn't she be afraid? The king wanted her dead.

Her mind replayed the conversation with her father.

Every shocking word. And the gut-wrenching screech from Tatiana when she'd learned that she'd been poisoned.

Luciana paused by the window overlooking the Southern Sea. The twin moons were setting in the west, where the Isle of Moon slept peacefully in the ocean. Out there was her home, her sisters. And here, assassins waited for their chance to kill her and her father.

Tears stung her eyes. All those years when she'd imagined true love and adventure beyond the convent, she hadn't realized what a safe haven it was. She reached a hand through the window, wishing she could touch her sisters.

Father had offered to send her back. He'd said he could tell everyone that she had died. Then he would secretly send her back. And she would be safe.

Home. With her sisters.

She sang softly, "My true love lies in the ocean blue. My true love sleeps in the sea. Whenever the moons shine over you, please remember me. My lonesome heart is torn in two. My grief runs deep as the sea. Whenever the waves roll over you, please remember me. Please remember me."

A tear slid down her cheek and angrily, she brushed it away. This was no time to be a homesick coward! She'd gone into this deception knowing it would be dangerous. She couldn't surrender to fear at the first sign of trouble.

"Why are you upset?" Tatiana wailed behind her. "I'm the one who was murdered!"

Luciana whirled around to find her sister with tears running down her cheeks. As soon as Tatiana had heard the news from Father, she'd screeched and promptly vanished. "Where did you go? I was worried about you."

"Were you really?" Tatiana gave her a dubious look.

"Of course."

Tatiana sniffed. "It's not fair. The king killed me just so he could get this moldy old castle."

"I'm so sorry."

"It should be a crime to kill someone young and beautiful like me!"

Luciana sighed. "It is a crime. But apparently, the king can get away with it."

Tatiana stomped a foot silently. "I should go to his palace in Ebton and sneak into his rooms. Yes!" She lifted her arms, her hands curled into claws. "I'll haunt him without mercy. He'll never know a minute of peace again!"

A sudden thought occurred to Luciana. "You can sneak into rooms."

"I know." Tatiana rolled her eyes. "I just said that."

"Father thinks the assassin could be a new guard."

"So?"

"Instead of haunting the king, you could sneak into the barracks and watch the guards." Luciana stepped toward her sister. "You are uniquely qualified to be a spy!"

"I am?"

"Yes. Tatiana, you could find the assassin!"

"Oh." Her eyes widened. "Y-you really think I could?"

"You could save Father's life. You could be a hero."

"Oh." With a sly smile, Tatiana curled a lock of hair around her finger. "Yes, I suppose I could." Her eyes lit up. "Why didn't I think about sneaking into the barracks before? I could watch the guards taking off their clothes!"

"Wait a minute. Don't forget your mission."

Tatiana clapped her hands together, then whirled in a circle. "I'm so excited!" She vanished.

"Wait—" Luciana sighed. Well, at least her sister was no longer upset. And she couldn't actually get into any danger.

There was a loud pounding on her door. "Are you all right, my lady?" Jensen yelled.

"Yes." She raised her voice so he could hear her through the thick door. "I was just talking to myself."

She roamed about the room. It was much smaller than Tatiana's bedchamber, but she liked it that way. It was cozy, and she enjoyed the fresh sea air that wafted through the windows. The wooden table and chairs in front of the hearth were simple in design. The bed was smaller than Tatiana's, but still bigger than she was accustomed to.

There was something odd about the wall across from the window that overlooked the sea. The interior of the tower room had been painted white, but this one section looked like it had been scorched. She ran a hand across the black-ened paint. Had someone held a torch against the wall?

Father had explained that her mother had found the du-ties of being a duchess rather daunting. So even though they loved each other very much and had shared a bed-chamber in the keep, she'd enjoyed having a private place she could escape to.

Luciana washed, using the bowl of water and towel that a guard had left for her. Jensen had sneaked into her dress-ing room to fetch a nightgown for her. As she slipped it on, she winced at how thin it was. There were no shutters on the windows, and the night air was rather cool. Fortu-nately, the bed had several blankets.

She crawled under the blankets and leaned back against the headboard. She was tired from being awake most of the night. But how could she possibly sleep when the king wanted her dead?

Unable to sleep, Leo paced about his tent. The more he learned about Tatiana, the more confused he became. Why had she sneaked off to a tower room for the night?

He opened his desk drawer and glared at the letter she'd written to Captain Bougaire. He hadn't opened it. The thought of reading endearments meant for another man was too wretched to bear. He'd rather take another light-ning strike than see proof that she loved another.

He slammed the drawer shut. That chapter in her life was officially closed. She belonged to him now.

He resumed his pacing. In all fairness, he couldn't begrudge the life she'd led before the betrothal. No doubt, she had never dreamed she'd be forced to marry the Beast.

Besides, he wasn't a virgin himself. Five years ago, a great drought had fallen over Eberon. With no rain or lightning for a year, his power had completely drained away. Even so, only one of the camp followers had dared to let him touch her. She'd been older than the other women and not as popular, but she'd been kind to Leo. Especially when he'd asked her how a man could please a woman.

For a few months, Leo had experienced a taste of what other men enjoyed regularly, but then the storms had returned.

He glanced down at his gloved hands. It was tempting, so tempting, to go to the nearby cliffs, remove his gloves, and shoot lightning bolts over the water until his power was completely gone.

Then he would be able to hold Tatiana's hand. Touch her cheek. Her hair. Her body. Woo her in bed like any other newlywed husband.

But with his power gone, how would he protect her?

"Leo?" the general yelled in front of his tent. "Are you awake?"

"Coming." Leo threw on his cloak, then lifted the flap and stepped outside. Dawn was breaking, streaking the eastern horizon with shades of gold and pink. "What news?"

"Your lady is safely ensconced in the southwestern tower." General Harden pointed at it, then looked Leo over. "You're still dressed. Did you never sleep?"

"I couldn't." Leo glanced at the tower. "I've been trying to figure her out."

The general snorted. "Take some advice from an old

man who's been married over thirty years. Never try to understand a woman. It will drive you insane, and you still won't understand."

"It can't be that bad."

The general gave him a wry look. "You're used to winning battles, aye?"

Leo nodded. "Of course."

"Then prepare yourself for defeat." The general chuckled as he sauntered toward his tent. "Get some sleep, boy. She's safe now."

Defeat? Leo frowned. He wasn't about to take the general's word on that. Tatiana would soon learn that he was in charge. He studied the tower. Safe, was she? He was tempted to see just how safe she really was.

When he'd studied the fortress earlier, he'd noticed a narrow strip of land between the outer wall and dry moat. The strip ended with a cliff about six feet before the southwestern tower loomed up from the edge of the rocky promontory. A metal drainpipe was fastened to part of the tower, probably used to carry waste from a privy to the sea below. A normal man could never reach the drainpipe from the cliff. He would plummet to his death on the rocks below.

But Leo was not a normal man. And he was tired of other men watching over Tatiana. She was his betrothed. His responsibility. His challenge.

He removed his gloves and stuffed them beneath his belt. Lightning power tingled his fingertips as he strode through the camp, headed for the fortress. When he passed a narrow pole, he wrenched it from the ground and tore the red-and-black flag off the top. At the edge of the camp, he broke into a run.

Power surged through his limbs, increasing his speed. If one of the guards on the wall spotted him, he'd be nothing more than a blur.

As he approached the dry moat, he leaped into the air, planted the pole in the ground, and catapulted himself across. Releasing the pole, he landed neatly next to the wall. Immediately, he took off, running along the narrow strip of land between the wall and moat. By the time he reached the cliff's edge, he was at top speed.

With a leap, he hurled himself through the air. The sea raged against rocks below. Sparks skittered around his hands, pulling him like a magnet toward the metal pipe that ran down the side of the southwestern tower.

He latched on to the pipe and dug his booted feet into the recessed mortar between the stones. Barely pausing to catch his breath, he climbed up the pipe. Near the top, he spotted some wooden beams protruding a few inches from the tower wall. No doubt, the beams provided the base for a wooden floor inside the tower.

He reached for the first beam, leaving the pipe behind. With his feet dangling, he swung to the next beam and the next. Now he was hanging above the wall walk. Above him, there was a window, too far to reach. He'd have to go down.

There should be a guard inside the tower. Leo whistled, and sure enough, an armed guard stepped out to look around,

Leo dropped on top of him, knocking the guard down. One touch of his hand on the guard's uniform, and the man was jolted unconscious. An accidental touch to the man's bare skin would kill him, so Leo quickly put on his gloves. He dragged the man into the tower before any other guards on the wall walk could notice.

Now inside the tower, he spotted a door and opened it. The privy. He headed up the spiral staircase to the top floor.

Peering around the center column, he spotted two guards by the chamber door. He moved with lightning speed, and by the time they saw him, it was too late for them to unsheathe their swords. He grabbed each man by his helmet and clashed them together with enough force that they were both knocked out. As they tumbled onto the wooden floor, Leo removed one glove and peered at the lock in the door. The key was on the other side.

Energy surged around his bare hand, then reached out to connect with the large, metal key. Slowly, he turned his hand to rotate the key till he heard a click. He'd unlocked the door.

His heart pounded. He pulled the hood of his cloak over his head and tugged his glove back on. Then he quietly opened the door.

Chapter Thirteen

❧

A whistling sound woke Luciana from a light slumber. Probably a bird, she thought as she peered around the dimly lit room. Dawn was breaking, but very little sunlight filtered through the windows that faced north and west.

There was no need to worry, she told herself. Jensen and another guard were just outside her locked door. And more guards were below. There were even some soldiers from the Lord Protector's army on the ground floor. Father had assured her that while she remained hidden for a few days, all three assassins would be discovered.

She closed her eyes. *No need to worry.*

A clashing noise jolted her wide awake. She sat up as loud thuds hit the wooden floor outside. Her guards? Her heart leaped up her throat. The assassin was back!

Goddesses, help me! She jumped out of bed. Surely, the assassin couldn't get in. She'd locked the door herself.

Slowly, the key turned as if an invisible hand were moving it. How was that possible? Terror seized her in an iron grip as she looked frantically around the room. No weapons. If she jumped out a window, it would probably kill her.

With trembling hands, she reached for the candlestick

on her bedside table. With her right hand she yanked out the lit candle. Then she grasped the brass candleholder upside down with her left hand. If the assassin drew near, she'd burn him with the candle and clobber him with the heavy base of the candleholder.

Goddesses, give me strength. She'd never used violence before. But what choice did she have?

The door opened slowly, and she pressed against the wall as a cloaked man slipped inside. She couldn't make out his face hidden in the hood, but there was something oddly familiar about him.

He was tall. Muscular. Strong. He stepped noiselessly into the room, his movement stealthy and controlled.

Now. I should attack before he sees me. She drew in a deep breath and eased forward.

He spun around to face her, and she froze. His hood kept his face in shadow, but she could feel his gaze on her. His head tilted as if he was looking her over inch by inch. Suddenly she was painfully aware that she was wearing nothing but a thin white nightgown. And he was still staring.

"I apologize for alarming you," he said softly. "I thought you would be asleep."

"You hoped to stab me in my sleep?" She extended the candle toward him. "Don't come near me."

He remained still, but she could feel an intensity radiating around him, as if he was filling the room with a great deal of energy that he somehow kept in check. "You should put the candle down before the wax burns you."

"You'll be the one getting burned." She widened her stance and brandished her weapons. "You should leave while you have the chance."

There was a flash of white teeth when he smiled. "You're brave. I like that."

She blinked. Since when did an assassin flatter a victim

before doing his deadly deed? "Make no mistake. I will hurt you." She raised her voice and yelled, "Guards!"

"They can't hear you." He strode toward the window that overlooked the Southern Sea.

Her mouth fell open in disbelief. He'd turn his back on her? How could he be so sure she wouldn't attack? Or was he so arrogant he assumed her attack would fail? She was tempted to clonk him on the head just to prove she could.

She slapped herself mentally. Why fight an assassin when she could escape? She eased toward the door.

He peered out the window. "No need for you to leave. Especially dressed like that."

She glanced down and winced. Tatiana's nightgown was embarrassingly sheer. Even so, survival was more important than modesty. She took another large step toward the door.

He turned toward her, and she stilled. "I came to make sure your room is secure."

What? "Why?"

"To keep you safe." He studied the hearth for a moment, then moved to the window above the wall walk.

Who was this man? Somehow, she felt as if she should know him. Even his voice sounded familiar.

He peered out the window. "This could be used to access the room. You'll need more guards below."

She winced as a bead of hot wax plopped onto her hand. Curse this man, she hated for him to be right. She ought to clobber him just for that. She shook herself. Why was she thinking about him when she should be escaping? She edged toward the door.

"Don't go."

Did he have eyes in the back of his hood? She knew he couldn't, but somehow, he seemed acutely aware of her. That alone caused the skin on her arms to prickle with goose bumps. The tone of his voice, so deep and intense, was strangely appealing. She found herself unwilling to move. As if she was waiting, anticipating . . . something.

He turned toward her, and his chest expanded as he took a deep breath. "You're beautiful. I like that."

Her heart lurched into a pounding rhythm. Who was this man? Where had she heard him before?

He strolled to the scorch mark on the whitewashed wall and touched it with a gloved hand. "What happened here?"

"I don't know."

He motioned to the door. "I'll have a bolt installed. The lock isn't enough." With a fluid movement, he bent over and whisked a dagger from his boot.

She gasped.

He straightened. "You need not fear me. I will not harm you."

She blinked as the familiar words clicked in her mind. "Ye—you're the false priest who listened to my confession."

His teeth flashed white again as he smiled. "You're clever. I like that."

She swallowed hard. Was he trying to kill her with compliments? At the rate her heart was hammering, he might succeed.

He tossed his dagger onto her bed. "Keep it by your pillow. Don't hesitate to use it."

"On you?"

Another flash of white as he smiled. "You could try." His smile faded, and she could feel his gaze moving slowly over her. The last remnant of her fear melted away, and a different sort of sensation crept into her, making her skin tingle and her heart flutter instead of pound.

She lowered her weapons, and the movement extinguished the flame on her candle. How could he affect her like this? With just a few words and a smile, he was rendering her defenseless.

"Tatiana," he said softly, and she swore she felt heartache in his voice. Or perhaps that was her own heart twisting, for he had called her by the wrong name.

He stepped toward her. "I promise I will do my best to never harm you."

"Who are you?"

"I'm—" Shouts rang out in the tower, and he sighed. "I'm out of time." He strode toward the window overlooking the wall walk. "I'll see you again soon."

Her jaw dropped as he climbed onto the stone windowsill. Surely he didn't plan to jump?

More loud voices sounded outside her door. Her unconscious guards had been discovered.

The cloaked man could barely fold his tall frame into the window. He glanced back at her. "I'll make sure you're safe, so get some sleep." His smile flashed again. "And if you dream, think of me."

He jumped out.

Luciana dropped her weapons and ran to the window. His cloak rippled in the air as he swooped down. He landed, immediately rolling forward in a somersault. When he rose smoothly to his feet, his hood fell back.

She gasped. Red hair. As if he'd heard her, he looked up.

It was him. Red and black. The man on the black horse. The man in the Great Hall. The man she'd intended to keep secretly in her dreams. He had been the one who had listened to her confession.

He lifted a gloved hand and smiled.

Her heart thudded so hard, she pressed a hand to her chest. Clattering noises sounded behind her as the guards rushed in. They talked to her, but their voices didn't register. She could only stare at the mysterious man who had invaded her room.

A guard moved beside her to peer out the window. He yelled, and the guards dashed from her room.

"Go," she whispered, but the redheaded man was already running down the wall walk. Guards from the gatehouse battlements started toward him. Soon, she saw her guards charging from the tower.

He would be surrounded.

Suddenly he leaped over the wall. His cape flapped in the wind, then disappeared.

Luciana inhaled sharply. How could he survive such a fall? But then he was no ordinary man.

She turned and leaned her back against the wall. Her hand was still pressed against her pounding heart.

And if you dream, think of me.

She sighed. "I believe I will."

"Tatiana! Are you all right? Tatiana!"

Luciana woke with a start.

Christopher's eyes widened. "You're alive!"

"Aye." She sat up in bed. Sunlight was pouring into the tower room now. She must have slept several hours.

"Oh, thank the Light." Christopher tried to bounce up onto the bed beside her, but slipped through the mattress. "I've been looking everywhere for you. I heard in the kitchens that you were dying. The servants are so upset."

Luciana winced. "I'm sorry."

"My mom was crying." Christopher stuck out his bottom lip. "You should tell her you're all right."

"I wish I could." Luciana hesitated, then decided the boy could handle the truth. He'd suffered much worse trauma than this. "The duke wants everyone to believe I'm at death's door."

Christopher blinked. "Why?"

"So the assassin who tried to kill me will leave me alone."

"What?" Christopher's form wavered.

"Don't worry. I'm fine," she reassured him. "And I'll stay fine as long as I remain hidden."

"Why?" Christopher's form grew more solid. "Why would someone want to kill you?"

"The king wants the Duchy of Vindalyn, and he's sent three assassins here to kill me and my father."

Christopher thought for a moment. "Then the king is a bad man."

"Yes, he is."

"And the assassins are bad, too."

Luciana swung her feet over the side of the bed as a thought occurred to her. She'd sent her sister to spy on the guards in the barracks. Perhaps Christopher could help, too. "Father believes one of the new priests could be an assassin."

Christopher's mouth fell open. "Really?"

"You could help me and the duke. If you watched the priests, you might discover which one is the bad one. You might even find proof. You could be a spy for me."

Christopher's eyes lit up. "A spy?" He bounced around the room, then stopped in front of her. "I haven't been this excited in ages!"

She smiled. "Then I will ask you to kneel." When he did, she took the dagger left behind by the redheaded man and pretended to tap the flat of the blade against the boy's shoulders. "You may rise, Sir Christopher."

With a giggle, he jumped to his feet. "I'm a knight!"

"And a fine one at that. Do you accept your mission?"

He nodded solemnly. "Don't worry, Tatiana. I'll find the bad man for you." His form wavered, then disappeared.

Luciana had barely risen to her feet when he popped back in. "Oh. That was fast."

Christopher laughed. "I forgot to tell you. I heard something else in the kitchens. They were busy making a fancy luncheon for your father and your betrothed."

Her heart lurched. "My . . ."

Christopher nodded. "Aye. The man you're supposed to marry. He arrived a few hours ago, and he's in the library with your father. My mom said it was so sad that he arrived just as you were dying."

"Oh." She'd thought he was delayed a few days. She'd thought she would have some time before having to meet him.

Christopher frowned. "Some of the servants called him the Beast, but my mom told them to hush. Why would they call him a Beast?"

Luciana swallowed hard, then waved a dismissive hand. "Nothing but gossip, I'm sure. Now, off you go. You have a mission, remember?"

"Aye, Captain!" Christopher saluted with a grin, then vanished.

Luciana made the sign of the moons. *Luna and Lessa, help me.* The Beast had arrived.

A knock on her door made her jump. Was he here already?

"My lady?" Jensen called. "Are you awake? I thought I heard your voice."

"I-I was talking to myself."

"Permission to enter?"

"Just a minute." She quickly put on the black gown she'd worn the night before. After braiding her hair and stepping into her shoes, she unlocked the door.

Jensen bowed. "We have orders to take you back to your bedchamber for a little while. Please wear your hooded cloak so no one will see you. And don't worry. We'll have guards posted at both entrances. You'll be safe."

"All right." She pulled on her dark cloak and followed Jensen down the spiral staircase. "I'm sorry you were knocked out. Again."

Jensen glanced back with an apologetic look. "You must think I'm incompetent."

"No, not at all. I appreciate what you're doing."

"Thank you, my lady. Keep your hood on so no one will see your face. While you're in the keep, we'll be installing a bolt for your door here in the tower."

She bit her lip. They were doing what the redheaded man had ordered? When they reached the ground floor, she asked, "Then I will continue to live in the tower?"

"Yes." Jensen gave her a worried look. "I don't wish to alarm you but your betrothed arrived early this morning. He's currently in the library with your father."

She nodded. "I understand."

"The Lord Protector requested a meeting with you," Jensen continued. "That's why we're taking you back to your dressing room. So you can get ready."

She swallowed hard. "I see." She pulled her hood up and started across the sheep meadow with Jensen and two other guards. Soon she would be meeting the Beast.

Jensen sighed. "The Lord Protector's arrival has changed everything. You'll be expected to spend time with him. And once the servants know you're alive and well, the news will spread quickly."

Her hands tightened their grip on her cloak. "I will be in more danger then?"

"You should be all right. Only a few guards know that you are sleeping in the tower. And no one would dare try to harm you when you're with the Lord Protector."

Because even the assassins feared him? Luciana took a deep breath to steady her nerves.

Back in her room, Gabriella burst into tears when she saw her. "My lady! I was so afraid something awful had happened to you!"

"I'm fine." Luciana gave her a reassuring hug.

With a blush, Gabriella stammered, "Th-thank you, my

lady." She wiped her cheeks. "We mustn't tarry. Your be-trothed wishes to see you soon."

For the next hour, Luciana was bathed and scrubbed and slathered with scented creams. Her hair was washed and braided with pearls. Gabriella decided on a gold brocade gown, claiming it would make her look like a princess.

The time flew by too quickly for Luciana, for she dreaded the moment she'd have to meet the Beast. By the time she was declared ready, her dread had grown into out-right fear. She could barely eat any of the bread or cheese that Gabriella had brought to her room. While her maid rushed off to let the duke's secretary know she was ready, Luciana paced about her room.

Her sister's warnings flitted through her mind. *I heard he killed his nanny and his mother. He fries people with his touch. Sizzle!* With a shudder, she paced toward the hearth. *Don't think about it!* She needed a distraction.

The letter from her sisters! She checked the opening in the upholstery of the chair where she'd hidden the note. It was still there. In two more days, she was supposed to leave a message on the rock offshore. How would she man-age that when she was being so carefully watched?

And what could she possibly write? That assassins wanted to kill her and she was about to marry the Beast of Benwick? She couldn't frighten them like that. She was frightened enough on her own—

She jumped when the door slammed open.

"Captain," Jensen protested. "You shouldn't be here."

"Stay outside," Captain Bougaire snarled as he shut the door in Jensen's face.

Oh, no! Panic bubbled up inside Luciana. What if the Beast came now? "You have to leave."

Alberto Bougaire spun around to look at her, and relief flooded his face. "Thank the Light. There's a rumor going around that you're dying. I knew it couldn't be true." He strode toward her.

She circled behind the chair to position it between them. "Please leave."

"No!" He reached for her, but she jumped back. "Tatiana, we have to go. Now! Before the Beast—"

"Stay away from me!"

He lunged for her and grasped her by the shoulders. "You promised you would run away with me. You love me!"

"No!" She struggled to get away, but he pushed her against a wall. Pinning her there with one hand, he gripped her chin with the other.

"Listen to me. No one gets between your legs but me. You're mine!" He rammed his mouth against hers.

With a strangled cry, she shook her head. *No, no!* This couldn't be her first kiss! She shoved with her hands, kicked with her feet, then suddenly he was wrenched off her and flying into a wall.

She gasped. The redheaded man was here! And he'd thrown the captain like he weighed nothing.

"What the hell?" Alberto scrambled to his feet. "How dare you come in here? Guards!"

"They no longer answer to you." The redheaded man flexed his gloved hands as he glared at the captain. "I informed them that you've been dismissed from your post."

"What?" Alberto eyed him with disdain. "You have no authority over me. And no right to attack me! I should kill you." He fumbled for his sword, but in only a second the redheaded man whisked a dagger from his boot and pointed it at Captain Bougaire's neck.

Alberto gulped.

"You truly wish to kill me?" the man said softly. "I'll give you the chance. Meet me in the courtyard at dawn. Your choice of weapons."

Luciana's breath caught. A duel?

"Fine." Alberto sneered. "I'm the best swordsman in the keep. When I win, I'll demand my position back. And I'll claim Tatiana as mine."

With a hint of a smile, the redheaded man lowered his dagger. "You will not win her."

Luciana stiffened. "Excuse me? I object to—"

"Don't worry," Alberto interrupted, slanting a wary glance in her direction. "I'll be sure to win you."

"Nobody is winning me," Luciana declared. "I object to being a prize at a tourney."

The redheaded man turned his head to give her a curious look.

His eyes are a beautiful green. Like new leaves in spring. Or a meadow at dawn— She pushed those thoughts away. "I appreciate you rescuing me from the captain's unwanted attention, but—"

"What?" Alberto huffed.

"I don't see why either of you should suddenly feel a need to kill each other," she finished.

"He insulted me!" Alberto pointed at the redheaded man.

"You insulted my woman," he replied.

Luciana scoffed. "I am not yours. I don't even know who you are. And both of you had better leave before my betrothed . . ." A niggling suspicion crept into her pores. Her eyes widened as she stared at the redheaded man.

One side of his mouth tilted up as if he found the situation amusing.

He couldn't be. This man had arrived with the army, and her betrothed had been delayed. Besides, this man was far too handsome to ever be called a Beast. His dark-red hair gleamed in the sunlight that poured through the windows. His square jaw and sharp jawline were shaded with whiskers a little darker than his hair. And his eyes, that beautiful shade of green, were focused entirely on her.

He arched a brow as if he were asking if she'd figured it out.

She shook her head. He couldn't be. If he was, then he'd lied. He'd been here all along. Tricking her.

"What's going on?" Alberto looked back and forth between her and the other man. "Who the hell are you?"

He slipped his dagger back into his boot. "I am Leofric of Benwick, Lord Protector of the Realm." He slowly smiled at Luciana. "And your future husband."

Her heart lurched. She didn't know whether to rejoice or crawl into a hole to die from embarrassment. He was the man of her dreams, but he'd played her like a fool. All the time that he'd spent watching her, taking her confession, sneaking into the tower, he'd always known who she was.

But he'd kept his identity a secret. So even though he'd made her heart flutter, he'd also caused her heart to ache, for she had believed she would be forced to marry someone else.

Had he found it all amusing?

Tears stung her eyes. "I should have clobbered you when I had the chance."

Chapter Fourteen

Leo's smile faded. This was not the reaction he had expected. Had he been wrong in believing their attraction was mutual? Was he so starved for affection that he'd misinterpreted every glance she'd aimed his direction?

"What?" Captain Bougaire regarded him in horror as he stumbled back a few steps. "You're the Be—Lord Protector?"

The bastard had come close to calling him the Beast. Leo cut him an annoyed look. "Leave us."

"Y-you should have warned us," the captain whined. "You should have told us who you are."

"Exactly," Tatiana ground out, her beautiful blue eyes glaring at him.

She was agreeing with the bastard? And how could she threaten to clobber her future husband? Leo stepped toward her. "Are you . . . angry with me?"

Her eyebrows lifted. "You're clever. I like that."

What the hell? She was using his own words against him. And there was no mistaking her sarcastic tone. No one dared talk to him like that. Only the general, Nevis, and Brody could get away with it, and only in private. Why, he could make hardened soldiers piss their pants with just a look—a sudden realization struck him.

She was standing up to him.

Since the age of five, he'd seen how people reacted when they learned he was a monster. They recoiled from him, cowered in fear, and refused to look him in the eye. But not Tatiana.

He moved closer and rested a gloved hand against the wall on one side of her head. Her eyes widened, but she didn't flinch or turn away. "You're bold. I like that."

Her eyes remained fixed on his, and his heart pounded in his chest. She was breathing quickly, the lovely upper curves of her breasts straining against the bodice of her gown. By the Light, he wanted to touch her. He wanted it with a fierceness that made his heart ache.

He searched her eyes, and there it was. A sense of time slowing down. A world melting away with only two souls remaining. An eternity of longing. Bittersweet and desperate.

Couldn't she feel it, too?

"Stay away from him!" Captain Bougaire yelled. "If he touches you, it will kill you!"

With a wince, she looked away, breaking the trance. *Don't be afraid of me, please.* Leo stepped back, lowering his hand. "I promised to do my best to never harm you."

"What about the duel?" Captain Bougaire whined. "It won't be a fair fight if you—"

"Enough!" Leo scowled at him. "I will not use my powers. It will be a test of skill. If you have any."

The captain snorted. "How can I trust the word of a Be—" He turned pale when Leo stalked toward him.

"Show up tomorrow. Or leave the castle now in disgrace. That is your choice."

The captain gulped. "I'll be there."

"Good. Leave us."

Captain Bougaire hesitated, casting a wary look at Tatiana.

Leo gritted his teeth. "*Go!*" He watched the bastard scurry from the room. "And shut the door behind you."

He turned back to Tatiana. She was glorious in gold brocade, as bright and beautiful as the sun, and thankfully the fire had returned to her eyes.

She lifted her chin. "You may go, also. I wish to be alone."

Was she giving him orders? His mouth quirked. This would be a duel he would enjoy. "I will stay. I wish to become better acquainted."

"Odd that you would say that, since you waited so long before introducing yourself."

He sauntered toward her. "This is only my third day here."

"More than enough time."

"Barely enough time for one of your very long baths." He breathed deeply. "Roses. I like that."

She crossed her arms, apparently oblivious that the action pushed her breasts higher against the low neckline of her gown. "You shouldn't remind me of your deception. Lying to me, pretending to be a priest—"

"I never said I was a priest—"

"You said the lines of a priest."

"And you said the lines of a confessor. Did you expect me to believe your long-bath story?" He scoffed. "We were both pretending to be someone we're not."

She closed her eyes briefly as she turned away.

Interesting. Had he touched a nerve? "The way I see it, there's no reason for you to be angry. I, on the other hand, have ample reason. I came here to introduce myself and found you kissing another man."

"I wasn't kissing him."

"His mouth was on yours."

She turned back toward him, her eyes glittering with emotion. "I didn't ask for it. Nor did I participate. If you were truly observant, you would have noticed I was shoving and kicking at him."

"Then you're not in love with him?"

"No! I can't stand the man!"

Leo smiled. "Excellent."

She gave him a wry look. "I didn't say that to please you. It was simply the truth."

"I wouldn't have it any other way. I think we'll do very well as long as we remain honest with each other."

She snorted. "Why did you invade my room in the tower and nearly frighten me to death? I thought you'd come to kill me!"

"I thought you would be asleep."

"You could have introduced yourself then."

"And you would have been even more frightened. You told me in confession you're afraid of your betrothed."

With a wince, she lowered her gaze to his gloved hands. "Am I wrong to fear you? Does your touch really . . . kill people?"

His hands curled into fists. He'd been a fool to think he'd enjoy this duel. It was a fight he couldn't win. "As long as I wear gloves and touch only your clothing, you should be safe. Leather and several layers of fabric normally serve as a protective barrier."

"And if you take the gloves off?"

His chest tightened. "My power is very strong right now. And mostly concentrated in my hands. If my bare hand touches your clothes, you could lose consciousness. If my bare hand touches your skin, my power would instantly transfer to you. It would . . . kill you."

She inhaled sharply, pressing the back of her hand against her mouth. "The king wants me dead, so he can take my inheritance. Are you part of that plan? Do you intend to marry me just to kill me?"

"No." He shook his head. "Actually, we have a sad thing in common. The king wants me dead, too."

Her eyes widened. "But why? He's your family."

"He's my uncle, but he's so paranoid, he doesn't trust anyone. He even had his son, Tedric, banished from court. As for me, he named me Lord Protector at the age of nineteen, hoping I would die in battle. He successfully got rid of my father, his younger brother, that way. And then I'm also Embraced, so I have a power Frederic doesn't have, and that angers him no end. He's tried several times to assassinate me over the years."

"That's . . . terrible."

"You needn't worry. I'll do my best to never harm you, and I'll protect you from the king." He rested a hand over his heart. "This I swear on my mother's grave."

With a wince, she eased away from him. "I-I heard . . ."

"What? What did you hear?"

With a deep breath, she visibly rallied her courage and looked him in the eye. "That you killed your mother."

He jolted back a step. "*What?* Who . . . who would say that?" He turned away, dragging a gloved hand through his hair. This had to be the king's doing. Uncle Fred wanted the people of Eberon to fear the Beast, so the king habitually started ugly rumors about his nephew. Frederic was so afraid Leo would rebel that he'd warned him repeatedly. If Leo ever marched on the royal court with the army, the king would have his personal guard murder every woman and child in the town of Ebton.

"It's not true?" Tatiana asked, watching him carefully.

Leo shook his head. "When my father died in battle, the king sent assassins to kill me. My mother flung herself in front of me. She took the sword meant for me." He closed his eyes briefly, then scoffed. "I suppose you could say I was responsible."

"No." Tatiana regarded him sadly. "How old were you?"

"Eight."

"You were a child." Her eyes brimmed with tears. "Don't ye dare say ye were responsible."

His heart squeezed in his chest. "You believe me?"

She brushed a tear away and nodded. "You had the most horrified look on your face. I felt the same way when someone told me I killed my mother."

His hands fisted. "Who would tell you something like that?"

"My mother died after giving birth to me."

"No one should blame an innocent babe for that. It's ridiculous."

Her eyes glistened with more tears. "That's what I keep telling myself."

"We have something else in common then." He took a deep breath. "Do you think you can trust me?"

"I'm trying to. I figure you could have hurt me in the chapel or when you sneaked into my room, but you didn't."

"That's right." Thank the Light she seemed to understand his good intentions. He walked over to the chairs in front of the hearth. "Let's sit for a while so we can discuss the marriage."

She shook her head. "How can we possibly be married?"

Shit. But he shouldn't be surprised. What woman in her right mind would want to marry a Beast? "We have no choice in the matter. The king has decreed—"

"But it won't be a marriage!" Another tear fell down her cheek. "Ye cannot be a husband. Not when ye can never touch me self!"

He froze, so stunned that his brain refused to work for a few seconds. Did this mean she actually wanted him to touch her? And what had happened to her accent? "Me *self*?"

With a gasp, she pressed her hands against her face.

"I-I must have spent too much time on the Isle of Moon recuperating."

He frowned. It couldn't have been more than two weeks. He stepped toward her. "Tatiana—"

"I-I can't do this now." She shook her head. "I just found out who you are. It's happening too fast." She ran to the door.

He let her go. Heard the door slam shut. *Dammit.* How could he win her heart when he was a danger to her? And why had her accent changed when she'd become upset?

"My dear child, you're trembling." The duke led Luciana toward the big armchairs in front of the hearth. "Come and relax by the fire."

Too upset to sit, Luciana began to pace. Jensen had escorted her to the library, claiming her father wished to see her. She'd been too distraught to disagree or even reply. How could she have let her accent slip? And the Lord Protector had noticed! Her heart thudded in her chest. Had he accepted her flimsy excuse?

She pressed a hand against her pounding heart. He'd still called her Tatiana. He couldn't suspect. Why would anyone suspect? No one knew Tatiana had a twin sister. She was safe. She had to be.

Taking deep breaths, she attempted to calm herself. It wasn't easy, though. Everything was happening too fast. It had been only two weeks and two days since she'd met her father. During that time, she'd focused most of her energy on successfully pretending to be her sister. She'd worried about her betrothal to the Beast, but it had been a vague and ominous thing in the future.

But now, the time had come. From now on, the deception

would require she do much more than speak like her sister
or wear her sister's gowns. It was she, Luciana, who would
become the Lord Protector's wife. It was she who would risk
death by being close to him. And every time he called her
by her sister's name, she would be reminded that she was
living a lie.

Red and black. The Telling Stones were still mocking
her. Two weeks after her prediction, she had met a tall and
handsome stranger. Red hair and a black horse. And each
time she'd seen him, she'd fallen deeper for him.

Should she rejoice that she was marrying the man of
her dreams? Or should she mourn that the marriage would
never be real? He would never know he was marrying Luciana. And he could never touch her. Or kiss her. She'd
never have children. In order to keep her deception a secret, she'd never be able to see her sisters again.

She brushed away her tears as she continued to pace.
This was not the time to feel sorry for herself. She needed
to be strong. And alert. So she wouldn't make a mistake
with her speech again.

The library was the most wondrous place in the entire
castle. Two stories tall, it took up the top two floors of the
keep and half of the eastern side of the square-shaped
castle. The huge cavern of a room housed over a thousand
books, and the sight and smell of them reminded her of
home and the workroom at the convent.

She paused in the middle of the room and closed her
eyes, letting the scent of books surround like a warm,
peaceful cocoon. *Knowledge is the true power,* her father
had told her when he'd first shown her this room. *And wisdom is knowing when to use it. Or when not to.*

She had more knowledge now. She knew the king
wanted to kill her and her father. She knew her betrothed
could kill her by simply touching her. He claimed he would

never hurt her, and she was inclined to trust him. In her heart, she wanted to.

A prick of shame needled her. Trust worked both ways. Why should he ever trust her when she was deceiving him?

To be honest with herself, she'd been attracted to him from the moment she first saw him. But she had to also admit that his strange power was frightening. What she needed now was the wisdom to make the right decisions without letting fear or attraction cloud her judgment.

"Feeling better?" her father asked softly.

She nodded. "A little."

He strolled to the sideboard and poured wine into two goblets. "I gather you met Leo."

"Leo?"

"Leofric of Benwick. He asked me to call him Leo." The duke smiled. "He seemed very friendly and down to earth. None of the arrogance of his uncle, the king."

So Father approved of her betrothed? Luciana strode toward the sideboard. "He admitted his touch can kill."

"Without his gloves, yes, so he's very careful. We had a long talk, and he explained a great deal to me. He's Embraced, and his gift is . . ." The duke shook his head. "I can't imagine having to live with something that horrendous."

She winced. "How does his gift work?"

With a frown, her father passed her a goblet. "He described it to me briefly. Whenever lightning strikes him, it fills him—"

"What?" Her hand trembled so badly she set the goblet down. "He's been struck by lightning?"

"Repeatedly. Since the age of five. He said there was no escape from it."

Her heart squeezed in her chest. By the goddesses, the pain he must have endured over the years.

"Remember the storm on the Isle of Moon?" the duke asked. "When it passed to the mainland, he was struck by lightning. So he is full of power right now."

He'd mentioned that his power was strong. And she recalled how she'd felt the energy emanating from him in the tower room. No wonder he could do things other men could not. "He retains power from lightning?"

Her father nodded. "He harnesses it. The power makes him incredibly fast and strong. He can attract or repel metal objects, and he can shoot lightning bolts from his fingers."

She swallowed hard, recalling his admission that his touch could kill her.

"Leo assured me that he knows how dangerous he is," her father continued. "Even with his gloves on, when his power is this high, if he touches someone's skin they can possibly receive a shock or, worse, lose consciousness. That's why he rarely ever touches anyone."

So he was never able to touch for affection? Since the age of five? Luciana's heart ached when she imagined how lonesome he must have been. She paced toward the chairs in front of the hearth. By the goddesses, she should be afraid the Beast would touch her. But she was much more upset by the wretched truth that he could never touch her. By marrying him, she was joining him in a life of loneliness.

Her father settled into a chair with his goblet of wine. "Leo swore to me he would never harm you. I believe he is sincere, so I agreed to let him meet you alone." He took a long drink. "Did the meeting not go well?"

She wandered back to the sideboard and took a drink from her goblet. "I wasn't alone when . . . the Lord Protector came." She wasn't comfortable calling him Leo. It seemed to denote an intimacy they could never have. "A few minutes before his arrival, Captain Bougaire barged in and demanded I elope with him."

"What?" The duke's eyes widened with horror.

"Did you know that he and—" Luciana drew closer to her father as she quickly glanced around the room to make sure no guards were nearby.

"Damn him," the duke growled, then lowered his voice to a whisper. "I warned her over and over to stay away from the captain. But it seemed like the more I objected, the more she was determined to thwart me." He jumped to his feet and picked up a poker. "I should have sacked him." He jabbed at the fire.

"The Lord Protector challenged him to a duel. Dawn tomorrow in the courtyard."

"Damn!" The duke stabbed at a log, then glanced back at her. "Was Leo . . . angry with you?"

Luciana thought back over the conversation. He'd certainly glared daggers at the captain, but his gaze at her had been . . . different. Filled with hunger and longing. Pain and anguish. "No, he wasn't."

"Ah, good." Her father returned the poker to its rack, then rested a hand on her shoulder. "I know it must be frightening for you, but it will all work out well. In order to keep you safe, Leo has agreed to be wed in name only. He will return to his duties as Lord Protector, traveling with the army and patrolling the border."

"I see." He would spend his life avoiding her so he wouldn't harm her. At the convent, she'd always dreamed that marriage would include love and joy. And children. Not a lifetime of loneliness.

"He has a small estate near Ebton. He said you were welcome to live there. But if you prefer, you could remain here." The duke squeezed her shoulder. "Of course, I would like for you to stay here."

Tears stung her eyes. "I would like that, too."

"Wonderful." With a smile, the duke drew her into his arms. "Then it's all settled." He patted her on the back. "Leo will be happy with the arrangement. He thought you would be safer here."

He would be happy? Did the man even know what happiness was? She buried her face in her father's shirt. Her dream man would never touch her, never be a true husband. And she would be safe.

She should be relieved. She could remain here at Vindemar with her father, and her every need would be taken care of. So why did she feel like crying?

Chapter Fifteen

❧

Hours later, Luciana was back in her room in the tower. The newly installed bolt was shot, and there were a total of six guards posted in the tower: two on the ground level, two on the floor below her where the privy was located, and two outside her door.

Before returning to the tower, she'd made a quick stop at her dressing room. Gabriella had helped her remove the gold brocade gown and put on a simple one she could handle alone. As soon as the sun had set, she'd donned the hooded black cloak, so she could secretly return to the tower. Jensen had warned her, though, that Captain Bougaire had spread the word that he was defending her honor at dawn. Soon everyone would know she was not at death's door. Including the assassins.

Alone now in the tower room, she paced about. A candle on the table cast flickering shadows on the walls. With a sigh, she stopped at the window where the Lord Protector had made his dramatic exit. Would he come see her again? What if something happened to him during the duel?

A surge of sympathy swept through her. The poor man. How many times since the age of five had he endured the pain of lightning strikes? At eight, he'd lost both parents. Seen his mother murdered by his uncle's assassins. Had there been no one who could embrace him while he'd mourned? Had he grown up never able to hug anyone? How terribly lonesome his existence must be.

As she put on her nightgown, she recalled how he'd said they had no choice but to marry. But now she wondered if he actually wanted to marry her. When he'd sneaked into the tower, his heated gaze had slowly wandered over her. She'd seen the hunger in his eyes. Oh, he had wanted to touch her. She'd felt it down to her bones.

A shiver ran down her spine, and she glanced down at her sheer nightgown. *Goddesses, help me!* She could see a hint of pink and the hardening tips of her nipples. Was it her imagination or could she actually glimpse the shape of her legs and the darker patch between them?

She pressed her hands against her hot cheeks.

You're bold. I like that.

She groaned. Not that bold. How would she ever look him in the face again?

Her sister suddenly appeared beside her. "Luciana!"

She gasped. "Must you always startle—" She noticed the distraught look on Tatiana's face. "What's wrong?"

"My poor Alberto is about to be slaughtered!"

"You mean the duel?"

"Of course!" Tatiana paced across the room, wringing her hands. "I heard them talking about it in the barracks."

Luciana perched on the edge of the bed. "I've been worried about it, too."

"You know it won't be fair, right? My poor Alberto will be murdered by that Beast!"

"The Lord Protector said he wasn't going to use his power, that it would be fair—"

"And you believe a Beast?" Tatiana screeched. She ran

toward the bed. "There's only one thing we can do. You have to beg the Beast not to kill Alberto."

Luciana winced. "I don't think—"

"You have to! If anything happens to Alberto, it'll kill me!"

"You're already—"

"It'll kill me again!" Tears filled Tatiana's eyes. "I'll be a lost spirit, wandering the earth, wailing for a thousand years."

"But how—"

"How can a love be as pure as ours?" Tatiana thumped a hand against her chest. "You might as well ask how does the sun rise in the west—"

"East."

"Whatever." Tatiana waved a dismissive hand, then gave her a pitying look. "You poor child. You'll never know a love as glorious as ours." She fell onto her knees. "So you must beg the Beast not to kill him!"

"It's late. I don't even know where to find him."

"You must find him! Ask the guards to take you to him. And be sure to wear that nightgown. He'll see everything."

With a groan, Luciana fell back onto the bed.

"And after you've dazzled him with your beauty—"

Luciana scoffed as she stared at the ceiling. "Are you saying I'm beautiful now?"

"Of course you are. You look like me. So, all you have to do is lounge on his bed like you're doing now, but try to look a little more lively than a beached whale, will you? And then he'll be so smitten, he'll grant you anything you ask for."

Luciana sat up. "Anything? As in sparing the life of my former lover? How could that possibly appeal to him?"

"You have to do something! *Please!*"

Luciana sighed. How could she leave her sister wailing for the rest of the night, much less a thousand years? "I'll send him a letter. No doubt one of the guards could deliver it."

"Wonderful!" Tatiana bounced up and down. "Thank you so much!"

"Did you learn anything else in the barracks?"

Tatiana stopped dancing and pressed a finger to her lips as she considered. "Oh, yes! It was quite shocking."

Luciana jumped to her feet. "You know who the assassin is?"

"No. But I discovered I've been wrong about something for years. I've always thought that the bigger a man was, the bigger his male . . . part would be. But that's not actually true."

Luciana's mouth fell open.

"I know." Tatiana nodded gravely. "I couldn't believe it, either, so I made a point of studying as many men as I could—"

"That's enough!" Luciana put on her black cloak to cover up the thin nightgown. "I need to ask Jensen to bring me some paper and ink."

Tatiana gasped. "And you wouldn't believe Jensen! I mean, he seems so ordinary, but—"

"I don't want to hear it! I have to be able to face him without blushing. Now, why don't you do something useful, like finding out who wants to kill me and Father?"

"Fine, fine." Tatiana waved a hand. "You're so bossy. And you'll send the letter?"

"Yes, I promise." When her sister vanished, Luciana drew the bolt and unlocked the door.

"My lady?" Jensen asked when she cracked open the door.

Her cheeks grew warm. "Could you bring me some paper and writing utensils?"

He bowed. "Right away." He glanced at the other guard as he headed for the stairs. "Don't leave your post."

Luciana closed the door and spotted a form taking shape by the window. "What now, Tati—"

The ghost spun around, a shocked look on her face.

"Mother." Luciana stepped toward her.

With a sob, her mother zoomed across the room and vanished through the door.

"No, wait!" Luciana flung the door open and ran outside.

"My lady." The guard bowed. "You shouldn't—"

"Th-there's someone in there!" She pointed to the room, and the guard dashed inside.

She hurried down the stairs, following the white wisp of her mother's spirit. "Don't go! Please!"

One floor down, her mother flew onto the wall walk headed south. One guard was across the landing at the northern entrance and the second guard was just coming out of the privy. They gaped in surprise as Luciana darted onto the wall walk.

"My lady! Come back!" They chased after her.

She sprinted along the wall walk, quick in her bare feet, the black cloak fluttering behind her. "Wait!"

Her mother reached a corner where the crenellated outer wall veered suddenly to the east, but instead of turning with it, she went straight through the wall into the night sky and vanished over the Southern Sea.

"No!" Luciana hit the corner, reaching out for her mother.

"What are you doing?" A gloved hand grabbed her arm and pulled her back. "Dammit, woman! Are you so averse to marrying me that you're trying to kill yourself?"

She gasped. What was the Lord Protector doing here?

Quickly he released her and stepped back. "Did I hurt you? Are you all right?"

"I—" Was she all right? Her arm was tingling where he'd touched her, but there was no pain. Her heart was pounding, she could hardly breathe, and there was a strange fluttering sensation in her stomach, but unfortunately she always felt that way whenever she saw this man.

By the goddesses, he looked so handsome. The light from the twin moons made the angles of his face seem sharper. His eyes appeared a darker green, and the stubble along his jaw more ruggedly masculine. The sea breeze had tousled his dark-red curls, making him look so adorable she longed to touch him.

But she couldn't. With a wince, she realized that was something she could never do.

"Dammit," he muttered. "I shocked you, didn't I?"

"No, I—" Goddesses help her, how long had she been silently gawking at him? With a twinge of embarrassment, she ducked her head. Oh, no, her nightgown! With another gasp, she quickly gathered her cloak around her.

He leaned toward her. "Are you sure you're all right?"

No, I'm mortified. "I'm perfectly fine. I should go back to my room now."

"You didn't feel anything at all when I touched you?"

Her cheeks flamed with heat.

"My lord." A voice spoke behind her, and she glanced back to see two guards.

"Leave us be," the Lord Protector ordered.

They bowed, then retreated to the tower. Clutching her cloak tightly around her, she started to follow them.

"Wait." The Lord Protector caught up with her. "We need to talk."

"I should go. I'm not properly dressed."

"I like the way you're dressed."

With a groan, she hunched her shoulders, huddling deeper into her cloak.

"Are you cold?" He removed his heavier black cape and

draped it around her shoulders. Holding the edges, he tugged her closer to him. "Now answer my question."

He'd trapped her. How dare he retain her against her will? Irritation flared inside her, but the fluttering in her stomach also increased. She'd never been this close to him before.

His hands fisted in the cloak. "Is it true? You would rather hurl yourself over the wall than marry me?"

He thought she was suicidal? Her irritation grew. "Of course not! Like you said before, we have no choice in the matter. So I have mentally prepared myself to go through with the ordeal."

His mouth thinned. "How noble of you."

"And what about you? Are you tempted to fall on a sword?"

He snorted. "Unlike you, I'm looking forward to the *ordeal*." He leaned closer. "And I'll be praying for a drought."

Her heart lurched. He wanted to marry her? And what did a drought have to do with them?

"I have another question." He gave her a wry look. "Actually I have many questions. Why did you leave your room? Why were you running at the wall?"

By the goddesses, how could she explain that? "I . . . wanted some fresh air."

"Try again."

She glanced down at his gloved hands, which still clutched the edges of his cloak and kept her trapped. How could she get free? Could she use his fear against him? She reached her hand toward the white shirt that covered his broad chest.

"No!" He jumped back, releasing her. "Don't do that. It's too dangerous."

"Nothing happened before when you grabbed me."

"There were several layers of insulation. My gloves, your cloak and nightgown." His mouth twitched. "Although your nightgown hardly counts as a layer."

Her cheeks burned with heat.

"I can never be sure how a person will react," he continued. "Especially when my power is this high. Even with my gloves on, my touch has caused some people to faint." His eyes glinted with humor. "Apparently, you're rather insensitive."

The rascal, now he'd asked for it. She lunged toward him, pretending she was going to poke him.

"Dammit, woman!" He leaped back.

She smiled to herself as she folded her arms across her chest. He wouldn't dare come near her now.

With a snort, he leaned against the wall. "You're too damned clever."

"I thought you liked that about me."

His mouth curled into a lopsided smile. "I do. So why did you run at the wall?"

"Why are you here? Shouldn't you be hunting down the assassins?"

His smile widened. "Another counterattack. Are you sure you're not a warrior?" He folded his arms, mimicking her stance. "Your father gave me permission to move into the southern tower. So now we're neighbors. And I can keep an eye on you to make sure you're safe."

She glanced at the tower behind him. It was the tallest tower along the curtain wall with an added turret on top. From there, he would have an excellent view of the sea and the entire fortress.

"As for the assassins," he continued, "I'm working on it."

"How?"

"I have a plan." He paused as if he was considering how much to tell her. "And my best spies are at work."

She blinked. Did he have spies watching her? "Who are they?"

"You needn't worry yourself over that."

She narrowed her eyes, then turned to gaze over the crenellated wall at the sea. "No doubt my spies are better. They'll find the assassins first."

"What? *Your* spies?"

"Yes."

He scoffed. "I don't believe it." When she merely shrugged, he stepped closer. "Fine. Who are they?"

She gave him a pointed look. "You needn't worry yourself over that."

His mouth fell open, then he grinned. "You know how to wrestle. I like that."

Her heart did a little leap as a vision popped into her mind of the two of them physically wrestling. And once he had her pinned down . . . but he couldn't. He could never touch her. By the goddesses, it was enough to make her learn how to curse. "I should be going now." She started toward the tower.

"Did you wonder why I'm praying for a drought?"

She halted. He'd come back with a counterattack of his own. An excellent one. For she *had* wondered.

His booted feet crunched on the stone wall walk as he approached her from behind. "No rain means no lightning. That means my power would slowly disappear."

The back of her neck tingled. "Why would you want to lose your power?"

"So I can touch you. Kiss you." His voice lowered to a whisper. "Bed you."

The tingle on her neck skittered down her spine. Then he might be able to touch her someday? And she hadn't imagined the hunger in his eyes. It was real. "You . . . want me?"

"Yes."

Her heart thudded as she turned to face him. "You hardly know me." He didn't even know her real name.

"I know you're clever, brave, bold, and beautiful. I know you're kind to servants. Kind to animals. You're not above working in the garden. You stand up to me. You intrigue me. I feel more . . . alive when I'm with you." He stepped closer. "Yes. I want you."

A sharp pang shot through her chest. He wasn't describing Tatiana. He was describing her. It was she, Luciana, that he wanted. "My lord—"

"Call me Leo."

She swallowed hard. "Leo. C-could you call me Ana?"

His eyes widened with surprise. "Does your father call you that?"

She shook her head. "It would be just for us." So she could feel that he was marrying her, not Tatiana. Tears stung her eyes, and she blinked them away.

"Is something wrong?" He stepped closer. "Ana?"

The goddesses help her, this man was making her heart ache. "I should go now." She headed toward the tower.

"Dammit," he grumbled behind her. "You never answered my questions."

She stopped and gave him a hesitant glance. "You shouldn't spend the night out here. You need your rest before the duel."

His eyebrows lifted. "Are you worried about me?"

Tatiana's request! She'd almost forgotten. "Could you do me a favor and not kill the captain tomorrow?"

"What? You're worried about *him*?"

Caw, caw. A seagull called out, and he muttered a curse.

She winced. "There are others who care about the captain. So I would appreciate it if you didn't kill him."

He gave her an exasperated look. "What do you think I am? I never planned to kill the bastard."

"Oh, thank you!" She ran into the tower as he growled a few more curse words.

"I'm not a Beast!" His voice echoed down the wall walk.

No, he was a man. Her eyes burned with tears as she hurried up the stairs. He was an amazing man. And he would be far too easy to fall in love with.

Chapter Sixteen

❧

Too tense to sleep, Luciana tossed and turned most of the night. Her mind fluctuated between replaying her last conversation with her betrothed and worrying about his upcoming duel. Slowly, as the hours dragged by, she grew accustomed to calling him Leo.

But the more she thought about him, the more she wished he'd cancel the duel altogether. If Leo planned not to use his powers, didn't he risk getting hurt? She didn't want him to be injured because of her. After being raised in a convent that valued peace and harmony, she simply didn't understand this need for violence.

And how was the duel supposed to protect her honor? Wouldn't it do the opposite and draw attention to her alleged affair?

Before dawn, her guards escorted her back to her bedchamber, and in her dressing room Gabriella helped her don the green velvet gown. As she left her bedchamber, her father was waiting in the hallway.

"We can watch from here," he said as he led her across the hallway to where the arched, open windows overlooked the courtyard.

A large circle had been marked off in the center of the courtyard, and around it, a crowd of people had already gathered.

Luciana's heart sank. It seemed the duel was really going to happen. "So many people," she murmured.

"Yes," her father agreed. "Everyone who works at Vindemar or lives close by has come to watch." He lowered his voice. "And the assassins will see that you are alive and well. You must be extremely careful from now on."

With a glance back, she noticed more than a dozen guards standing behind them, all dressed in Vindalyn blue and white. Other guards were stationed along the gallery where they watched the crowd, and more soldiers were in the courtyard, making sure no one was carrying any weapons.

To her surprise, some people were pointing at her and cheering. She spotted Yulissa and her kitchen help and waved. Tearfully, they waved back.

It warmed her heart to see how much support she had, but it was still hard to forget that somewhere in the crowd, three assassins wanted to kill her.

Suddenly the crowd below her parted, and a small group of soldiers marched through the western gate into the courtyard. Captain Bougaire was in their midst, dressed in leather breeches and a chain-mail shirt, topped with a blue-and-white tunic cinched around his waist with his sword belt. In the crook of his elbow, he carried a steel helmet adorned with three white plumes.

He marched into the circle, and the crowd began to murmur about the Beast, their speculations becoming louder and louder till Luciana could hear every word.

"The Beast is going to kill you!" one man shouted at the captain.

"The Beast will fry you like bacon!" another yelled.

Luciana winced as she recalled Leo's words from last
night. *I'm not a Beast!* Where was he? Could he hear
what these people were saying?

Shouts of alarm sounded below. People scurried out of
the way as General Harden and his son, Captain Harden,
marched through the south gate. After the crowd had
parted to make a wide passage, Leo strode in alone.

A sudden hush fell over the courtyard. No one dared say
a word about the Beast in his presence. Some turned their
back to him, afraid to even look at him. Others wrapped
small children in their cloaks and held them close.

Luciana swallowed hard. How long had he lived like
this? Shunned and feared by people. His face was devoid
of expression, but she knew he must be hurting inside.

How many times growing up at the convent had she felt
rejected and abandoned? But at least she'd had her adopted
sisters and Mother Ginessa. She'd received love and warm
embraces. How lonesome Leo must have been over the
years.

Her sympathy grew into alarm when she realized he
wasn't wearing any protective armor. He was simply
dressed in black breeches and boots, a white shirt, a vest
in the royal colors of red and black, and his usual black
leather gloves. His left hand rested on the hilt of his
sword.

General Harden exchanged a few words with him, then
headed toward the west wing of the keep.

"I asked the general to watch the duel with us," Luciana's father told her.

Leo walked into the circle and, along with Captain Bougaire, faced Luciana and her father and bowed.

The duke raised a hand in greeting. "Lord Leofric of
Benwick, Lord Protector of the Realm, has challenged
Captain Alberto Bougaire to a duel. Each opponent is
allowed one sword. The battle will commence at the drop

of the red banner and it will end when one opponent either succumbs to death or surrenders."

"Death?" Tatiana screeched, and Luciana started at her sister's sudden appearance to her right.

"Or surrender," Luciana whispered.

"My Alberto will never surrender!" Tatiana wailed. "He's doomed. Doomed!"

"Calm down. He'll be fine."

"What's going on?" Father whispered.

Luciana glanced back at the guards, then leaned close to her father on the left. "We're not alone."

His eyes widened. "Tatiana?" When she nodded, he asked, "Where?"

Luciana motioned to her right. "She's—"

"Did you write the letter?" Tatiana interrupted. "Did you beg the Beast to spare my darling?"

"I asked him in person," Luciana whispered. "He said he wouldn't kill Alberto."

"Oh, thank you!" Tatiana's eyes filled with tears. "But how can we trust the word of a Beast?"

"Tatiana," Father whispered. "My dear, please know how much I miss you and that I love you with all my heart."

When Tatiana sniffled, Luciana said, "She feels the same way."

"Are you two getting along now?" he whispered.

Luciana patted his arm. "We're becoming good friends."

"Ha!" Tatiana scoffed. She looked at the courtyard and shuddered, her image wavering. "I can't bear to watch."

Luciana glanced down at the courtyard. Leo was watching her, his head tilted with an inquisitive look. She bit her lip. Had he noticed her talking to an empty space?

"Good morning," General Harden said in his booming voice as he approached them on the balcony.

"Thank you for joining us," the duke said.

Luciana curtsied. "Excuse me, General, but is it possible to cancel the duel? I don't want any harm to come to my betrothed."

"Or my Alberto!" Tatiana wailed.

The general smiled. "It's sweet of you to worry about Leo, but the duel needs to happen. It's part of his plan."

"What plan is that?" the duke asked.

"Oh, look." The general moved close to the railing. "They're about to begin."

Luciana's heart stilled. Leo and the captain were facing each other in the circle about ten yards apart, their swords pointed at each other. A soldier holding a red banner stood at the circle's edge.

Tatiana sighed. "Doesn't Alberto look magnificent?"

Luciana didn't answer. She thought he looked rather silly wearing a helmet with foot-long plumes.

The soldier with the red banner whipped it down to the ground, then quickly moved back as the two opponents began to circle each other. The crowd cheered, and Luciana tensed. She'd never witnessed a swordfight before, but this didn't seem right. Why did the captain have chain mail and a helmet, when Leo didn't?

"Why isn't Leo wearing any armor?" she asked.

"He normally would in a real battle," the general told her. "But his power is so high right now, if he wore any metal it would become infused with his power. If Bougaire struck his armor with a sword, the power would travel up the captain's sword and most likely kill him."

Luciana winced. So Leo had to put himself at more risk in order to keep Captain Bougaire safe?

The captain made the first move, bellowing out a war cry as he charged toward Leo. Luciana held her breath as the captain's sword sliced down. A clashing sound echoed through the courtyard as Leo blocked the blow and forced Alberto back.

The captain attacked again. And again. He pranced about, displaying his skills, his sword flashing in the sun. He leaped. Spun about. Sliced high at Leo's head, cut low at his knees. No matter what he did, Leo remained calm, smoothly fending off one attack after another.

Luciana frowned. Did Leo not know any of the fancy moves that the captain was showing off? He didn't seem to be trying very hard, for he was repelling each attack with a minimum of movement. She couldn't decide if he was lazy or incredibly skilled. "Excuse me, General. Is this a . . . normal swordfight?"

The general and her father chuckled.

"Leo looks a bit bored," the duke said with a wry smile.

The general nodded. "He's biding his time."

Tatiana snorted. "He's no match for my Alberto."

Luciana sighed. At this rate, the fight would last until the sun went down or Alberto finally gave out from exhaustion. Even the crowd was starting to grow bored and restless. Some of them pulled bread and cheese from their knapsacks to snack on.

The two swords of the duelists clashed together, and with a screech, they scraped against each other till the two men were only inches apart. With a push, Leo shoved the captain back, then sliced the air above Alberto's helmet, neatly cutting the three plumes in half. As the feathers fluttered to the ground, the crowd roared, once again excited about the match.

With an angry shout, Alberto ripped his helmet off and tossed it aside. "I'll kill you for that!"

Leo merely sauntered to another spot and readied himself for the next attack. In his new position, Luciana could see his face. He did, indeed, seem bored.

"What is this plan you mentioned before?" her father asked.

The general rubbed his beard. "If you will recall the night the assassin stabbed your daughter's bed, his scent was picked up by Brody."

"Brody?" the duke asked. "Who is that?"

"He's over there with my son, Nevis." General Harden pointed to the right side of the courtyard.

Luciana surveyed the crowd till she spotted Captain Harden. "Oh, he has Pirate with him." She'd been wondering where the dog had disappeared to.

"Pirate?" the general asked.

"My pet dog," Luciana explained. "I call him Pirate because of the black patch over one of his eyes."

General Harden snorted. "His name is Brody, and he came here with my son before the army arrived. Leo knew you were in danger, so he sent Brody to guard you."

Luciana's mouth dropped open. "Then Pirate, I mean Brody, is Leo's pet?"

The general chuckled.

Luciana didn't know how the general could find anything amusing at a time like this. She glanced at Leo to make sure he was all right. The captain was spinning about and performing a series of leaps while the crowd applauded. Leo was watching with a wry look on his face.

The general cleared his throat. "As you know, we suspected the assassin was one of the guards. So yesterday morning, before Leo met Your Grace, he and Nevis took Brody through the barracks, so Brody could sniff out the assassin."

"Did the dog find him?" the duke asked.

"No." General Harden shook his head. "Then they took

Brody to sniff around the chapel in case the assassin was one of the new priests. No luck there, either."

"So the first assassin is neither a guard nor a priest," her father concluded.

"That's right," the general agreed. "And that's one of the reasons Leo challenged Captain Bougaire to a duel. He knew it would draw everyone here."

"And then Brody could detect the assassin." The duke smiled. "Brilliant."

Luciana glanced over at Captain Harden and Brody. They were carefully weaving through the crowd.

"And that's why Leo is biding his time," the general continued. "He can't let the duel end until Brody has uncovered the assassin."

So this was the plan Leo had mentioned last night, Luciana thought. She glanced at him. *You're clever. I like that.* "You said this plan was one of the reasons Leo had for the duel. What are the other reasons?"

General Harden grinned. "Isn't it obvious? He wants to be rid of the bastard."

Tatiana gasped. "I knew it! He wants to kill my Alberto."

Down in the courtyard, Brody barked and leaped on a man. As the man tried to scramble away, Captain Harden jumped on him and pinned him down.

"We got him!" General Harden announced.

The duke leaned forward, his eyes narrowed. "I think he's from the stables."

Luciana's heart raced. One of the assassins had been found! She glanced over at Leo to see if he'd noticed.

He had. He leaped into action, charging toward Alberto, and within seconds the captain's sword was flying across the courtyard. It landed with a clatter as Leo knocked Alberto onto his back and pinned him down with a booted foot on his chest. Leo grasped his sword's hilt with both hands and lifted the sword in the air with the point aimed at Alberto's neck.

Luciana gasped, her hand pressed to her heart. Leo was magnificent, even without his powers.

"Surrender or die!" Leo shouted.

Tatiana screeched.

Chapter Seventeen

❦

"I surrender," the captain mumbled.

Leo leaned over, putting more weight on his booted foot that ground into Bougaire's ribs. "What was that? I couldn't hear you over all the cheering for your defeat."

"I surrender!"

"Good choice." Leo lowered his sword so the tip rested on the pavement stones of the courtyard. "Now here's the deal. You pack your shit up, leave by noon, and keep going till you cross the Duchy of Vindalyn's border. You're banished for life. Got it?"

"Damn you!"

Leo scraped his sword along the stones till the edge was a mere inch from the captain's face. "Are you in a position to make me angry?"

Bougaire grimaced. "Do whatever the hell you want. My life is over as it is. I've lost my Tatiana."

"I'm glad you realize that."

The captain snorted. "Not the way you think. She's truly gone. I don't know what they did to her."

Leo straightened. "What are you saying?"

Bougaire's eyes gleamed with malice. "I'm saying you'll never have *my* Tatiana."

"Bastard." Leo knelt beside the man and gripped his throat with a gloved hand. There was a risk of shocking him, but at this point, Leo didn't give a damn. The asshole had been defeated, but was still trying to jab at him. "She will be mine."

The captain gritted his teeth. "That woman will be yours." He motioned toward the gallery where the duke and his daughter were standing. "But she is not Tatiana."

Leo was so stunned, he released the bastard for a few seconds. The man gasped for air, then Leo tightened his grip again. "You lie."

Bougaire shook his head, his face turning red. "I knew . . . when I kissed her . . . not Tatiana."

Leo let go and sat back on his knees. "I have no reason to believe you."

Bougaire breathed heavily. "I know. I didn't want to believe it, either." He motioned toward her. "That . . . that woman looks just like Tatiana. But she didn't kiss—"

"She no longer wants you. That's why she resisted."

"She didn't taste the—" Bougaire hesitated when Leo drew back a fist. "She doesn't act the same. And something about her speech seemed different."

Leo lowered his fist. *Dammit.* He'd noticed her speech, too. He shook his head. "There are reasons for her different behavior. And she looks like Tatiana because she is her. Everyone, including her father, acknowledges her as Tatiana."

The captain sighed. "I don't know what's going on. I just want to know what happened to *my* Tatiana."

"She's exactly the same, except she no longer wants you." Leo rose to his feet and sheathed his sword. "You will leave by noon and never speak of her again."

While Bougaire slowly stood, Leo called a few of his soldiers over. "Watch Bougaire and make sure he leaves."

His men saluted and followed Bougaire toward the western gate and the barracks that lay outside the keep.

Leo's gaze drifted up to the gallery. The general and duke were applauding and beaming proudly at him. His heart softened. He'd been fortunate to grow up with General Hard-Ass on his side. Now another good fortune had befallen him. His future father-in-law seemed wise, powerful, and supportive. And the best fortune of all—his betrothed was the brave, beautiful, and clever Tatiana.

His eyes met hers. With a shy smile, she lifted a hand in greeting.

He raised his hand, then placed it over his heart, a sign that he was pledged to her, and with blushing cheeks she ducked her head. By the Light, he would swear she was unaccustomed to receiving attention from men. Somehow, she seemed completely innocent.

Dammit. Did she have an affair with Captain Bastard or not? Was she really Tatiana or not? It was quite possible that the captain had lied to him out of spite, but unfortunately the bastard had planted the seeds of doubt in Leo's mind, and now he was finding them hard to ignore.

How could this woman be an imposter? She'd asked him to call her Ana. Why? Was she really Tatiana, but she simply wanted a different name to signify a new start with a new man? Or was she an imposter who felt uncomfortable whenever he called her Tatiana?

Unease tickled the back of Leo's neck as more thoughts flitted through his mind. There had been a time when her speech had sounded like an islander. And then there was the odd message delivered to her by seals. Before the duel, she'd been talking to her father, but she'd kept looking to her right as if there'd been someone else taking part in the conversation. Who? The spirit of a dead person?

Leo shook himself mentally. Even if there was some

strange shit going on, that didn't mean she was an imposter. The weird stuff was easily explained if she was Embraced. Everyone, including her father, accepted her as the Lady of Vindalyn. That meant she was still his betrothed. She was also the woman he wanted, the woman he had sworn to protect.

He narrowed his eyes, watching her. The next time they met, she needed to answer his questions. He had to know the truth, the whole truth, if he was going to protect her.

"Has he said anything?" Leo asked as he entered the dungeon.

"Yes." Nevis stood in front of the prison cell, glaring through the iron bars at their prisoner. "His name is Willem. He works in the stable. And guess what—he claims to be innocent."

"I am!" Willem cried from the back of the cell. His wrists were shackled to chains screwed into the stone wall. "I was just minding my own business when a rabid dog jumped on me!"

Brody scoffed. He was now in human form and casually dressed in baggy breeches and shirt, his feet still bare. He was sitting on the corner of the jailer's desk, eating from a tray of food. "He's the one," he mumbled with his mouth full. "Definitely."

"Who the hell are you?" Willem demanded. "I've never seen you before in my life. How would you know anything?"

Brody ignored him and kept eating.

Leo motioned to the empty chair at the desk. "Where's the jailer?"

"We sent him to get more food and wine," Nevis replied, then scowled at the prisoner. "Not for you, though. If you want to eat, you'll have to talk."

"I am talking!" Willem insisted. "I'm innocent."

Leo strode up to the iron bars. "We believe you are guilty. The punishment is death."

Willem gasped. "But I didn't kill anybody! The Lady of Vindalyn isn't dead. I just saw her at the duel."

Leo glanced at Nevis. "Did you tell him the identity of the intended victim?"

Nevis shook his head. "No. Funny how he knows—"

"What?" Willem's eyes widened with panic. "No! Everyone was saying she'd been murdered. That's how I knew. Besides, she's not dead. She wasn't even in bed when I—" He gulped. "I didn't do anything. I'm innocent!"

"You just confessed," Leo growled. "I'll have some gallows erected in the courtyard. It should take a day or two to complete. When it's done, you will hang."

"No!" Willem lunged forward, but the chains halted him with a jerk. "You can't kill me for stabbing a few pillows!"

"It must be annoying, having to die for something you failed at." Leo leaned forward, holding on to the bars. "But there is a way you could come out of this alive."

"What? I'll do anything!" Willem wailed.

"Tell me who the other two assassins are," Leo said.

Willem's eyes darted about, then he licked his lips. "Th-there are two more? I-I don't remember—"

"Not a problem. I know exactly how to jolt your memory." Leo slowly removed a glove. "Perhaps you have heard about me?"

Willem's eyes bulged. "You're the B-b-b-"

"Damn." Nevis affected a shudder. "I'd better leave before the lightning bolts start."

"Hmm." Brody swallowed his food. "So scary."

"*Please!*" Willem dropped to his knees. "Don't hurt me! I think one of them is a soldier. That's all I know. Please, my wife and children will be murdered if the duke and his daughter don't die. Please help me!"

Leo exchanged a glance with his friends as he tugged his glove back on. "Are you saying your family is being held hostage to force your cooperation?"

"Yes! I've never killed before. I'm a poor farmer."

Leo sighed. He wouldn't be surprised if Uncle Fred had actually done something this despicable. "Where is your family being held?"

"Our farm. It's about a two-hour ride north from here. Can you help me?"

"I can't make any promises until I check out your story," Leo told him. "Nevis, take a troop of men to his farm. If his family is being held hostage, rescue them and bring them back here."

"Oh, thank you, my lord!" Willem cried.

Leo gave him a stern look. "This doesn't mean you are forgiven. You attempted murder, and you will pay for that. The duke is your lord and master. You should have informed him immediately what was happening."

Willem hung his head. "Yes, my lord."

"And if this is a trap my men are riding into, you will suffer for that, too," Leo warned him.

While Nevis asked the man for directions to his farm, Leo wandered over to the desk where Brody was sitting.

"Have you learned anything new?" Leo helped himself to a piece of cheese off the tray of food. "Any clues who the other two assassins could be?"

"I'm betting on a soldier and the young priest, but we have no way of confirming that until they do something." Brody gave him a wry look. "How did the duel go? I assume you won."

"Aye. The captain has been banished." Unfortunately, Leo couldn't banish the seeds of doubt that Bougaire had planted.

"I was surprised yesterday when you made your presence known. I thought the plan was for you to pretend to be delayed so the assassins would make their move."

Leo sighed. "That was the plan, but after the attempt on Tatiana's life, I couldn't bear to sit back and do nothing. She's my betrothed, my responsibility."

"Ah. So you're smitten with her already?"

Leo considered physically wiping the smirk off Brody's face. "Have you noticed anything else about her that seems . . . off?"

Brody shook his head. "Haven't seen her much since yesterday. I've been guarding the entrance of the tower while she's up in her room." His eyes glinted with humor. "Apparently, you've seen her more than I have. I heard some guards were knocked unconscious when a mysterious stranger sneaked into her room to be alone with her."

Leo shrugged. "A simple security check, nothing more."

"Right. Well, the guards never reported it. They were too embarrassed by how easily you breached their defenses—or was it her defenses?"

Leo gave him a pointed look. "Watch how you talk about my betrothed."

Brody grinned. "Oh, you're smitten all right." He tilted his head, considering. "All I've heard lately is that she talks to herself quite a bit. The guards think it odd, but we already know she talks to spirits. And I've heard that the tower is haunted. Last night she ran from her room, yelling, *Wait!*"

And then she'd run at the wall, reaching for something. Or someone. Leo took a deep breath. No wonder she'd refused to tell him why she was on the wall walk. She didn't want to admit she was talking to dead people. "There must be a ghost she's anxious to talk to." Her mother?

Another thought occurred to Leo. "If the tower is haunted, then that must be why she went there the night Willem stabbed her pillows."

Brody nodded. "She was hoping to talk to the resident ghost."

Nevis sauntered over and grabbed a small loaf of bread off Brody's plate. "I'll be going now."

"Be careful. It could be a trap," Leo warned him. "And have your men dress as a band of thieves. We can't attack the king's guards as soldiers. Uncle Fred would take it as a rebellion."

"Got it." Nevis strode from the room as the jailer came in with another tray of food and bottle of wine.

"Thanks." Brody opened the bottle and took a long drink.

"The duke wants to see your lordship in his library," the jailer told Leo.

"Very well." Leo grabbed a grape off the tray and popped it into his mouth. "Post additional guards and be extra vigilant. The other two assassins might consider our prisoner a liability."

The jailer nodded. "Yes, my lord."

Luciana dipped her quill into the ink bottle as she considered what to write next. Luckily, she already had paper and ink since Jensen had delivered them to her tower room the night before. She hadn't needed to write to Leo after all, but this evening she had to compose a letter for her sisters. Tomorrow morning at dawn, she was supposed to place the bottle with the new letter on the rock offshore. Then the seals would deliver it to Maeve.

After the duel, her father had invited her to a midday meal with him, the general, and Leo. She'd declined. After Leo's confession last night of wanting to bed her, she felt too flustered to be in his presence. How could she sit calmly beside him and eat a meal when her stomach was fluttering and her mind was racing with questions? Was she really falling in love? How could her heart be filled with longing for a man whose touch could kill her?

So she'd hurried back to her dressing room to change into a more comfortable gown and hide the bottle with the Telling Stones in her pocket. Now she was alone in the tower room, seated at the table, writing to her sisters.

She'd started with a greeting and confession of how much she missed them. And then she'd stopped, overwhelmed for a moment with homesickness. By the goddesses, she yearned for her sisters. If only they were here now. They would listen to her and help her make sense of the confused jumble of emotions she was feeling.

With a deep breath, she refocused on her letter. She didn't want to frighten them with news about assassins or a betrothed who could kill people with his touch. She needed to write something happy.

You won't believe it! My sister didn't remain at the convent, but followed me here. We're becoming good friends.

Luciana winced. That was a bit of an exaggeration. Her gaze fell on the bottle she'd placed nearby on the table. She uncorked the bottle and shook the Telling Stones into her hand. The number two, red and black.

She placed the pebbles on the table and ran her fingers over them. They would remain with her here, a physical link to her sisters. Touchstones that would bring her comfort whenever she felt overwhelmed. She picked up the quill and began again.

Something wondrous has happened. Two weeks after we played with the Telling Stones, I met a man with red hair and a black horse, exactly like the stones predicted! His name is Leofric of Benwick, and we are to be married. He seems quite strong and dependable, honest and trustworthy. And I find him extremely handsome. His hair is a dark red, but he doesn't have the freckles that Sorcha feared

*he would. His skin is tanned from being in the sun. His
eyes are a beautiful green like the new leaves of an oak tree
that unfurl in spring. Though at night, they seem a darker
green like a pine—*

Luciana paused, her eyes widening as she realized how
lovesick her words looked.

A blob of ink stained the paper, and she quickly moved
the quill aside. Was she truly in love? Maybe it was
simply an infatuation. After all, she'd been raised in a
convent, so she'd never seen that many men. Especially
young, healthy men.

But the ship had been full of them. And the fortress of
Vindemar had plenty. She'd even been kissed by Tatiana's
lover. And she'd felt nothing. No flutters, no yearning.

She groaned. Why not let her sisters think she was happily in love and her life was rosy and perfect? It was better than making them worry.

*Soon, I will be going to the royal court in Ebton to be
wed, so you may not hear from me for a while. I will
send notice in my father's next wine shipment to let you
know when I have returned to Vindemar so we can resume our correspondence. Even though I will be away,
distance can never separate us. You will always be with
me in my heart.*

Missing you and loving you always,

Luciana

When the ink dried, she folded the letter up, slipped it
inside the bottle, and squeezed the cork in as tightly as she
could. The letter was too incriminating to be left out in
the open, so she hid the bottle beneath her pillow. Her gaze
lingered on the dagger Leo had given her.

Would there ever come a time when she could tell him
the truth? Or would her deception make him feel so betrayed that he would turn on her and her father? The minute the king learned of their deception, their lives were

over. With a sigh, she realized there was no help for it. She'd have to carry her lies to the grave.

Remain strong, she reminded herself. Right now she had a more immediate problem. How was she going to place the bottle onto the rock offshore at dawn?

She unlocked the door and cracked it open a few inches.

Jensen bowed. "Was there something you needed, my lady?"

"Yes. If you recall a few days ago, I took a morning swim. I would like to do it again tomorrow at sunrise."

He frowned. "My lady—"

"I've been cooped up here too long," she continued. "The exercise will do much to revive my spirits."

"I understand. But there are still two assassins—"

"They would never suspect I would be at the beach at dawn."

Jensen shook his head. "I can't take that chance."

"I'll have my father approve it."

"Actually, the Lord Protector has taken charge of your safety. He would need to approve—"

"Oh." She waved a dismissive hand. "There's no need for him to know—"

"Know what?" Leo's voice called out from the spiral staircase.

Luciana's heart lurched as he came into view.

"My lord." Jensen bowed.

Leo nodded at the guard, then gave Luciana a wry smile. "No need for me to know what?"

She swallowed hard. "It's a trifling request, not worth bothering your lordship about."

He stepped closer, his eyes watching her intently. "That's a relief. I'd hate to think you were keeping secrets from me, Ana."

Her fingers dug into the door as she looked away. "Of course not."

"My lord," Jensen began. "Her ladyship has requested permission to take a short swim in the sea at dawn."

"Yes." Luciana nodded. "The exercise will do me good. And I don't believe the assassins would ever suspect I would be at the beach at dawn. I'm sure I'll be perfectly safe." She glanced at Leo and found him still staring at her. Her cheeks grew warm.

"Could you wait a few days till after we catch the assassins?" he asked.

She winced. "I have my heart set on tomorrow morning."

His eyebrows rose. "It has to be tomorrow?"

"Yes." More heat poured into her face.

"Perhaps I should go swimming with you."

She tensed. "That won't be necessary. I prefer to swim alone. For modesty's sake."

His eyes narrowed. "I will agree with certain conditions." He turned toward Jensen. "You may do as she requests. I want you and two guards to accompany her. Do not tarry on the beach for long."

"Yes, my lord."

Leo glanced back at her. "I have a matter to attend to, then I'll return to fulfill the rest of my condition."

She swallowed hard. "What would that be?"

He stepped close to her and lowered his voice. "We will talk. And you will answer my questions."

Chapter Eighteen

❧

Back in the southern tower, Leo waited in his room for Brody to arrive. After leaving Tatiana's tower, he'd asked the dog shifter to meet him here. On the ground floor of his tower, he'd found two of his personal guard and his squire, Edmund, sharing a meal.

"Brody will be coming soon," Leo had told them. "Can you spare some food for him? And some clothes?"

When they agreed, Leo headed up the stairs to his room. Now he paced about the small, circular chamber. It was much the same as Tatiana's room, furnished with a bed, a table, and two chairs. One window overlooked the Southern Sea, and the other one gave him an excellent view of the southwestern tower where Tatiana was living.

He stopped at the second window to scowl at her tower. *Morning swim, my ass.* She was exchanging messages with someone. And she didn't want her future husband to know about it.

There was a knock at the door, then Brody peered inside. He was dressed in a spare uniform from one of the guards below. "Did something happen? Has Nevis returned?"

"Not yet." Leo motioned for him to enter. "Did you get something to eat?"

Brody shut the door behind him. "They didn't have much left downstairs, so Edmund ran to the kitchens to get some more. What's going on?"

Leo crossed his arms as he gazed out the window. "The seals will be back in the morning."

"The ones that brought my lady a secret message? How can you be sure?"

With a wave of his hand, Leo motioned toward her tower. "She asked permission to go swimming. It has to be tomorrow. At dawn. And she wants to be alone."

"Damn," Brody whispered. "What is Lady Tatiana up to?"

If she was Tatiana. Though now, she wanted to be called Ana. Leo dragged a gloved hand through his hair. *Dammit.* After the duel was over, she'd been invited to lunch with him, the general, and her father, but she'd refused. Was she avoiding him in order to keep her secrets?

With Captain Bougaire's accusation still ringing in his head, Leo had wondered how her father would react. So he'd mentioned it during their luncheon in the library.

"Bougaire said something odd when he surrendered." Leo had pretended to be engrossed in his roast beef. "He claimed your daughter was not actually Tatiana."

General Harden had chuckled. "What a sore loser."

But the duke had instantly turned pale, and his hand had trembled slightly when he'd set his wine goblet down. "What nonsense." He'd cleared his throat. "As if I wouldn't know my own daughter."

Dammit to hell. Leo paced across the tower room. He couldn't bring himself to tell Brody about his latest suspicions, but it seemed clear that the duke and his daughter were both hiding something. "I need to know the truth about her."

A knock sounded at the door. "I have your food, my lord," Edmund called out.

"Bring it in," Leo ordered. He continued to pace while his squire set a basket on the table, then left, closing the door behind him.

Brody retrieved a bottle of wine and two pewter mugs from the basket. "Here. Have a drink." He poured the two mugs full.

Leo took a sip. "I've spent my entire life on land, so I don't know much about sea creatures. Do you think it's possible to track the seals?"

Brody ran a fingertip around the rim of his mug, apparently deep in thought. Finally he took a deep breath and looked up. "It could take a few days, but I'll do it."

Leo blinked. "You can do it? How? Do you need to rent a boat? I can give you the money for that. And you can take as many soldiers as you need. Or hire as many sailors—"

"Don't worry about it. I'll take care of it." Brody took a long drink.

Leo narrowed his eyes. Was he becoming paranoid, or was Brody withholding information again?

Brody removed a platter of cold meats and cheeses from the basket, along with several small loaves of bread. "The prisoner hasn't said anything yet?"

"No, Willem has refused to talk until he knows his family is safe."

Brody ripped open a loaf and stuffed it with meat and cheese. "And Captain Booger? Did he leave like he was supposed to?"

"Yes." Leo suspected Brody was trying to steer the conversation away from his mission of tracking the seals. "What do you think she's up to?"

"Lady Tatiana?" Brody bit into his makeshift meal.

"Who else?"

"Well," Brody mumbled with his mouth full, "I don't know whom she's communicating with, but they must be very important to her. The last time the undertow was strong enough to pull her off her feet. She put herself in danger in order to reach the bottle."

Leo recalled seeing a bottle before in her bedchamber in the keep. "There were pebbles in the bottle."

Brody shrugged. "Don't know what that means." He took another bite.

"You'll be ready at dawn?" When Brody nodded, Leo continued, "We can't let her know that we're following the seals."

"Right." Brody swallowed. "You know, you could try trusting her. If you're truly smitten with her."

Leo scoffed. "Or she could try trusting me enough to tell me the truth."

"We already know almost everything. She's worshipping the moon goddesses. She talks to the dead. That's a strange ability, so we're assuming she's Embraced. The only thing we don't know right now is who is on the other end of these messages, but I'll uncover that soon."

There was also the question of her identity, but Leo didn't want to admit to that. "I'm to be her husband. She should tell me everything."

Brody took a long drink. "Look at it from her point of view. Why would she ever tell anyone she's Embraced, when it could get her killed? And get her father killed for hiding it?"

"I need to know the truth so I can protect her!"

"You're a member of the royal family, so as far as anyone knows you're loyal to your uncle."

Leo shook his head. "I told her the king has tried to assassinate me, too."

"Why should she believe that when she hardly knows

you? The king wants her dead, so he's demanding she marry you, and everyone knows you're . . ."

Leo closed his eyes briefly. "A monster? Is that what you were going to say?"

Brody sighed. "You're potentially dangerous. She's known you for only a few days, so you can't expect her to totally trust you. No doubt, she's heard some bad things."

Like he'd murdered his own mother. Leo wandered over to the window to gaze at her tower. There was something between them, something pulling them together. He could swear she was feeling it, too. Couldn't she trust in that?

By the Light, he wanted her. The first time he had seen her in that flimsy nightgown, he'd had to turn away to keep her from seeing the swelling in his breeches. He was aching to touch her. But she'd said it herself. How could they possibly marry when his touch would kill her? "Why would she want to marry the Beast?"

"Give her some time," Brody said.

Leo rested his gloved hands on the windowsill. "Fine." He would send Edmund over to her tower to inform her that he'd given her a reprieve for the rest of the day. The questions could wait till tomorrow.

The next day before dawn, Leo crouched behind some bushes on the bluff that overlooked the beach. As he waited for Tatiana and her guards to arrive, he assured himself that his main purpose here was to protect her. It wasn't that he was spying. He had his bow and arrows with him in case the remaining two assassins attempted an attack.

He sighed. *Admit it, you're spying.* But wasn't it normal for a man to want to know everything about the woman he was to marry?

As the twin moons descended toward the western horizon on the far side of Vindemar, the beach below him fell more into shadow. Patches of mist hovered over the dark sea and rocky shore.

In the distance, Leo spotted a light, moving slowly through the mist. As it came closer, he could see it was an oil lamp. Jensen was using it to illuminate the path to the beach. Tatiana and two more guards followed close behind.

All three guards were well armed. They wore sword belts, their swords sheathed. Jensen had a spear he was using as a hiking stick, while the other two had bows and quivers of arrows slung across their backs. Tatiana was dressed in a simple black gown tied around the waist with a strip of leather. Her dark hair was braided, her face pale as she concentrated on the steep path down to the beach.

Leo narrowed his eyes. Her left hand was lifting her skirt a few inches, but her right hand was hovering over a pocket as if she was protecting something inside. Was it the bottle? Was she sending a message today instead of receiving one?

Leo glanced toward the sea. The mist was heavy farther out, making it harder to see, but still, there was no boat in sight. Was Brody keeping his distance so Tatiana wouldn't suspect? By the time she and her guards reached the beach, the sky in the east was brightening with muted shades of gold and pink. Soon the sun would peek over the horizon.

The second and third guards sprinted along the beach, checking behind rocks to make sure no one was hiding nearby. From Leo's position above them, he couldn't see anyone else. To the right, close to Vindemar, there was a jumble of massive boulders, shrouded in mist. Somewhere, hidden in those rocks, was the secret tunnel that led to the catacombs. The duke had told him it was an emergency escape route in case the fortress ever fell.

While the guards looked around, Tatiana removed her

shoes and began wading into the dark water. When Jensen followed her, she shooed him off.

He returned to dry sand and stood there, one hand on the hilt of his sword, the other gripping his spear, as he surveyed the length of the beach. When his gaze lifted to scan the bluff, Leo kept perfectly still behind the bushes.

The sun continued to rise, and Tatiana strode deeper into the water. Leo winced, imagining how cold it must be. A wave swept out and nearly took her with it. She skidded a few feet but kept her balance.

He tensed. *Dammit.* He should go down there now and stop this nonsense before she was carried out to sea.

She headed toward a large, flat rock, wading deeper until the sea was higher than her waist. The next time the sea retreated, she let it pull her straight to the rock. Leo grimaced, afraid she'd smash into it. She caught herself, then gripped the rock with her left hand.

As the sun continued to rise, he saw a flash of light reflect off the glass bottle in her right hand. She hefted herself up, then planted the bottle near the center of the rock.

So she was sending a message this time. Leo quickly scanned the foggy horizon, but no sign of a boat. Where the hell was Brody?

When the waves roared toward the shore, Tatiana released her grip on the rock and let them carry her toward the beach. Thankfully, she managed to have her feet firmly planted before the sea pulled back out. She slipped a bit, but kept her balance. Soon she was splashing into shallow water that only reached halfway to her knees.

Leo exhaled in relief. She was safe for now.

Jensen joined her, saying something to her that Leo couldn't hear, but he assumed Jensen was making sure she was all right. She was being clever, Leo noted. She was positioned so that Jensen's back would be to the rock when he talked to her. That way, he wouldn't notice the bottle. The other guards were scanning the bluff.

Suddenly the water around the rock became frothy and agitated. A seal leaped onto the rock, followed by another and another till a dozen seals flopped around, barking, their sleek bodies glistening in the sunlight.

Leo shook his head. Unbelievable. Whoever had arranged this had to possess the ability to communicate with animals, or at least seals.

Jensen's exclamation was loud enough for Leo to hear. All three guards were now watching the seals. Luciana waved and called out a greeting. There was no reason for her to worry about the guards seeing her bottle, for it was completely hidden in the midst of the sea creatures.

While Tatiana and her guards remained focused on the seals, Leo spotted a movement on the beach, far to the left. Something moving from behind a rock, partially hidden by the mist. He reached for his bow and arrow, then stopped when he realized it was Brody.

What the hell? How could he track the seals as a dog? Brody slipped into the water, unnoticed by Tatiana and her guards, who were watching the seals dive back into the water.

Soon the rock was bare, the bottle gone. One of the seals had it for sure. The surface of the sea frothed as the dozen seals started their journey.

Leo glanced back at Brody. He dove underwater, and a few seconds later Leo spotted the sun glistening off a slick black body as it broke the surface and made another dip underwater.

What the hell? Leo stood up and frantically scanned the surface of the sea. Where the hell was Brody? Was he in trouble, or had he actually transformed into a different creature?

When Tatiana and her guards started back toward the

fortress, Leo hunched down behind the bushes. *Holy shit.* He could have sworn Brody had become a seal. Did that mean he could shift into any creature he wanted to?

Leo ran a gloved hand through his hair. Tatiana wasn't the only one keeping secrets from him.

Leo remained distracted for the rest of the morning. He made a quick trip to the dungeon to check on the prisoner, but Willem still refused to talk. Leo assured him Nevis would return soon, but also reminded him that as soon as the gallows were built, Willem was scheduled to hang.

In the courtyard, Leo inspected the scaffold that had been erected near the south gate. It was nearly complete.

His gaze wandered toward the western wing of the keep. No doubt, Tatiana was in her dressing room, changing into dry clothes. Perhaps having one of her long baths. He smiled to himself. He was beginning to like hot baths, too.

On the ground floor, below the library, there was a communal bath, one for men, another for women, with large pools of heated water. After spending most of his life on the road with the army, Leo was enjoying his daily bath and a real bed to sleep in. But this sort of lifestyle wasn't something he could grow attached to. As soon as the assassins were discovered and dealt with, he would have to escort Tatiana and her father to the court in Ebton. After the wedding, he would return them to Vindalyn and resume his duties as Lord Protector. He would rarely even see his new wife.

When he entered the southern tower, two of his personal guard were on duty. They jumped up to salute. Edmund handed him a letter from the duke.

"Thanks." Leo's stomach rumbled as he headed for the stairs. He'd been in such a hurry to spy on Tatiana this morning that he'd neglected to eat breakfast.

Edmund chuckled. "Food again?"

Leo smiled. "If you don't mind."

While Edmund dashed to the kitchens, Leo went up the stairs to his room to read the letter. The duke had ordered a celebration for that night in the Great Hall. Dining, music, and dancing. Both Leo and Lady Tatiana were requested to attend.

He smiled to himself. Ana couldn't avoid him now.

After a few minutes, Edmund knocked on his door, then entered with a tray of food.

"Thanks." Leo dropped his bow and quiver onto the bed while Edmund set the tray on the table. There were two plates, one heaped with bacon, sausages, and eggs, and the other filled with bread, butter, and jam. Leo's mouth watered as he took a seat. "This looks excellent."

Edmund grinned. "My lady fixed these for you."

"My—you mean, Lady Tatiana?"

"Yes, my lord. She's helping out in the kitchens. They're very busy getting ready for the celebration tonight."

"Ah." So she wasn't lying about in a bathtub. She was working.

"She should be safe," Edmund continued. "Jensen and two guards are outside the kitchen door. Usually Brody is with her, too, but I haven't seen him today."

Leo nodded. "I asked him to take care of a matter for me. He'll be gone for a few days."

Edmund bowed and left, closing the door behind him. Leo removed his gloves, and while he ate his mind kept replaying the vision of a sleek black body diving into the water. Brody had become a seal? Why had Brody never mentioned that he could shift into different animals?

It had been five years ago when Brody had wandered into camp as a dog, looking exhausted and hungry. After Nevis had given him a bone to chew on, the dog had followed Nevis into his tent, and there he had shifted into human form, scaring the crap out of Nevis. But once he convinced Nevis he had news from the royal court, Nevis had thrown him some clothes and taken him to meet Leo.

Leo had hired him, and over the years Leo had started to rely on Brody's reports and good advice. Brody was the only other person he knew who was Embraced, so they had that in common. But Brody was gone most of the time, gathering information, and even when he was around, he could only be human for a limited time, and that time was normally used for business. Leo had to admit now that he actually knew very little about Brody.

A knock sounded on his door and Edmund peeked inside. "My lord, I thought you might want to know . . ."

Leo rose to his feet. "What?"

"I saw it from the entrance to the tower. Lady Tatiana has moved to the kitchen garden to work."

Was Jensen crazy? She shouldn't be out in the open like that. Leo stuffed his gloves under his belt, then grabbed his bow, quiver, and a long coil of rope. "Tell Jensen she needs to be inside. Take my guards with you."

While Edmund ran downstairs, Leo dashed up the stairs to the top of the turret. The sun was halfway to its midday point, so it had to be midmorning. All the mist had burned away, and the sea was a brilliant blue. From this position, Leo could see most of the keep and inner bailey. He spotted Tatiana in the garden on her knees, digging up vegetables. Jensen and two guards were a short distance away, their backs to her as they surveyed the surrounding area. Edmund and two of Leo's guards ran toward them.

Quickly, Leo scanned the curtain wall. The guards were looking outward, none of them focused on Tatiana. He shifted his gaze to the battlements on top of the keep.

There. A Vindalyn soldier was watching Tatiana. He reached back for an arrow from his quiver.

Dammit. "Jensen! Edmund! The keep!"

Chapter Nineteen

Luciana slammed onto her back hard enough to knock the air out of her lungs. The fact that Jensen had suddenly tossed her aside and pounced on her was shocking enough, but she barely noticed his body covering hers. It was the arrow that had struck the ground a few feet away that held her attention.

That arrow had been meant for her.

It quivered from the force of impact. Enough force to have pierced her through.

"My lady!" Jensen lifted his weight off her. "Are you all right?"

She shifted her gaze to the brilliant, blue sky overhead, and with a gasp she resumed breathing. But too quickly. The clouds swirled, and for a moment she had trouble focusing. "I—I . . ."

Above her, something shot across the sky. Another arrow? She blinked. Now there was a rope going from the keep to the turret on the southern tower. The rope shook as it was pulled taut.

"What—" As the initial shock faded away, she found her senses suddenly sharpening to a keen edge as if an inner, instinctual need for survival had seized hold of her.

In a few seconds, the time it took her to sit up, she understood everything that was happening.

The second assassin had shot an arrow at her from the battlements atop the keep. Jensen had saved her, and two of Leo's personal guard and his squire, Edmund, had joined her other guards. She now had a total of six men circled about her to protect her. Three wore the blue and white colors of Vindalyn, while the other three wore the red and black of the royal army.

As she scrambled to her feet, she spotted movement on the top of the southern tower. Her heart lurched. By the goddesses, had Leo lost his mind? He had looped a belt over the rope and was swooping down it, his feet dangling in the air. He zoomed past them, then swung his body over the crenellated battlements to land on top of the keep.

Is he trying to kill himself? Luciana thought. "How does he do that?"

Edmund chuckled. "That's normal for the Lord—"

"My lady," Jensen interrupted. "We should take you to the tower immediately."

"I'll be safe as long as I'm with you." Luciana dashed toward the south gate to the keep. "It's more important that we help Leo catch the assassin."

"But, my lady—" Jensen jogged to keep up with her.

"Where do you think the assassin will go?" Luciana asked as the six men entered the courtyard and surrounded her.

"He'll head down the stairs to the courtyard," Jensen replied.

"Then we should close the gates!" Luciana motioned for the men to go. "Hurry!"

Four of her companions sprinted toward the gates, yelling at the soldiers posted there to bolt them shut. Jensen and Edmund remained at her side, their swords drawn.

Luciana looked around. The newly built scaffold was next to her, the hangman's noose dangling from the top beam. Workers in the courtyard stopped what they were doing when they noticed swords being drawn and gates being shut. A few ran inside the keep, no doubt intending to spread the news that something was about to happen.

With a gasp, Luciana spotted Leo on the western side of the keep. He was sliding down the steep slate roof, his bare hands shooting sparks as they controlled his descent. His feet went off the edge. She cried out, afraid he'd plummet to the stone courtyard three floors below. His body kept skidding off the roof till he caught himself with his hands. His boots found a foothold on the upper frame of a window below him.

Luciana watched, stunned and breathless, as he fell downward and stopped, his hands catching on a stone windowsill. He dropped again, this time his hands grabbing onto a stone arch above the gallery. His boots landed on the stone balustrade. He ducked his head and jumped onto the black-and-white-tiled floor of the gallery. He was now one floor up. And safe.

Luciana pressed a hand to her racing heart and resumed breathing. She didn't know whether to be amazed by him or angry that he couldn't take the stairs like a normal, sane person.

He shouted at something across the courtyard. Luciana turned sharply and spotted the assassin entering the gallery on the eastern side of the keep. He'd taken the stairs, so he was a few seconds behind Leo. He stiffened at the sight of Leo and ran back to the stairwell. One flight of stairs and he would reach the courtyard.

Leo dashed along the gallery, his speed so fast, his form became a blur. He reached the southern side of the gallery, just above the newly constructed gallows, then jumped onto the stone balustrade.

Luciana gasped. He leaped off the balustrade, caught the top beam of the gallows, then swung forward to land on the wooden platform. As soon as his feet hit, he ran forward then jumped off the edge. After a somersault in the air, he landed in the courtyard and kept running.

He was halfway to the door on the eastern side of the keep when the assassin emerged. With a stunned look on his face, the assassin dashed toward the north gate, no doubt hoping to get through it to the gatehouse.

The assassin skidded to a stop when he noticed the northern gate was bolted shut. Two Vindalyn guards and one of Leo's personal guard fanned out, blocking the assassin. He whirled about and froze at the sight of Leo only a few yards away.

A tense silence fell over the courtyard. Workers had lined the perimeter of the courtyard to watch. Servants were standing along the gallery. Everyone waited to see what would happen next.

"Surrender," Leo said quietly, though his voice carried over the hushed courtyard.

The assassin looked frantically about, his face growing ashen, his hands trembling.

"Surrender," Leo repeated louder as he tugged on a pair of gloves.

The assassin shook his head, then fiddled with a ring on his hand. When he lifted it to his mouth, Leo shouted and lunged toward him.

"No!" Leo wrenched the man's hand away from his mouth.

Too late. Luciana grimaced as the man's body shook with convulsions. He collapsed onto the pavement stones, writhing and frothing at the mouth till he finally grew still.

Leo stood nearby, his fists clenched. He didn't need to say a word, for Luciana could feel the waves of frustration coming off him.

Then the whispers began. Like dead leaves scurrying

with a wind, the words drifted down the gallery and across the courtyard.

"The Beast killed him."

"If the Beast touches you, you die."

"No," Luciana whispered. They couldn't blame this on Leo.

"Take the body to the dungeon," Leo ordered the soldiers.

As the soldiers picked up the dead assassin, the whispers grew louder. Fingers pointed at Leo. And he stood there alone, his gloved hands balled into fists, while the people called him a Beast.

"Stop it!" Luciana cried, but only a few nearby heard her.

She scrambled up the stairs to stand on the gallows. "The Lord Protector saved my life!"

A few more heard her and stopped whispering.

She pointed at the dead man being carried away. "That man tried to kill me. He took poison to avoid being captured. You saw it! The poison was in his ring! The Lord Protector tried to stop him!"

More voices hushed. She waved her arms, attempting to draw everyone's attention, and raised her voice as loud as she could. *"He's not a Beast!"*

Silence fell once again, and Luciana panted to catch her breath. Then she saw him. Saw the astonished look on his face.

And her heart wrenched. "He's not a Beast," she whispered. And in that moment, while he watched her in amazement, all her doubts withered away and she knew with a certainty what she should have known for days.

She loved him.

Somehow, he seemed to sense the realization that had come to her, for his gaze grew more intense and heated. His expression turned from wonder to smoldering hunger as he strode toward her.

Tears sprang to her eyes. How could she not love him? He was stealing her heart, invading her thoughts, and ripping into her soul. With each step he took toward her, her resistance melted away. Her pulse raced, and her skin flushed hot as if a fever had taken hold of her.

"My lord!" A guard ran toward him and whispered some news.

Leo stiffened, then motioned to her guard. "Jensen, get her to the tower now! Edmund, bring the general!"

Edmund dashed toward the north gate, while Jensen grabbed Luciana's arm and escorted her off the scaffold. A group of Vindalyn guards surrounded her, their swords drawn.

Something had gone terribly wrong, but Luciana couldn't tell what. All she could see was Leo running toward the dungeons as she was bustled back to her room in the tower.

Leo ordered his personal guard to step outside when the general arrived at the dungeons. There was no danger for them, since the other occupants were all dead.

"What the hell?" General Harden surveyed the underground room. "I take it the third assassin did this?"

"I believe so." Leo shut the iron door, so he and the general could speak in private. "While we were focused on catching assassin number two, the third one used that time to eliminate any threats."

The general muttered a curse as he glanced down at the bloodied corpse lying near the door.

"The first jailer." Leo motioned to him. "Stabbed through the chest at close range. No defensive wounds. He was taken by surprise."

General Harden nodded. "He let the killer in. He must have known him."

Leo wandered over to the body of assassin number two.

"This is the one who shot an arrow at Lady Tatiana. I chased him down, but he took poison before we could capture him. I had him brought here."

"Blue-and-white uniform," the general observed.

"One of Vindemar's new recruits, just like we suspected. I was told his name is Dax." Leo motioned to the dead body inside the jail cell. "Assassin number one, Willem. His throat was cut. The cell was opened with keys taken from one of the jailers."

General Harden grimaced. "He was still chained to the wall. Couldn't defend himself."

"He must have known the identity of the third assassin, so he was silenced." Leo sighed as his gaze shifted to the second dead jailer. "I warned them that this could happen. They weren't vigilant enough."

"Obviously, the killer was someone they trusted."

Leo strode toward the second jailer's body. "His sword is drawn. I figure he saw his companion murdered by the door, then he drew his weapon to fight with the assassin."

"A fight that he lost," the general mumbled.

"There's some blood on his sword, so we know the assassin has been wounded. That should help us to locate him."

The general snorted. "There's an easier way to—" He hushed when the door burst open and the duke strode into the dungeon with two guards.

"Your Grace," Leo greeted him. "You should remain in your quarters. The third assassin is still at large, and as you can see, he's extremely dangerous."

The duke grew pale as he looked around the room. His gaze rested on the second assassin. "This is the man who made an attempt on my daughter's life? Is she all right?"

"Yes," Leo replied. "She was escorted back to the tower."

With a heavy sigh, the duke knelt beside the body of

the second jailer. "This was a good man. He was in my employ for over twenty years." He glanced at the first jailer. "And he grew up here at Vindemar. His father was a soldier before him."

"We'll capture their killer soon," Leo assured him.

The duke rose slowly to his feet. "I appreciate your help."

"You and your daughter will be my family," Leo said quietly. "I will do everything in my power to keep you both safe."

"I will hold you to that promise." The duke gave the deceased Willem a resigned look. "Captain Harden and his party have been spotted. They'll be here shortly. They have Willem's family with them."

Leo nodded. "The king's men may have been holding them hostage to force Willem's hand."

"I'll look after them." The duke squared his shoulders. "I'll inform the families of the deceased and make arrangements for the funerals. Obviously, the festivities to celebrate your betrothal to my daughter will have to be postponed. Tonight, we will have a funeral feast to honor the two men who served me so well."

"I understand," Leo murmured.

The duke strode from the dungeons, followed by his guards.

The general made sure the door was shut, then whispered to Leo, "The easiest way to catch the third assassin is to have Brody sniff around in here. He can catch the killer's scent, then point him out to us."

Leo groaned inwardly. "Brody's not here. I sent him on a mission."

"What?" General Harden gave him an incredulous look. "What the hell did you do that for? Bring him back. Now!"

Leo clenched his fists. "I don't have a way to contact him."

"Damn!" The general grimaced.

Leo closed his eyes briefly. He should have done as Brody said and trusted Tatiana. But no, he'd decided it was more important to investigate her. He'd put uncovering her secrets ahead of protecting her. If something happened to her now, it would be his fault. "I made a mistake. I've been a bloody fool."

The general snorted. "Don't be so hard on yourself. We'll find the killer."

Leo shook his head. He should have trusted her. *He's not a Beast!* Her shouted words had pierced him through. She believed in him. She'd taken his side against the crowd. Her heart was opening up to him. He could feel it.

And he wanted her with a desperation that stole his breath away.

He should have trusted her. Now Brody was gone, and it would take longer to discover the identity of a third assassin who had just gone on a murderous rampage.

Tatiana was in more danger than ever.

Chapter Twenty

❧

When Luciana returned with Jensen to the tower, they passed by the two guards at the ground-level entrance and began their climb up the spiral staircase. When they reached the floor where the privy was located, she excused herself.

Jensen bowed. "I'll go upstairs to make sure your room is safe."

Alone for a few minutes in the privy, Luciana's thoughts fled back to that moment where she'd stood on the scaffold, announcing to everyone that her betrothed was not a beast, then realizing that she loved him. Even now, her heart raced when she recalled his reaction, the way he'd stalked toward her with that desperate, hungry look in his eyes.

Her face burned with heat as she washed her hands in the basin. Was she being ridiculous to love a man who couldn't touch her?

As she left the privy, she heard an odd moaning sound emanating from the stairwell. Was that Tatiana? Was she hurt? Could a dead person even feel pain?

She hurried up the stairs, then halted with a jerk midway up. Tatiana was moaning all right, but not from pain. Captain Bougaire had pinned her against the wall, and he was dragging his mouth down her neck as if he were devouring her.

Luciana gasped. The captain was dead? She blinked a few times to make sure she was seeing this. Apparently, two ghosts could touch each other, and these two were heartily proving that fact. She grimaced when her sister grasped the captain's rump and pulled him closer. He growled in response and yanked the bodice of her red gown down to expose a breast. Then his mouth latched on to her nipple.

Did men actually do that? Luciana was so stunned she nearly toppled down the stairs. "By the godde—get yourselves to a bedchamber!"

They broke apart. The captain scowled at her, while Tatiana merely looked annoyed as she tugged her bodice back in place.

"Go away," Tatiana grumbled. "Can't you see we're busy?"

"How—" Luciana winced at the gaping wound in Captain Bougaire's chest. His white shirt was stained with blood. "How can you be dead?"

He snorted. "How do you think? Your precious Lord Protector had me killed."

Luciana flinched. "No." *No, he gave his word that he wouldn't kill the captain.*

"I told you we couldn't trust the Beast!" Tatiana shouted.

But she'd believed Leo. She'd trusted him. Luciana shook her head. "There must be some sort of explanation . . ."

"Of course there is," the captain growled. "The bastard had me killed because I told him you weren't the real Tatiana."

Luciana's heart lurched. "Ye—you told him that?" By the goddesses, had Leo believed it?

The captain sneered. "I knew you were an imposter the

minute I tried to kiss you." He gave Tatiana a wry smirk. "She kisses like a dead fish."

Tatiana scoffed. "She'll never know a love as glorious as ours."

The captain's smirk twisted. "It could have been glorious. We could have had everything, dammit. Why did you have to get yourself killed?"

Tatiana blinked in surprise. "Excuse me? You think I wanted to be poisoned?"

"If you had just gotten pregnant, I could have convinced your father to let us marry. Dammit to hell!" Captain Bougaire slammed a fist against the stone wall, but his hand passed through. "Shit! Now I'm dead, and I have nothing!"

"You have me!" Tatiana placed her hands on his chest. "We can be together now for all eternity."

He shoved her hands away. "You think it was you that I wanted? I was so damned close to getting my hands on the duchy. But you ruined everything, you stupid bitch."

Tatiana gasped. Luciana gasped, too, and watched with horror as her sister slowly realized the truth about her glorious love affair. As Tatiana's eyes filled with tears and her body wavered, Luciana felt her blood surging hot with raw anger.

The captain barked out a laugh. "It was ridiculous how easy you were to fool, how easily you spread your legs—"

"Enough!" Luciana stepped between them so she was mere inches from his face. "Don't ye dare talk to my sister like that. Ye were banished from Vindalyn, so ye'll leave now and never come back."

He snorted. "Can you make me?"

"Aye, I can," Luciana growled. "I'll find every living member of yer family in this duchy. Yer mother, yer brothers and sisters, yer cousins. I'll strip them of their homes and every possession they own, and kick them out, penniless and starving. And I'll let them know that all their suffering is because of you."

His face grew pale. "Y-you wouldn't dare—"

"Don't try me," she hissed. "If I ever hear of yer presence in my duchy again, I will unleash hell on yer—"

"I got it! I'm leaving." He lifted his hands in surrender and shot Tatiana a disgusted look. "It's not as if I have anything to lose here." His form vanished.

With a muffled sob, Tatiana disappeared.

"My lady?" Jensen called from above. "Are you all right?"

"Yes." Luciana took a deep breath and exhaled slowly. *Stay calm. Don't let your accent slip again.* "I'll be right there." Her hands trembled as she gathered up her skirts to climb the rest of the stairs to the top floor.

Jensen eyed her warily. "Are you sure . . . ?"

How much had he heard? "I-I was pretending to fuss at the assassin who tried to kill me. I thought it might release some of the stress."

"Ah." Jensen nodded slowly. "Well, it has been a difficult day for you. Perhaps you should get some rest."

"I will." She stepped into her room. "And thank you, Jensen, for saving my life."

He blushed. "Yes, my lady."

She shut the door and locked it, then discovered her sister was pacing back and forth, her feet gliding noiselessly on the wooden floor.

"I can't believe it!" Tatiana wailed. "All this time, he was using me!"

"I'm so sorry," Luciana murmured.

"I gave my virginity to that bastard!" Tatiana waved her arms wildly. "I hate him! I hate him!"

"I'm sure you do."

Tatiana whirled and planted her hands on her hips. "I hate all men!"

"Well, I wouldn't go that far—"

"Even that Beast is a bastard! How dare he kill my Alberto!"

Luciana winced. She didn't want to think that Leo had broken his word. "I thought you hated Alberto."

"I do! He's lower than swine. He's the scum coming out of a privy pipe! *I hate him!*" Tatiana screamed as she swiped her arm across the table and sent the brass candlestick holder flying across the room.

Luciana gasped. "Did you see that? By the goddesses, look at what you did!"

Tatiana glanced at the candlestick holder rolling on the floor, then at her arm. "How—how did I do that?"

Luciana picked up the candlestick holder. "I've never seen a spirit that could move objects before."

"Neither have I."

Luciana grinned. "You're the most marvelous ghost ever!"

Tatiana giggled, then curled a strand of hair around her finger. "Well, yes, I suppose I am."

"Can you do it again?" Luciana placed the candlestick holder back on the table.

Tatiana swiped at it, but her hand passed through. "Oh, no. What happened?"

"You were extremely angry before. Perhaps you should picture Captain Booger's face on the candlestick."

Tatiana's eyes narrowed. "You bastard!" She knocked the candlestick holder across the room. "I did it!"

Luciana clapped her hands together. "You're amazing."

Tatiana gave her a sheepish smile. "No, you're the amazing one. You were right up in his face. *Don't ye dare talk to my sister like that.* By the light, you were fierce!"

Heat flooded Luciana's cheeks. "Well, I can't let anyone insult one of my sisters."

"I'm your only . . . oh." Tatiana sighed. "I guess you miss your sisters at the convent."

"I do. But I'm very happy to have my sister here."

Tatiana's eyes filled with tears. "I haven't been that nice to you. I was a little jealous, I guess. You grew up with such close friends, and I didn't. I had Christopher for a while, then . . ."

"You could still be friends with him. And you have Mother. And me. Father, too. I'd be happy to relay your messages to him."

Tatiana nodded and wiped a tear from her cheek. "I'm going to be the best spy in the world now. I'll keep you and Papa safe. You'll see."

Luciana blinked back tears of her own. "Thank you."

With a sniff, Tatiana's form wavered and disappeared.

Feeling emotionally drained, Luciana stretched out on her bed. The day was only half over, but so much had occurred. She'd hardly slept the night before, too worried that if she did doze off, she'd miss the seals at dawn and her chance to send a message to her sisters.

Other shocking things had happened, like the assassination attempt, but of all the memories of the day, it was the look on Leo's face when she'd defended him that had struck her the most. If he were able to touch her, would he act like the dead captain had with Tatiana? Would Leo tear off her clothes and suckle her breasts?

Images flitted through her mind, making her heart race, then with a frustrated groan she shoved the thoughts aside. Why bother to even imagine such things? Things like Leo's mouth nibbling down her neck, his hands roaming her body. It couldn't happen. Not unless there was a serious drought. Was she supposed to wish failed crops and starvation for the Eberoni just so she could be kissed?

She punched a pillow. She shouldn't allow herself to

become lovesick over a man she hardly knew. Could he truly be trusted? What if he'd had Captain Booger killed? What if he knew she was an imposter? Would he turn her in to the king? Thoughts swirled in her mind till she finally fell into an exhausted sleep.

When she woke, she slowly became aware that she'd curled into a ball, for the room was chilly. And she was being watched.

With a jerk, she sat up, and her mother's ghost retreated across the room with a smooth glide.

"Don't go!" Luciana jumped out of bed.

Her mother, Ariana, hovered by a window, gazing at her sadly.

Tears welled in Luciana's eyes. "Please don't leave. I'm so happy to see you."

A tear rolled down Ariana's face. "My baby girl. You've grown up to be so brave and beautiful."

Luciana's heart squeezed and her tears overflowed. When her mother's form wavered, she reached out her hand. "Please stay."

Ariana grew solid again. "Forgive me. This is difficult. When I think about all the years that you must have thought you were abandoned . . ." She wiped tears from her face. "If only I could have let you know how much you were loved."

"I do know now."

"I'm sorry I wasn't able to be with—"

"Don't say that!" More tears poured down Luciana's cheeks. "I'm the one who's sorry. You died giving birth—"

"Hush now." Ariana whooshed toward her and framed Luciana's face with her hands.

Luciana reached up to touch her mother's hands, but her fingers passed through to her wet cheeks.

Ariana sighed. "I wish I could hold you. I held you when you were a baby, and I thought my heart would burst with joy." Her gaze grew more stern. "Don't you ever for a moment blame yourself. You were an innocent child, born from love. And I am so proud of you."

Luciana pressed a hand to her mouth as a sob escaped.

"Shh." Her mother passed a hand over Luciana's head as if she were stroking her hair. "You must be strong now. You're in grave danger."

Luciana sniffed and nodded.

With a sigh, Ariana glided back a few steps. "My poor Tatiana was killed, and now they're trying to kill you. How could Lucas bring you here? I'm so upset with him now. You were supposed to always be safe."

"He begged me to stay on the Isle of Moon. But I couldn't once I learned the truth. If Father fails to do as he was ordered, he'll be executed."

Ariana frowned. "I fear you and Lucas will never be safe. I saw what happened today in the courtyard and the dungeons."

"The dungeons? What happened there?"

"I only saw the aftermath, and I was so shocked, I didn't stay long." Ariana grimaced. "While the second assassin was being chased down, the third one slipped into the dungeon to murder the first one. And he killed the two jailers who were there."

Three murders? Luciana made the sign of the moons, then fisted her hands. No wonder Leo had insisted she be brought back to the tower immediately.

"The Lord Protector is trying very hard to keep you safe," Ariana continued. "I like him."

"You do?"

Ariana nodded, her eyes softening. "I believe you like him, too."

Luciana's cheeks flared with heat.

Ariana chuckled. "You remind me of your father. He loved me, even though there were terrible rumors about me and my family."

"Really?" Luciana sat on the bed. "Can you tell me how you met?"

Ariana moved to the window to gaze at the Southern Sea. "I came from a village along the coast. I never knew my father. My mother and grandmother were feared by all the local people, who called them witches." She smiled sadly. "In truth, they were great healers and people thronged to them when they were sick. But when they were healthy . . ."

"They spread rumors about them?" Luciana asked.

Ariana nodded. "My grandmother was famous for being able to predict the future, and that frightened people."

Luciana's gaze wandered to the Telling Stones on the table. "Your grandmother could predict the future?"

"Yes. I inherited the sight, too, but to a lesser degree. Tatiana never seemed to have it at all." Ariana gave her a curious look. "Are you able to see the future?"

"Maybe, a little." Luciana explained about the Telling Stones. "And it happened just like I said. Two weeks later, I met a tall and handsome stranger with red hair and a black horse."

"Interesting." Her mother glided to the table and ran her hand over the stones, her fingers passing through them. "Have you seen anything else?"

"No, but I haven't really tried." Luciana wondered if the predictions she'd given her sisters would also come true.

Ariana sighed. "I never saw my own demise, but there were a few things I knew for certain. I knew I would give birth to twins, both girls. We didn't need to be psychic to know how dangerous that was, but it gave us time to prepare for your safety. And I knew, somehow, that this room was important. I assumed it meant I would give birth here, so I had the room furnished. But I never realized . . ." Her voice trailed off as she gazed at the scorched wall across from the window.

A chill ran down Luciana's back. "What . . . ?"

"I think I understand why it happened now," Ariana whispered.

"What happened?"

Ariana turned and gave her a sad smile. "You wanted to know how I met your father?" When Luciana nodded, she continued, "When Lucas asked the king for permission to wed, the king insisted he marry me. He probably thought Lucas would be afraid to touch a notorious witch like me, and then there would be no heirs. But Lucas didn't let the rumors stop him. He treated me with respect and kindness, and before long we were madly in love."

Luciana smiled. "That's beautiful."

Ariana gave her a wry look. "That's why you remind me of your father. You're not letting rumors about the Beast stop you from falling in love."

Luciana's cheeks heated up once again.

Tatiana suddenly appeared. "I found out what happened—oh, hello, Mama. I-I know what happened in the dungeons."

"I've already told your sister." Ariana gave Tatiana a stern look. "I heard Captain Bougaire's ghost was saying foul things about you in the catacombs before he left."

Tatiana winced and hung her head.

Ariana crossed her arms, frowning. "I warned you about him. You should have listened."

"Yes, Mama." Tatiana glanced sidelong at Luciana. "So you two are talking now?"

Luciana nodded.

Tatiana bit her lip. "I said some things I shouldn't have."

"You were upset about being dead," Luciana told her softly as more tears gathered in her eyes. "But we're all together now."

Tatiana gave her a teary smile and nodded.

A knock sounded on the door.

"Ana?" Leo called.

Luciana's breath caught, and she quickly wiped her face dry. "Yes?"

"May I see you?" Leo asked.

Tatiana glared at the door as she floated away from it. "Why is the Beast here? He's spoiling our family reunion."

"He's going to be family," Ariana said with a smile.

"Ha!" Tatiana crossed her arms. "He can't be trusted."

Luciana ran to the door, unlocked it, and cracked it open. Her heart leaped at the sight of Leo. She hadn't seen him since her shouted defense of him in the courtyard. He must have just bathed, for his red hair was damp and curling around his ears. His breeches and shirt were clean and smelled of soap and fresh ocean breezes. The wolfish hunger was gone from his eyes, replaced by a gentle, friendly look. Was the Beast pretending to be a sheep? Even if he was trying to make her feel more comfortable, she could still sense the heat of his desire, simmering just below the surface. Ready to boil over at any moment.

She had a strange and sudden desire to be singed.

He smiled and lifted a basket for her to see. "I realized I hadn't eaten since that wonderful breakfast you packed for me, and I thought perhaps you hadn't eaten, either. So how about having luncheon with me?"

Her pulse raced even faster. "All right." She opened the door, and he strode inside.

"It's chilly in here. Shall I start a fire for you?"

"I-I think it will warm up soon." Luciana glanced at her mother and sister.

"I'll leave you two alone." Ariana smiled, then vanished.

"Well, I'm not leaving," Tatiana announced, her hands planted on her hips. "I don't trust him. And I want to know the truth about him killing Alberto!"

Chapter Twenty-one

She looked like she'd been crying. Leo fought an urge to pull her into his arms, but he couldn't risk shocking her with lightning power. As he set the basket on the table, he wondered what had upset her.

No doubt the assassination attempt had frightened her. And she could be unnerved by something he didn't know about. She had so many damned secrets. Was she even who she claimed to be?

Not that her true identity mattered that much to him. Whoever she was, he wanted her. He'd lusted for her from the beginning, but now that she'd taken a stand for him, yelling to the crowd that he wasn't a Beast, he ached to claim her as his own.

He glanced at her, and a pang shot through his chest. It wasn't just her body he wanted. He wanted her heart. Wanted to know her thoughts, her secrets. And that meant he needed her trust.

As he placed a bottle of wine and two wooden cups on the table, he noticed the three stones resting there. Two were painted with colors, red and black, and one had some sort of figure—an upside-down number two?

Were these the pebbles he'd seen in the bottle she used

for her secret messages? He reached out a gloved hand to turn the third pebble around. Definitely a number two. "What is the meaning of this?"

"Oh. It's . . . nothing." The sudden paleness of her face belied her words. "Thank you for bringing all this food." She quickly finished emptying the basket. "I was starving."

She was changing the subject. Leo opened the bottle and poured wine into the cups while she set out the rest of their luncheon. There was a round wooden platter of sliced cheese, cold ham, and grapes. Wrapped in a linen cloth was a hot loaf of bread. She set a crock of butter beside it along with a small knife.

When he offered her a cup, she didn't notice. Her gaze had turned toward the window, and she was frowning. "Ana?"

She jumped. "Oh, thank you." She accepted the cup.

He lifted his own cup and touched it against hers. "To us."

She smiled shyly, her cheeks blooming a pretty pink.

"May we have a long, happy life together," he continued, "trusting each other in all manner of things."

Her hand trembled slightly.

He drank from his cup, watching her. She took a sip, then her gaze shifted once more to the window.

"There's a definite chill coming in." He refilled his cup. "We could have curtains installed."

"It's fine as it is." With a hesitant smile, she sat at the table.

He glanced at the window once more. There was no discernible breeze, and no reason why a summer afternoon in southern Vindalyn would produce such a chill. Unless . . . the chill was caused by something else. Or someone else. *Damn.*

When he'd knocked on the door, he'd heard her inside, talking to someone. Was there a ghost here bothering her?

He didn't know how well he could protect her from a spirit, but it prompted him to move his chair close to her. She stiffened slightly. "Do I make you nervous?"

"No, not at all." She grabbed the loaf of bread, tore off a piece, and slathered it with butter.

She wasn't a very good liar. He sat beside her. "The assassination attempt must have frightened you."

She paused a moment, then shot him an annoyed look. "Do you know what frightened me the most? Seeing you flying through the air, hanging on a rope, and falling down the side of the keep. You could have broken your neck! Next time, take the stairs!"

He blinked in surprise, then rested an elbow on the table, grinning. "You were worried about me?"

She scoffed, then stuffed the buttered hunk of bread into his mouth.

"Careful," he mumbled, leaning back. He bit off a small piece, then removed the bread with a gloved hand. "I appreciate that you no longer see me as a Beast, but I'm still too dangerous for you to touch."

"I know," she muttered as she ripped another hunk of bread off the loaf.

Was she upset that they couldn't touch? Did he dare hope that she wanted him? "Ana."

She glanced up at him, and her eyes widened, locked with his for a tense moment. By the Light, he wanted her. His gaze drifted down to her mouth. If only he could kiss her.

He held his piece of bread up to her mouth, nudging it against her rosy pink lips. Her mouth opened, accepting it. When she bit down, he leaned forward to bite off the other end. Their eyes met.

So close, but still impossible. Even so, his groin swelled

and began to harden. *Not now*, he mentally warned himself, as if his cock ever listened. Damn, if he was ever able to kiss her, it would nearly kill him.

He leaned back, leaving the bread in her mouth.

She took a bite and set the bread on the table in front of him. With a slight wince, she glanced toward the window.

A chill skittered down Leo's spine. Had their ghostly guest disapproved?

Her gaze drifted toward the bed.

Was the ghost moving? He wanted to ask her, but figured she'd clam up if he pushed too hard. Maybe if he started with something small. He motioned to the pebbles. "Why are they painted? Do the colors mean something?"

"They're not important." She busied herself buttering a second piece of bread.

"They're important enough that you keep them."

She shrugged. "They mean whatever you want them to mean. It's nothing but a silly game."

His mouth twitched. "A game of stones?"

She set the knife down and gave the pebbles a wistful look. "They're called Telling Stones. It's a game to predict the future. I learned how to do it when I was on the Isle of Moon."

"When you were recovering from being poisoned?"

A muscle in her jaw quivered. "I thought you were hungry." She moved the platter closer to him and selected a slice of cheese for herself.

While she ate, he gathered up the stones in his gloved hand. "Red, black, and the number two. What future did these foretell?"

She swallowed. "It was simply a game to keep us entertained."

His fist closed around the pebbles. "Then there's no harm in telling me."

She studied his face for a moment, then nodded slowly.

"All right, then. When I drew those three stones, I said in two weeks I would meet a tall and handsome stranger with red hair and a black horse."

Damn. He set the stones down, gazing at them in wonder. "They told the truth."

She gave him a dubious look. "Only if I actually consider you tall and handsome."

He arched a brow at her.

Her mouth twitched as she plucked a grape off the platter. "Well, you are tall."

"You think I'm handsome."

"Do I?" She popped the grape in her mouth.

"Yes, you do. You were staring at me the first time we saw each other."

"I was staring because the prediction had come true."

"Ah. So you do think me tall and handsome."

"I don't think it." She picked up another piece of cheese. "I know it."

He grinned. "I knew you were exceptionally intelligent." She smiled back, and he ran his fingers over the three stones. "It seems like a fun game. May I have a turn?"

She nodded as she ate.

He pointed at each stone in turn. "A beautiful woman with black hair will meet a man with red hair—make that a tall and handsome man with red hair."

When she snorted, he picked up the stone with the number two. "This means the two will become one." He set it down and looked at her. "Is that a future you can accept?"

Her cheeks grew pink, and she fiddled with her cup of wine. "I—perhaps." She winced as she glanced toward the bed.

"Something wrong?"

"No." She took a drink of wine.

"You were hoping I could bed you now?"

She sputtered, her eyes watering as she coughed.

He hesitated, wondering if it was safe to pat her on the back. With her gown and his gloves, there were two layers of insulation. Tentatively, he touched her. Her coughing continued unabated. No shock, then.

He patted her.

"I'm all right." She wiped her eyes.

He let his hand rest on her back.

She drew a deep breath. "I could use more wine."

"Of course." He stood to grab the wine bottle from across the table, then sat again to refill their cups. "Ana, I need you to be extra careful until we catch the third assassin."

"Do you have any idea who he is?"

"I'm having someone watched." Leo suspected Father Rune, but it would be hard to prove at this point. They knew the assassin was wounded, but the young priest had a nasty habit of inflicting wounds on himself. "Whoever he is, he's extremely dangerous. He broke into the dungeons and killed the first assassin and the two jailers there."

She nodded, and he realized she wasn't surprised by the news.

"You already knew?"

"I . . . heard." Her gaze shifted toward the bed. "Were there any clues left behind? Can you do like before and use your dog to track down the killer?"

"You mean Brody? He-he's on another mission right now."

Her eyes widened. "You send your dog on missions?"

Leo winced inwardly and decided to change the subject. "Your father is arranging the funeral for this afternoon. It should be happening soon, but I would prefer that you not attend. It will be hard enough to keep your father safe. We'll have to keep him surrounded and insist he wear a helmet."

"I understand."

"How do you conduct your funerals here at Vindemar?"

A look of alarm glinted in her eyes. "Oh, th-the usual way." Her gaze darted toward the bed, and she quietly fiddled with the grapes before turning to him. "The dead are burned on pyres along the cliffs overlooking the sea, then the bones are interred in the catacombs."

That wasn't the usual way for the rest of Eberon. Leo had a strange feeling that she'd just repeated the answer word for word.

Her gaze shot toward the bed once more. "It's a shame no one can talk to the ghosts of the dead jailers. The ghosts would know the identity of the man who killed them."

"An interesting strategy," Leo murmured. But for whom was she suggesting it?

Her jaw shifted as if she was annoyed by something, then she turned toward him. "I have a question for you."

"Go ahead."

Her eyes narrowed as she watched him closely. "Did you have Captain Bougaire killed?"

Leo sat back. "What? I banished him. That's all."

She continued to study him. "You didn't order some-one to kill him?"

"No. As far as I know he's—" Leo leaned toward her. "Are you saying he's dead?"

She nodded. "You seem genuinely surprised."

"I am. I told you I wouldn't kill him, and I kept my word."

She sighed, a flicker of relief crossing her face. "I didn't think you could have done it."

Leo tensed. How could she know that the captain was dead? And if he was dead, did that mean someone had murdered him to keep him from talking? Had Captain Bastard told the truth, and the woman sitting with him now was an imposter?

She bit her lip. "Who would have killed him then?"

Leo swallowed hard. He'd told only the general and the duke what the captain had said. The general had laughed it off, but the duke had looked alarmed. Alarmed enough to kill? *Dammit, no.*

She tilted her head, watching Leo. "You know who did it?"

"I . . . suspect someone. I'll check into it for you." Although he doubted he could ever tell her that her father had done it. If he was her father. Leo shook his head. What the hell was going on here? He was losing patience with all these damned secrets. "Why do you want me to call you Ana?"

She shrugged and fiddled with the grapes. "It's short for my name."

What name would that be? "Tell me, *Ana*, how do you know the captain is dead?"

A touch of panic glimmered in her eyes before she shuttered her expression. "I told you. I have spies."

"So do I. But I have yet to hear about the captain's death."

She plucked a grape off the tray. "I guess my spies are better than yours."

"Apparently so." Now it was his turn to watch her carefully. "Are your spies, by any chance, *dead*?"

She flinched, and the grape popped out of her hand. "Oh!" She reached for the grape as it fell, catching it just as it landed on his lap.

He hissed in a breath as his groin reacted.

"Oh!" With a gasp, she jerked her hand away, and the grape went flying. "I'm sorry!"

He grabbed her forearm, his gloved hand encircling her sleeve. "You gasped. Were you in pain?"

"No, I . . ."

"It didn't hurt you?" When she shook her head no, he

slapped her hand against his cock once more and held it there. "That doesn't hurt you?"

She gasped again, her eyes wide. "What are you doing?"

"Do you feel a shock?"

"Of course!" Her cheeks flamed with heat as her gaze shifted downward with a look of horror. "There's something hard in your breeches, and I think it's moving!"

"Not that! Are you feeling a shock from lightning?"

She shook her head. "Am I supposed to?"

Only one layer of insulation, and she was all right.

A knock sounded, then the door cracked open. Leo released her, and they jumped apart so fast their chairs fell over.

"My lord?" Jensen's eyes widened, and he quickly looked away as Leo righted his chair. "The funeral has begun, and His Grace has requested your presence."

"Of course." Leo bowed his head to Luciana. "I will see you later at the funeral feast."

She nodded, her gaze riveted to the floor.

He softened his voice. "Will you be all right?" When she nodded again without looking at him, he groaned inwardly. He may not have shocked her physically, but he'd certainly given her an emotional shock. "Lock and bolt the door behind me." He strode from the room.

After shutting the door, he waited to hear the click of the lock and slide of the bolt. "Jensen." He motioned the guard to join him by the stairwell. "I've posted nine more guards below. If the assassin believes all of our attention is focused on the funeral and the duke, he might decide to strike here instead."

"I understand, my lord."

Leo gave him an encouraging look. "I'm counting on you."

Ten guards had to be enough, Leo thought as he hurried down the stairs. Four of his own personal guard were one floor down, and the remaining five from Vindalyn were on the ground floor. Three of the guards had horns they would blow at the first sign of trouble. With his lightning speed, Leo could return before the assassin managed to get through ten soldiers and a heavy, bolted door.

His Tatiana would be safe. Or was she simply Ana? He hated to think he was being fooled, but he had to admit she might not be Tatiana. The way she'd reacted to his cock made her seem far too innocent to have been involved with Captain Bougaire. And it looked like the captain had been killed to keep him from telling the truth.

At the bottom of the stairs, the five guards bowed as he passed by.

He hesitated at the tower entrance. "How long have you been here at Vindemar?"

The answers were all different, varying from eight years to thirty-five.

"Then you have all known Lady Tatiana for a long time." When they agreed, Leo continued, "Has she changed at all recently?"

"Ah, you must have heard the rumors." The oldest guard waved a dismissive hand. "Pay them no heed, my lord."

"What rumors?" Leo asked.

The men exchanged glances, then the oldest explained, "She has been acting a bit kinder of late. Not that she was ever unkind," he added quickly.

"But she looks exactly the same?" Leo asked.

"Of course, my lord," the oldest guard replied.

"I think she's a bit thinner," the youngest one mumbled.

"She almost died." The oldest one gave him an annoyed look. "Would you expect her to be fatter?"

"I'm counting on you all to keep her safe," Leo reminded them, then strode from the tower.

On the way to the drawbridge, he thought over the problem. If Ana was an imposter, then there were two options.

The first: The whole castle was in on the hoax. This he seriously doubted. The second option: Only Ana and the duke knew. But in order to fool everyone in the castle, Ana had to look, talk, and act just like the real Tatiana.

How was that possible? And what had happened to the real Tatiana?

Was Ana like Brody, but instead of shifting into animals, she could take the form of another human? Leo shook his head. He'd never heard of anyone with that kind of power.

It was more likely that she was related to Tatiana. A sister, perhaps, who looked just like her.

Leo stopped with a jerk.

A twin.

Chapter Twenty-two

❧

"Enough," Luciana muttered as Tatiana continued to giggle.

"Oh, there's something hard in your breeches!" Tatiana repeated for the fifth time in a high, squeaky voice.

"I didn't sound like that," Luciana grumbled as she poured herself more wine.

"Ack! It's moving!" Tatiana struck a dramatic pose, the back of her hand against her brow. "What will become of me? How will I survive your enormous lightning rod?"

Luciana flinched, afraid that her sister's jest might be too close to the truth. She gulped down some wine. Whatever she'd felt in his breeches had seemed rather rod-like. And rather large. She finished the cup. "You shouldn't have eavesdropped on a private conversation."

"Private, all right. *His* privates. I can't believe he pressed your hand against him like that."

"I don't want to talk about it."

Tatiana gave her a knowing grin. "So you made him hard, huh?"

Made him? "Are you saying I was somehow responsible for his condition?"

Tatiana's grin turned into a grimace. "By the Light, are you truly that ignorant?"

Luciana bristled. "I am quite well educated. I speak and write all four mainland languages—"

"Whatever." Tatiana waved a dismissive hand. "Thank the Light you have me around to explain things. I am a bit of an expert, you know."

Luciana shifted her weight. "Is it normal for a man to be hard?"

"Only when he wants to bed you."

Luciana blushed as a series of images flashed through her mind. Leo touching her, kissing her. And whatever else a man did with a woman. She wasn't quite sure of the details, but apparently it had something to do with the hardness of his male private parts.

Tatiana snorted. "You liked touching him, didn't you? And that thing you did with the bread—"

"How could I enjoy any of it with you constantly screeching that he was going to fry me like a pork chop?"

Tatiana huffed. "The thanks I get for looking out for you." Her expression grew sympathetic. "You know you can't actually bed the man, right? Even a kiss would probably kill you."

A pang struck deep in Luciana's chest. "I know."

"You actually like him, don't you?"

Luciana nodded. "Is it wrong to fall for him so quickly? I've known him only five days."

Tatiana shrugged. "I fell for Alberto even faster than that." She sighed. "I guess we're both unlucky in love. At least you have me. You wouldn't have known how to answer his funeral question if I hadn't helped you."

"Thank you for that. And I did what you asked," Luciana reminded her sister. "You heard Leo's answer. He didn't kill your captain—"

"You believe the Beast?"

"Yes, I do." When her sister scoffed, Luciana continued, "Now it's your turn to do as I ask. Go to the funeral for the jailers, see if you can find their ghosts, then ask them who killed them."

Tatiana rolled her eyes. "Fine. You just stay here and enjoy some real food while I do all the work."

"Exactly." Luciana smiled as she picked up another grape.

"Oh, there's something hard in your breeches!" Tatiana squeaked once more.

Luciana threw the grape at her, and with one last giggle Tatiana vanished.

Sighing, Luciana retrieved the fallen grape and set it back on the table. Her gaze lingered on the piece of bread that she'd shared with Leo. It was as close as she'd ever gotten to an actual kiss from him.

She ran her fingers over the three pebbles, pausing on the one decorated with the number two. *This means the two will become one*, he'd said.

How could she become one with Leo? Tears stung her eyes. She did want him to touch her. She wanted a real husband and a home with him. She wanted to feel safe enough that she could invite her sisters to come see her and her children. But how could she ever have a baby if Leo couldn't touch her? How could she ever lie in his arms and kiss him? Would she have to wait for a drought? What if one never came?

Would she have to live the rest of her life like the ghosts of her mother and sister, existing but not able to experience the real joys of life? Waking in the arms of the man she loved. Holding his babies against her breast. Celebrating life's milestones surrounded by those she loved.

How could she even tell him she was in love with him? It would only cause him more torment since he couldn't touch her. And if he tried to touch her and accidentally hurt her, he would blame himself and suffer for it. How could she do that to him?

With a sigh, she realized it was best to keep her distance and not tell him she loved him. It would be one more secret that she had to keep.

Are your spies, by any chance, dead?

She shivered. He was far too clever. She would have to be very careful from now on and guard her secrets closely.

The smell of smoke crept through the open windows of the tower. The funeral had begun. She sent a prayer to Luna and Lessa that the goddesses look over the bereaved families and keep her father safe.

A while later, Tatiana appeared.

"Did you find the jailers?" Luciana asked.

Tatiana shook her head. "They've already moved on to the Realm of the Heavens."

Luciana's shoulders drooped as she sat in a chair at the table. "I thought they would stay with their families for a while."

Tatiana shrugged. "Most people do move on right away. The only ghosts I know here, besides me, are Mama and Christopher. Mama stayed behind to be with Papa and me. And Christopher doesn't want to leave his mother."

"Did you see him?"

Tatiana nodded. "He was so surprised to see me. And really sad that I'd died. But now he seems happy to have more company."

"He told me there were more ghosts in the catacombs."

Tatiana shuddered. "I'm never going there. Mama warned me not to. Christopher told me the ghosts there are mean and vicious. They were bad people when they were alive, and now they refuse to move on to the Realm of the Heavens for fear they'll be punished."

Luciana grimaced. Growing up, her worst fear had

always been the possibility of being trapped with evil ghosts. "It sounds like a horrible place."

Tatiana nodded. "There were four bodies at the funeral. The first two assassins were burned, too. I didn't see their ghosts. I thought maybe they had moved on, but Christopher thinks they went to the catacombs."

A shiver ran down Luciana's back. She couldn't ask her sister or Christopher to venture into such a horrid place. "Then we have no way of figuring out who the last assassin is. We'll have to rely on Leo to catch him."

"Why don't we just lock the damned priest up in the dungeon?" Nevis asked as he and Leo crossed the drawbridge, headed for the keep and the funeral feast.

"We have no proof he's an assassin," Leo replied. "And if the news gets out that we've imprisoned one of the king's precious priests, he could label us heretics."

Nevis grimaced. "I'd rather not be burned at the stake."

"Exactly." Leo sighed. "Uncle Fred is always looking for a reason to be rid of me. I'd rather not give him one."

"He's a royal pain in the ass," Nevis grumbled. "No offense."

"None taken. Besides, we can't actually be sure Father Rune is the assassin. We were wrong about the first one, Willem. But then we were right about the second one. Dax was a new guard just like we suspected."

"I heard it was awesome how you chased him down." Nevis made a sour face. "All the excitement happened while I was gone."

"You had some excitement, too, when you rescued Willem's family."

Nevis scoffed. "Not really. We dressed up like a gang of thieves and planned an elaborate attack, but the king's men took one look at us and ran away. We spent most of our time bringing Willem's family here, because the children wanted to stop every five minutes to take a piss. And the baby kept crying. I'd rather fight a horde of elves than endure that again."

"You'll probably get your wish."

"Felt a bit sorry for the widow, though," Nevis mumbled. "She came all this way just to find out her husband had been murdered."

"The duke said he'd take care of the widow and children," Leo said as they passed through the north gate into the courtyard.

"That's good." Nevis motioned toward the gallows at the south side of the courtyard. "So they finished building it. Hopefully, we'll be hanging that damned priest soon."

"If he's truly the assassin." Leo smiled to himself as he recalled how Ana had stood on the platform, yelling at everyone that he wasn't a Beast. Now whenever he saw the gallows, he would no longer think of death. Because of Ana, he would think of courage and loyalty. And desire. By the Light, he wanted her something fierce.

Beside him, Nevis asked, "Where the hell is Brody? He could verify if the priest is guilty."

Leo winced. "He's not here."

"Where did he go?"

"He's on a mission." Leo slapped himself mentally once again for sending Brody away. Now there was no one left who could identify the last assassin.

But could one of his dead victims point him out? Ana had suggested that, but Leo had had a strange feeling that her words had not been meant for him. Had there been a ghost in the room with them? It seemed that Ana could truly talk to the dead, but he wished she would trust him enough to admit to it.

His heart sped up as they started up the stairs to the Great Hall. He would be seeing her again in a few minutes.

"By the Light, I can smell the food already." Nevis took

the stairs two at a time. "All I've had the last few days was some dried beef and stale bread."

Leo snorted. "You don't look like you went hungry."

"This is muscle!" Nevis slapped his belly as they arrived at the double doors.

The Great Hall was already filled with people, busily finding a place to sit at the long tables while servants filled goblets with wine and set out baskets filled with bread. Nevis started to sit, but Leo nabbed a handful of his cape and dragged him toward the dais.

"But I'm starving!" Nevis objected.

"You should greet my betrothed first." Leo had spotted her on the dais, talking to her father and General Harden.

"You're referring to Lady Tatiana?" Nevis asked.

"Yes." Or perhaps not. Whoever she was, she was everything he wanted. As if she felt his presence, she turned her head and looked right at him.

His heart lurched in his chest. By the Light, she was stunning. And she was wearing that blue gown again, the one where her breasts were practically popping out.

"That looks tasty," Nevis said.

Leo halted, his hands fisting as he shot his friend a warning look. But Nevis was focused on a platter of raw oysters that a servant was setting on a long table.

Damn. Leo released the iron grip he had on Nevis's cape. He'd nearly clobbered his best friend. He'd never felt so strongly about a woman before.

It's more than lust, a quiet voice warned him. *More than possession. More than desire.*

He shook himself mentally. "Come." He motioned for Nevis to follow him up onto the dais.

Leo bowed his head. "Good evening, Ana."

"My lord." She curtsied.

"Leo," he reminded her, and she smiled shyly. "Have you met my best friend?" He motioned to Nevis.

"Yes, I have." Her smile widened as she offered Nevis her hand. "Captain Harden, thank you for watching over Leo."

"My pleasure." Nevis took her hand and bowed over it, giving her knuckles a light kiss.

Leo's chest tightened. The gesture came so easily for his friend, but it was something he didn't dare attempt.

"Hear, hear!" The duke drew everyone's attention as he raised his goblet in the air. "Before we begin the feast, I'd like to give a toast."

"I'll see you later," Nevis whispered, then he scrambled off the dais and rushed to an empty spot at a table where everyone was rising to their feet.

Leo lifted his goblet along with everyone else.

"To the brave men who lost their lives today. May they always be remembered," the duke said, then everyone gave an enthusiastic shout and took a drink.

The duke glanced at Leo, smiling. "And another toast to welcome my daughter's betrothed and the future Duke of Vindalyn, Leofric of Benwick!"

This time the shout was halfhearted at most. Leo winced inwardly. Apparently, it would take some time before the people of Vindalyn saw him as anything but a Beast.

"Let the feast begin!" the duke announced, then sat. As everyone took their seats, the servants began filling bowls with soup.

"Allow me." Leo drew Ana's chair out for her.

"Thank you." When she sat, he gently pushed her forward, letting his gloved fingers graze her sleeves.

No gasp of pain. He sat beside her, wondering if he dared touch her bare skin. But if he ended up hurting her, then he really would feel like a Beast.

"I enjoyed our luncheon together," he whispered to her.

She glanced at her father, who was busily slurping down soup, then whispered back, "I enjoyed it, too."

"Really? I was afraid I might have shocked you."

Her gaze flickered to his lap before bouncing back to his face. "I'm quite all right." She grabbed a loaf from the nearby basket and tore off a hunk. "Would you like a piece of bread?"

He accepted it. "Shall we share it like before?"

Her cheeks bloomed a pretty pink as she tore off a second piece. "Not now."

"Later then?" He leaned closer. "Shall I come see you?"

"I—" She stiffened suddenly, her eyes wide and focused in front of her. "Chris—" She glanced quickly at Leo, then tore a piece of crust off her bread. "Crispy."

What the hell? She was staring again at an empty space in front of the table. Chilly air wafted toward Leo.

He tensed. "Ana?"

Her hands flinched, crushing the bread. "D-don't eat the soup."

"What?" He glanced down at his bowl.

She jumped up from her chair and grabbed her father's hand as he brought another spoonful of soup to his mouth. "Stop." She looked at General Harden. "Please stop."

The duke set his spoon down. "The soup?"

She nodded. "It's only the tureen for our table."

Leo rushed over to her father and the general. Their faces were turning ashen. The general's hand trembled as he dropped his spoon on the table.

Dammit. Leo was grateful that Ana was safe. But he wasn't so sure about her father and the general. They had halfway finished their bowls of poisoned soup.

Chapter Twenty-three

❧

"Men," Luciana muttered to herself as she paced across her small room in the tower. At the first sign of trouble, they always wanted to isolate her here like she was some sort of delicate flower that might wilt at the first sign of danger. Very aggravating, especially when she was the one who had alerted them of the danger in the first place. Now she didn't know how her father or the general was faring. She didn't even know what Leo was doing.

She stopped at the window that overlooked the wall walk. *I should be out there helping Leo catch the assassin.* The next time she saw him, she'd let him know that when it came time for them to marry, she would not accept the role of a do-nothing, know-nothing, say-nothing wife.

And if he was afraid that touching her might hurt her, she'd just take the matter into her own hands. The next time she saw him, she'd touch him wherever she wanted.

"I'm not going to live my life afraid." She winced as soon as the words came out because she was afraid. Afraid that her father was dying. Surely, if he was, he would ask her to be by his side?

With a groan, she started pacing again. How could she

bear to lose her father? She'd known him for only a few weeks.

After she'd stopped her father from finishing his bowl of soup, he'd stood up to make an announcement to all the people in the Great Hall. An important matter of state had suddenly come up, and he needed to confer with the Lord Protector and general. Everyone else was to remain and enjoy the feast. Then he'd ordered Jensen to take her to the tower while he and the other men rushed off to his private rooms.

"Men," she grumbled once again.

"Does that include me?" a young voice asked.

She whirled to find Christopher standing by the window. Smiling, she rushed toward him. "How could I be angry with you? You're my hero!"

Christopher grinned. "Well, you did make me a knight."

"That's right, Sir Christopher." She curtsied, which made him grin even wider. "I am deeply indebted to you. Thank you so much."

He ducked his head, blushing.

"Do you have any news? Is my father all right?"

Christopher nodded. "He has a stomachache, but the physician says that he'll live."

"Oh, thank the goddesses." Luciana made the sign of the moons.

Christopher gave her a curious look. "Tatiana told me you're from the Isle of Moon?"

"Yes." She lowered her voice to a whisper. "I was sent there as a baby. I didn't even know I had a twin sister till a few weeks ago."

Christopher stuck out his bottom lip. "I was a little mad at first that you had tricked me. But Tatiana said you and the duke would be killed if anyone found out."

Luciana nodded. "I'm sorry I couldn't tell you. But I'm

glad you know the truth now and that you're friends again with my sister."

Christopher smiled shyly. "I have two new friends now."

"That is true. Is the general all right, too?"

"Yes. His son took him back to his tent. I don't think they liked our physician." Christopher wrinkled his nose. "I don't like him, either. His stuff is nasty. It made the duke throw up."

Luciana grimaced. It did sound bad, but perhaps it had been the best way to get the poison out of her father's stomach. "Do you know where the Lord Protector is? Is he hunting down the assassin?"

Christopher shook his head. "He was busy talking with your father. But he doesn't need to do any hunting. I know who poisoned the soup. I saw her. That's how I knew—"

"Her? The assassin is a female?"

"It was Rowena. One of the scullery maids. I think she did it because she was angry. Dax was her boyfriend."

"Oh, I see." So the assassin who had killed himself was Rowena's lover. Luciana bit her lip. The poisoning could have been an act of revenge. Rowena might not be the last assassin after all.

"I'll let Leo know." Luciana smiled to herself. "It'll irritate him no end that my spies are better than his."

Christopher grinned. "Yes, we are!"

"Another excellent spy reporting in," Tatiana announced, and they turned to find her standing by the bed.

"Hi, Tatiana!" Christopher bounced over to her.

She patted the boy ghost on the back. "You saved my papa's life, you know."

Christopher blushed once again.

"How is Father doing?" Luciana asked.

"He's expected to make a full recovery," Tatiana said. "Mama wanted me to tell you so you wouldn't worry."

"Thank you."

Tatiana gave her a sympathetic look. "And I'm supposed to warn you that the physician is on his way here."

"Why?" Luciana asked. "I didn't eat any of the soup."

"Papa doesn't know that. He's afraid you could be sick, too."

Luciana groaned. "If they would just let me see him—"

A knock sounded on the door, and Jensen called out, "My lady, the physician is here to see you."

Christopher shuddered. "He's nasty. I don't want to see him again," he whispered, then vanished.

Tatiana grimaced. "Prepare yourself."

"How bad can it be?" Luciana's only experience with a healer was the sister at the convent who was renowned for her expertise and pleasant manner. But the gagging face her sister was making seemed to indicate a different story here at Vindemar. She swallowed hard and unlocked the door.

Jensen regarded her with a look of sympathy. "The physician is here. Master Wormwood."

"I have no need of a physi—"

"Stand aside, man," a gravelly voice ordered Jensen. "This is a matter of life and death."

"I'm not dying," Luciana began as Jensen stepped aside to reveal a portly man in a filthy tan robe that ended in tatters above dirty feet encased in leather sandals.

His eyes were black beads, embedded in a puffy red face. Beneath his red button nose, his greasy mustache descended into a long, scraggly beard. Long hanks of hair were plastered across the top of his balding head. His looks were bad enough, but the stench emanating off him nearly bowled her over.

She coughed, her eyes watering.

"Aha! A sure sign the poison is at work," Master Wormwood announced. He strode toward her, his smell wafting ahead of him like a sulfuric cloud.

Instinctively, Luciana reeled back, but that only gave him access to her room. He marched inside while Jensen hovered by the door, frowning.

"I'm not sick!" She rushed over to the window to inhale some fresh air.

"Ah, but you are." Master Wormwood studied her, nodding his head knowingly. "I can tell that the poison has taken effect. Your complexion is turning green."

"I didn't eat any of the soup!"

"Of course you did." He waved a hand dismissively, and she cringed at how dirty his fingernails were. "How else would you have known the soup was tainted?"

Luciana winced. She couldn't very well say that a boy ghost had warned her. "It didn't look or smell right. I really didn't eat—"

"Luckily for you, I have brought a special tonic that will save your life."

"I'm not dying! Jensen, take me to my father now."

Master Wormwood put up a hand to stop Jensen. "She will see His Grace after she has taken the tonic. Those were the duke's orders."

Jensen gave her a pitying look.

Master Wormwood retrieved a vial from his filthy robe, along with a wooden cup. He pulled the cork out with his yellow teeth, filled the cup with his tonic, then spit the cork onto the floor. "Here, my dear. You are fortunate to benefit from my years of extensive scientific study and remarkable skill."

Next to the bed, Tatiana was pretending to choke herself.

"I'm perfectly fine," Luciana tried again. "Once I see my father—"

"After the tonic." Master Wormwood offered her the cup.

She took it, and the smell alone made her gag. She covered the top with her hand and leaned against the window to inhale some fresh air. "What is in the tonic, if I might ask?"

"Some medicinal herbs, along with desiccated chicken gizzards, bull testicles, and my special ingredient to make it extra potent—cat urine."

Luciana coughed. No wonder her father had thrown up and the general had run back to the army camp. She couldn't do this. There had to be something . . .

With a gasp, she pointed at her sister. "A ghost!"

Master Wormwood scoffed. "You think to fool me? I'm a man of science, and I can tell you without a doubt that ghosts do not—"

Tatiana knocked the candleholder off the bedside table, and it went flying across the room to land on the floor with a clatter.

"A ghost!" Master Wormwood turned to stare at the bed in horror.

Luciana emptied the cup out the window while Tatiana gave a shout of victory.

Down below on the wall walk, a voice yelped. "What the hell?"

Jensen snorted, then glanced warily at the candleholder rolling on the floor.

Tatiana spun in a circle, laughing. "Oh, that was fun!"

Master Wormwood turned to look at Luciana. "What is going on here?"

Luciana shrugged. "Haven't you heard the rumors that this tower is haunted?" She handed him the empty cup. "Now I would like to see my father."

He eyed the cup and her suspiciously. "You don't feel a need to purge?"

"Oh, yes!" She ran for the door. "I'll be in the privy!"

Jensen followed her down the stairs. "I'm not sure how you did it, but well played, my lady," he whispered.

"Thank you." She shut the privy door, then took her

time relieving herself. Afterward, she poured fresh water from the pitcher into the bowl to wash her hands and face.

When she emerged, Jensen told her, "You're safe now. I told the physician you were throwing up, so he left."

"Thank you. Let's go see my father now."

The Duke of Vindalyn was sitting up in bed, looking pale and tired, when Luciana entered his bedchamber.

"Father!" She ran toward him. "Are you all right?"

"Yes, my dear." He reached a hand out to her. "How are you?"

"I'm fine." She took his hand and perched on the side of his bed. On the far side of his bed, her mother, Ariana, smiled at her. Another form appeared. Tatiana.

Luciana released her father's hand as she quickly surveyed the room. Across the room, close to the fireplace, the duke's secretary was seated behind a desk, reading some papers. Leo was nowhere in sight.

"Father," she whispered, then angled her head toward her mother and sister. "We're not alone."

He glanced to the side. "I thought it was chilly." With a louder voice, he addressed his secretary. "Percy, you may bring Father Grendel now."

"Yes, Your Grace." Percy bowed and headed for the door.

"Father, are you sure you're all right?" Luciana asked. "Why do you need a priest?"

"For the ceremony."

"What cere—"

"I'll explain later." Her father waited for the door to shut, then whispered, "Is Tatiana here?"

"Yes." Luciana motioned to side. "And my mother."

"Ariana?" The duke's eyes filled with tears as he extended a hand. "Ariana, I have missed you so much."

She smiled sadly at him, her eyes glistening. "Tell Lucas that I've always been by his side."

As Luciana repeated her mother's words, Ariana touched her husband's hand.

His fingers curled, reacting to the cold. "Was that her?"

"Yes." Luciana blinked away tears.

He dragged in a shaky breath. "Ariana . . . I love you so much."

Luciana wiped her cheek as a tear escaped. How lovely it would be if she and Leo could have a love as enduring as this. But even though she knew she loved him, she had no idea if he felt the same way. He'd admitted to wanting to bed her, but that didn't seem quite the same as love.

Tatiana cleared her throat. "What about me?"

Luciana motioned to her. "Tatiana saved me from having to take the physician's tonic."

"That's right!" Tatiana boasted. "You should have seen me, Mama. I knocked a candleholder across the room! Scared that nasty Wormwood to death!"

"That's amazing!" Ariana gave her an astonished look.

"Well, yes, I am." Tatiana smoothed back her hair.

"You didn't take the tonic?" the duke asked Luciana.

She shook her head. "I didn't need to. I didn't eat any of the soup."

"Oh, thank the Light." The duke heaved a sigh of relief. "I was afraid you would need a purgative. That is the only thing Master Wormwood is good at."

Luciana grimaced. "Why do you have such an awful physician?"

"He is nasty, isn't he?" Her father rubbed his sore stomach. "The king sent him here, so I dare not reject him. He's a gift, according to Frederic, but I swear it's just one more way the king is trying to kill us."

Luciana shuddered.

"If you didn't eat the soup, how did you know—"

"Christopher told me," Luciana explained.

"Yulissa's boy? He died years—ah." The duke nodded. "I understand."

"He saw a scullery maid put something in the silver-plated soup tureen for the high table, so he came to warn me. Her name is Rowena, and she and the second assassin were lovers."

"I see." The duke considered a moment. "So the poisoning was an act of revenge?"

Luciana nodded. "And the last assassin is still unknown. Where is Leo? We should tell him."

"He'll be here shortly. He needed to fetch a few things from his tent." The duke leaned back against his pillows, studying her. "This latest incident made me realize just how vulnerable you are. If an assassin succeeds in killing me—"

"That won't happen," Luciana interrupted.

The duke took her hand. "Hear me out. If I were to die, the king would become your guardian, meaning he could remove you from Vindemar, take you away someplace, and you would never be seen again. I spoke with Leo at length, and we came up with a plan to keep you protected."

Luciana pulled her hand away. "You made plans for me without consulting me?"

"My dear, nothing has changed for you but the timing. You will still marry Leo. He was destined to become the duke when I passed on. We're simply speeding that up. Tonight, he'll become the Duke of Vindalyn and take responsibility for you. I'm signing over the title to him."

Luciana sat back, stunned.

"What?" Tatiana screeched. "How can Papa give everything to the Beast? Luciana, you have to stop him!"

"Father," Luciana began, but he interrupted her.

"I realize it comes as a shock, but while I lay here in pain, fearing I would die, I was reminded of what is truly important—you, and all the people I have been responsible for over the years. Leo will take the title, but I will continue to run the duchy as always, protecting the land and my people. I will simply be the steward."

"The Beast will take over and kick us out!" Tatiana yelled.

"Father." Luciana took his hand. "Vindalyn means everything to you. How could you—"

"It means a great deal to me, yes." He squeezed her hand. "But you mean even more. This is the best way to keep you safe, my dear."

"Safe?" Tatiana scoffed. "The Beast will kill you both!"

"No." Ariana shook her head. "I think Lucas is right. The Lord Protector will not harm them."

Luciana hoped her mother was right, but even so, her father's solution seemed too drastic.

"What does Ariana think?" her father asked.

"Mother agrees with you. Tatiana doesn't." Luciana sighed. "I think you might be overreacting."

"Perhaps, but I still think this is for the best. Leo has been kind enough to agree—"

"Why wouldn't he?" Luciana asked. "He'll have everything!"

"Yes, including the king's wrath." The duke gave her a stern look. "Don't you realize what he's doing? The minute he acquires the duchy, he alone will stand in the way of what the king wants for himself. We will be out of the picture. Leo is protecting us by making himself the lone target."

Luciana swallowed hard. Leo was trying to save her and her father?

The door opened and Leo strode inside.

Her heart fluttered as it usually did whenever she saw him. He was formally dressed in his army uniform—black breeches, a red-and-black tunic topped with a black cape, his sword sheathed in a black leather scabbard, his hands covered in black leather gloves. His black boots looked recently polished, his clothes clean and pressed, and his handsome face recently shaven.

The fire from the hearth lit his hair golden red, and she felt a tightening in her chest when she realized he'd tried to tame the curls with a comb.

He dropped a large knapsack on the floor, then looked at her, his gaze narrowed, the sharp angles of his jaw clenched tight.

Her breath caught. Why did he look so . . . intense?

"Don't trust him," Tatiana whispered behind her.

The secretary entered and shut the door after Father Grendel shuffled inside. The elderly priest headed for an armchair close to the warmth of the fireplace.

"Thank you for coming, Father," the duke said to the priest as he eased out of bed.

"Careful." Luciana reached out to steady him. He was still dressed in the clothes he'd worn to the funeral feast. But then, so was she.

"I'm fine," her father assured her. "Are the papers all in order?"

"Yes, Your Grace." Percy circled behind the desk. "Once the contract is signed and sealed, it will go into effect the minute the ceremony has concluded."

As Leo strode toward the desk, he drew a signet ring from his pocket.

"My lord." The duke raised a hand, and Leo paused. "I will remind you once more in front of these witnesses that you have sworn a sacred oath to protect my daughter and my right to rule the duchy as I see fit."

"You have my word." Leo bowed his head, then dipped a quill into the ink bottle. He glanced up at Luciana. "She has agreed?"

"Of course," the duke replied.

Agreed to what? Luciana wondered as Leo signed his name, then pressed his signet ring into a glob of hot wax.

Father Grendel rose from the armchair. "We will begin now. My lord, did you bring a ring for the ceremony?"

"Yes." Leo pulled a second ring from his pocket and placed it on the desk. "It was my mother's."

"Excellent." The priest took the ring. "Now if the bride will come forward."

Luciana stiffened. "B-bride?"

Leo's jaw shifted. "She doesn't know?"

She turned toward her father, her heart racing. "What . . . ?"

The duke lowered his voice. "Remember it is a marriage in name only. And you've already agreed to it. Nothing has changed but the timing."

"But—"

"The wedding must occur for the contract to go into effect," her father said. "It is the only way Leo can take responsibility for you. You must marry him tonight."

Tonight? Luciana's quick breaths pushed her breasts hard against the bodice of her blue brocade gown. And yet, she still felt as if she couldn't breathe.

"Don't do it!" Tatiana yelled.

"Shh," Ariana hushed her. "She likes him."

Luciana's heart pounded in her ears. Yes, she did like him. Earlier today, she'd even felt certain that she loved him, but now her thoughts were spinning so fast, she didn't know what to think.

"Ana," Leo said quietly, and she whirled to face him.

"You have my word," he said as his intense gaze bore into her. "I will protect you and your father. I will not harm you. Will you trust me?"

She gulped and her gaze flitted nervously around the room. Five days. She'd known him only five days.

"I will marry you as Ana," Leo whispered, and her gaze shot back to him.

How much did he know? Captain Bougaire had warned him that she wasn't Tatiana. Was this Leo's way of telling her he would marry her no matter who she was? How could he agree to wed her and protect her when he didn't know her any better than she knew him? "D-do you trust me?"

He nodded slowly. "I do. Will you marry me?"

A buzzing sound hummed in her ears as her nerves suddenly grew calm. Time seemed to slow down as if she were lulled by the steadiness of his gaze. *It's really very simple*, an inner voice filled her mind. *Do you love him? Do you want him?*

"Yes," she whispered.

Chapter Twenty-four

❧

Leo paced across the floor of Ana's bedchamber. *My bedchamber, too.* Hell, the whole damned fortress was his now. Not that he cared about being a duke. It was simply the best way to protect Ana and her father. Once the news spread, the king's assassins would start pointing their arrows at him.

He would send a courier in the morning to deliver the news to the king. Although Leo would couch the message as good news, that he'd brought the duchy into the royal family, he knew Uncle Fred would be royally pissed. The king's orders had been for Leo to bring the duke and his daughter to his palace at Ebton. Leo would still take them, but no doubt the king had expected his assassins to kill the duke and daughter before the wedding could happen.

With Leo now in the way, Uncle Fred would most likely try to arrange some sort of accident for him. He'd have to be extra careful. If he died, Ana and her father would be homeless.

The amount of trust they were placing in him astounded him. By the Light, he would not, he could not let them down. He halted a moment in his pacing as the shock of tonight's events skittered through him once again. He now had a wife. And family.

He shook his head. As much as he wanted to embrace this new idea of having a family and home, he knew he was too dangerous to live with. He would need to return to his life as Lord Protector, traveling with the army and guarding the borders of Eberon.

The former duke would still run the duchy, and Ana would live here safely with her father. Everything would be the same as before.

Except now he was married.

He resumed his pacing while his new bride hid in the dressing room. *Dammit.* Maybe it wasn't as bad as he suspected, and she wasn't actually hiding. But he'd seen the look of panic on her face when she'd learned she was to marry him tonight.

It had taken her a few minutes to agree to it. Had she acquiesced to please her father? If that was true, it was damned annoying.

Somehow, he had hoped that she would want to marry him. When she'd defended him earlier today, screaming to the crowd that he wasn't a Beast, he'd thought she truly cared about him. But just because she railed against injustice didn't mean that she loved him.

Dammit, he wanted her to love him. But that just frustrated him even more because he couldn't touch her. Not her bare skin. He was a married man who could not consummate his marriage.

"Shit." He dragged a gloved hand through his hair. How could he be so dangerous and pathetic at the same time? Perhaps it was just as well. He wasn't sure Ana would even welcome his touch.

Never touch the Beast.

Never let the Beast touch you.

He'd promised to keep her safe. That meant he would

have to keep his distance. He couldn't be a husband. He was nothing more than her bodyguard.

A knock on the door made him scowl. He'd left four of his personal guard outside with orders that he and Ana were not to be disturbed. He unlocked the door to find Edmund outside with a basket and a stuffed knapsack.

"Congratulations!" Edmund beamed at him, then glanced back at his personal guard. "He's still dressed."

They chuckled.

Leo arched an eyebrow. Apparently, he'd spent too many years with Edmund and his personal guard, for they had lost all fear of him. "Is there a reason for this disturbance?"

"I brought wine and food." Edmund lifted the basket. "In case you've worked up an appetite."

"Thanks." Leo nabbed the basket.

"Aye, you need to keep up your strength." Edmund exchanged an amused look with the guards. "It'll be a long night, but I'm sure he's *up* to it."

They all snickered.

Leo groaned inwardly. "What's in there?" He motioned to the knapsack.

"The clothes you left in the tower." Edmund leaned to the side to try to peek inside the room. "Shall I put them away for you?"

"I'll take care of it." Leo grabbed the knapsack.

Edmund elbowed the nearest guard. "He wants to be alone. I wonder why?"

They all grinned at him like the fools they were. Had they forgotten he was a Beast? "Stay extra vigilant," he ordered his guards. "There is still an assassin at large, and he will be targeting this room."

"Aye, my lord." The guards bowed.

Edmund snickered. "And you'll be somewhat distracted, I wager."

"Edmund, go away." Leo shut the door before he could

be subjected to more of their inane chuckling. He dropped the knapsack on the floor and kicked it. "Dammit."

"Is it true?" Ana's voice carried softly across the room, and he looked up to see her standing in the doorway of the dressing room.

She was beautiful, so beautiful, that he stopped in his tracks just to look at her. Her face was a bit pale, as if she was nervous, but then why wouldn't she be nervous? She'd just married the Beast.

Her hair was loose, falling to her waist in shimmering black waves that he couldn't touch. Her slender body was covered from the neck to her bare ankles—a voluminous blue velvet robe on top of a white nightgown. He wondered briefly how sheer her nightgown was. If it was like the one before—just the memory of it caused his groin to tighten.

Stop that, he ordered himself. Her big blue eyes were watching him so closely, he couldn't afford to swell up like a randy goat.

He positioned the basket in front of his breeches as he strode toward the table near the hearth. "I have food. You might be hungry like me. We didn't get to eat at the funeral feast."

She eased into the bedchamber while her maid hovered by the doorway. "Is it true that the assassin will target this room?"

"They might try." Leo retrieved two goblets and a bottle of wine from the basket. "But don't worry. There are four guards at each door and two outside below the windows. A total of ten."

"Shouldn't we stay in the tower? I thought it was safer there."

He poured wine into the goblets. "It was safer for you there when you were alone. But now you have me." He set the bottle down with a clunk. "Your guard dog is on duty."

She blinked. "Guard . . . *dog*?"

"Precisely." Time to set things straight. "Don't think of me as a husband. I'm too dangerous for that. Don't even think of me as a man. I am a vicious dog who will destroy anyone who tries to harm you."

Her eyes had grown wide, but she didn't cower in fear. Not his brave and beautiful Ana.

She lifted her chin. "I won't have you speak of yourself that way."

"Do you need a demonstration?" He ripped the glove off his left hand and stepped closer to the fireplace, where a few half-burned logs remained in the hearth. He reached out his hand, and sparks sizzled and popped around his fingers. A small bolt shot out and struck the logs, scattering a few wood chips before engulfing the wood in flames.

Leo heard the maid's screech as he slowly tugged his glove back on. Steeling his nerves, he prepared himself to see the horror on Ana's face.

To his surprise, she was hugging her maid.

"Shh, Gabriella." Ana patted her on the back. "He's not going to harm us." She shot him an annoyed look. "For some reason, he felt compelled to try to frighten us."

"Aren't you afraid? You said in confession that you're afraid of me. And I saw the panic on your face when you learned we would marry tonight."

"I was caught by surprise." She glared at him. "And it occurred to me that I've known you only five days. There is too much I don't know about you."

He snorted. "There is even more that I don't know about you." He lifted a goblet as if to make a toast. "To the beginning of our life together, and to the end of our secrets."

Her face grew even more pale. Now he really had frightened her.

"Gabriella," he addressed the maid. "Please bring some extra blankets."

"Yes, my lord." Gabriella ran for the exit to her small room.

Leo drained his goblet. "I will not be sharing your bed. Even an accidental touch might kill you."

Ana approached the table. "Why are you acting like an ogre?"

"Because I am one." He refilled his goblet.

She shook her head. "You're a man, and a terribly confusing one at that. On one hand, you try to frighten me and push me away. But at the same time, you claim you want to bed me, and you press my hand against your—" She motioned toward his breeches.

"Cock?" He took a drink.

She narrowed her eyes. "Lightning rod."

He choked. After a minute of coughing and sputtering, he wiped the moisture from his eyes and found her calmly filling two plates with cold chicken, cheese, and strawberries.

"Ana, you should be afraid of me."

"Why? You've told me over and over that you'll never harm me. Shouldn't I believe you?"

He winced. How could he explain that he had two warring factions going on inside him? One that longed for her to trust him and love him, and another that feared if she did, he wouldn't be able to resist her. And then he would end up hurting her or even killing her.

He was the one who was afraid, dammit. And the only solution was to keep her at a distance.

He sat at the table. "Tomorrow morning I will investigate the poisoning."

"Oh, I've been meaning to tell you. A scullery maid in the kitchens did it. She was the second assassin's lover, so I believe it was an act of revenge on her part and not even related to the third assassin."

Leo sat back, staring at her as she nibbled on a piece of chicken. "You know all this for a fact?"

She nodded. "I have an eyewitness who saw her. You needn't worry about her. My father told me after the wedding ceremony that he would take care of the matter so we could relax and . . . enjoy ourselves."

Enjoy? Leo snorted. He couldn't imagine a wedding night more awkward than this. "I would like to question your eyewitness."

She winced, then gulped down some wine. "He's not available at the moment."

Leo tapped a gloved finger on the table while he studied her. "Is he one of your spies?"

She nodded and bit into a strawberry.

"And he works in the kitchen?"

She nodded again.

Leo thought back. Hadn't Brody told him she had talked to the ghost of a boy who had died years ago in the kitchen? He had to be the ghost who had warned her in the Great Hall.

She ripped a small loaf of bread in half and offered him a piece. "May I ask you a question now?"

"Yes." He topped his bread with a slice of cheese and took a bite.

"Why are you so determined to keep my father and me safe? Why are you endangering yourself in our stead and risking the wrath of the king?"

Leo swallowed hard. Because it was the right thing to do. The noble thing. Because she deserved to live long and be happy. He could give her countless reasons, but deep in his heart he knew the truth.

The Beast wanted to be loved.

And it had to be her. He cared about her.

He snorted. He wasn't even sure who she was.

The dressing room door opened, and Gabriella eased inside, giving him a fearful look.

He stood and motioned to the floor between the table and the bed. "While you lay out the blankets, I'll put away my clothes and check on the guards."

"Yes, my lord." The maid scurried out of his way as he brought his knapsack into the dressing room.

He tossed it in the corner next to the knapsack he'd brought from camp, then headed through the maid's room to the servants' corridor. There he found Jensen and three more guards.

After they bowed and swore they would be extra vigilant, he returned to the dressing room. As he opened the door, he spotted Ana and froze. She had moved close to an upholstered chair. She glanced quickly over her shoulder at the maid whose back was turned to her as she spread blankets on the floor.

Ana leaned over to peer closely at the upholstery. Her fingers skimmed over the fabric, then with a look of relief, she straightened. As her gaze lifted, Leo stepped to the side out of view.

More secrets? *Dammit.*

He poured fresh water into the basin to wash his face and hands, then dried off with a linen towel. His gaze drifted around the room, taking in the shelves lined with Ana's gowns, a stack of folded white shifts, another stack of nightgowns, a basket filled with ribbons and pins for her hair. In the middle of the room, a large copper tub sat with a spigot for draining the water into buckets.

He smiled to himself. This was where she took her infamous long baths. Nearby, a small table stood with more baskets containing scented soap, lavender, and rose petals. He lifted a glass bottle and uncorked it to take a sniff. Scented oil.

If he were a normal newlywed husband, he would take this to bed and slather her sweet body with it, touching and tasting every inch of her, using it to make her legs slick as they wrapped around him, her thighs warm and welcoming.

But he was not normal. The lightning power was still strong, sizzling beneath his skin, eager for release. Unfortunately, his cock didn't know that and had another sort of release in mind.

Lightning rod? *Damn.* That might be too close to the truth.

With a sigh, he corked the bottle and set it back on the table. He pulled his gloves back on and a cape from one of the knapsacks. The loose material might help to conceal the bulge in his breeches.

When he entered the bedchamber, Ana was back at the table, seated and finishing her plate of food.

"That is all, Gabriella," he told the maid. "You may retire for the night. Be assured there are guards outside your door to keep you safe."

"Yes, my lord. Thank you." She curtsied, then ran into the dressing room, closing the door behind her.

He sat at the table and wrenched off one boot, then the other. "I will be gone during the day for the next few days. Your father is showing me the nearby villages and castles, introducing me to his vassals—"

"Your vassals."

Leo dropped a boot with a loud clunk. "The tour is to help spread the word that I'm the new duke. The sooner everyone hears the news, the safer you will be."

"The last assassin might still be here."

"I know." Leo unbuckled his sword belt and laid it next to the blankets. "You'll be guarded as usual." He glanced up at her. "Be careful."

"You, too." She stood. "Did you want to sleep now? I'll fetch you a pillow." She rushed over to the bed and grabbed one. "Here."

"Thank you." He dropped it at the top of the blanket. "I know this isn't the sort of marriage you probably dreamed about—"

"Don't." She regarded him sadly. "Don't apologize for who you are."

"You had to marry a Beast."

"I married an amazing man."

His heart lurched. "Ana." He stepped toward her.

"Good night, Leo." She blew out the candle next to her bed, then quickly took off her robe.

In the firelight, he could see the shape of her body beneath the white nightgown. The material wasn't quite as sheer as the other nightgown he'd admired, but he was still able to detect the roundness of her rump as she climbed into bed.

"Good night," he whispered as he settled onto the blankets. He stretched out, his back to her, his cape wrapped around to conceal his swollen groin. It was damned uncomfortable sleeping in overly tight breeches.

Rustling sounds from the bed tormented him as he imagined her long legs stretching beneath cool sheets. He watched the fire in the hearth, the flames slowly dying till the logs glowed with an amber light.

More rustling sounds. A soft, feminine sigh.

"Leo," she whispered. "Are you awake?"

"Yes." He rolled onto his back to glance at the bed.

She was sitting up and watching him. "Maybe we should use this time to get better acquainted."

He gave her a wry look. "Are you going to reveal your secrets?"

She smoothed her fingers over the embroidered coverlet. "I was curious about you."

"I see." He took a deep breath. "What would you like to know?"

"Does it hurt? When the lightning strikes you?"

He scoffed. "What do you think?"

"I think it must hurt something fierce."

"That's about right."

She stretched out, her head toward the foot of the bed so she could see him. "You told me how your mother died. How did your father pass away?"

"He was killed in battle with a Norveshki dragon."

"When you were eight?"

"Yes."

"What happened to you then?"

"General Harden rescued me from the assassins, and I started my training as a soldier. Nevis was my sparring partner. That's how we became friends."

"That seems so young to be with the army."

Leo shrugged. "The general knew I had to excel as a warrior if I was going to survive."

"When did you have your first battle?"

He paused. "I was fourteen."

She paused even longer. "That's so young to have to kill someone."

He sat up, his gaze focused on the fireplace.

"Leo? Are you all right?"

His hands fisted around his cape. *Don't tell her.* But he wanted her to know what a monster he truly was. "I killed my first person at the age of five." He heard her quick intake of breath behind him. Good, she would know to stay away from him.

"That was the first time the lightning found me. It was hardly even raining yet. We were in a meadow, having a picnic, when a light shower began. We laughed, gathering up the blankets and food. Then, out of nowhere, a bolt of lightning shot out of the sky and hit me so hard, it sent me flying across the meadow. I landed, my body twitching. I thought I was on fire. I could barely hear my mother and the servants screaming. My nanny was the first one to reach me. She touched me." Leo closed his eyes as the memories flooded his mind. "She died."

"I'm so sorry."

He heard more rustling sounds. He'd probably made her uncomfortable. "And that's when people started calling me a Beast."

"It must have been terrifying for you."

"You mean terrifying for everyone around me."

"No. I mean you. You were only five."

He stiffened when he felt her hand on his back. "What are you doing?"

Both her hands pressed against his cape. "I swore to myself earlier today that I wouldn't be afraid to touch you."

He gritted his teeth. "You should be afraid. I just told you I killed my own nanny. Don't you see how dangerous I am?"

Her hands skimmed around to his chest. "You shouldn't blame yourself. It was an accident."

"You need to stop," he warned her as her hands moved past the edge of his cape and onto his shirt. One thin layer of insulation. "Are you all right?"

Her arms were now fully wrapped around him, hugging him. "I'm fine. You're the one who's hurting." She rested her head against his shoulders.

His heart clenched in his chest. How long had it been since he'd received a hug? He couldn't even remember. He glanced down at her hands. On her left hand, the gold of his mother's ring glinted in the firelight. The ring that now belonged to his wife. Dammit, this was making his eyes burn, making him weak. He should put a stop to it.

"Ana."

"Shh. Let me stay here a moment."

As time stretched out, he slowly relaxed, slowly learned to accept her embrace. He could now feel the shape of her face nestled against his shoulder blades. With each breath, her breasts nudged gently against his back.

"Ana. I'll always remember how you defended me in the courtyard. It meant a great deal to me."

Her grip around him tightened. "It meant a lot to me, too."

"I'm honored by the amount of trust you and your father have placed in me. I won't let you down."

"I know." Her face moved against his back as if she were caressing him.

Did she actually care for him? Did he dare touch her bare skin? But his hands—most of his power was concentrated in his hands. Even with his gloves on, he sometimes gave people a shock.

But maybe he could touch her nightgown. Maybe he could caress her as long as she remained dressed. His groin grew harder just at the thought.

Dammit. He'd promised to protect her. Why would he risk hurting her? And why drive himself to despair, growing hard from wanting her when it was impossible?

He swallowed hard. "Good night, Ana."

She slowly released him and backed away. "Good night, Leo."

Chapter Twenty-five

❧

A few hours before dawn, Brody arrived in the shallow waters near the Isle of Moon. It had been a hell of a long swim—all day and most of the night. The seals he had followed looked exhausted as they flopped onto the sandy beach.

At first, they had been wary of his presence, but he'd communicated to them that he meant no harm. A few times during the long journey, they had rested by floating on their backs, and he'd busied himself catching fish to eat. After he offered them some fish, they'd welcomed his company.

Now they dozed off in the sand, their black hides glistening in the light of the two moons. He shifted from a seal into a dog and moved away to shake himself dry. After finding a soft, grassy spot behind a rock, he curled up for a nap.

Sometime later, he woke to the sound of a female singing above him on the bluff.

"My true love lies in the ocean blue. My true love sleeps in the sea. Whenever the moons shine over you, please remember me. My lonesome heart is torn in two. My grief runs deep as the sea. Whenever the waves roll over you, please remember me. Please remember me."

It was the same song he'd heard Lady Tatiana sing the first time the seals had come. But this was a different voice, one that was so sweet and lyrical he wondered if he was dreaming it.

"Ye came! Oh, my darling dears, how can I e'er thank ye enough?"

The seals replied with a barked greeting.

Brody peered around the rock. The sun was rising in the east, painting the sky with rosy colors and making the sea sparkle. A woman, dressed in the cream-colored wool of a nun's habit, was descending the path to the beach. She held up her skirt with one hand, and in her other hand, the handle to a wooden bucket. When she made a final jump onto the beach, water sloshed over the brim of the bucket, dampening her gown.

"Are ye hungry?" She rushed toward the seals. "I brought ye some fish."

As she approached, Brody realized she wasn't quite fully grown. She had the height of a woman, but the willowy body and youthful face of a girl perhaps fifteen or sixteen years old. Her long black hair was plaited in a ponytail, although silky strands escaped to curl around her face.

Surely she was too young to take the vows of a nun. Perhaps she was simply being raised at a convent. In that case, she was most likely an orphan.

She set down the bucket and began flinging fish at the seals. When they caught them in midair, she laughed.

The sound was musical. Breathtaking. It flooded his senses, immediately making him crave more.

Suddenly suspicious, he inched closer. A breeze wafted her scent toward him, and he froze.

A shifter. The scent was faint. Barely there. Most likely

she'd not yet experienced her first shifting, but she would soon. And since she could apparently communicate with the seals, that probably meant she would be shifting into a seal.

A selkie. That explained the special allure of her voice. And the beauty she already possessed. In another year or two, she would be stunning.

Men would find her hard to resist. Sailors would wreck their boats to find the source of her song and laughter, and once they saw her, they would risk drowning to catch her. Luckily for sailors, a selkie was extremely rare.

"Did ye bring the bottle with you?" she asked the seals.

The seals barked in reply, and one of them tossed the bottle toward her, the glass sparkling in the sunlight. With another musical laugh, she caught it.

"Thank ye so much!" She hugged the bottle to her chest, then leaned over to pet the seals. "What was that? Ye made a new friend?" She looked around and spotted Brody.

Damn. He hadn't expected the seals to tattle on him. Had they said he was a shifter? He crouched down low to look unthreatening and gave her his best sad-eyed, puppy face.

"Aww." The girl gave him a sympathetic look. "Ye poor thing. What happened? Are ye lost?"

Brody woofed, then sat and lifted a paw. That move usually worked wonders.

She smiled as she slowly approached. "Ye're so sweet."

Brody grinned back, letting his tongue loll to the side of his mouth.

"And so pretty with yer bright blue eyes." She shook his paw. "I think I'll call ye Bettina."

He gulped so fast, he nearly bit off his own tongue. Who the hell named a dog Bettina?

People usually called him Spot or Patch because of the black fur around his eye. Lady Tatiana had been a bit more original, calling him Pirate. He'd liked that name. But never in his twenty-one years had someone given him a *girl's* name. He gave out a low growl.

"Oh." She drew back. "Ye don't like it?" She regarded him seriously for a moment. "I know! Julia. I've always loved that name."

Dammit. Was he going to have to lift a leg? Not that he normally exposed himself to young women. But why the hell couldn't she tell he was male?

"Look what I have, Julia!" She showed him the bottle. "My sisters are going to be so excited! Come on!" She grabbed the empty bucket and ran toward the path. "After we read the letter, I'll try to find ye an old bone."

Sisters? Brody scrambled up the path after her. Did she mean real sisters or other nuns? Apparently, Lady Tatiana had written them a letter. Were these the nuns who had nursed her back to health?

At the top of the bluff, he trotted alongside her as she ran across an open field, headed for a group of buildings. The scent of freshly cooked breakfast emanated from the first building.

Bacon! Brody stopped and whimpered, affecting his best pitiful look. *Let's go to the kitchens for bacon!*

She motioned for him to follow. "Come on! We have to read the letter first."

Dammit. He loped behind the girl as she ran past a chapel and into a graveyard. Next to a new grave, three young women were waiting.

Brody lurked behind a stone statue while he studied them. They were all dressed alike in their cream-colored habits, but they were definitely not real sisters. One had the white-blond hair and ears of an elf from Woodwyn. Another had the red hair of a Norveshki, and the third, the golden-blond hair of a Tourinian.

"Maeve!" the redhead called to her. "Did ye get it?"

"Aye!" The selkie plopped down onto the ground at the foot of the new grave. "Here it is!"

The Tourinian girl sat next to her and grabbed the bottle. "I'm the oldest now. I'll read it."

"Hurry, Brigitta," the redhead urged her as she and the elfin girl sat across from them.

While Brigitta fished the letter out, Brody inched closer till he was hidden behind the gravestone.

"*My dear sisters*," Brigitta began. "*Thank you so much for writing! I love you and miss you more than I can say.*"

"I miss her, too," Maeve grumbled.

Brody peeked around the gravestone so he could see the four girls. Why would Lady Tatiana refer to them as her sisters? If she'd stayed here to recuperate from her illness, it could have been only about two weeks, hardly enough time to act like this was family.

"*I have safely arrived at Vindemar*," Brigitta continued. "*The fortress is huge! It is surrounded on three sides by water, and whenever I gaze at the sea, I think of you.*"

The elfin girl sighed. "I wish we could see it."

"I know." Brigitta resumed reading, "*You won't believe it! My sister didn't remain at the convent, but followed me here. We're becoming good friends.*"

"What? Tatiana didn't stay here?" The redhead's gaze shifted to the grave, and all the girls gave the dirt mound a wary look.

Brigitta scoffed. "And here we thought we were doing Tatiana a favor by reading the letter by her graveside so she could hear it. But she's not even here!"

Brody's thoughts swirled. Lady Tatiana was buried here? Then who was at Vindemar with Leo?

"I hope this means Tatiana is being nice now," the elfin girl said.

"*Something wondrous has happened*," Brigitta continued. "*Two weeks after we played with the Telling Stones,*

I met a man with red hair and a black horse, exactly like the stones predicted! His name is Leofric of Benwick, and we are to be married."

With a squeal, Brigitta lowered the letter. "She's getting married!"

"How exciting!" The redhead clapped her hands.

"But then she'll ne'er come back," Maeve mumbled.

The elfin girl patted the selkie on her knee. "It doesn't mean we'll ne'er see her again."

Brigitta hugged the letter to her chest. "I wish we could go to the wedding."

The elfin girl tilted her head. "'Tis strange how her prediction came true. I wonder if she has some kind of power other than seeing the dead."

"Ye think she can see the future?" the redhead asked. "Then all of her predictions might come true?"

"Oh, I hope so!" Brigitta's eyes lit up. "She said I would have seven suitors vying for my hand."

The redhead snorted. "Like that would e'er happen."

"It could," Brigitta protested.

"Read the letter!" Maeve yelled.

"Fine." Brigitta studied the letter. "Where was I?

"He seems quite strong and dependable, honest and trustworthy. And I find him extremely handsome. His hair is a dark red, but he doesn't have the freckles that Sorcha feared he would."

"Well, that's a relief," the redhead grumbled.

Apparently the redhead was Sorcha. Brody continued to listen as the letter went on to describe Leo in glowing terms. Whoever the writer was, this lady pretending to be Lady Tatiana, she was clearly attracted to Leo.

"Oh, my," the elfin girl said. "Luciana sounds like she's smitten!"

Brigitta giggled. "I think ye're right, Gwennore."

Luciana? Was that the name of Lady Tatiana's imposter? Brody listened to the rest of the letter, and sure enough, it had been signed with the name Luciana.

The four girls chattered excitedly as they stood up.

"I'm famished!" Sorcha announced. "Let's go eat."

"Oh, I promised some food for my new friend." Maeve spun around till she spotted Brody half hidden behind the gravestone. "Julia! There ye are!"

He winced.

"Good goddesses." Sorcha looked him over. "Where did ye find the dog?"

"Down on the beach." Maeve patted Brody on the head. "I named her Julia. Isn't she adorable?"

Gwennore grinned. "I think he's more of a Julian."

"No, she's not!" Maeve huffed. "Look at her pretty blue eyes."

Brody whimpered, and the other girls laughed.

"Come on, Julia." Maeve rubbed his ears. "I'll find ye an old bone to chew on."

I'd rather have bacon. Brody hesitated while the four girls headed for the kitchens. Then he circled to the front of the gravestone to read the name engraved there.

LUCIANA.

His eyes narrowed. Tatiana and Luciana. One was buried here, and the other was about to marry the Lord Protector. He needed to hurry back to Vindemar to warn Leo.

After he had some bacon.

Chapter Twenty-six

❧

"Father Rune has disappeared," Nevis told Leo in the privacy of his tent. "His room is empty, and the other priests have no idea where he is."

"Is he no longer at Vindemar?" Leo asked. He'd been traveling all day with Ana's father, visiting nearby villages and vassals. Upon their return to Vindemar, he had gone to his tent to remove his chain mail and helmet. Normally, he only wore armor if he was going into battle, but it had seemed necessary now that he'd made himself a target. With his lightning speed, he could usually avoid an arrow. But only if he saw it coming.

"We were having him watched," Leo insisted as he hung up his armor. "What happened to the soldier—"

"He was found asleep outside the chapel." Nevis held up a hand to stop Leo's angry reaction. "He was drugged. Someone grabbed him from the back, put something over his mouth and nose, and everything went black. I believe him, for he was staggering about even after we woke him up."

Leo narrowed his eyes. "Then the priest knows about potions."

"It looks that way," Nevis agreed. "I had the keep and grounds searched, but there was no sign of him."

Leo paced about his tent. His gut warned him that Father Rune had been responsible for yesterday's murders in the dungeon. The jailers had trusted the priest enough to let him in, and the first jailer had died without any defense wounds for he'd been caught entirely by surprise.

"Everyone in the vicinity should know by now that I've taken over the duchy," Leo thought out loud as he paced. "If the priest has truly left, then Ana and her father may no longer be his targets."

Nevis gave him an exasperated look. "Why did you make yourself the target? That damned priest could be planning to kill you while you travel around."

"That's what I'm hoping for."

Nevis groaned. "You're endangering yourself for a woman you've known for only a few days."

"Shouldn't a man protect his wife?"

Nevis snorted. "It's a marriage in name only. You can't even touch her. And she's already had one affair. What makes you think she'll—"

"Enough!" Leo shot his friend a warning look. "You will not speak of her that way. She's mine."

Nevis blinked. "Holy shit. You're in love with her."

"Don't be ridic—" Leo stopped. Was he? No, not possible. Not when he didn't know who exactly she was. Not when she didn't trust him enough to tell him the truth.

"Leo!" General Harden barged into the tent. "A soldier just arrived from the troop we left on the Woodwyn border."

"Where is he?" Leo headed for the exit.

The general put up a hand to stop him. "I took him to the medic. He's wounded, but he told me everything before he passed out. A band of elves attacked. We suffered heavy casualties, but managed to capture an elf, and he boasted that their army is about to launch a massive attack—"

"How massive?" Leo asked.

"Don't know, but we should move out—"

"I understand." Leo paced across the tent. As Lord Protector, his first job was to protect the country. But at the same time, he didn't want to leave Vindemar until the matter of the last assassin was taken care of and he knew Ana and her father were safe. And then he had orders from the king to deliver them to court at Ebton.

He turned toward the general. "Are you fully recovered from the poison? Can you lead?"

General Harden snorted. "I should box your ears for even asking. I taught you everything you know, you little whelp."

Leo smiled. This was the General Hard-Ass he knew and loved. "Then you're in charge. Move out at dawn. The entire army, except for Nevis's troop and my personal guard."

"Aye, my lord." The general gave him a curt salute, then left the tent.

Nevis looked annoyed. "I have to stay behind?"

"I thought you were worried about my safety," Leo told him wryly. "I have to take my bride to Ebton without getting us killed."

Nevis rolled his eyes. "I could be killing elves, but I have to play chaperone for the newlyweds."

"Jealous?"

"I can shake her hand. Can you?"

"Bastard."

With a smirk, Nevis strolled from the tent. "I suggest you take a bath before meeting your wife."

Leo glanced down at his dirty and sweaty clothes. It had

been damned hot with all the armor on. And all his clean clothes were in the dressing room.

He strode through the camp with four of his personal guard following at a discreet distance. All through the camp, soldiers were busily packing up for the march at dawn. Part of him wished he were going with them. Life with the army was all he'd known since the age of eight.

But now he had a wife. And a home. He studied Vindemar as he approached. It was one of the largest fortresses in Eberon, as large and fine as the royal court at Ebton Palace.

With an inward wince, he realized just how big a threat he was to his uncle. He had a huge amount of land and wealth now at his disposal. He had the vassals and men of Vindalyn who owed their allegiance to him, and he had the loyalty of the royal army. He was more dangerous to Uncle Fred than the elves of Woodwyn, pirates of Tourin, or dragons of Norveshka.

This could only mean that the assassination attempts would never stop. No matter how many times he pledged his loyalty to his uncle, the king would still want him dead. If he openly attacked the king's men, it would be treason, and that would give his uncle a legitimate reason for executing him. Not that Leo would ever accept that without a fight, but he was reluctant to plunge the country into civil war, not when there were three neighboring kingdoms that would invade at the first sign of weakness.

No matter what happened, he didn't want to end up like his cousin Tedric, the heir to the throne. Five years ago, Tedric had been banished from court and sentenced to live in a crumbling old castle with a handful of guards, essentially a prisoner, waiting for his father to die.

As Leo crossed the drawbridge, the Vindemar guards saluted him, a silent reminder that he was now in charge. In the courtyard, the men bowed, the women curtsied. But he didn't miss the wary glances cast his way or the worried whispers. Even though Ana's father had assured everyone at breakfast in the Great Hall that the transfer of power was his idea and had his blessing, there were still some lingering suspicions as to why the Beast had suddenly become the Duke of Vindalyn.

Ana's guards were not outside the bedchamber, which could only mean that she wasn't there. As he entered, he heard voices coming from the dressing room. With his hand on the hilt of his sword, he peeked through the door.

It was Edmund, flirting with Ana's maid as they made room for Leo's clothes on the shelves.

"That's not necessary," he said, leaning against the doorjamb.

They both jumped and quickly made a bow and a curtsy.

"I should start fetching water for my lady's bath." Gabrielle grabbed a bucket and ran into her adjoining room.

Edmund sighed. "You scared her away." His nose wrinkled. "You'll scare your wife, too, looking like that."

Leo snorted. "Amazing how all my bachelor friends are suddenly experts on marriage."

Edmund grinned. "Are you saying I'm one of your friends?"

"Sod off." Leo scowled as he eyed the bottom shelf. Two of Ana's linen gowns had been folded up to make room for his shirts and breeches. "You shouldn't have done this. I won't be here that long."

Edmund motioned to the folded gowns. "Gabriella said it didn't matter, that those were her work clothes. We didn't disturb her fancy gowns."

Next to Leo's stack of shirts was a stack of Ana's nightgowns. Seeing them side by side made his heart tighten. He was truly married.

He dragged a gloved hand through his sweaty hair. "What did Lady Tatiana do today? Do you know?"

"She slept till noon." Edmund chuckled. "I heard she fussed at Gabriella for not waking her up earlier."

"I told her maid to let her sleep late." Leo had figured Ana needed more rest after all she'd endured the day before. She'd narrowly missed an arrow meant for her and a poisoning, and then she'd been coerced into a sudden wedding.

"She spent the afternoon in the library reading," Edmund continued. "Gabriella said she plans to take a bath here before meeting you at supper in the Great Hall." He gave Leo a skeptical look. "You're planning to bathe, too, right?"

"I'm on my way to the bathhouse," Leo growled as he stuffed clean clothes into a knapsack. "Why don't you make yourself useful and help Gabriella bring water up here?"

"Yes, my lord!" Edmund dashed through the bedchamber and out the door, no doubt eager to resume his flirtation.

Alone now in the dressing room, Leo dropped the knapsack, then dug through the stack of Ana's nightgowns till he found the extra-sheer one. With a smile, he placed it on top.

Knapsack in hand, he headed into the bedchamber. He slowed as he passed the upholstered chair, recalling how oddly Ana had acted when she thought no one was looking.

He tossed the sack onto the seat, then ran his fingers over the same area she had touched. There was definitely something hidden in the upholstery, and it had been inserted through an opening in a seam. Slowly he pulled it out. A folded sheet of paper.

Was it a love letter like the one in his desk drawer in his tent? But if his wife wasn't Lady Tatiana, like Captain Bougaire had claimed, then she hadn't written that letter.

Slowly Leo opened the note.

Our dear sister, Luciana . . .

The first line came as such a shock, he stood frozen for a few seconds. When he read it again, a swarm of questions swooped across his mind like a horde of bats fleeing a cave. Was this his wife's real name? Was that why she'd asked him to call her Ana? Was Ana short for both Luciana and Tatiana? Had his suspicions been correct? Were the two of them twins?

He quickly read the rest of the letter, searching for clues. The four females who had signed the letter considered Luciana their sister. If Ana had grown up with them on the Isle of Moon, it would explain why she'd made the sign of the moons. And if there had been twin girls, it would make sense that Lucas Vintello had hidden one of them. Twins, especially girls, were never allowed to live in Eberon.

But if Luciana had taken Tatiana's place, where was Tatiana? Hiding or . . . dead?

And Ana could speak to the dead.

A chill ran down Leo's spine. Surely his imagination was going wild, and none of this could be true.

In the letter, the four sisters wrote about the Game of Stones and Ana's prediction of meeting him. Their story matched the one Ana had told him, so that much appeared to be true.

How much was true? How much was deception? When she'd defended him in the courtyard, was that how she truly felt? When she'd hugged him last night, had that been sincere?

By the Light, he hoped so. He wanted it too much for it to be a lie. He wanted her. He wanted her to love him.

Dammit to hell. What was happening to him? He couldn't allow himself to get weak over some sappy feelings. Not when the king would keep trying to kill him. He had to remain strong if he was going to survive.

He folded the letter up and inserted it back into the hole. Out of sight, out of mind. He wouldn't mention it to Ana. If she didn't trust him enough to tell him the truth, then so be it. He just needed to keep his distance.

After all, it was a marriage in name only. He could never actually live with her. It was foolish to hope for more.

Her new husband was ignoring her.

Luciana pushed her food around her plate and took another sip of wine. The Great Hall was packed tonight with nearby vassals, merchants, and tradesmen who had come to swear allegiance to the new duke and toast the newlyweds.

The atmosphere at Vindemar was tense with excitement. The level of curiosity was so high that no one even attempted to hush their voices. By the time Luciana had walked to the Great Hall, she'd heard most of the gossip. Everyone was wondering if somehow the Lord Protector had coerced her father into giving up the duchy. Had he threatened the poor duke with his Beastly powers?

And she hadn't missed the sympathetic glances aimed her way. How on Aerthlan had Lady Tatiana survived a wedding night with the Beast?

Now from her seat at the high table, she could spot the furtive glances. Once everyone realized she was somehow miraculously alive, they turned their attention to Leo.

She did, too. He looked as handsome as ever. His dark-red hair was still damp and curling around his ears. Was it as soft as it looked? Were those dark whiskers lining his jaw soft or prickly? How would she ever know if she couldn't touch him? With a pang of annoyance, she drank more wine.

He was definitely ignoring her. He'd left the bedchamber this morning without even telling her good-bye. Now, at her father's insistence, he was sitting in the larger chair at the center of the dais—the duke's chair. Luciana was seated at his right, and her father at his left.

She'd tried to look her best tonight. Freshly bathed, wearing her golden gown, her hair gathered at the nape of her neck in a sparkling golden net. But Leo had hardly seemed to notice.

With a sigh, she reached for her wine goblet. During the entire meal, he'd been engaged in deep conversation with her father. Apparently the army was leaving in the morning. She'd tensed for a moment, believing Leo was leaving, too, but he appeared to be staying. Relieved, she took a long drink of wine.

Perhaps it was a good thing that Leo and her father were getting along so well. It would help to dispel the rumors that the Beast was forcing them into compliance.

The dinner dragged on as more and more toasts were offered. At first, the guests simply wished her and Leo a long and happy life. Then a guest wished them a healthy child. *As if that could ever happen*, Luciana thought with dismay as she drained her goblet.

Not to be outdone, the next toast wished them three children. The next toast half a dozen. The next one ten. Each time the cups were emptied, the servants refilled them, and the guests became more rowdy.

"Two dozen children!" a red-faced merchant yelled, and everyone gave a cheer, then drained their cups.

Two dozen? May the goddesses help her. Luciana drank more wine.

When the singing started, her father stepped off the dais to join some old friends in song. Luciana shook her head as the noise reverberated painfully in her head. *Ouch*. That hadn't helped. Now the room was swirling.

"Let me take you back to our room," Leo whispered.

She blinked and turned toward him. "Why? The dinner's not over yet."

"You hardly ate. But you've had a lot of wine."

"Ye mean ye noticed?" She pressed her knuckles against her mouth. Had she messed up her accent? Surely not.

"I notice everything you say and do . . . Ana."

Was he inferring something? With her clouded mind, she couldn't tell.

"Let's go," he whispered. "No one will question why the newlyweds want to retire early."

She frowned, trying to decipher that. "Oh, I see. They'll think we're getting started on the two dozen children. But don't they know . . ." She slapped a hand against his chest. "This is all we can do."

He circled a gloved hand around the sleeve of her forearm. "Do you wish we could do more?"

"Now, there's a pointless question." Her gaze met his. He had the loveliest green eyes. "Ye—you're far too pretty to be a Beast."

The corner of his mouth lifted. "You're not making me sound very manly."

"Oh, you're very manly." She pressed her fingers against his rock-hard chest. "But pretty, too. I tried to look pretty for you tonight."

"You're more than pretty. You're absolutely beautiful."

She smiled, and a giggle escaped. "Oh." She covered her mouth. "I'm not used to drinking so much wine. We always water it down at the con—" She winced. "I'd better go to bed."

He stood. "I'll take you."

"There's no need." She waved a dismissive hand as she rose to her feet. When she stumbled, he swooped her up in his arms. She gasped and the Great Hall filled with cheers.

Leo announced to the crowd, "We bid you good night."

As the cheers rose in volume, Luciana buried her face against his shirt. By the goddesses, this was embarrassing.

Still carrying her, he stepped down from the dais and headed for the nearest door.

"Leo, put me down. I can walk."

"I like carrying you." He strode down the hallway toward the bedchamber. "I dream about holding you in my arms."

What a sad pair they were, she thought as she leaned her head against his shoulder.

Before she knew it, he had deposited her in the dressing room and closed the door. Gabriella helped her out of the golden gown and into a nightgown. After washing her face with cold water and brushing her hair, she felt much more clearheaded.

"Good night, Gabriella." When the maid retired to her room, Luciana cracked the door and peered into the bedchamber. Leo had lit a fire in the hearth, and he was already stretched out on his blankets on the floor. Maybe he was already asleep. He'd put in a long day, unlike her.

She tiptoed toward the bed.

"I like that nightgown."

With a gasp, she turned toward him, then glanced down. Good goddesses, it was the sheer nightgown again. "Good night." She ran toward the bed and slipped underneath the coverlet.

"Are you feeling better?" he asked.

"Yes." She stared at the canopy overhead.

"Then we can talk."

She winced. "About your day?"

"About you."

Oh, no. She pulled the coverlet up to her chin.

"I told you about myself. How my parents died and my nanny died. I'd like to know about you."

She bit her lip, trying to figure out what she could safely say. "My mother came from a family of witches who could foresee the future. I may have inherited a bit of that, since I predicted you with the Telling Stones."

"I see. And your mother passed away a few days after giving birth to you?"

"Yes."

After a pause he asked, "Do you still see her?"

Luciana's breath caught.

"Ana, do you see the dead?"

She looked toward him, but could barely see him in the dim light of the fireplace. "That would be . . . too strange."

He sat up. "I'm Embraced. My gift, or curse if you prefer, is the power of lightning. And you?"

Was he asking if she was Embraced? How could she admit it? She'd been warned all her life never to say it, first by Mother Ginessa and all the nuns, and then by her father. "'Tis—it's common knowledge that you're Embraced."

He rose to his feet and came close to the bed. "Ana, I'd like for you to trust me."

Even though his face was in shadow, she could feel him watching her. By the goddesses, she was tempted to tell him everything. But she wasn't the only one at risk. How could she endanger her father? If the truth about her deception ever surfaced, she and her father would both be executed.

If only she and Leo were alone on an island. But they weren't. They were surrounded by enemies. "I—I'm sorry."

He sat on the edge of the bed and looked around. "Are we alone now?"

Was he still trying to get her to admit to seeing the dead? "I . . . believe we're alone."

"That's good." He placed a gloved hand on the coverlet where her foot was. "I have fought armies of elfin warriors." His hand slid to her ankle, then her calf. "I have faced fire-breathing dragons."

"That must have been terrifying." Her heart raced as his hand skimmed up her thigh and over her hip.

"Do you know what terrifies me even more?" His hand moved past her waist, then paused just below her breasts.

She clenched the top edge of the coverlet in her fists. "It was a dragon that killed your father. What could terrify you more than that?"

"The possibility that I might hurt you."

Her eyes burned. "I know you don't mean to hurt me."

"Do you?" His hand curved around her breast, and she gasped. Gently, he squeezed.

A tingling sensation stole over her, making her breasts feel heavy and her whole body ache to be touched. "Leo . . ." A whimper escaped as his gloved fingers teased at her nipple, causing it to harden into a tight bud.

"You have no idea how much I want you." He leaned close enough that she could see the determined glint in his eyes. "At first, I thought it was only your body I wanted. But something about you has made me greedy as hell. I want everything. Your love. Your mind. Your secrets. Your soul."

He released her, then returned to his blankets on the floor. "Good night, Ana."

She pressed her hands against her hot cheeks as a tear escaped. By the goddesses, she did love him. She loved him so much her heart ached. But how could she tell him her secrets? How could she bare her soul to him?

He wanted more than she could ever give.

Chapter Twenty-seven

❧

When Luciana woke the next day, she discovered her head was aching and her husband was missing. Once again, she'd overslept and he'd left without telling her good-bye. It was hard to be annoyed with him, though, when Gabriella admitted that he'd asked her to be very quiet and let her ladyship sleep, since she might not be feeling well.

On the way to the kitchens, she was surprised to find only Jensen accompanying her, but he explained that the suspected third assassin had left the fortress, so she was no longer in grave danger. If that was supposed to relieve her, it didn't, for she knew the danger still existed. It had only shifted to Leo. She said a silent prayer, beseeching Luna and Lessa to keep her husband safe.

With Jensen standing guard at the kitchen door, she entered with a cheerful greeting. Christopher was sitting in a corner with a worried expression. She gave him a smile before turning to his mother. "I'm afraid I missed breakfast. Could you spare me something to eat?"

"Of course!" Yulissa grabbed a wooden plate and began heaping food on it. "You didn't need to come here, my dear. We would have brought it to your room."

"This is fine." Luciana sat at the table. "I plan to work in the garden after I eat."

Yulissa poured some apple cider into a cup. "We're so sorry about Rowena poisoning the soup." She handed her the cup with an apologetic look. "I hope you weren't too sick."

"I'm perfectly fine," Luciana assured her. "And Father is, too."

Yulissa and her workers murmured how relieved they were, then an awkward silence fell upon the room. Luciana ate while they busied themselves, but she could see them exchanging wary glances.

"Did my father handle the . . . situation?" Luciana asked.

The scullery maid dropped a platter, and another cook accidentally nicked her finger with a knife. Yulissa turned her back to check a pot over the fire.

Luciana set down her fork. "Where is Rowena?"

"The dungeons," the scullery maid muttered.

"And where else would she be?" Yulissa asked with an exasperated tone. "She poisoned the soup for the high table."

Silence fell over the room again. Luciana motioned for Christopher to come closer.

"Did I do a bad thing?" he whispered. "I thought it was right to warn you about the soup, but now Rowena is in big trouble." He glanced at his mother and the workers. "They're afraid she'll hang."

Luciana's breath caught. Even though Rowena had clearly committed a serious offense, she'd only made two people slightly ill. Her father had been well enough to ride the next day. The general had marched off with the army this morning.

"I'll see what I can do for her," Luciana offered, and everyone turned toward her with hopeful looks.

"Bless you, my lady." Yulissa's eyes glimmered with tears. "You have a kind heart."

"Oh, please forgive me!" Rowena cried. She'd fallen to her knees the minute Luciana and Jensen had entered the dungeons.

The girl was younger than Luciana had expected, no more than seventeen. Her face was streaked with dried tear tracks, and she was kneeling on old rushes that should have been cleaned out months ago. There was no cot, not even a blanket, and the smell from the chamber pot nearly made Luciana gag.

She approached the bars of the cell.

The jailer jumped up from his chair behind the desk. "You should stay away from her, my lady. She could be dangerous."

"I'll be all right." Luciana noted two trays of food on the jailer's desk. Was he eating both of them?

He poured wine into the second cup and offered it to her. When she declined, he offered it to Jensen.

"Not while I'm on duty." Jensen frowned at him.

"Very well, then." The jailer sat back down and resumed eating.

Luciana crouched down in front of the jail cell. "Are you all right?"

"I'm so sorry." Rowena licked her chapped lips. "I'd heard that the Beast had killed my Dax, so I thought I would make his belly ache. I never meant any more harm than that. But it was wrong of me. Please forgive me."

Luciana figured the girl was telling the truth since her father and the general had not suffered too much. "Have you had anything to eat or drink?"

She shook her head and cast a wary look at the jailer. "Yulissa sent me some food, but I wasn't allowed to eat. Or drink."

Luciana straightened and turned toward the jailer. "Are you refusing her food and water?"

With a snort he poured more wine into his cup. "Is she whining again? Pay her no heed, my lady. She is far beneath you. Besides, there's no point in feeding her if she's just going to hang."

Rowena whimpered and a tear ran down her face.

"Have you been telling her that?" Luciana marched toward the jailer, her temper rising. "It is not your decision to make."

The jailer gave her a condescending smile. "Of course, my lady. Either the old duke or the new one will be making the decision. But since she tried to kill them both, it's a safe bet that she'll swing." He shrugged. "It's better for her to know the truth, so she'll have time to accept it."

Luciana gritted her teeth as she motioned to the second tray on the desk. "Is that her food you're eating?" When the jailer shrugged, she picked up the second cup of wine. "Jensen, will you go to the kitchens and bring back food and water for Rowena?"

Jensen hesitated. "I shouldn't leave you alone."

"I'm not alone." She tilted her head toward the jailer. "And it won't take you very long."

"Very well." Jensen headed out the door.

Luciana passed the cup of wine through the bars, and Rowena rose to her feet to accept it.

"Thank you, my lady." She gulped it down.

"Do you have parents or family close by?"

Rowena shook her head. "Mama died from a plague when I was a babe, and Papa died at sea." She hung her head. "I shouldn't have gotten involved with Dax. I was just so happy not to be alone."

Luciana sighed. How fortunate she'd been to grow up with the nuns and her four sisters. "Everyone in the kitchens is very worried about you. From now on, think of them as your family. They can give you good advice."

"Yes, my lady."

The jailer gave out a loud belch. "Beggin' your pardon, my lady, but you shouldn't fill her head with false hope. No way is she going to live."

Rowena flinched, and more tears fell. "I'm so afraid."

Luciana couldn't let this girl suffer any longer. "I'm going straight to the library, where I'll inform my father's secretary that I have given you my word that even though you may receive some kind of punishment, you will not come to any bodily harm."

Rowena's eyes widened. "Can you really do that?"

"Yes." Luciana turned toward the jailer. "And you, sir, should start treating this woman with respect." She strode toward the door. "I'll be back soon."

She shut the door behind her and headed down the stone corridor for the stairwell that led up to the courtyard. Just as she reached the first stair, a noise behind her made her stop. Before she could turn around, an arm looped around her waist, pulling her back. Another hand pressed a strange-smelling handkerchief against her nose and mouth.

Panic streaked across her senses as she struggled to break the person's hold. A swift kick backward elicited a muttered curse. A male's voice.

The third assassin? She shook her head, trying to dislodge the handkerchief, but the drug crept into her senses. Within a few seconds the staircase blurred before her eyes and her legs grew weak.

Goddesses, help me! Her legs gave out, and everything went black.

When Luciana opened her eyes, she felt disoriented for a few seconds. Her head throbbed as she pushed away the fog in her mind. The assassin! Panic took root in her chest, but she quickly squashed it down. If she was going to survive this, she needed to keep her wits about her.

Where was she? Where was her kidnapper? Would it be best to pretend she was still unconscious?

She was lying on her back in a dimly lit place. Stale, musty air filled her lungs as her vision adjusted. A stone ceiling arched overhead. Hard stone beneath her. She stretched her arms and legs. No pain. No restraints.

She turned her head slightly to the right, her gaze following the arch of the stone ceiling till . . . good goddesses.

Bones. Thousands of bones. Shelf after shelf. Skulls staring at her with empty eye sockets. The flickering light of a nearby torch danced across the skulls in hues of red and gold, contorting the facial features until they looked as if they were possessed by demons.

Panic welled up inside her once more. This had to be the catacombs. Where the dead were buried and the ghosts of evil men lingered. She squeezed her eyes shut and clenched her fists. *You must remain calm.*

"I know you're awake."

Her eyes flew open.

"Get up," the kidnapper ordered. "I haven't much time."

As she slowly sat up, she looked around. To the left was another wall of bones and skulls. Behind her, more bones and a torch attached to the wall. In front, an iron gate extended across the width of the room. On the other side, another torch lit another room. More shelves with bones and skulls. In the distance, she spotted a man dressed in the black robes of a priest. Father Rune.

"Oh, look," a voice whispered behind her. "A live one has come to visit."

Luciana stiffened as a wisp of cold air floated across her back. *Don't turn around.* It would be better not to let these ghosts know she could see and hear them. *Ig-*

nore them. She rose to her feet and approached the iron gate.

"Yessss," another voice hissed like a snake. "We could have fun with her."

Panic threatened once again when she noticed the padlock on the gate. She was trapped in this chamber with some evil ghosts. Goddesses help her, this was her worst nightmare.

Father Rune chuckled. "I can see by your expression that you have realized the full extent of your situation."

She took hold of the iron bars, and barnacles of old rust bit into her palms. "What do you hope to achieve by this? My husband and father will be furious."

"She's locked in with usss," the snake-voiced ghost whispered, then chuckled with his dead companions.

She gave the bars a shake, but the lock held tight.

The priest sneered. "There's no way out. You will remain there until someone finds you. Hopefully, it will be the Beast. I have arranged a small surprise for him."

"Oh, she's pretty." Icy-cold ghostly fingers stroked her arm, passing through her gown and causing her skin to prickle with gooseflesh.

"I like them pretty." A ghost giggled with a manic, high-pitched tone that chilled her to the bone.

By the goddesses, that one sounded mentally unhinged. Once again she struggled against the panic flaring inside her. "The Lord Protector won't let you get away with this."

The priest waved a dismissive hand. "He's far away. While I was hiding down here, I planned it all out. First, the castle guards will look for you. And then, they'll send an envoy to let your father and husband know you're missing. By the time the Beast can ride back to Vindemar, I'll be gone."

Father Rune sighed. "Such a shame that I'll miss it, but

I can imagine how it will unfold. Your rescuers will rush through the dark tunnels of the catacombs, desperate to save you, and there in the distance a single torch, a shining beacon, will illuminate you, the damsel in distress. Then the Beast will charge toward you."

Father Rune motioned to two thin threads stretched across the corridor about a foot above the stone floor. In the dim light, they were barely visible. "Whoever trips the first wire will release a dozen arrows. The second wire will release a dozen more. I'm hoping, of course, that your husband will be among the dead."

Luciana tightened her grip on the bars. In the seven days since she'd first met Leo, she'd grown to love him so much. She couldn't bear to lose him. He wouldn't die if she warned them about the trap, but she didn't want to tell Father Rune that. He might decide to gag her or tie her up. So she gave him what she hoped was a forlorn, defeated look. "Why are you doing this?"

"It's very simple. The king pays well." The priest shrugged. "Of course, it's possible that the Beast will survive this. But if he hunts me down, I'll be ready with another trap. Sooner or later, the Beast will die."

"Never. Leo is too smart for you."

Father Rune chuckled. "You actually like him, don't you? Well, you can always pray that he won't find you here. Then he would be safe. But if that happens, you'll be left here to die a slow death." He sauntered away with the torch. "The Light be with you."

As he disappeared around a corner, the room became darker, now lit by only one torch behind her.

"We're alone with her now," a ghost whispered, and a draft of cold air enveloped her.

There had to be half a dozen of them that surrounded her. One ghost had clearly died from a chest wound. The one with a snake voice appeared to have been hanged, for a line of mottled bruises crossed his throat. She closed her eyes briefly to keep from looking at them.

"So pretty." The high-pitched giggle grated on her nerves.

A shot of cold penetrated her chest as the manic giggler tried to grope her breasts. She backed away, crossing her arms across her chest.

"I think she can feel usss," the hanged man whispered.

"I hope she's been left here to die," the one with a chest wound said. "Once she becomes a ghost like us, we'll be able to touch her."

Another giggle. "If she dies, I'm fucking her first."

Goddesses, help me! Luciana looked frantically about. There. A rib bone with a sharp, pointed end. She grabbed it and inserted the point into the opening on the padlock.

"Hey, that's mine!" the hanged ghost protested.

The padlock refused to open. She grabbed a stronger thigh bone and wedged it into the iron loop that connected the padlock to the gate. If she could wrench the lock off the gate, she could escape. After a few heaves, the brittle old bone snapped in two.

The padlock was too strong. She examined the hinges, then each bar, searching for a weakness.

"Luciana! I found you!"

She whirled toward Christopher with a surge of relief, then a realization that she must have alerted the ghosts that she could see and hear them.

"Crispin, you ugly piece of toast." The ghost with the chest wound pushed the boy so hard he stumbled back. "What are you doing here?"

The hanged ghost caught Christopher from behind and gripped his neck as if to strangle him. "Too bad you're already dead, and we can't kill you."

"Look!" A ghost who carried a severed head in the crook of his arm pointed at Luciana. "She can see us."

Luciana turned away, but it was already too late.

The chest-wounded ghost sneered. "Then she can watch us beat up the boy."

"I think we should bugger him," the giggler announced.

"Christopher, leave!" Luciana shouted.

The boy pulled away from the hanged ghost. "I don't want to leave you here."

"Tell my mother and sister I'm here. Please go!" Luciana exhaled in relief when he disappeared.

"Bitch!" Chest-Wound snarled at her. "You took away our fun."

The giggler floated toward her, grinning. "Let's grope her till she screams."

Luciana grabbed the broken femur and whirled in a circle, slicing it through the ghosts. "Back off!"

"How can you make us?" Severed-Head smirked.

She tried the tactic that had worked on the dead Captain Bougaire. "When I'm rescued, I'll track down all your families and make them suffer!"

The ghosts chuckled, the giggler two octaves higher.

"You think we care what happens to the living?" Chest-Wound smirked as he pointed at the hanged ghost. "Why do you think they executed him?"

Hanged-Man grinned. "I killed my wife and baby."

"Let's get her!" the giggler announced, and the gang of ghosts closed in.

"I'm a witch!" Luciana tried a new strategy. "I'll put a curse on you for all eternity!"

They paused.

"C-can she do that?" Giggler asked.

"We're already dead," Chest-Wound growled. "What can one witch do to us?"

"How about two witches?" Luciana's mother asked as her form solidified.

"The duchessss," Hanged-Man hissed, and they all floated back.

"Leave her be," Ariana ordered. "Or I'll have my husband clean all the bones out of here, throw them in the sea, and fill these tunnels with sand."

"We'll have nowhere to go," Giggler whined.

Luciana ran to her mother's side. "Thank you."

Ariana smiled. "Thank Christopher. He told me where you were. Jensen has the entire castle guard looking for you. I asked Tatiana to come up with a way to contact them." She cast a disgusted look at the ghosts. "Meanwhile, I'll take you away from the filth."

"The priest said there was no way out."

Ariana snorted. "He lived here only a few weeks. He may know about the main escape route, but I know a secret one. Your father showed it to me years ago." She motioned to the torch on the back wall. "Take that with you."

Luciana pulled the torch from the wall bracket. "I'm not sure I should leave. If anyone comes down here to rescue me, they could be killed in the trap that Father Rune set. I need to stay here to warn them."

Ariana shook her head. "They've just begun to search the keep and towers along the outer wall. We can be out of here before they even start on the catacombs." She pointed to a skull with a red X painted on its brow. "Underneath this skull is a lever. Pull it."

Luciana did as she was told, and with a loud creak, a section of shelves swung back to reveal a narrow opening. She held the torch aloft and spotted a steep, stone staircase descending into a dark pit.

"Let's go." Ariana glanced back at the ghosts. "Do not follow us, or I'll have the catacombs destroyed."

Luciana took one last look at the trap on the other side of the iron gate and said a silent prayer that she was making the right decision.

Down into the darkness she went, planting her feet carefully on each damp stone step. She couldn't afford to slip. How far she would fall she had no idea. But she couldn't afford to go slowly, either.

She was in a race against her rescuers. If she didn't reach them first, they could venture down into the catacombs and die.

Chapter Twenty-eight

❧

After charging across the drawbridge, Leo reined in his horse and quickly dismounted. He removed his helmet as Nevis and Edmund ran toward him. "Have you found her?"

"Not yet." Nevis glanced at the drawbridge. "Where are your personal guard? And the rest of your party?"

"A few miles behind me." Leo pulled off his chain mail and handed it and his helmet to Edmund. "Did you send out some trackers in case she's been taken away from the fortress?"

"Yes," Nevis replied. "But it's hard to detect anything when the army left behind so many tracks when they moved out this morning. And dammit, Leo, why didn't you stick with your guards?"

"They're too slow. And you're too slow. Get everyone in the fortress involved in the search."

Nevis huffed with annoyance. "Don't you realize Father Rune may have taken her just to lure you out and make you easier to kill? And you played right into it!"

"I don't give a shit!"

"Do I have to knock some sense into you?" Nevis yelled.

Leo dragged a gloved hand through his hair. He didn't want to admit it but Nevis was right. He'd made himself vulnerable by riding ahead of his party. It wasn't like him to behave this recklessly. Even in battle, he always remained in control. But the second he'd heard that Ana was missing, something crazed and desperate had seized hold of him.

Ana's father was distraught, too, but he'd been unable to keep up with Leo. He'd charged ahead like a madman, pushing his horse to the limit. "Edmund, will you take care of Fearless?"

"Aye, my lord." As Edmund took the reins, he gave Leo a hopeful look. "Maybe Father Rune doesn't have her. Maybe she just went to a secret place to be alone for a while."

"And not tell anyone?" Nevis grumbled. "Why would she do that?"

Leo didn't dismiss the idea like Nevis, not when he knew Ana had secrets. Could she have gone to the sea to send another message by seals? "Did you check the beach?"

"No. Hey, where are you going?" Nevis shouted as Leo dashed back across the drawbridge. "Dammit, you're not wearing your armor!"

Leo kept going. As long as he was running at lightning speed, an assassin would find it difficult to hit him with an arrow. He darted down the path to the beach.

The flat rock where the seals gathered was empty. He sprinted along the beach, calling her name. No reply. She wasn't among the boulders.

Had she been caught by the undertow? Swept out to sea?

Panic ripped through him so hard, he fell to his knees. *No!* He couldn't lose her. Not beautiful, brave, and clever Ana. She was the one who believed in him, the one who gave him hope that he could be a man and not a Beast.

He needed her. She was the strength of his body, the

beat of his heart, and the yearning of his soul. The thought that she could be suffering or afraid paralyzed him with a fear he'd never felt before. And there on his knees, the truth struck him hard.

He loved her.

An eternity had happened in the seven days since he'd first met her. An eternity that had bonded her soul with his.

"Leo, what are you doing?" Nevis called as he descended the path to the beach.

He had to find her. Leo jumped to his feet and sprinted back to the path. "We need to enlarge the search. Have you gone into the wine cellars or catacombs?"

"Not yet. They're—" Nevis lifted a hand to shield his eyes as he gazed out at the sea. "What is that?"

Leo spun toward the water. *Please don't be a body.* "Where?"

"There." Nevis pointed at something black moving through the waves. "Oh, don't worry about it. It's just a seal."

A surge of hope replaced the panic that had sizzled through Leo. Could it be Brody? In dog form, he'd be able to track Ana's scent. "What perfect timing!"

"Huh?"

Before Leo could explain, the seal shifted into a dog.

"What the hell?" Nevis stiffened, a stunned look on his face. "Is that . . . *Brody*?"

"Yes." Leo grinned as he started down the path. "He's back!"

"Huh?" Nevis followed him. "He went somewhere as a bloody seal? You knew about this, and you didn't tell me?"

"Not a word to anyone," Leo warned him.

Nevis scoffed. "Who the hell would believe me?"

Brody splashed through the shallow water, then halted with a jerk when he spotted Leo and Nevis coming toward him.

"Thank the Light you're back," Leo told him.

Brody shifted into human form and sat in the shallow water, breathing heavily. "Now you know."

Nevis gave him an incredulous look. "I don't know what the hell you are. No offense."

"We'll discuss it later," Leo said. "For now, I want—" He stopped when Brody collapsed onto his back. "Are you all right?"

"Exhausted."

"I bet!" Nevis continued to stare at him. "How far did you swim? How many animals can you turn into?"

"Later!" Leo shot him an annoyed look. "Right now—"

"There's something important you need to know," Brody interrupted.

"It can wait. I need—"

"But it's about Lady Tatiana," Brody insisted as he sat up. "She's not—"

"I don't want to hear it!" Leo yelled, surprising Brody and Nevis and even himself. Brody might have uncovered Ana's secrets, but Leo wanted to hear the truth from her first. He wanted her alive, and he wanted her trust.

If only he had trusted her from the beginning. Then he wouldn't have sent Brody away, and the dog shifter would have been here to track down the remaining assassins before Ana could have been exposed to danger.

"Ana is missing," Leo told Brody. "We believe she's been kidnapped by the third assassin, and we need to find her. Can you do that?"

"Sure." Brody ran a hand through his shaggy black hair. "What happened to the second assassin?"

"Dead," Nevis replied. "Along with the first."

"We'll explain later." Leo headed back to the path. "Meet me in the courtyard. I'll bring something Ana wore to help you detect her scent."

With lightning speed, he dashed back to the keep and

into the dressing room he now shared with Ana. He stuffed one of her work gowns and slippers into a knapsack, then ran back to the courtyard.

Nevis was there with Brody, back in dog form.

"Here." Leo emptied the knapsack, and Brody sniffed at her clothing.

"Where was she last seen?" Leo asked Nevis. "We should start there."

"The dungeons," Nevis replied, and all three headed across the courtyard as Jensen joined them.

"Any sign of her?" Leo asked.

The guard shook his head. "I left her for only a moment in the dungeons. The jailer said she was going to the library, but she never arrived. I-I'll accept whatever punishment you—"

"We'll discuss it later." Leo opened the door to the dungeons.

Brody trotted down the stairs, then wandered toward the dungeon door. He paused, then retraced his steps to the stairs.

"Did she leave?" Leo asked.

Brody turned and padded back down the corridor, this time passing the dungeon door and continuing down some steps into the darkness.

"What's down there?" Leo asked.

"The catacombs," Jensen replied.

"Get some torches," Leo ordered. "We're going in."

By the time Luciana reached the bottom of the stairs, it felt like the narrow stone walls were closing in. Now she and her mother were inching along a dark tunnel. She'd been forced to slow down because the ceiling occasionally dipped down so low, she had to stoop to get through.

Her footsteps echoed eerily about them, along with

scurrying sounds that she suspected were rats. "How much farther?"

"I'm not sure," Ariana replied as she floated along behind her. "I never had to use this passage."

"Can you tell me more about yourself?" Luciana asked, eager to take her mind off the rats and the prospect of her rescuers being killed in the catacombs.

"Well, let me see," Ariana began. "After I realized I was giving birth to twin girls, we started making preparations. We sent for a midwife and wet nurse from the Isle of Moon, for we knew they would worship the twin goddesses and consider you and your sister a blessing. We knew they could be trusted to keep your existence a secret."

"So no one else knew you were having twins?" Luciana asked.

"Not a soul. We couldn't let anyone else know, or your lives would have been in danger." Ariana sighed. "Everything was planned out so well. The oldest daughter would remain here as the heiress, raised by Lucas."

"And that was Tatiana."

"Yes. And the second daughter, you, would travel with me to the Isle of Moon, where I would raise you in secret."

Luciana halted and looked back at her mother. "You were planning to go with me?"

Ariana smiled. "Yes, my dear. Your father and I couldn't bear the thought of either of you being raised without a loving parent, so—"

"You were going to separate?"

Ariana nodded. "It was the only way."

"But you and Father love each other so much," Luciana protested.

"We didn't arrive at that solution easily. The thought of separating was heart-wrenching—"

"Mother, I'm so sorry."

"My dear child." Ariana reached out to touch Luciana's

cheek, but her fingers passed through like a cold shiver. "Someday you will have children, and you'll understand. There was nothing we were not willing to bear in order to give you and your sister the love you deserved. I'm just so sorry that I—"

"No, don't say that. You gave your life for us."

Ariana nodded slowly. "If only I had foreseen the lightning."

"What?"

Ariana motioned toward the darkness in front of them. "We must keep going. I'll tell you what happened."

Luciana continued along the tunnel as she listened to her mother's story.

"I was in the tower room, sewing baby clothes, about a week before you were due, when a storm began. The rain was coming in the windows a bit, but I thought it best to stay there rather than run back to the keep in the rain when I was so heavy. Everything was fine until a light flashed outside the window overlooking the sea, and a streak of lightning shot straight through."

Luciana glanced back at her mother. "That's what left the scorched mark on the wall?"

"Yes. Unfortunately, the lightning splintered and a shard struck me—"

"You were hit?" Luciana whipped around.

Ariana nodded. "Knocked unconscious. When I came to, I realized my water had broken and my labor had begun. When the storm finally stopped, Lucas found me in bed, having contractions. He immediately brought in the midwife and nurse. Tatiana and you were born that night."

"When the twin moons embraced."

"Yes. We knew, then, that you would also be Embraced, so you were both in great danger. Unfortunately, the lightning strike had left me extremely weak—"

"It was a wonder it didn't kill you," Luciana said.

Ariana smiled sadly. "It did, eventually. But you and Tatiana survived. I was so heartbroken when I realized I would not be making the trip to the Isle of Moon with you."

"Mother, please don't feel bad. I had a very happy life at the convent."

She nodded with tears in her eyes. "The midwife and nurse took a sacred oath to protect you. The nurse remained here and became Tatiana's nanny. The midwife promised she would take you to a safe and loving place on the Isle of Moon where she would watch over you."

"Then I know her?" Luciana asked. "What is her name?"

"Ginessa. Do you remember her?"

Luciana exhaled with a short laugh. "Of course! She took me to the Convent of the Two Moons, and now she's in charge. She's Mother Ginessa." With a smile, Luciana resumed her trek through the tunnel. No wonder Mother Ginessa had sent all her practice pages and illustrations to Father. She was already acquainted with him.

"I'm so relieved it worked out all right for you," Ariana said with a sniffle.

"It did." Luciana glanced back with a grin. "I grew up with four sisters. We're all Embraced, so we were taken to the convent as babes so we would be safe."

"Tell me about them," Ariana urged.

"Well, Brigitta is the oldest of the four, just six months younger than me." Luciana rounded a corner and narrowed her eyes. "Is that a light up ahead?"

"I believe so."

"We're almost there!" Luciana lifted her skirt in one hand and the torch in the other as she rushed forward.

The light grew until it began to take the shape of an arched entrance. As they approached, she spotted bars. A gate?

The stone floor gave away to sand, and the sound of seagulls reached her ears.

"It's the beach!" Luciana ran to the gate. She passed the torch to her left hand to push the gate open with her right.

It wouldn't budge.

A quick inspection showed no locks. Apparently, the water level had risen high enough in the past to flood the tunnel, and the gate had rusted shut.

She found a crack in the wall where she could wedge the torch, then she attacked the gate with both hands, shoving with all her might. Still no luck.

"Hello! I'm here!" she screamed as loud as she could, but she couldn't be sure if anyone in the fortress would hear her.

"Help me!" she yelled, pushing at the gate. If she threw the torch through the bars, would anyone see it? No, she couldn't risk losing her only source of light in case she had to go back to the catacombs. And the terrible ghosts.

Panic threatened to return full force. "Goddesses help me, what should I do?"

"We'll think of something," Ariana said.

"If I can't get out, I'll have to go back to catacombs. I need to warn Leo before he and the others are killed!"

"Stay calm. I'll see what I can do." Ariana shimmered and vanished.

Luciana gave the gate another shake, then yelped as a big rat ran past her onto the beach. *Calm?* If anything happened to Leo, it would kill her.

Chapter Twenty-nine

❧

Leo was grateful he'd thought of marking their descent into the catacombs. For half an hour, they'd been winding through passages lined with shelves stacked with bones. These were the more recent dead, Jensen had explained, for over the years, people had grown reluctant to venture into the depths of the catacombs for fear they would be lost down there forever.

It was a legitimate concern, Leo thought, as they veered one way, then another each time the path forked. Father Rune could have hidden down here for weeks without being detected.

Nevis had tied one end of a ball of twine to the entrance of the catacombs, and he'd been unfurling it as they went. Already, he'd gone through three balls. Brody could probably sniff his way out, but they'd all agreed that having a second lifeline was for the best.

Brody was in the lead, his nose to the ground, while Leo and Jensen held torches to light their way. They had finally reached a series of large chambers, each one lined with shelves of more bones.

The air was chilly, as it usually was underground, but Leo wondered if part of the chill came from the presence of ghosts. If that was the case, then poor Ana had to be terrified.

Up ahead, he spotted an iron gate extending across the room, separating this room from the next. He held his torch up high. The next room had a back wall, so it was a dead end. She should be here.

"Ana!" His voice echoed about the chamber.

Brody suddenly halted with a jerk.

Arrows burst out of shelves in the chamber walls. With lightning speed, Leo jumped back, pulling Jensen with him. The arrows thudded into bare wooden shelves on the opposite side, passing several feet above Brody, who had flattened himself on the stone floor. A human would have been killed.

"Is everyone all right?" Nevis asked.

"Yes." Leo lowered his torch and spotted another wire. "There's a second trap. Move back."

Brody scooted back to join them, then Leo tossed a bone at the second wire.

Another barrage of arrows shot across the room.

Jensen eased closer to the side to inspect the walls. "Someone emptied the bones from this section of shelves and fastened several crossbows."

"I knew it," Nevis muttered. "That damned priest kidnapped Lady Tatiana so he could lure Leo to his death."

"But where is she?" Leo demanded. The next room was empty.

Loud footsteps echoed in the distance as someone hurried toward them. He must have been following their lifeline.

Nevis and Jensen drew their swords.

"Identify yourself!" Leo yelled.

"It's me, Edmund!" His voice sounded in the distance. "Come quick!"

Leo ran with the others, following the trail of twine.

After a few minutes, they found Edmund coming toward them.

"Lady Tatiana's father arrived," Edmund reported. "He went up on the wall walk to look around and spotted something strange happening on the beach."

Leo took off at lightning speed while Nevis yelled, "Wait for us! It could be another trap!"

As soon as Leo cleared the catacombs, he dropped his torch into a pail of water and kept going. He darted across the courtyard and drawbridge, headed for the beach.

At the top of the path, he halted. A line had been drawn in the sand, parallel to the shore. He scanned the beach, but there was no one there. Then another line began to appear, and his breath hitched. A stick was digging through the sand, but it was moving on its own. Was one of Ana's ghostly spies at work?

He eased slowly down the path, not wanting to frighten the ghost away from its chore, for he had no doubt that this was somehow the key to finding Ana.

The new line connected to the tip of the straight line, then another line began. An arrow? If so, it was pointed at the rocks at the base of the promontory. Had Ana found the tunnel leading from the catacombs?

"Ana!" he shouted as he raced down the path. The line stopped, and the stick fell to the ground.

"Leo!" Ana yelled. "I'm here!"

His heart surged with a mixture of relief and joy as he charged toward the rocks. He skirted a few boulders, then found the narrow opening in the rock wall of the promontory. A few feet in, an iron gate crossed the tunnel, and behind it, Ana was jumping up and down, grinning.

"Leo!" She reached through the bars.

"Ana!" He ran toward her, grabbing her arm with his gloved hand.

"I was so worried about you." She pulled her arm back to clasp his hand with her own.

"Careful."

"I'm fine." She interlaced her fingers with his. "See?"

He could touch her bare skin with his gloves? "Ana." He reached his left hand through the bars to touch her face for the first time. "By the Light, I was so afraid I'd lost you."

She nuzzled against his gloved hand, her eyes twinkling. "You, the mighty warrior, afraid?"

"Hell, yes. I was scared shitless." He glanced at the gate. "What's wrong? Is it locked?"

"Rusted shut. I was trying to escape so I could warn you. Father Rune left a trap—"

"We found it. Don't worry, everyone's fine."

She exhaled with relief. "Thank the goddess—I mean—"

"You can thank the goddesses. Hell, I'll thank them, too. I'll thank every deity I can think of, as long as you're safe."

Her smile wobbled as tears filled her eyes. "I-I wish I could hold you."

His breath caught. He wished he could do a lot more than holding. "I'll get you out." He grasped the bars and gave the gate a shake. It held fast.

She sighed. "I tried heating up the hinges with my torch, but it didn't work. It was so frustrating, because I wanted to stop you before you found the trap."

His brave, beautiful, and clever Ana. "Step back. Way back. I'm going to blast the gate open."

As she retreated down the tunnel, he removed the glove from his right hand. Lightning power built inside him, surging down his arm till sparks crackled around his fingertips.

He extended his hand toward the first hinge and let

loose a streak of energy. With a small explosion, the hinge shattered.

"Leo!" Nevis shouted behind him.

He glanced back to see Nevis, Jensen, Edmund, and his personal guard rushing toward him with their swords drawn. Ana's father was with them, and Brody trotted beside them, barking.

Leo lifted his hand, sparks flickering around his fingers. "I'm breaking open the gate. Keep your distance."

They stopped and peered around some boulders to watch him as he blasted away a second hinge, then the latch on the other side. Grasping two bars, he ripped the gate out and tossed it aside.

"Leo!" Ana ran toward him and threw her arms around his shoulders.

He caught her in his arms, angling his head away so his bare skin wouldn't touch hers. "Ana."

He could hold her forever, and it wouldn't be enough. Should he tell her he loved her? Not now, when they had an audience. Brody was still barking, and the other men were cheering.

Go away, he thought, tightening his hold on her and swaying from side to side. She was warm. And soft. *And mine*. His groin swelled.

You can't bed her, he reminded himself. *You can't*—he stiffened with a sudden realization. His right hand was still bare. It was pressed against her back between her shoulder blades. Perhaps her gown was protecting her, but her long braid of hair was brushing against his bare skin each time they swayed.

"My dear!" Lucas Vintello approached them with tears in his eyes.

"Father!" Ana released Leo and hugged the former duke.

"I was so afraid." Tears ran down her father's face.

"I'm fine. I—" She lowered her voice. "I'll tell you more later."

Leo figured she was referring to her ghostly spies, like the one who had drawn the arrow. But her secrets were not foremost in his mind right now. He kept thinking about her hair brushing against his bare skin. Did this mean he could touch her without killing her?

She hadn't reacted at all. How could that be when a touch from his bare hand would kill anyone else? He thought back to all the times he had touched her. The first time he'd grabbed her arm to pull her away from the curtain wall, he'd been wearing gloves and she'd had on a cloak and nightgown. Three layers of insulation, so she hadn't felt any pain. Later, in the tower room, he'd taken hold of her arm. His glove and her sleeve had made two layers of insulation. And when he'd pressed her bare hand to his cock, only his breeches had separated them. In her bedchamber, she'd hugged his back, her bare hands pressed against his thin shirt. She'd never felt a shock. And just now, he'd touched her bare skin with his gloved hand. That would have caused most people to lose consciousness.

But not Ana.

Even so, he would have never risked touching her with his bare hand. Yet he had touched her hair, and she was unharmed. Could he touch her skin? He stared at her as he tugged on his glove.

"Pirate, you're back!" Ana leaned over to give Brody a hug.

Jensen knelt on one knee and bowed his head. "Forgive me, my lady. I have failed you."

"Nonsense." She grabbed his arm to pull him to his feet. "I'm the one who sent you away." She turned toward Leo. "Please don't punish him. It was my fault I was captured."

Leo could only nod in silence, for his mind was still reeling. If he could touch Ana, he could make love to her.

"Was it Father Rune?" Nevis asked.

"Yes." Ana nodded. "He left the trap so he could escape before Leo returned. Oh, I should warn you. He said if you survived his trap and go after him, he'll have another trap ready for you."

"Bastard," Nevis muttered.

"We'll catch him," Edmund boasted, then glanced at Leo. "Right, my lord?"

Leo nodded as he flexed his gloved hands. "Nevis, take your men and half of my personal guard. Edmund can go, too, if he likes. And Brody, if you're up to it."

The dog woofed.

Nevis's eyes narrowed. "Aren't you coming?"

Leo shifted his weight. He couldn't admit in front of everyone that he was more desperate to bed his wife than catch an assassin. "I want to make sure Ana and her father are safe before I leave. Send Edmund back once you find the priest's trail, and I'll join you then."

"Aye, my lord." Nevis motioned to Leo's personal guard. "Let's go!" They ran toward the path leading to the fortress with Brody chasing after them.

"Give Brody some food before you leave!" Leo yelled after them. The dog shifter had to be exhausted, but perhaps he could shift into human form for an hour or so and ride a horse.

"Come, my dear." The former duke wrapped an arm around Ana's shoulders and led her up the path, with Jensen following close behind. "You've had a frightful day."

She shuddered. "I've seen more bones, spiders, and rats than I ever cared to. All I want to do now is soak in a hot tub."

Her father nodded. "You should stay in your room and rest. I'll have some food brought up for you."

Leo followed behind them, making his plans. If all went well, his marriage would be consummated tonight.

Thirty minutes later, Leo had bathed, shaved, and dressed in clean clothes in the communal bathhouse. On the way across the courtyard, he slipped on his gloves. His power was still high, so he'd have to be careful. Dammit, if he hurt Ana, he'd never forgive himself.

Outside Ana's bedchamber, he found Jensen standing guard. "No disturbances for the rest of the night."

"Yes, my lord." Jensen gave him a sheepish look. "I won't fail you again."

"I believe you." Leo let himself in the room and bolted the door. The room was empty, but the sound of splashing and female voices came from the dressing room. She was probably still bathing. A basket of food had been left on the table in front of the hearth, along with a bottle of wine and two goblets.

Leo started a fire, using his lightning power, then opened the bottle and filled the goblets. His gaze kept drifting toward the bed as his thoughts kept returning to the way her hair had brushed against his bare hand. Surely that meant he could touch her. If he could touch her, he could kiss her. He could make love to her.

His groin swelled. What was taking her so long? Was this one of her infamous long baths?

He pulled off his boots and draped his jacket across the back of a chair. The splashing noises continued. Dammit, he couldn't wait any longer.

He cracked open the door to the dressing room. The maid was pouring a bucket of water over Ana's head, and suds were streaming down her hair and bare back.

When he walked in, the maid yelped and dropped the bucket with a noisy clatter. "My lord." She quickly curtsied.

With a gasp, Ana sank deeper into the tub of sudsy water.

He skirted the tub, taking in Ana's stunned look and attempt to cover her breasts with her hands. Her long hair floated around her shoulders, and her bare knees stuck out above the water.

He was so tempted to touch her, but he knew from experience that his lightning power was somehow amplified in water. Instead, he rested his gloved hands on the side edges of the tub as he leaned forward.

Ana's eyes widened as she pressed back against the tub. Was she afraid of him? He didn't want her fear. He wanted her to ache for him as much as he ached for her.

"Was there something you needed? Some clothing?" She glanced toward the shelf where his clean clothes were stacked.

He let his gaze wander down her body, half hidden in the sudsy water. A slim waist that flared into rounded hips. Soft white thighs pressed together but not completely hiding the triangle of dark hair. His groin swelled thicker.

When his gaze returned to her face he didn't hide the hunger he was feeling. "I need my wife."

Her mouth parted with a quick breath that made her breasts rise. And his cock grow harder.

Slowly he straightened and handed a towel to Gabriella. "Help her out of the tub. No need to dress her. Then you are dismissed for the night."

"Yes, my lord." The maid took the towel and gave Ana a worried look.

Leo strode back into the bedchamber and paced in front of the fire. Could he touch her? Soon he would know.

He heard a door closing, the maid's door. Then the dressing room door opened and Ana appeared in the doorway, her long hair loose and wet about her shoulders, her hands fisted around the towel to keep it wrapped around her. She hesitated, biting her lip.

"Come in." He cleared his throat, for his voice had sounded harsh.

She stepped closer. "You look like you took a bath, too. Would you like something to eat?"

"Later." He reached out a gloved hand to touch a strand of her wet hair. She looked wary, but not in pain. He touched her bare shoulder. "You're all right?"

"Yes." She bit her lip. "I should finish dressing."

"No." He removed his gloves.

She stiffened, her eyes widening. "Leo, what are you doing?"

"Trust me." He reached a hand forward, and she turned her head, squeezing her eyes shut as if she was expecting a shock. By the Light, he hoped she wasn't right.

His fingers touched her hair. She remained still, her eyes tightly shut. She hadn't run away or stopped him. Even though she was clearly afraid, she'd let him touch her. Hell, she'd just risked death for him.

A surge of emotion nearly bowled him over. "Ana, I love you."

With a gasp, her eyes flew open.

"Look." His fingers glided down her hair. "I'm not hurting you, am I?"

"No." She watched his hand and gasped again when he touched her forearm. Slowly he grazed his fingers up her arm to her shoulder.

"Leo." Her skin prickled with goose bumps.

"I can touch you." His groin grew harder as his fingers skimmed along her collarbone. "I can kiss you."

He let his fingertips descend to the edge of the towel that was wrapped around her, that she still held in place with a clenched fist between her breasts.

"Say yes." He curled his fingers around the edge of the towel.

Her breasts pushed against his hand as her breathing grew more labored.

"Say yes."

Her gaze met his, her eyes glittering with emotion. He wasn't sure if it was fear, worry, or desire, but as long as she said yes—

"Yes."

With a victorious growl, he ripped the towel off her and pulled her into his arms.

Chapter Thirty

❧

There was something hard in his breeches again. And it was growing, pressing against her lower belly, easy to feel since she was naked. Completely naked. Luciana buried her face in his shirt. Good goddesses, she'd never felt so exposed before.

Her mind reeled with a thousand thoughts. How was Leo able to touch her? How come he was fully dressed when she was fully naked? Did married couples actually do this sort of thing in daylight? What shocking thing was he planning to do next? Right now, his hands were skimming up and down her back—her bare back because she was totally naked!

Don't panic! She clutched his shirt with her fists. *You survived the catacombs and your worst fear. You can do this.* Thank the goddesses her mother had vanished with Tatiana before Leo had whisked off her towel. Apparently her mother had known what was coming next.

But I don't! Luciana had said yes, but she wasn't quite sure what she'd agreed to.

"Ana."

She stiffened. "Yes?"

"Relax. You're breathing as fast as a frightened rabbit.

There's nothing to worry about. We've already established that I can touch you without hurting you."

She ventured a glance up at him. "How can that be?"

"I don't know." He brushed her wet hair back from her face. "And right now, I don't care. I've wanted you since the minute I first saw you." He smiled, his green eyes twinkling with warmth. "I knew you would be beautiful. And you're softer than I ever imagined."

Heat invaded her cheeks. Maybe being naked wasn't so bad after all. It had probably been ages since the poor man had been able to touch anyone. She bit her lip. Were they able to touch because they were both Embraced? Or did it have something to do with her mother being struck by lightning? Had she somehow become immune to lightning?

"You're frowning." With his thumb, he stroked the skin between her eyebrows. "Why not be happy that we don't have to wait for a drought?"

"I was trying to figure out why—"

"No." He smoothed his fingers over her brow and down the curve of her face. "No more thinking. For the rest of the night, you should do nothing but feel."

"But I have a theory—" She stopped when he placed a finger on her lips.

"Feel as I make love to my wife."

She swallowed hard. Maybe she should tell him the truth now. Shouldn't he know who exactly his wife was? But what if he felt betrayed by her deception?

"You're frowning again."

She took a deep breath to prepare herself, but that caused her bare breasts to push against his chest in such a delicious manner that her thoughts scattered momentarily before she was able to focus once more. "There's something I should tell you."

"Later." He rubbed his thumb along her lips, and once

again she fell prey to an intriguing sensation. All her awareness centered on the tingling of her lips and a sudden, urgent desire to be kissed.

"For now, there are only a few words I want to hear." He pressed gently on her lower lip. "You can tell me faster, slower, harder, and—" He leaned closer till his mouth was only a breath away from hers.

Sweet goddesses, yes. Please kiss me.

He pressed his lips lightly against hers, then pulled back to look at her. "Softer."

Was that it? She needed more.

"Then there's my favorite—" He cradled her head with his hands. "—don't stop."

Her hands slipped up to his shoulders. "Don't stop."

He smiled, then leaned over to give her a slow, languid kiss, one that made her feel cherished and warm, as if she could gently melt into him. And the more she melted, the more she wanted to feel. There was the sweet pressure and nibbling he was doing to her lips, the strength of his broad shoulders beneath her hands, the softness of his hair as it curled around her fingers. Her breasts felt oddly full and heavy, and heat gathered between her legs, filling her with a need so demanding, she was sorely tempted to press against the hardness in his breeches.

At first thought, that didn't seem like a wise thing to do. But the more she fought the need, the more intense it became. Perhaps he wouldn't notice a tiny, little rub, just enough to ease the torment building inside her.

He noticed. With a growl, he thrust his tongue into her mouth.

Stunned, she reared back, breaking the kiss. "What are you—"

He planted his hands on her bare rump and pulled her hard against him.

She gasped. "Leo?"

"Let me in."

She blinked. "In? Where?"

"Here." He ground his hardness against her. "And here." He cupped a hand around the back of her head and kissed her once more.

If the first kiss had melted her, this one set her on fire. It was no gentle wooing of a lady, but a victor claiming possession. He demanded entrance. He invaded. His mouth devoured hers, and with each stroke of his tongue, he rocked her against the hard length in his breeches.

Moisture seeped from her womanly core, and a quivering, aching need escalated inside her till she blatantly squirmed against him.

A noise sounded deep in his throat. He broke the kiss, grabbed her around the waist, and set her on the nearby table.

"The food," she murmured as her hip brushed against the basket. He transferred the basket and corked bottle of wine to a nearby easy chair, his movement so fast, it blurred before her eyes.

"Here." He handed her one goblet and downed the second one.

She took a few sips of wine, then halted with the goblet halfway to her mouth when he yanked off his shirt. His shoulders were incredibly broad, the skin smooth except for one scar across his left shoulder. Dark-brown hair curled in the center of his chest, then made a line down to the swelling in his breeches.

"Done?" He took the goblet from her, noticed it was still half full, then with a crooked smile, he shoved her onto her back.

"Leo?" She gasped when he fondled a breast, then leaned over to draw her nipple into his mouth. Good goddesses, the things this man could do with his tongue.

"Now for a feast." He poured the rest of her wine over

her breasts, then down her ribs and belly, finishing the last drops between her legs. After tossing the goblet aside, he began with her breasts, licking and suckling till she was whimpering with pleasure.

"Leo." She dug her fingers into his soft hair, then rubbed her hands across the bare skin of his shoulders and back. When he dragged his tongue down the wine path to her belly, she squeezed her thighs together as the raw need in her womanly core intensified to nearly frantic levels.

She gasped when his fingers delved into the curls between her legs. Was he supposed to be touching her there?

"I want to see you." Before she could object, he lifted her legs and spread them wide.

"Leo!" Good goddesses, was he supposed to be looking at her?

"Beautiful." He hooked a foot around a chair leg and dragged it closer. Then he sat with her legs draped over his shoulders. "I think you'll taste like woman and sweet wine."

She blinked. Taste? Surely he wasn't supposed to taste her! "Leo, this can't be right—" She gasped when his fingers skimmed over her folds.

"You're so pink and soft. And wet. Ah, this is especially pretty." He tickled a spot that made her jolt. "Hang on." He grasped her thighs and leaned in.

She cried out when his mouth enveloped her. Holy goddesses, she didn't care if this wasn't right, she wanted more of it. He suckled gently, then teased her with his tongue.

"Faster," she breathed, and he complied. "Harder." The pleasure spiraled upward, taking her with it. "Don't stop!"

She screamed as she shattered. Delicious throbs racked her body, and she squeezed him with her thighs. Good goddesses, if this was making love, she'd want to do it every day.

Closing her eyes, she stretched. "That was lovely. Could we have a bite to eat afore going to sleep?"

"You want a taste of this?"

She opened her eyes, then gasped. "Oh, my . . . *what*?" He'd dropped his breeches, and an enormous . . . thing was pointing upward. Holy goddesses, it was the lightning rod!

"You'd better not have a taste right now. I'm about to explode."

"What?" Could he actually explode? She jolted when he parted her folds and inserted a finger inside her.

He gave her a lopsided grin. "It'll be a tight fit."

Huh? Surely he wasn't intending to put the lightning rod inside her? "Tha—that's not going to work."

"It will." He inserted a second finger. "Relax."

Who was he kidding?

"You're so beautiful." His fingers stroked her inside, while his other hand teased the sweet spot he'd suckled earlier. "Soft, wet, and swollen. Does it feel good?"

She whimpered.

"I want to make you scream again. Ah, do you hear that?" He waggled his fingers inside her. "The sound of more juice."

She moaned. The aching need was coming back stronger than ever.

He removed his fingers and licked them. Just the sight of that made more moisture seep from her.

"Leo . . ."

"Yes?" He wrapped her legs around his waist.

"Don't stop."

A corner of his mouth curled up. "My favorite words." He nuzzled his cock against her and pushed slowly in.

She pressed her heels against his back, her muscles tensing as he eased inside. When a twinge of pain made her cry out, he stopped.

"By the Light." He closed his eyes briefly as he breathed heavily. His grip on her hips tightened.

"Is something wrong?"

He opened his eyes. "You're a virgin."

She huffed. "Did ye think I wouldn't—" Her breath caught. Oh, dear goddesses, no. Was he taking this as proof that she wasn't Tatiana? She hadn't realized a man could detect something like virginity. Would he reject her now for her deception?

He leaned over her, his gaze burning into hers. "There is only one thing I need to know. And I will have the truth, understand?"

Tears welled in her eyes as she nodded.

"Do you want me as your husband?"

Relief rocked through her, for that was so easy to answer. "Yes. Yes, I do."

"Good." He grasped her hips and plunged inside her. She cried out.

"It'll be all right." He kissed her cheek as her tears overflowed. "It won't hurt again."

She shook her head. "It's not just the pain. It's . . . regret. I should have told you before."

"No regrets." He held her face with his hands and wiped her tears with his thumbs. "Don't you see? You're the only one I can touch. We're supposed to be together."

She touched his hair as another tear escaped. *Red and black. And the two will become one.* Even the Telling Stones had said they were destined for each other. "I love ye so much, Leo."

"I love you, too." He slowly pulled out, then pushed back in. "Are you all right?"

"Yes." She clutched his shoulders as he slid out and in once more. The pain was quickly subsiding, and a wonderful feeling of friction and fullness was taking its place. "Faster."

He quickened his pace, and soon she was caught in a whirlwind of sensation. Hot and glorious.

"Don't stop!" Her fingers dug into his back. She lifted her hips to meet each thrust. She needed him deeper. Hotter. He was part of her now, emblazoned on her heart, and she was burning from the inside out.

With a shout, he pumped into her. She moaned, so close to exploding with him. He reached between her legs, pressing against her special spot, then giving it a tug.

She cried out as all her senses burst. He pulled her into his arms, holding her tight as the throbbing slowly subsided.

"Holy Light, Ana." He rubbed her back. "I'll never get enough of you."

She wrapped her arms around his neck. "I didn't know it could be like that. But is it normally done on a table?"

With a grin, he released her. "Stay put." He strode into the dressing room.

As if she had the energy to move. Besides, the view of his buttocks as he walked away was quite mesmerizing.

He returned, carrying a damp washcloth in his hand.

"I—" She blinked. "What happened to your lightning rod?"

He snorted. "It's finally at peace. After seven days of blue balls."

She tilted her head, studying his male part. It seemed more pink than blue. Still rather long, but much friendlier looking.

"I appreciate your sudden fascination with my cock, but if you keep staring, I'll be wanting more."

She gave him an incredulous look. "There's more?"

"Yes, but you'll be too sore for some things." He stepped closer. "Spread your legs."

She did a little, but he pushed them wider apart and

wiped her thighs with the washcloth. "What are you doing?"

"Cleaning off the blood. Your virgin blood."

She swallowed hard. "I-I can explain."

"I've been waiting for the truth." He folded the washcloth and pressed a clean side against her vagina.

She sucked in a breath at the coolness against her heated skin.

"I've been waiting for you to trust me." He rubbed ever so slowly and gently. "*Luciana*."

Chapter Thirty-one

Leo watched as one emotion after another flitted across her face—shock, fear, worry, shame, regret. How had she ever hoped to succeed with this deception when her face gave everything away?

Alarm skittered through his chest. It had taken him less than a week to figure out she was not Lady Tatiana. If her lies were exposed at the royal court, the king would have the perfect excuse for executing her. "I need to know everything, so I can protect you."

She winced. "Aren't you angry with me?"

"Well, let me think. I have a brave, beautiful, formerly virginal wife who can somehow miraculously touch me and make love to me, but she's not very good at lying." His mouth twitched as he continued to stroke her with the washcloth. "Do you think I should be angry?"

"I—" She moaned. "I can't think at all when you do that."

His hand stilled. "Tell me everything, so I can figure out what to do with you."

She blinked. "What does that mean?"

"It means I'm not sure what to do. I'd like to tease you until you climax again, but should I use my hands or my mouth?" He heaved a sigh. "Tough decision."

Her mouth fell open.

His gaze shifted to her mouth. "Or maybe I should enjoy the sweetness of your lips."

"You mean more kissing?"

"Not exactly." He glanced down at his cock, then back to her mouth.

She looked down, then back up, her eyes widening. "Ar—are you serious?"

He nodded.

She glanced down once again. Her head tilted as she bit her lip.

"Luciana?"

"Yes."

"So you admit that's your true name?"

"Oh." She sat up. "Shame on you. I was distracted by your . . ."

"Cock." He rubbed the washcloth against her clitoris. "You're easily distracted."

Her eyes glazed over. "Is this an interrogation technique?"

He smiled. "Maybe."

"Mmm. Then I'll make a full confession." She closed her eyes briefly. "I asked you to call me Ana, so it would feel like you were marrying me instead of my sister."

"Then you really wanted to marry me."

"Yes, I did." She reached out to touch his cock.

His breath hissed. "Luciana."

"Is this allowed?"

"Hell, yes."

"Ah." Her hand circled him. "It's softer than I thought it would be."

"Not for long." He gritted his teeth as she gently squeezed.

"How do you know my name?"

"I read the letter you hid in the—" He stiffened. By the

Light, she'd turned the tables on him and was now inter-
rogating him. With a snort, he took her hand off his cock.
"You're a clever one."

Her eyes twinkled with humor. "We'll have very clever
children."

"True. Will you tell me more while we eat?" When she
nodded, he lifted her off the table and gave her his dis-
carded shirt to wear. While she put it on, he slipped his
breeches back on.

She talked, confirming most of his suspicions, as they
unloaded the basket of food. She and Lady Tatiana were
indeed twins. Their mother had died after giving birth to
them on a night when the moons embraced. They both
shared the gift of seeing the dead.

"Where is your sister now?" he asked as he refilled their
goblets with wine.

With a sigh, Luciana sat at the table. "She passed away
after she was poisoned. Father was bringing her to the convent on the Isle of Moon, since he knew from his correspondence with Mother Ginessa that we had a gifted healer
there."

Leo drew a chair close to her and sat. "Didn't your
father correspond with you?"

She shook her head. "I was raised as an orphan for nineteen years. I never knew I had a father or sister until they
arrived."

"I'm sorry." He set a piece of cold roast chicken on her
plate. "It must have been lonely for you."

"No, not at all. I was raised with four other girls who
became my sisters."

"The ones you correspond with using seals?" He bit into
a slice of chicken.

Her eyes widened. "You know about that?"

He nodded as he chewed and motioned to the easy chair
where she'd hidden the letter.

She sighed. "I miss them so much. We were all raised as orphans, but now I wonder if they actually have family like me."

He drank some wine. "So you agreed to risk your life for your father when you had just met him?"

She nodded and took a bite of cheese. "He tried to talk me out of it. He'd already lost Tatiana, so he didn't want to lose me. But how could I send him away, knowing he would be executed if he failed to follow the king's order?"

"You're incredibly brave." He refilled his goblet. "I'm sorry you lost your sister before you were able to meet her."

Luciana smiled. "Actually, we've become good friends. Her spirit followed me here. She's the one who drew the arrow in the sand for you to see."

"Lady Tatiana is one of your spies?"

"Yes. I see her often." She ate some chicken.

He cast a wary glance around the room. "She's not here now, is she?" When Luciana shook her head, he drank some wine in relief.

"She was here, but she left with my mother."

He choked. "Your mother was here?"

Luciana grinned. "They disappeared before you ripped the towel off me."

"Oh." He cleared his throat. "Thank the Light."

"Mother helped me escape the catacombs. And Christopher told me about the poisoned soup. Oh, that reminds me, I need to make sure Rowena isn't harmed."

"And who are Christopher and Rowena?" he asked.

After she explained, he promised to take care of the matter. Then she told him about her theory to explain why they could touch.

"The scorch mark in the tower is from a lightning strike?" he asked.

"Yes. And since I survived it before I was born, I believe I must be immune."

He squeezed her hand. "It's been years since I was able to touch anyone."

She smiled. "I've told you everything. Have you decided on my punishment now?"

"Ah. How should I bring about your next climax?"

"Is that what you call it?"

"Yes, climax, orgasm, those blissful few minutes when you scream and throb and look so wild and beautiful that all I want to do is make love to you all over again."

Her smile widened. "Well, as a dutiful wife, I will gladly encourage your endeavors."

"As a dutiful husband, I will gladly make you scream."

She ran her fingers through his hair. "I should warn you. Women who have been raised on the Isle of Moon are strong and independent. We consider ourselves equal to men in every way."

His brows lifted. "Does that mean you're planning to boss me around?"

She skimmed her hand down his neck to his bare chest. "It means I plan to do to you whatever you do to me."

His mouth ran dry. "I can live with that."

"How very open-minded of you."

With a grin, he stood. "You're a challenge. I like that." He swooped her up in his arms. "So do you have a preference? Hand? Or mouth?"

Her cheeks blushed a pretty pink. "I like them both."

Still grinning, he carried her to the bed. "Then you shall have both." He dropped her on the coverlet. "The night has only begun."

The following week was, in Leo's opinion, the best week of his life. He spent the days touring the duchy with his new father-in-law, who enjoyed having a young man to mentor. Whereas General Harden had taught Leo everything he knew about war and self-defense, Lucas Vintello taught him how to govern with wisdom.

In the evenings, he returned to Vindemar, where he spent half the night making love to Luciana. After years of sensory starvation, he couldn't get enough of touching her. When they ate, he sat close enough to rub his leg against hers. When they fell asleep, he continued to hold her. In private, he called her Luciana, for it made her smile, and as besotted as he was, he loved making her smile.

The news soon spread that the new duke was sharing his duchess's bed, and somehow, she had miraculously survived it. The people of Vindemar swelled with pride, for it was their lady who had tamed the Beast of Benwick. And since it was clear that the Beast was cherished by both his wife and the former duke, the people began to accept him, too. For the first time in Leo's life, the common folk greeted him with smiles instead of fearful cringing.

He knew, however, that this idyllic time could not last. Soon, he would have to take Luciana and her father to court, and during that trip the king would probably try to kill them.

At the end of the week, he received news from General Harden. The Eberoni army had successfully pushed the elfin army back. Unfortunately, news had come down from the north that the Norveshki dragons were raiding once again. So the general had left several troops behind to guard the border with Woodwyn, and was now taking the rest of the army north. Leo sent the envoy back to the general with a letter expressing his thanks and approval.

The next day, Nevis returned with his troop of soldiers and an exhausted Brody. Father Rune had managed to elude them in the marshlands along the Ron River.

Leo suspected the priest was waiting for him to take Luciana and her father to court in Ebton. He'd sent an envoy to the king after his wedding, so he was expecting a reply soon.

The king's envoy arrived two days later. Leo was ordered to bring his wife to court immediately. There was no mention of her father, so apparently, the former duke was no longer of interest. Leo had successfully made himself the target.

Lucas Vintello suggested they travel by ship. That way they could avoid any traps set by Father Rune on the land route. But when Leo accompanied his father-in-law to the nearby port to book a ship, they were met by some disturbing news. The infamous Tourinian pirate, Rupert, was terrorizing the villages along the coast of Eberon. No ship could travel to the Ebe River without being seized and boarded.

Back at Vindemar, Leo ordered Nevis to take his troop and Leo's personal guard to protect the villages along the western coast.

"Bad idea," Nevis protested. "You need us to guard you on your journey to court."

"I'll have Brody, Jensen, and Edmund. And I'll keep one of my personal guard—"

"Not enough!" Nevis growled. "Father Rune is still out there, and the king may have hired even more assassins. It's my job to protect you."

"And it's my job to protect the people of Eberon. Go to the coast and try to capture that pirate. Meanwhile, I think we'll draw less attention to ourselves as a small group. We'll pack light, dress plainly, and move quickly. If we stay off the main roads and avoid villages and inns, no one will even know where we are."

Nevis gave him a skeptical look.

"And don't forget that my power is still high. I'm very difficult to kill."

"Difficult to win an argument with," Nevis grumbled.

"You can accompany us as far as the Ron River," Leo conceded. "Then you will leave for the coast, and we'll head north to Ebton."

Five days later, they parted at the ferry crossing for the Ron River. The journey through the Duchy of Vindalyn had been smooth since Leo was now the duke and possessed castles along the way for spending the night.

There'd been one awkward moment when they'd left the fortress of Vindemar. After hugging her father good-bye, Luciana had been greeted by the stable master, who had readied her favorite horse for the trip. One look at his wife's face, and Leo had suspected Luciana didn't know how to ride.

"Lady Tatiana will ride with me for now," Leo had announced. "We will bring her horse with us, so she can ride it later if she so desires."

She'd given him a relieved smile as he'd pulled her up in front of him.

"Thank you," she whispered.

He wrapped an arm around her waist and pulled her tight against his chest. Her sweet bottom nestled against his groin. "My pleasure."

When Vindemar was out of sight, he whispered in her ear, "You never learned how to ride?"

She shook her head.

"You'll be expected to know how at court." After giving her instructions for a while, she tried riding her horse slowly beside him.

She improved each day, and each night he massaged her sore legs and buttocks, as well as other places that made her writhe with pleasure. Then he teased her that she also needed to learn how to ride her husband with great skill.

Leo smiled to himself. She was a fast learner.

After crossing the Ron River, they moved quickly through

the countryside, staying off the main roads. Jensen traveled in front with Brody, who remained in dog form during the day. He remembered Father Rune's scent from the catacombs, so he preferred to remain as a dog so he could detect if the priest was nearby.

Leo rode beside Luciana, the two of them dressed simply, though he had a sword under his cloak and numerous daggers hidden in his clothes and boots. Edmund remained close by, and behind them, his personal guard Stanley brought up the rear.

Leo estimated it would take four more days to reach Ebton. The first day went smoothly, but on the second day it began raining just after noon. He eyed the sky carefully. There was no sign of lightning. This was nothing more than a summer shower, but still, they were soon drenched and miserable.

Jensen stopped at a farm to ask if he and his friends could have some food and take shelter in the barn for a few silver coins. The elderly couple was thrilled to earn some money with a barn they no longer used and happily sold him two loaves of bread, a wheel of cheese, a roasted chicken, and five bottles of ale.

Leo and his companions settled in the barn, taking care of the horses first. Edmund took the first tour of guard duty, standing outside under the eaves while the rain continued to pour.

Leo took his and Luciana's saddlebag up to the loft where she was waiting in her soaked gown. They changed into dry clothes, then joined the others below to eat.

At sunset the rain finally stopped, and Leo used his lightning power to light an oil lantern so they could see inside the barn. Stanley took his turn as guard.

Leo was hugging his wife on a makeshift bed of hay in the loft when she suddenly sat up with a gasp.

"What's wrong?" He shivered as frigid air surrounded them.

"Tatiana," she whispered. "What are you doing here?"

"Your sister's here?" Leo asked.

Luciana nodded. "She wants to see the court at Ebton. And she's peeved that I didn't pack any of her beautiful gowns."

"We needed to travel light. I'll have some new gowns made for—" He stopped when Luciana held up a hand to hush him.

She frowned as she listened to her sister, then she gave him a worried look. "She says Stanley ventured off into the woods nearby, and he's talking to some strangers. It's dark and they were wearing hooded cloaks, so she couldn't see their faces, but Stanley called one of them Father."

Leo stiffened. Father Rune? But that would mean Stanley was betraying him. "That can't be right. Stanley has been with me for four years. He wouldn't—" Leo fisted his gloved hands. *Dammit.* He knew from experience that many men would do anything for the right price. "Did your sister see how many?"

Luciana listened for a while, then said, "She didn't count them, but she believes there are about a dozen."

Leo glanced at the blank space where his wife was staring and bowed his head. "Thank you, my lady." He handed one of his daggers to Luciana. "Remain here until it's safe."

She nodded. "Be careful."

He descended the ladder and gathered Edmund, Jensen, and Brody to explain the situation.

Edmund's mouth fell open. "Stanley? I don't believe it."

"I don't want to, either," Leo admitted. "Even so, we must be ready. Saddle the horses. Gather your weapons."

Brody shimmered, then shifted into human form.

Jensen jumped back. "What the hell?"

Up in the loft, Luciana gasped. "Pirate?"

Leo moved in front of the naked Brody to block his wife's view. "Nothing to see here." He glanced back at Brody. "Now you decide to shift?"

"I can't wield a sword without hands," Brody grumbled. "Edmund, can you hand me my breeches?"

"Right." Edmund rummaged through his saddlebags and tossed Brody's breeches to him.

"What the hell?" Jensen repeated, still staring. "How come I didn't know about this?"

"Because you were too busy snoring." Brody fastened his breeches. "I've been shifting every night during my guard duty, but you always sleep through it."

Leo glanced up at the loft where Luciana still looked stunned. "Throw down the saddlebags."

She did. "I've never heard of people who can become animals."

"Brody is Embraced like us," Leo explained as he collected their saddlebags. "His gift is the ability to shift into a dog." Or a seal, but he saw no reason to divulge all of Brody's secrets.

Luciana gave the dog shifter a wary look. "But I've kissed him and rubbed his ears."

Brody bowed. "Much appreciated, my lady."

Leo groaned inwardly. At least she hadn't rubbed his belly. "Jensen, snap to. We need to saddle the horses."

"Aye, Your Grace." Jensen went to work, and quickly they had all the horses packed and ready to go.

Suddenly a barrage of fire arrows shot through a window at the back of the barn and landed in a pile of hay. As the flames took hold, Edmund attempted to smother them with an old blanket. The horses reared, sensing danger, but Jensen and Brody caught their reins to settle them down.

Luciana ran to the ladder. "We'd better go!"

"You should remain hidden for now," Leo warned her. "The assassins will be waiting outside for us."

Another barrage of fire arrows zipped through the back window, forcing Edmund to retreat. The fire began to spread.

Jensen ran to the front door and slid the bolt. He pushed, but the door wouldn't budge. "It's blocked!"

Edmund dashed around the flames to the back door. "This one is blocked, too!"

Luciana gasped. "We're trapped in here?" Her eyes widened with terror as she watched the growing fire.

"Not for long," Leo called up to her. He removed his gloves and wedged them under his belt. Sparks flickered around his hands. "This will be over soon. Men, prepare for battle."

Jensen and Edmund mounted their horses, while Brody took Luciana's. All three men drew their swords.

Leo extended his hands toward the front doors. Two bolts of lightning shot out and blasted the doors open. He drew his sword and ran. "Charge!"

Chapter Thirty-two

❦

Luciana gasped at Leo's display of power. After sharing his bed for over two weeks, she'd forgotten how dangerous he could be. With his sword in his right hand, and his left shooting out lightning, he'd dashed through the doors so quickly, he'd become a blur before her eyes.

Jensen, Edmund, and Brody charged after him on horseback.

Tatiana whooped with glee. "This is so exciting!"

Luciana gave her an incredulous look. "Exciting? They could be killed!" She motioned to the growing fire. "And we could burn to death!"

Tatiana scoffed. "Speak for yourself."

With a growing sense of panic, Luciana wondered what to do. She couldn't stay inside a burning barn, but the only exit led straight into a battle. Already she could hear the sound of swords clashing and the screams of wounded men. *Please, Luna and Lessa, keep Leo and my friends safe.*

"Pardon me for having a bit of fun," Tatiana grumbled. "It doesn't happen that often since I'm *dead*."

Down below, Leo's horse whinnied and tugged at the reins that tied him to a post. Poor thing, he was as afraid as she was. Luciana wedged her dagger under her belt and started down the ladder.

"Where are you going?" Tatiana floated beside her. "I swear you don't have any time for me anymore. Every time I try to visit, you're romping about naked with the—"

"What?" Luciana halted halfway down the ladder.

"Beast," Tatiana finished. "Don't look at me like that. I don't stay to watch." She shuddered.

"Thank you for that," Luciana muttered as she resumed her descent.

"So does his touch not hurt you at all? Or does all that power make him sizzling hot in bed?"

"I have other concerns right now." Luciana glanced at the fire as she reached the ground. The back wall of the barn was now completely ablaze, and smoke was filling the air. She crooked her arm against her nose and mouth as she approached Leo's horse.

"I'll take that as a yes." Tatiana grinned. "And you thought you were so well educated. I bet the Beast has been giving you a few lessons!"

Luciana patted Fearless, murmuring words of comfort, and he nudged her shoulder. "Don't worry. I'll get us out of here."

"So tell me," Tatiana continued. "Is the Beast an animal?"

Luciana gave her a wry look. "He's all man. Apparently, the animal is Brody."

Tatiana's eyes widened. "Oh, I know! Can you believe it? I was so shocked!"

"Me, too." Luciana took Fearless's reins to lead him, but he practically dragged her through the opening. The fresh air was glorious, but she wasn't sure how safe it was. Halfway hidden behind Fearless, she peered out.

A number of cloaked men lay dead on the ground. A few had attempted to run away, but Jensen, Brody, and

Edmund were chasing them down. Leo, with his gloves back on, was tying a bruised and bleeding Stanley to a tree.

"The priest is getting away!" Edmund pointed in the distance at a robed man on horseback.

Leo whistled and Fearless trotted over to him. "Ana, come on!" He mounted as she ran toward him, then he hauled her up in front.

"Hold on!" he shouted, and she gripped the saddle horn. He pulled her tightly against him and spurred his horse into a fast gallop.

Father Rune was racing across a meadow, illuminated by the burning barn and the twin moons overhead. Hooves pounded as Leo, Luciana, and their three male companions charged after him.

"Wheee!" Tatiana flew alongside them.

The priest whipped into an old forest, his horse weaving among the trees.

They followed him in, but soon it grew too dark to see him well.

"I think he's headed for the South Fork of the Ebe River," Leo said. "Brody, can you smell him?"

"Aye." Brody took the lead, riding Luciana's horse.

After a few minutes, there was a wide clearing where the ground dipped into a grassy ditch and the twin moons were able to give them some light.

"The South Fork used to flow through this channel," Leo said softly.

"There he is." Luciana pointed at the priest, who was urging his horse up the far side of the ditch. "He's about to enter the woods again."

"I see him." Leo removed a glove and extended a hand.

The priest glanced back, and when the lightning bolt shot out, he pulled his horse sharply to the side. The bolt struck an old oak tree next to them, causing a thick branch to plummet to the ground. The horse reared, dumping Father Rune on the ground before galloping away.

Leo urged his horse down into the ditch. Luciana could see the frightened look on the priest's face as he scrambled to his feet.

"Surrender," Leo called out.

Father Rune ran into the woods.

"Hold on." Leo held Luciana tight as Fearless crossed the ditch, then leaped over the branch to chase after the priest.

Soon they reached the South Fork, and Leo reined his horse to a stop. The other men halted beside them.

The twin moons shone down, casting silver sparkles on the slow-moving river. Father Rune was already halfway across, the water up to his chest.

Leo dismounted. "Everyone, stay back." He strode to the riverbank. "This is your last chance. Surrender!"

The priest turned to give him a disdainful look. "They should have killed you as a child. You're a monster!"

"Then prepare for a monstrous death." Leo leaned over and put his bare hand into the water. Dead fish popped to the surface close to the shore, then farther and farther into the river.

Tatiana floated along the riverbank. "Oh, a fish fry!"

With a terrified look, the priest desperately scrambled for the other shore, but soon the wave of energy caught him. He flailed about, screaming, then sank into the water. His body floated back to the surface, facedown, then slowly moved downstream with the current.

With a sigh, Leo put his glove back on, then trudged back to his horse.

As Luciana watched him, tears stung her eyes. "You're not a monster."

He hefted himself into the saddle behind her and held her tight. "Have I told you recently that I love you?"

"I knew it!" Tatiana grinned at Luciana. "He's sizzling hot!"

Back at the barn, Leo discovered that Stanley had managed to escape, since the elderly farm couple had untied
him after he'd convinced them he was one of the good
guys. The burning barn had caused them to rush from
their home, but fortunately the rain that afternoon had
drenched the land enough that the fire had fizzled out.
Their distress immediately disappeared when Leo gave
them a gold coin.

"I am the Duke of Vindalyn," Leo introduced himself,
not mentioning he was the Lord Protector, since most
country folk feared the Beast of Benwick. "And this is my
wife."

After that, the farmer and his wife insisted they spend
the rest of the night in their home. Leo was glad Luciana
had a warm pallet next to the fire to sleep on, but he regretted he couldn't make love to her in the small one-room
house.

The next morning, they set out for Benwick Castle,
where Leo's cousin Tedric had lived since being banished
from court five years earlier. Luciana was riding her horse
again, for Brody was back in dog form.

"Remember the South Fork from last night?" Leo asked
his wife. "Benwick Castle is close to where the South Fork
joins the Ebe River. From there, we'll follow the Ebe River
west to Ebton."

"Will we be safe with your cousin?" she asked.

Leo nodded. "Tedric and I have always gotten along.
He's nothing like his father, the king."

"How so?"

Leo sighed, recalling the last time he'd seen his cousin.
Tedric had spent the entire time encamped in his library,
barely taking time to eat. "He doesn't have a mean bone

in his body. He has a kind heart and an unswerving sense of justice."

"I heard that as a child, he was bullied and beaten by his father," Edmund said as he rode behind them.

"True," Leo agreed. "That's why Tedric took refuge in books. He can seem a bit distant at times, but that's because his mind is always thinking about whatever books he's currently reading. He has an enormous library."

Luciana smiled. "I like him already."

Leo nodded. "He's the most educated man I know. Someday he'll be a wise king."

"But not a strong one," Edmund muttered. "I heard he can barely lift a sword."

Leo gave his squire a pointed look. "He'll have us to guard the borders and go to battle for him."

Edmund snorted. "We do all the work."

"We have fun, too." Leo winked at Luciana.

She grinned back. "Is your cousin married?"

Leo winced. "He was, but you probably shouldn't mention it."

Her smile faded. "Why? What happened?"

"She ran off with a servant!" Edmund piped in. "And then they both drowned in the Ebe River!"

Luciana gasped. "How awful."

"Yes." Leo shot his squire a wry look. "Some people don't know when to shut their mouths."

Shortly before sunset, they arrived at Benwick Castle. It had been three years since Leo had last visited, and he noticed how the oldest tower appeared to be crumbling. A quick glance around assured him that the rest of the castle was in good shape. The moat looked recently dredged and clean enough that a few ducks were swimming happily about. A few guards along the curtain wall were watching him closely.

He drew his party to a halt in front of the drawbridge, and a guard yelled through the portcullis for them to identify themselves.

"Leofric of Benwick, Lord Protector of the Realm," Leo called back. "I wish to see my cousin."

The guard scurried off, and soon the portcullis was heaved up.

Leo and his party crossed the drawbridge, passed through the gatehouse, and came to a stop in the courtyard. He glanced around as he dismounted and helped Luciana from her horse. There was the usual bustle of activity. Servants rushed about, making chickens squawk when they got in the way. Some stonemasons were halfway finished sealing up the entrance to the old tower.

"Leofric!" Tedric called from the top of the steps leading to the Great Hall. "Good to see you again."

"And you." Leo was a bit surprised when his cousin used his full name, but then Tedric tended to be overly formal at times. He looked much the same as before, with the red hair and green eyes that all men of the Benwick line possessed.

Leo took Luciana's hand and led her forward. "I'd like to introduce my wife, Ana, the Duchess of Vindalyn."

"Welcome, Your Grace." Tedric gave her a quick look, then his gaze focused on their clasped hands.

Luciana curtsied. "Your Highness."

"Can we beg a room for the night, cousin?" Leo asked. "We're on our way to Ebton. The king has requested our presence at court."

Tedric's mouth thinned. "Has His Royal Majesty tried to kill you yet?"

Leo blinked. Tedric had never been this blunt before. "The latest attempt was yesterday. I'm sure my wife would appreciate a hot bath and warm bed—"

"Of course." Tedric motioned for a servant to approach.

"Please take Her Grace to the blue room and prepare a bath for her."

Leo gave her a peck on the cheek. "I'll see you soon."

She smiled at him, then gave Tedric a nod as she followed the servant up the stairs. "Thank you, Your Highness."

Tedric joined Leo at the foot of the stairs and whispered, "So she's the heiress of Vindalyn?"

"Yes."

"And you're able to touch her?" When Leo nodded, his cousin muttered, "Lucky bastard."

With a smile, Leo motioned toward the old tower. "Why are you not repairing it? If it crumbles any more, it could affect the integrity of your curtain wall."

Tedric snorted. "Spoken like a warrior. We're in the middle of Eberon. Who's going to attack us? Besides, I don't have the money . . ." His face grew harsh. "Yet."

Leo gave his cousin a closer look. Had five years of banishment soured his disposition?

Tedric suddenly smiled like he used to. "Come, cousin, let's have a drink and catch up on news."

Leo followed him into the Great Hall, then through a door on the left to his library.

"Whiskey?" Tedric asked as he filled two goblets.

Leo paused before saying, "Sure." The last time he'd visited his cousin, Tedric had imbibed only watered-down wine, claiming that anything stronger interfered with his studies.

Leo accepted a goblet and strolled along a wall lined with bookshelves. "I've always admired your library."

"Thank you." Tedric settled into the chair behind his desk. "Come, have a seat."

As Leo turned back toward the desk, he suspected that his cousin didn't want him wandering about. But it was already too late. Leo had spotted the layer of dust coating the books. What would have caused his cousin to eschew his favorite pastime?

"I didn't realize you had married," Tedric began.

Leo sat across from him. "King's orders, though I'm delighted with the result."

"No doubt. She's a beauty." Tedric frowned. "So my father has even more reason to kill you now. He can finally snatch up the Duchy of Vindalyn."

"I'm sure that's his plan."

Tedric took a sip of whiskey. "I'm surprised you're traveling with such a small party."

"I thought it best not to draw any attention to ourselves."

Tedric snorted. "Once my father decides to kill you, nothing deters him. You should have brought your army with you."

Leo shrugged. "They're busy. There was a battle with an elfin army last week, and now they're fighting the Norveshki."

Tedric took another sip. "And who is leading the army in your absence?"

"General Harden."

"A friend of yours?"

"Yes. He's like a father to me." Leo wondered where this was going. Tedric had never shown any interest in the military before.

"So you have the loyalty of the army, but the king wants you dead." Tedric set his goblet down with a clunk. "The solution seems rather obvious, don't you think?"

Leo arched a brow. "That . . . solution seems rather drastic. Not to mention traitorous."

Tedric scoffed. "Are you seriously trying to remain loyal to a king who has tried numerous times to kill you?" He leaned back in his chair. "I'm beginning to think your visit here is quite fortuitous. After all, I'm the heir, and you have the army."

Leo sipped from his goblet. "You never seemed this ambitious before."

Tedric suddenly leaned forward, his green eyes blazing with anger. "I've been stuck here for five years. I'm sick of waiting for the old man to die. All you have to do is take the army to Ebton, and he'll crater . . ."

"The minute I do that, he'll have every woman and child in Ebton slaughtered."

Tedric waved a hand impatiently. "You have to expect a little bloodshed at a time like this."

Leo inhaled sharply.

"Are you with me?" Tedric's eyes narrowed. "Or not?"

Leo had a bad feeling that if he declined, he and his party would be part of the bloodshed. For now, he would try to buy some time. "I'll think it over. Come up with some plans. We'll have to be very careful."

"Excellent." Tedric's smile didn't reach his eyes.

Leo stood. "If you don't mind, I'd like to wash up before dinner. And spend some time with my wife."

Tedric snorted. "Lucky bastard."

Not lucky at all, Leo thought as he left the room. They'd escaped one dilemma only to land in another one far more dangerous.

Chapter Thirty-three

❧

Luciana leaned back and closed her eyes, enjoying the tub of hot water and peaceful solitude. A week on horseback had been tough on her legs and backside. And it seemed like ages since she'd had a moment completely alone.

"Luciana!"

Not alone, after all. She opened her eyes and discovered her sister hovering nearby.

Tatiana huffed. "You're naked again. At least this time you're not performing acrobatic stunts in bed."

Luciana gave her a wry look. "Jealous, are you?"

With a shrug, Tatiana turned away. "I need you to get dressed. There's someone you have to meet."

"You mean a . . . ghost?"

"An important one." Tatiana waved a hand impatiently. "Come on, hurry! I'm your best spy. You should trust me."

"I do trust you." Luciana climbed out of the tub and quickly dried off. "And you're much more than a spy to me. You're my sister. And my friend."

Tatiana turned toward her with tears in her eyes. "Thank you. I'm sorry I've been such a grouch lately. I just felt a little . . . neglected." She sighed. "And jealous, too, I guess."

"Tatiana—"

"I know, I know. You're newly wed and madly in love. I'm happy for you, really. Now get dressed."

Luciana slipped into a robe that the maid had left for her. "Who is this important ghost?" She wrapped the towel around her wet hair to squeeze it dry.

"You'll see." Tatiana called out, "You can come in now."

As a spirit sifted through the closed door, Luciana gasped and dropped the towel to the floor. How could this be? She'd seen this man earlier, and he'd been alive. She curtsied. "Your Highness?"

Tedric of Benwick's eyes lit up. "Then it's true! You can see and hear me?"

"Yes." Luciana gave her sister an inquisitive look.

Tatiana nodded. "It's really him. The prince. I found him moping about the Great Hall."

Tedric stepped toward them. "I've been desperately trying to contact the living so I can right this terrible injustice. And now, thanks to the two of you, I have hope that we can succeed." He smiled at both of them. "You truly do look exactly alike."

Tatiana sighed. "Not exactly, since I'm dead."

Tedric tilted his head, studying her. "You still look beautiful to me."

With a small gasp, Tatiana glided over to Luciana. "Did you hear that? The prince thinks I'm beautiful."

"You are," Luciana whispered, then cleared her throat. "Excuse me, Your Highness, but how can you be dead, when I just saw you downstairs?"

"The man you saw is an imposter," Tedric explained. "And the one who murdered me. As far as I can tell, he can take on any human form. He masqueraded as one of my personal guard for several days, but when I discovered the guard's dead body, I confronted him, and he killed me."

"Then he took on your form?" Luciana asked.

Tedric nodded. "His kind is extremely rare among the Embraced. Most people don't even believe they exist. I've read of only one other documented case. They are referred to as Chameleons."

The door swung open and Leo strode inside, walking straight through his dead cousin. "There you are." He pulled Luciana into his arms. "Why are you dressed?"

"Leo—"

He nuzzled her neck. "It's been three days since we made—"

"Leo!" She pushed him back.

"All right. I'll bathe first. Is the water still warm?" He pulled off his shirt.

"We're not alone."

He glanced around. "Your sister again?"

"Yes. And this time, she brought company."

He winced. "Your mother?"

"No." Luciana gave her giggling sister an annoyed look. Even the prince was smiling. "This is serious."

Tedric instantly sobered. "Quite so. You must be certain that no one overhears the conversation you are about to have."

"I understand." Luciana ran to the door and peered out. No one in sight. Then she checked the privy and looked outside the window. The sun was nearing the horizon, and servants were lighting torches down below in the court-yard. No one was hovering close by to listen in.

"What's going on?" Leo asked. "Who else is here?"

Luciana drew close and whispered, "There's a problem with your cousin."

Leo winced. "I know. He . . . he's changed somehow."

"He's dead."

"No, I just saw him—"

"His ghost is here." Luciana gestured toward him. "The man downstairs is an imposter."

Leo narrowed his eyes at what was an empty space for him. "I—no, how can that be?"

Tedric nodded. "I anticipated this reaction. Tell him, when we were young, he called me Drick and I called him Frick."

Luciana repeated his words, and Leo's eyes widened. When Tedric told her more, she said, "When he was seven, the king broke his arm, and you asked him if he wanted you to give the king a little shock, but he said no."

"Not a mean bone in his body." Leo glanced toward the empty space as a glint of pain shimmered in his eyes. "Tedric? By the Light, man. What happened?"

"The imposter killed him." Luciana quickly explained all that Tedric had told her.

A knock on the door startled them.

"Leo?" Brody called, and Leo quickly let him in.

Brody was barefoot and dressed in some of Edmund's spare clothes. "I smelled something off, so I shifted so I could tell you about it."

"Shifted?" Tedric asked.

"He turns into a dog," Tatiana explained.

Tedric glided over to study him. "Fascinating."

Brody stepped closer and lowered his voice. "There's another shifter here. I'm not sure who yet—"

"He's the man who murdered my cousin," Leo whispered. "Tedric's ghost is here, and he told Ana everything. The murderer is masquerading as Tedric. Have you ever heard of a shifter who can take on any human form?"

Brody stiffened with a wary look.

"They're called Chameleons," Luciana added.

Brody winced. "We need to stop him. Obviously, this is part of his plan to take over the throne."

"Quite so," Tedric agreed. "And he'll get away with it since he looks exactly like me. In my opinion, the only way to foil his plan is for you to uncover my dead body."

"Where is your body?" Luciana asked. After he answered, she turned to her husband. "He and the dead guard are on the top floor of the old tower."

Leo snorted. "No wonder the Chameleon is having the tower sealed up. Brody, find Edmund and Jensen. I'll meet you there shortly." He turned to Luciana. "I want my cousin to join us there. And I need you dressed and by my side. As dangerous as this imposter is, I dare not leave you alone."

Leo tamped down on his power. The energy had been surging inside him, threatening to break loose, ever since he'd learned that his cousin had been murdered.

Now, as he strode across the courtyard with Luciana by his side, his mind waffled between shock and anger. Part of him wanted to reject the notion that his cousin could be dead. Not Tedric. He was a scholar who would never harm a soul. But at the same time, Leo knew it had to be true. The imposter had said things that his innocent cousin would never have said. That damned murderer.

Anger spiked so fiercely, Leo could barely control the power that begged for release. His skin crackled with energy and his hair stood on end. People in the courtyard scurried away from him with whispers of the Beast.

The stonemasons halted their work and watched with alarm as he neared them.

"Stand aside," he growled.

"Y-your Grace." Their leader bowed. "His Highness wanted this job finished by sundown." He motioned toward the setting sun. "It's almost—"

"Do you know who I am?" Leo removed his gloves and stuffed them beneath his belt. As he lifted his bare hands, sparks sizzled around his fingers.

The stonemasons dropped their tools and ran.

"You won't make any friends that way," Edmund muttered as he approached with Brody and Jensen.

"Wait," Luciana whispered. "Your cousin says you shouldn't blast through the stones. The tower is too fragile and might collapse. Then you would never find his body and be able to prove his murder."

Leo groaned. Right now, he had a need to blast something to tiny bits.

"Tedric recommends you use the door on the wall walk," Luciana continued. "It hasn't been sealed with stone yet."

"Very well," Leo grumbled. He gave Brody, Jensen, and Edmund a stern look. "Guard my wife well." He dashed toward the stone staircase that led up to the wall walk. Halfway up, he heard the imposter yelling at him.

"What are you doing?" The false Tedric glared at him from the entrance to the Great Hall.

Leo paused on the staircase. "As the Lord Protector, I have the right to inspect your defenses."

The Chameleon's eyes narrowed. "Access to the tower is forbidden."

"Why? What are you hiding there?" Leo continued up the stairs.

"Guards!" the Chameleon yelled at his soldiers on the wall walk. "Stop him!"

The nearest guard on the wall walk approached the top of the stairs and drew his sword. Leo used his power to rip the sword from the guard's hand and pull it toward him. It landed with a clatter on the step in front of him.

The guards on the wall walk backed away.

The Chameleon ran down the steps into the courtyard. "Guards, arrest the duchess!"

Leo tensed as half a dozen guards advanced on Luciana with drawn swords. "Brody!" He grabbed the sword from the step in front of him and tossed it to the dog shifter.

Brody caught it while Edmund and Jensen drew their swords. All three men surrounded Luciana as she held up the dagger Leo had given her. The soldiers paused in a stalemate. In the midst of his fear for her safety, Leo's heart squeezed at the sign of Luciana's courage.

"Only a simpering coward would attack a woman." Leo slipped his gloves back on as he descended to the foot of the stairs. "Or hide behind a false face. We know what you did, you murdering bastard." He drew his sword. "You're not leaving here alive."

With a roar of anger, the Chameleon unsheathed his sword and ran toward Leo. Slashing downward, the Chameleon attempted to cleave Leo's head in two.

Leo blocked it and pushed the Chameleon back. "You just proved you're not my cousin. Tedric doesn't know how to fight. You pathetic coward, you killed a defenseless man."

The Chameleon slashed again at Leo. He defended himself but fell back, pretending he was being forced up the stairs. He continued to hurl insults at the Chameleon to keep him angrily attacking. Near the top of the stairs, Leo jumped onto the wall walk and dashed toward the tower at lightning speed.

"No!" The Chameleon raced after him.

The tower entrance was blocked with a wooden door and padlock. Leo ripped off his right glove to blast the lock away. After keeping his power suppressed, too much energy burst out, and the whole door exploded, causing the tower to tremble.

Leo cursed inwardly. He needed the tower to remain intact until he located his cousin's body. As soon as he crossed the broken doorway, he smelled death. *Tedric.*

He darted up the spiral staircase as the tower swayed. A step crumbled beneath his feet, but at the speed he was going, it didn't stop him. The stench grew heavier as he approached the top floor. Behind him, he could hear the labored breathing and cursing of the Chameleon, who still followed him.

"Tedric." Leo covered his mouth and nose as he gazed down on his cousin. The body was stretched out on the wooden floor next to a guard. Blood stained their shirts where they'd been skewered through the chest.

The tower shook as the Chameleon sprinted up the crumbling stairs. Leo could blast him, but then, the tower would collapse on them both. First, he needed to make sure everyone saw Tedric's body.

He picked up his cousin and headed up the last flight of stairs till he emerged outside on the top of the tower. "People of Benwick Castle!" He stopped in front of the parapet that overlooked the courtyard and lifted his cousin in the air. "Behold Prince Tedric, murdered by the Chameleon who has been posing as him!"

The people in the courtyard reacted with shouts of anger and wails of grief. The guards who had surrounded Luciana and his friends lowered their weapons.

"Watch out!" Luciana shouted.

Leo glanced back just as the Chameleon charged toward him and shoved him hard against the parapet. The stone barrier plummeted to the courtyard below as the people screamed and ran to avoid being crushed. As Leo scrambled not to fall, he lost his hold on his cousin's body, and Tedric fell, landing on top of the rubble in the courtyard. Leo's legs went over the edge, but he caught himself by grasping onto a protruding stone that managed to remain firm. He heard Luciana's scream from below.

With a triumphant laugh, the Chameleon stomped on Leo's left gloved hand to make him lose his grip. But Leo's right hand was still bare, so he grabbed the Chameleon by the ankle and sent a shock wave through him.

With a scream, the Chameleon fell onto his back.

Leo swung his legs over the edge and hefted himself back onto the tower floor. From a crouching position, he reached for the Chameleon's leg to give him another shock.

The breeches were empty.

"What the hell?"

Suddenly an enormous eagle burst from the Chameleon's shirt and flew right at Leo's face. He fell back on his rump. Caught by surprise, he was a second late shooting out a bolt of lightning. He missed the eagle's body and hit one of its clawed feet.

The eagle screeched, then circled in the air to attack him once more. At the last minute, the bird dove below the tower, and Leo's bolt of lightning struck a section of the parapet. The stones plummeted to the wall walk, and the tower shook.

The eagle rose again, soaring above Leo. He ran toward it, releasing another blast of lightning. The tower swayed beneath his feet and he grabbed onto the parapet to keep his balance.

With a triumphant squawk, the eagle soared away. *Dammit to hell.* Leo clenched his teeth. How would he ever catch his cousin's murderer when the damned Chameleon could shift into anything? He didn't even know what the bastard looked like.

The parapet gave way as the tower began to implode beneath his feet. With only a second to spare, Leo leaped off the edge overlooking the moat.

He hit the water hard, but welcomed the pain since it meant he was still alive. As he swam to the bank, he passed some dead fish and realized his power had killed everything in the moat. With a muttered curse, he hefted himself up onto the bank.

Shouts drew his attention to the drawbridge where all the people were spilling out of the castle. His wife and friends led the crowd, and Luciana collapsed onto her knees, crying, when she saw he was alive.

"Don't cry." He slipped his glove back on so he wouldn't accidentally hurt anyone, then motioned toward the moat. "On tonight's menu, fried duck."

With a laugh, she ran toward him, and he caught her in his arms. "Leo!" She wrapped her arms around his neck. Then she pulled back and thumped him on the chest. "You scared me to death! Don't you dare do that again!"

"I was scared, too, that you would be hurt. Are you all right?"

"I'm fine." She ran her hands over his chest and arms. "You're not injured? The fall didn't break anything?"

"I'm not that easy to kill." With a grin, he patted his stomach. "This is pure muscle."

Brody scoffed. "Where have I heard that before?"

Leo smiled at his friends. "Thank you for protecting her. Are you all right?"

"Aye," Edmund answered, then bowed.

Beside him, Brody and Jensen also bowed, and behind them, the crowd of people knelt and curtsied.

Leo inhaled sharply as he realized the full import of his cousin's death.

He was now the heir to the throne.

Chapter Thirty-four

❦

Luciana woke to the sweet sensation of her husband caressing her breasts. Leo was curled against her back, nuzzling the back of her neck. She moaned softly as her nipples pebbled in response to his fingers.

"Are you awake?" he whispered against her ear before drawing her earlobe into his mouth.

"Barely." She'd slept only a few hours for they'd made love half the night.

He rubbed the hardened tip of a nipple between his forefinger and thumb. "I can't get enough of you."

"Mmm." After two and a half weeks of marriage, she knew that to be true. Her poor husband had grown up starved for touch. Not that she ever complained. The things he did with his fingers and mouth were magical. He seemed to know her body better than she did. He'd certainly explored every inch of her, and each time he brought her to climax, she screamed his name and begged for more.

She stretched, entwining her legs with his. He tugged gently on her nipple, and moisture pooled between her thighs. Good goddesses, she wanted him to touch her. She was as insatiable as he was. "Can we stay here for a few days?" *And never leave the bed?* "I'm so sore from all the riding."

"Poor, pretty bottom." He moved his hand to her buttocks and gently massaged. "I wish we could stay here, but we need to take my cousin's body to court. If we don't provide proof of his demise, then the Chameleon could impersonate Tedric again and claim that I'm lying about his death in order to inherit the throne. The king would probably believe him and try to have me executed."

Luciana nodded. "I can see why the king would believe him. What father would want to admit his son is dead?"

"Right. So we'd better take the body to court before it deteriorates any more."

"I'm so sorry about your cousin." Luciana rolled onto her back to look at her husband. "Won't you be safe once the king realizes you're his only heir?"

"I should be." His hand stroked her belly. "You should be safe, too, since you could be carrying a future king."

She wrapped her arms around his neck. "You mean future queen."

With a smile, he patted her belly. "I think our firstborn should inherit the throne, then the second can be the next Duke of Vindalyn."

"You mean Duchess."

He gave her a wry look. "Are you intending to give me only daughters?"

"Is that a problem?"

His hand slipped down to play with the curls between her legs. "They would, no doubt, be as brave, clever, and beautiful as their mother, but I do foresee a problem."

Her smile faded. "How so?"

"There would be no men anywhere on Aerthlan who would be good enough for them."

"Ah." Her smile returned. "Are you worried about becoming king someday?"

"Not as long as I have you." He stroked her gently, and she opened her thighs so he could make her squirm.

"You will always have me." She pressed herself against his hand. Already she was wet and eager to feel him inside her. "I love you, Leo."

He moved between her thighs as she wrapped her legs around him. "And I will always love you."

She reached for him as he slid inside.

An hour later, just after sunrise, they were dressed and ready to leave. Their party was larger now, Luciana noted, since her husband was taking a handful of castle guards with them to protect the deceased prince. A wooden casket was now carrying Tedric's body, and it would be taken by cart to Ebton Palace. The guards would also serve as witnesses that the Chameleon had killed Tedric in case the king tried to pin the murder on Leo.

As the guards loaded the casket onto the cart, Luciana saw her sister floating toward her with a happy smile on her face. She moved to an isolated spot beside the stables so she could talk to Tatiana unnoticed.

"Are you excited that we'll be at court in a few hours?" Luciana asked.

Tatiana gave her a sheepish look. "I'm not going."

"What?"

"Tedric asked me to stay here with him! Can you believe it? A real prince!"

Luciana's mouth fell open. "You and Tedric are . . . ?"

"We're just friends for now." Tatiana clasped her hands together and whirled in a circle. "But I do believe I am falling for him. Do you know what we did last night? We sat on top of the battlements over there and he pointed out all the different stars and constellations. You wouldn't believe how knowledgeable he is!"

Luciana smiled. "That sounds lovely."

"And I made him laugh! Especially when I told him his favorite constellation looks like a man with an erection. Tedric said I made him laugh more last night than he's ever laughed in his entire life."

"That's wonderful."

"And he told me the strangest thing. He thinks we are mistaken to worship either the sun or the moons because who made the sun? Or the moons? He believes there is one Creator who made everything in the Heavens. Plus every living thing on Aerthlan."

"Oh." Luciana blinked. "That's . . . interesting."

"I know! Ted—he said I could call him Ted—he's not like anyone I've ever met before. He wanted to read some of his favorite books to me, but he said he wasn't able to open the books or turn the pages, so I told him I would give it a try. We went to the library, and I did it!"

"That's amazing."

"That's what he said I was. And he's so intelligent!" Tatiana sighed with a dreamy look on her face. "I never realized before how attractive a smart man is!"

Luciana grinned. "That's true."

"I was such a fool." Tatiana winced. "I used to think it was brute force and aggression that made a man attractive. But that only means he's an ass. Tedric is a real gentleman. He kissed my hand and said I was so lovely, he was tempted to give up going to the Realm of the Heavens so he could spend eternity with me."

"Oh, my. That's beautiful."

"I know." Tatiana's eyes filled with tears. "So as much as I would love to stay with you and be your spy—"

"No, you must stay here. You deserve to have your own life. And your own love."

A tear rolled down Tatiana's face. "We'll come see you at court every now and then. Ted says he would be happy to provide counsel for his cousin if he would accept it."

"I'm sure Leo would love that." Luciana blinked away tears. "And I would love to see my sister. You've grown into a beautiful woman."

Tatiana laughed. "Better late than never."

On the way to Ebton, Leo surveyed the land surrounding them as he was accustomed to doing as a soldier, but this time, he also observed the sky in case the Chameleon was in eagle form, keeping an eye on them. After discussing the new enemy with Brody, Jensen, and Edmund, they had all reached the same conclusion. The Chameleon had demonstrated too much determination to take over the Eberoni throne. He would not give up easily.

Leo suspected that by now, the Chameleon could have already infiltrated the court at Ebton, perhaps taking the place of a guard like he had at Benwick Castle. Brody claimed that he could pick up his scent. Leo glanced over at the shifter, who was currently in dog form and hitching a ride in the cart. The Chameleon might also walk with a limp, Leo thought, since he had managed to scorch the eagle's right foot with a bolt of lightning.

As Leo surveyed the sky once more, his thoughts turned to what Luciana had told him about Tedric's new idea. One Creator who had made everything in the Heavens and on Aerthlan. The theory appealed to Leo's military-trained sense of logic and organization. There could be only one commander, or your troops would be in chaos. But if this Creator was real, why had he neglected to show himself to the people of Aerthlan? They could certainly use some heavenly guidance. The countries were continuously at war, not only with one another but also within their borders.

Leo looked again at the blue summer sky, and the way the sun sparkled off the Ebe River to his right. To his left, the rolling hills boasted green meadows and stately forests. The world was beautiful, a creative work of art. Perhaps the Creator had made himself known after all.

He pushed the philosophical thoughts aside as they reached the summit of a high hill and the town of Ebton stretched out before them.

On the outskirts, poorer homes lined dirt streets that were still muddy from the recent rain. The wooden houses had thatched roofs, and every bit of fenced-in yard was dedicated to growing food. Farther into town, the streets were paved with cobblestones and flanked with larger buildings of brick and stone, two and three stories high, roofed with gray slate. Along the river, small ships had docked at the numerous piers, and merchandise was being carted to and fro.

From their vantage point on the hill, he could see the town squares where merchants ran their shops and vendors set up stalls to sell fruits and vegetables. The streets and squares were crowded with people, and the noise they made sounded like a dull roar. They had no idea, Leo thought, that their king used them as hostages in order to keep him and his army from rebelling.

The bell tower of the Church of Enlightenment rose above the town, its gold-plated bells glowing in the sun. And just beyond the town, the outer curtain wall of Ebton Palace stretched for miles to encircle the enormous fortress. Inside the wall, the huge square-shaped keep overshadowed numerous smaller buildings. Attached to the fortress, a long bridge spanned the river with a wooden drawbridge in the middle for boats to pass through.

Beside him, Luciana gasped. "There are so many people. And I didn't realize Ebton Palace was so huge."

Leo nodded. "My family built the drawbridge over the river several centuries ago. Any boat that wishes to sail through must pay a toll. That was the beginning of the Benwick family's wealth and power."

She bit her lip and gave him a worried look.

He reached out to take her hand. "We can do this."

With a nod, she squeezed his hand. "Together."

Chapter Thirty-five

❧

Slowly they rode through town. Without his uniform, Leo garnered only a few curious looks. The townspeople were far more interested in the coffin being escorted by a few soldiers. As the people pressed closer, asking who had died, Leo worried that one of them would get too close to him and accidentally receive a shock. As nice as it was not to be feared for a change, he couldn't risk injuring anyone.

He motioned to his squire. "Edmund, you'll need to announce me, not as a duke but . . ."

"Aye, I understand," Edmund muttered, then forged ahead through the jostling crowd. With a loud voice, he yelled, "Make way for Leofric of Benwick, Lord Protector of the Realm!"

By the time Edmund repeated the announcement twice, the crowd had reacted with shouts of panic. Some ran away, while others pressed against buildings, watching with expressions of terror as Leo passed by. Uncle Fred had done a good job of making sure people feared him. The path before them was now clear, and whispers of the Beast floated through the air.

Luciana gave him a sympathetic look.

"I'm used to it." He motioned toward the fortress. "The news of our arrival will reach the king before we do."

Sure enough, when they arrived at the gatehouse, the guards there waved them on through. As they pulled to a stop in the courtyard, the king's chief minister, Lord Morris, rushed toward them.

"Morris," Leo greeted him as he dismounted. He'd never cared much for the minister. Morris, a former priest and spy, had been rewarded with land and a title. A scrawny man with beady eyes, he'd risen to power due to his willingness to do the king's dirty work. No doubt, he was the one who had dispatched the assassins to kill Leo and Luciana.

"Lord Benwick." Morris sketched a small bow. "I see you have brought the Lady of Vindalyn as ordered."

"Yes." Leo helped Luciana off her horse. "But my title is now the Duke of Vindalyn, and my wife is the duchess."

Morris smirked. "I would not press that matter, if I were you. Your recent letter to His Majesty angered him greatly. He was reading it again just moments ago." He bowed to Luciana. "My lady."

She curtsied. "My lord."

"I have urgent news for the king," Leo said. "If you will escort us—"

"In good time." Morris waved a dismissive hand. "The king is enjoying his midday meal at the moment and doesn't wish to be disturbed. He requested that you wait here."

Leo clenched his gloved hands. Not only was Frederic making them wait, but he was purposefully not inviting them to join him at his table. To be even more insulting, he was not having them shown to some rooms where they could wait in comfort. Unfortunately, it was typical behavior for dear Uncle Fred.

Morris motioned to the coffin. "Did one of your men die on the journey? You should have buried him—"

"I had intended to tell the king first," Leo interrupted. "As I said, the matter is urgent. I have brought the body of Prince Tedric."

Morris blinked. "That can't be. I saw him here at court just a few hours ago."

Leo tensed. "He was here?" When Morris nodded, Leo continued, "That was an imposter. The real prince is here in this coffin. He was murdered."

Morris gasped. "You—you killed him?"

Leo gritted his teeth, while Luciana huffed.

She glared at Morris. "My husband would never kill his cousin. Or any innocent man, for that matter."

Leo's heart warmed at the way his wife defended him. "Let me explain what happened." He reported all that had transpired at Benwick Castle, but Morris gave him a skeptical look.

"The murderer changed into an eagle and flew away?" Morris snorted. "That was convenient."

Edmund, Jensen, and the Benwick guards corroborated Leo's story, but Morris still looked unconvinced.

"Men who can shift into animals?" Morris scoffed. "Inconceivable."

Brody sat up in the cart and barked to get everyone's attention. When he shifted into human form, Morris shrieked and backed away.

"Believe me now?" Leo asked drily.

"Wh-what is that?" Morris pointed at Brody as he shifted back into a dog. "He must be Embraced, an abomination before the Light! He should be put to death!"

Brody growled, and with lightning speed, Leo grabbed the minster's vest and yanked him forward. "No one touches him. Understand?" He shoved Morris back.

With a huff, Morris adjusted his vest. "Hardly surprising

that you would surround yourself with abominations since you're one, too."

"He's the heir to the throne, you ass," Edmund muttered, then smirked when Morris glared at him.

Leo motioned toward the coffin. "Shall we open it so you can verify the body?"

"I'll inform His Majesty and send the royal physician." Morris scurried off to the keep.

After a few minutes, the royal physician arrived with some soldiers, and they pried the lid off the coffin.

"It is the prince," the physician said sadly. "We should take him to the chapel. Come." He motioned for the soldiers to carry the coffin.

After a long wait, six of His Majesty's personal guard arrived to escort them to the king.

"His Majesty wishes to see only the Lord Protector and his wife," the captain of the guard announced as he gave Leo a stern look. "And you must leave all your weapons here."

As Leo unbuckled his sword belt, Edmund drew near. "I don't like this."

"It's a standard request." Leo handed him his sword, then the dagger from his boot. "Don't worry. My power is my best weapon. And I'll have some help." He waved at Brody, and the dog shifter jumped down from the cart.

Luciana handed Jensen her dagger.

As Leo and his wife followed the guards into the keep, he glanced back to make sure Brody was trailing them at a safe distance. Once inside the keep, the dog shifter could sniff out the Chameleon, if he was there.

The guards led them up the grand staircase and down a gallery decorated with portraits of former kings and queens. Brody slunk behind them, keeping in the shadows.

When they arrived at the king's sitting room, the captain knocked and opened the door.

"We'll be fine," Leo whispered to his wife as he strode inside.

She followed, her face pale, but her chin lifted with determination. Brody dashed in before the door shut. Three guards remained outside in the gallery, while the other three came inside. Brody sniffed at them, and the captain nudged him aside.

There were already five dogs in the room, so no one objected to Brody's presence. But it seemed odd to Leo that the king's dogs were hovering by the door to his bedchamber. One of them whined and scratched at the door.

"You may speak," Frederic grumbled.

"Your Majesty." Leo bowed, and Luciana curtsied.

Frederic had aged since Leo had last seen him. There was more gray than red in his long hair and beard, and the skin around his eyes and jowls was puffy and gray. He sat at the head of a long table covered with platters of food.

The dogs approached him, snarling and growling.

"Hush!" He threw a ham bone in their midst, and they snapped at one another as they fought for the prize.

Apparently, Frederic had eaten his fill, for he tossed more food to the dogs. It was a statement, Leo realized. His uncle wanted them to know he'd rather share his food with dogs than with them.

Frederic scowled at him. "I hear you brought my son's body."

Leo bowed his head. "My sincere condolences."

Frederic snorted. "As if Tedric's death has saddened you in any way."

"He was a good man—"

"He was a fool!" Frederic ripped a leg off a roasted chicken and threw it at his dogs. Brody circled the group of dogs, sniffing.

"He was too weak to be king." Frederic took a long drink of wine, then slammed the goblet on the table as he glared at Leo. "I suppose you'll do well enough. At least you know how to make people fear you, Beast that you are."

"I would not wish to govern through fear," Leo said.

"Then you are as big a fool as Tedric. If the people do not fear you, you will have chaos." Frederic scoffed. "I should have killed you years ago."

"You certainly tried," Leo said drily.

Frederic barked a laugh, then gave Luciana a curious look. "So you're the heiress of Vindalyn. I heard you were pretty."

Luciana curtsied. "Your Majesty."

Frederic gave Leo a sour look. "So you helped yourself to the duchy."

"If I hadn't, I feared my wife and the former duke would suffer some sort of accident," Leo replied.

Frederic grabbed a knife off the table and threw it at Leo, but he dodged it with lightning speed. "You bastard. I ought to go ahead and kill you. With your freakish powers, you can never have children. Our line will perish." With a smirk, he filled his goblet with more wine. "Perhaps I should bed the wench for you."

Leo clenched his fists. "You will not."

Luciana looped her arm through his. "We are truly man and wife. I am already with child."

Leo stiffened with surprise and searched her eyes. Was she just saying that, or was it true?

She went up on tiptoe to kiss his cheek.

"She touches you and lives?" Frederic eyed him closely. "Then your power must be depleted. Guards! Arrest him! Arrest them both."

Leo pushed Luciana behind him. "For what reason?" He pulled off his gloves as the guards drew their swords.

"Do I need a reason?" Frederic laughed. "How about

this one? I'll feel safer if you wait for my throne in the dungeons."

Sparks sizzled around Leo's fingers, and the guards halted their advance. "As you can see, my power is intact. I will decline your offer of hospitality, Uncle. If you have no wish to see me again, I will gladly return to the army or to Vindalyn with my wife."

Brody suddenly barked and snapped at the king.

"Get back!" Frederic threw a goblet at Brody.

When Brody barked again, the king stood, his eyes narrowed on the dog shifter. "Guards, kill that dog."

The three guards advanced, but hesitated when Brody slipped into the midst of the other dogs as they all began to snarl at the king.

"Which one?" the captain asked.

"Why are they acting like this?" another guard asked.

"Dammit, I'll do it myself." Frederic grabbed another knife off the table and approached the snarling dogs. With a limp.

Leo sucked in a quick breath. There were bandages around the king's right foot. And the dogs knew he was an imposter. "He's the Chameleon!" He lifted his hand to shoot a bolt of lightning.

The guards jumped in front of the false king to protect him.

"Kill him!" The Chameleon pointed at Leo. "He's trying to kill me!"

"He's not the real king!" Leo moved to the side, trying to get a clean shot at the Chameleon.

"Kill the woman first!" the Chameleon shouted, then ran with a limp toward the bedchamber.

The guards advanced on Luciana, and Leo used his power to rip the swords from their hands. They drew their daggers and continued to advance. She grabbed a fallen sword and hurried to Leo's side.

Meanwhile, the Chameleon had rushed into the bed-chamber, followed by the group of growling dogs.

The captain swiped at Leo with his dagger. Leo dodged it, then tapped the man on the back. With a yelp, he fell to the ground and passed out.

"Cease!" Leo yelled at the other two guards. "I have no wish to harm you."

The door flung open and the three guards who had remained outside barged in with Lord Morris.

Leo lifted his hands. Sparks still swirled around his fingertips. "Stay back."

"Where is His Majesty?" Morris shouted.

"I don't know," Leo said. "The Chameleon has taken his place. Come!" He grabbed Luciana's arm and ran into the king's bedchamber. The dogs were scrambling around the bed, whining and scratching.

The Chameleon was nowhere in sight. Leo opened a door and peered inside. The privy was empty.

"Look!" Luciana knelt beside a pile of clothes. "He must have undressed."

Lord Morris ran into the room, followed by the guards. "What is going on? Where is the king?"

Leo pointed at the dogs. "I think you'll find him underneath the bed. The Chameleon killed him, then took his place."

Morris scoffed. "Then where is this Chameleon? How do I know you didn't kill—"

"We just arrived!" Luciana yelled.

"They didn't harm the king," a guard added.

While Morris peered under the bed, Leo went at lightning speed to check the dressing room and every spot in the room where the Chameleon could be hiding.

Morris joined him by the fireplace. "You were correct. The king is dead. But where is the Chameleon?"

The guards pulled the king's body out and laid it to rest on the bed. The dogs milled about, whimpering.

"The dogs," Luciana said. "There's one more than before."

One of the dogs dashed into the sitting room, his gait uneven from an injured leg. Brody gave chase, barking at him.

"That's him!" Leo ran into the sitting room, but the sight there brought him to an abrupt halt. There were two Brodys. Identical.

Luciana stopped beside him. "Which one is the Chameleon?"

"What the hell?" Lord Morris whispered as he entered the room.

Sparks flickered around Leo's hands as he tried to decide which dog to strike.

One dog shimmered, then shifted into human form. "I'm the real one. See?"

Leo tried to remember if the Chameleon had seen Brody's human form. Yes, he had.

The second one shifted. "No, I'm Brody!" He quickly covered his private parts. "Begging your pardon, my lady . . . Luciana."

Leo aimed a lightning bolt at the first Brody just as the imposter made a leap for the balcony window. The bolt struck the wooden frame and set the curtain on fire.

The Chameleon burst onto the balcony and leaped into the air as he shifted into an eagle.

"No!" Leo ran onto the balcony and shot a lightning bolt at the eagle.

Fire singed a wing, and the eagle screeched. It dove into the midst of town.

"Dammit." Leo didn't dare shoot lightning into the town. He'd set the place on fire and probably injure some people in the process.

"He's getting away!" Luciana cried beside him.

Leo banged a fist on the balcony railing. How could he track the bastard down when he didn't know what he looked like? He turned around and found one of the guards had ripped the burning curtain down and stuffed it into the nearby fireplace. Brody had helped himself to a pair of the king's breeches from his dressing room.

"You saw the Chameleon, right?" Leo asked Morris and the guards. "You agree that he murdered the king and impersonated him?" He didn't want any rumors starting that he had killed his uncle or his cousin.

"Yes, Your Majesty." Morris bowed low, and the other guards followed suit.

Leo swallowed hard. He was now the king.

Beside him, Luciana curtsied.

"Wait." He took her hands and led her down the balcony out of everyone's sight. "I don't want you to bow to me."

"But I'm supposed to—"

"No. The position will be burdensome enough as it is. When I'm with you, I want to simply be your husband, the man who loves you more than anyone."

Her eyes glistened with tears. "I'm so proud of you."

He shook his head. "I'm not perfect. I've made mistakes. I should have known the Chameleon would come straight here. I should have stopped him before—"

"How?" She rested a hand on his chest. "You're not an eagle that can fly by night. We left right after sunrise and came as quickly as we could. You mustn't blame yourself for this."

"I should have stopped—"

"No, the guards should have stopped him. That was their job." She touched his face. "My dear heart, you can't take responsibility for every evil act in the world."

He searched her eyes, then nodded. "You're right." He

took her hand and kissed her palm. "Are you really with child?"

She smiled. "I'm one day late for my courses. Too early to know for sure, but—"

He pulled her into his arms. "Have I told you recently that I love you?"

"I believe you did this morning."

"I love you more each day." He stepped back to gaze into her lovely face. "And I need you. I'll need your calm wisdom, your bravery, your love and support."

A tear rolled down her cheek. "You're the king now."

"And you're my queen." He kissed her forehead. "More than my queen. You're my heart and soul, and you will never bow to me for you are my equal in every way."

She sniffed. "Oh, Leo. I love you so much."

He pulled her in for a long kiss.

When he drew back, he became aware of loud, shouting voices. *Damn.* He'd thought he'd found a private place, but the courtyard below was filled with people cheering him on.

"Shit," he muttered.

Luciana laughed and gave him a hug. "It's all right. We just gave the people proof that their new king is not a Beast after all."

Down below, the people began to chant, "Long live the king! Long live the queen!"

Apparently, while Leo had been busy kissing his wife, the news had spread. "It won't be easy," he warned her. "There will be factions who want to kill us, and other countries that will want to destroy us."

"We'll be fine. We have good friends." She motioned to Brody, who lurked in the doorway, grinning at them. Down in the courtyard, Jensen and Edmund were cheering the loudest.

Leo nodded. "We have your father, Nevis, and General

Harden. A few friendly ghosts and an army on our side, too."

"And we have each other." She smiled, then glanced at Brody. "How did he know my real name? Did you tell him?"

"No, I . . ." Leo winced. "It's a long story. I'll tell you later. After I give you the crown jewels."

Brody scoffed. "You should have trusted her."

"What?" Luciana gave him a questioning look.

With a sigh, Leo glanced at Brody. "Do you have any room in the doghouse?"

Epilogue

❧

ONE MONTH LATER . . .

"I can't believe it!" Brigitta hugged Luciana as soon as they entered the privacy of her enormous sitting room. "Our sister is a queen!"

"How does it feel?" Gwennore hugged her next.

"Exhausting," Luciana replied with a tired laugh. "I thought the coronation would never end."

She and Leo had just been crowned in a ceremony that had lasted five hours. Afterward, he'd rushed off to his study for a private conference with General Harden, Nevis, and her father, while Luciana and her sisters had come to the queen's official sitting room.

"This thing is heavier than I thought it would be." She lifted the crown off her head.

"I'll help." Sorcha took the golden crown inlaid with pearls and precious jewels, then with a mischievous grin, she set it on her own head. "How do I look?"

"Queen Sorcha." Luciana curtsied, and they all laughed. "Do you know what is the best part of the coronation?"

"The jewels?" Sorcha placed the crown carefully on a nearby table.

"Having the beautiful new gowns ye gave us?" Brigitta

whirled around, letting the skirt of her blue silk gown swish around her.

"Knowing that ye'll have a baby in eight months?" Gwennore asked, her lavender-blue eyes twinkling.

"That is a close second," Luciana conceded.

Maeve looked at Luciana with tears in her eyes. "The best part is that we're all back together again."

"Exactly." Luciana hugged the youngest of her adopted sisters, and soon they were all hugging one another.

Brigitta sniffed. "We missed ye something terrible."

"No tears now," Luciana warned them. "We still have the ball to attend tonight. Have you been practicing the steps I showed you?" Her sisters and Mother Ginessa had arrived two days earlier, and Luciana had spent every spare minute with them. She had wanted to include them in today's ceremony, but Mother Ginessa had insisted they only watch from a balcony.

Maeve stuck out her bottom lip. "Mother Ginessa said we can only watch the ball."

"What?" Luciana gave her sisters an incredulous look. "But I had beautiful ball gowns made for each of you. And I thought—" She didn't want to mention it, but she had hopes of matching her sisters with eligible young noblemen.

"Mother Ginessa insists we remain hidden," Brigitta grumbled.

"Where is she?" Luciana asked.

"She went to her room," Gwennore answered. "She said the ceremony was too tiring, and she needed to rest."

Sorcha scoffed. "She's still keeping secrets from us. It makes me so angry!"

Brigitta sighed. "What is wrong with us that we have to hide away?"

Gwennore winced. "In my case, I look like an elf, and people will think I'm an enemy. But I don't know why the rest of ye can't have fun at the ball."

Maeve shrugged. "Mother Ginessa said we mustn't be noticed."

"That's ridiculous." Luciana sat down with a huff. "You're the four most beautiful women in court. Even if you hide on balconies behind pillars, people will notice you."

"That's right!" Maeve looked at Brigitta. "Remember that man that came up to ye during the ceremony?"

"A courtier approached you?" Luciana asked.

Brigitta waved a dismissive hand. "He was not tall and handsome. I have no interest in him."

"He was certainly interested in yerself," Gwennore said. "He even asked if yer name is Brigitta. And when ye said yes, he scurried away."

"Scurried?" Luciana asked.

"Aye, scurried," Brigitta grumbled. "Because he was short and scrawny and old enough to be my father."

Luciana tapped her fingers on the arm of her chair. "How was he dressed?"

Brigitta sat beside her on a settee. "A blue vest and cape, lined with gold silk."

The royal colors of Tourin. Luciana bit her lip. She suspected the man had been the Tourinian ambassador. But how had he known Brigitta's name?

Gwennore sat on the settee next to Brigitta. "I'm so happy ye were crowned as Queen Luciana. Now ye don't have to pretend to be yer sister."

"What happened to Tatiana?" Maeve sat on the rug, her pink silk skirt billowing around her, and Sorcha sat next to her in her new gown of green silk.

Luciana told them her sister's story.

"She found a prince!" Brigitta clasped her hands together with a dreamy look.

"Luciana did, too," Maeve insisted.

Sorcha nudged her with an elbow. "Leo's a king. That's better than a prince."

"I heard he's passed some new laws," Gwennore said.

"*We* have," Luciana corrected her. "First, we decreed it is no longer a crime to be born Embraced or a twin."

Sorcha snorted. "Well, that gets us off the hook."

"Exactly," Luciana agreed. "And we gave religious freedom to all the Eberoni people. We can now make the sign of the moons without fearing for our lives."

"Didn't that anger the priests that follow the Light?" Gwennore asked.

Luciana nodded. "Yes, but we disbanded them. The Eberoni are now free to hire their own priests who will actually care for them instead of spying on them. We believe a person's religious beliefs should not oppress him, but set him free."

"I like it!" Gwennore smiled.

Luciana smiled back. Leo's cousin Tedric had helped with that decision. Unfortunately, the disgruntled ex-priests were now ganging up with Lord Morris to cause trouble, but she didn't want to spoil the day with bad news. "So now you are free to live here with me. We can all be together again."

Her sisters exchanged sad looks.

Luciana's smile faded. "What's wrong?"

"Mother Ginessa says 'tis not safe for us on the mainland," Brigitta mumbled.

"She said we need to go back to the Isle of Moon in a few days," Gwennore added.

"And she won't tell us why!" Sorcha clenched her fists. "I hate that!"

Luciana's heart sank. She had so wanted to live with her sisters again.

"Maybe Luciana can tell our future," Maeve suggested. "She predicted her own. She could do ours."

Luciana sighed. "I don't really know—"

"Ye could try!" Brigitta jumped up and ran to the trunk that the girls had brought from the Isle of Moon. It contained their woolen gowns from the convent.

Brigitta dug beneath the gowns and pulled out a linen bag closed with a drawstring. "I brought the stones!"

"Excellent!" Sorcha jumped to her feet. "We can play the Game of Stones!"

Gwennore dashed over to the table, where she emptied the fruit from a brass bowl. "We can use this bowl."

"Let's play by the fire." Maeve headed across the enormous room, then stopped with a gasp. "Ye have a dog?"

Luciana's mouth fell open. Brody was curled up in front of her fireplace, fast asleep. She hadn't realized he was back at court. For the last month, he'd been away, hunting the Chameleon. The poor guy had to be exhausted if he'd slept right through their conversation and the coronation ceremony.

"Julia? Good goddesses, is that you?" Maeve ran across the room, squealing so loudly she woke Brody up. He blinked sleepily at her.

"It is you!" Maeve pulled him into a hug. "Julia!"

Brody growled low in his throat.

Luciana bit her lip to keep from laughing at the mortified look on the dog shifter's face. "His name is Brody."

"I told ye he's male," Sorcha muttered.

"Julia is too pretty to be a boy," Maeve insisted as she rubbed his ears.

"Wait a minute." Luciana frowned. "Are you saying you've met this dog before?"

"Julia was on the Isle of Moon. I gave her bacon." Maeve gave the dog a perplexed look. "Julia, how did ye get here?"

"Brody was at the convent?" Luciana asked.

With a whimper, Brody slipped out of Maeve's arms and slunk behind the settee.

Luciana snorted. Now she knew how Brody had known her real name. Leo, that rascal, had been dodging the question for a month now.

"Let's play the game." Gwennore set the bowl of Telling Stones on the rug and sat, tucking her lavender-blue silk skirt around her.

Luciana and the rest of her sisters sat in a circle around the bowl. Gwennore covered the bowl with a linen napkin.

"You should go first, Brigitta," Luciana said.

"All right, but ye should pick the stones for me. Ye're the one with the gift of foresight."

When the other girls agreed, Luciana reached underneath the napkin and gathered a handful of stones.

Eight, seven, blue, and gold.

"O Great Seer," Sorcha whispered, "reveal to us the secrets of the Telling Stones."

Luciana cleared her throat. "In eight months, you will meet a tall and handsome stranger."

Brigitta snorted. "Of course I will. 'Twill be yer newborn son."

Luciana shook her head. "You mean daughter. And I doubt she'll be very tall."

"Aye." Sorcha grinned. "But she could be strange."

Luciana swatted her sister's arm, then laughed. "Och, but I have missed ye all."

"There's the seven again." Brigitta pointed at the second numbered stone. "Does it mean I'll have seven suitors vying for my hand?" When Luciana nodded, she squealed with excitement.

Gwennore rolled her eyes. "Do ye truly wish to be the prize for some kind of contest?"

Brigitta frowned at her. "I wish to be wanted. Is that so bad?"

Maeve gave her a worried look. "Be careful what ye wish for."

Brigitta waved a dismissive hand. "'Twill be glorious, just ye wait and see. And the blue and gold stones, do they mean the tall and handsome stranger will have blue eyes and blond hair like me self?"

Sorcha snorted. "Aye, he'll be yer cousin."

"Or brother," Gwennore muttered.

Brigitta huffed. "That's not true! He'll be wonderful just like Luciana's husband. Right, Chee-ana?"

Luciana bit her lip as she studied the blue and gold stones. "They do not mean a physical description. These are the royal colors of Tourin."

Brigitta gasped. "Then he'll be a prince?" With a squeal, she jumped to her feet and whirled about.

Luciana shook her head. "I'm not sure. I'm not trained to do this, you know, so you shouldn't take this to heart."

With a groan, Brigitta sat back down. "All right, but it is fun to pretend, don't ye think?"

Luciana gave the stones a wary look. She wasn't sensing any definite details, only an uncomfortable feeling of danger.

"What's wrong?" Gwennore asked. "We only meant to have fun with yerself, but ye're frowning."

Luciana dropped the stones back into the bowl. "Ye're right. 'Tis only a game. And I don't need the stones to make a prediction I know must come true. You must all come back here when I give birth."

"Of course," Brigitta agreed. "And Mother Ginessa will come, too, since she's the best midwife on the Isle of Moon."

Luciana smiled, remembering how Mother Ginessa had been present at her own birth. Still, that feeling of future danger pricked at her. "I'll make sure you are safe on the journey. We'll send some ships from the royal navy to escort you here."

"How exciting!" Maeve clapped her hands.

Sorcha grinned. "I cannot believe ye have so much power now."

Brigitta took Luciana's hand. "Ye have the power to make it safe for us to see each other."

"And the power to change the world for the better," Gwennore added.

"Did ye hear the latest prediction from the Isle of Mist?" Maeve asked. "The Seer said a new wind is sweeping across Aerthlan, from the Isle of Moon to the Eberoni shore. And the first change in the New World is the new king and queen of Eberon."

From behind the settee, Brody barked his agreement.

Luciana smiled. "It's good to be queen."

Acknowledgments

Any author starting a new series is bound to feel a mixture of excitement and apprehension. For while it's exciting to embark on a new journey, there's always the worry that I'll be making the voyage alone! So first of all, I must acknowledge my readers. If you have joined me here as my travel companions into a strange new world, you are my heroes and heroines. Thank you! I sincerely hope you'll enjoy your new story.

While I do my best to provide the entertainment onboard, there is a team of people behind the scenes, steering the boat. My thanks to everyone at St. Martin's Press: my editor Rose Hilliard, her assistant Jennie Conway, and the art, marketing, publicity, production, and sales departments.

I doubt I would survive the writing of any book without my friends and family on the home front. My thanks to my husband, Don, and our kids, for always believing in me and feeding me whenever I'm under deadline. My thanks, also, to my critique partners, who have been with me for over seventeen books, scouring each and every page that I write and kicking my ass as needed. Miraculously, we are still the best of friends, and somehow, they manage to keep me reasonably sane. Admit it, M.J., Sandy, and Vicky: that last line made you snort.

In order to create a new world, I picked bits and pieces from our world that especially appealed to me. For instance, the setting for the fortress at Vindemar is based on the lovely castle of Dunnottar in Aberdeenshire, Scotland. My thanks to fellow writers/traveling companions Cathy Maxwell, Lorraine Heath, Elizabeth Essex, Deborah Barnhart, Denise Coyle, and Bonnie Tucker. Our trip to Scotland was magical! Thank you for sharing it with me. And my thanks to all the readers who came to see us in Glasgow! Meeting you was such a hoot!

The castle keep and catacombs at imaginary Vindemar were inspired by Kronborg Castle in Helsingor, Denmark. Kronborg, also known as Hamlet's castle, has a long history of providing inspiration. The castle's strategic location enabled the kings of Denmark to collect tolls from any ship entering the Baltic Sea. This idea found its way into my book, where the ruling house of Eberon collects tolls from any boat traveling up the Ebe River. Many thanks to Erik, Kate, and Stephan Nielsen for driving me around Denmark, showing me so many wonderful sites, and even venturing into the spooky catacombs with me. Thank goodness the passages weren't stacked to the ceiling with bones like the ones in this book. And luckily, we didn't run into any ghosts (that we know of).

My thanks to any new readers who are giving this series a chance. For all my readers, old and new—welcome to the world of Aerthlan. May it bring you hope, joy, and the comforting warmth of remembering those we have loved.

In another time on another world called Aerthlan, there are five kingdoms. Four of the kingdoms extend across a vast continent. They are constantly at war.

The fifth kingdom consists of two islands in the Great Western Ocean. These are the Isles of Moon and Mist. On the Isle of Moon, people worship the two moons in the night sky. On the Isle of Mist there is only one inhabitant— the Seer.

Twice a year, the two moons eclipse. Any child born on the night the moons embrace will be gifted with some sort of supernatural power. These children are called the Embraced. The kings on the mainland hunt and kill the young Embraced, and any who seek to protect them. Some of the Embraced infants are sent secretly to the Isle of Moon, where they will be safe.

For as long as anyone can remember, the Seer has predicted more war and destruction. But recently a new king and queen have ascended to power in the mainland kingdom of Eberon. King Leofric and Queen Luciana are both Embraced, so they have declared Eberon a safe haven for those who are born on the night the moons eclipse.

Because of the new king and queen, a new prophecy has

emerged from the Isle of Mist. The Seer has predicted a wave of change that will sweep across Aerthlan and eventually bring peace to a world that has suffered too long.

And so our story continues with Queen Luciana's four adopted sisters, who grew up in secret on the Isle of Moon. They know nothing of their families. Nothing of their past.

They only know they are Embraced.

Chapter One

❧

"I cannot play," Brigitta told her sisters as she cast a wary look at the linen bag filled with Telling Stones. Quickly she shifted on the window seat to gaze at the Great Western Ocean. The rolling waves went on for as far as she could see, but her mind was elsewhere. *Calm yerself. The prediction will ne'er happen.*

At dawn they had boarded this ship, accompanied by Mother Ginessa and Sister Fallyn, who were now resting in the cabin next door. This was the smallest vessel in the Eberoni Royal Navy, the captain had explained, sturdy enough to cross the ocean, but small enough to travel up the Ebe River to the palace at Ebton. There, they would see their oldest sister, who was now the queen of Eberon.

According to the captain, Queen Luciana had intended to send more than one ship to safeguard their journey, but at the last minute, the other naval ships had been diverted south to fight the Tourinian pirates who were raiding villages along the Eberoni shore. But not to worry, the captain had assured Brigitta and her companions. Since the Royal Navy was keeping the pirates occupied to the south, their crossing would be perfectly safe.

Indeed, after a few hours, it seemed perfectly boring.

"If we don't play, how will we pass the time?" Gwennore asked from her seat at the round table. "'Twill be close to sunset afore we reach Ebton."

"I wish we could wander about on deck," Maeve grumbled from her chair next to Gwennore.

Sorcha huffed in annoyance as she paced about the cabin. "Mother Ginessa insisted we remain here. I swear she acts as if she's afraid to let anyone see us."

"Perhaps she fears for our safety because we are Embraced," Gwennore said.

Sorcha shook her head. "We're safe now in Eberon."

But only in Eberon, Brigitta thought as she studied the deep blue waves. Being Embraced was a death sentence anywhere else on the mainland. The other kings abhorred the fact that each of the Embraced possessed some sort of special power that the kings themselves could never have.

When Brigitta and her adopted sisters were born, the only safe haven had been the Isle of Moon. They'd grown up there in the Convent of the Two Moons, believing they were orphans. But almost a year ago, they'd discovered a shocking truth. Luciana had never been an orphan.

Since then, Brigitta had wondered if she had family somewhere, too. Had they hidden her away, or worse, abandoned her? She feared it was the latter. For in all her nineteen years of life, no one from the mainland had ever bothered to contact her.

You are loved, she reminded herself. She'd grown up in a loving home at the convent. Her sisters loved her, and she loved them. That was enough.

It had to be enough. Didn't it?

Sorcha lowered her voice. "I still believe Mother Ginessa knows things about us that she won't tell."

Brigitta silently agreed. She knew from her special gift that most everyone was hiding something.

"Let's play the game and let the stones tell us," Maeve

said. "I need to do something. This cabin is feeling smaller by the minute."

Brigitta sighed. Sadly enough, this was the largest cabin on board. Captain Shaw had lent them his quarters that had a large window overlooking the back of the vessel.

The ship creaked as it rolled to the side, and Sorcha grabbed the sideboard to steady herself.

"Have a seat afore ye fall," Gwennore warned her.

"Fine." Sorcha emptied the oranges from a brass bowl on the sideboard and plunked the bowl onto the table as she took a seat. "Let's play."

Brigitta's sisters gave her a questioning look, but she shook her head and turned to gaze out the window once again. It had been twelve years ago, when she was seven, that Luciana had invented the game where they could each pretend to be the Seer from the Isle of Mist. They'd gathered up forty pebbles from the nearby beach, then had painted them with colors and numbers. After the stones were deposited in a bowl and covered with a cloth, each sister would grab a few pebbles and whatever colors or numbers she'd chosen would indicate her future.

"We'll just have to play without her," Sorcha grumbled. A clattering noise filled the cabin as the bag of Telling Stones was emptied into the brass bowl, a noise not quite loud enough to cover Sorcha's hushed voice. "Ye know why she won't play. She's spooked."

Brigitta winced. That was too close to the truth.

She could no longer see the Isle of Moon on the horizon. As the island had faded from sight, a wave of apprehension had washed over her, slowly growing until it had sucked her down into an undertow of fear and dread. For deep in her heart, she believed that leaving the safety of the convent would trigger the set of events that Luciana had predicted.

But how could she have refused this voyage? Luciana

would be giving birth soon, and she wanted her sisters with her. She also needed Mother Ginessa, who was an excellent midwife.

"I'm going first," Sorcha declared, and the stones rattled about the bowl as she mixed them up.

"O Great Seer," Maeve repeated the line they always said before each prediction. "Reveal to us the secrets of the Telling Stones."

"What the hell?" Sorcha grumbled, and Maeve gasped.

"Ye mustn't let Mother Ginessa hear ye curse like that," Gwennore warned her.

"These stones are ridiculous!" Sorcha slammed them on the table, and out of curiosity, Brigitta turned to see what her sister had selected.

Nine, pink, and lavender.

Gwennore tilted her head as she studied the stones. "In nine years ye will meet a tall and handsome—"

"Nine *years?*" Sorcha grimaced. "I would be so old!"

"Twenty-seven." Gwennore's mouth twitched. "Practically ancient."

"Exactly!" Sorcha huffed. "I'll wait nine *months* for my tall and handsome stranger, and not a minute more." She glared at the colored stones. "I hate pink. It looks terrible with my freckles and red hair."

Maeve's eyes sparkled with mischief. "Who said ye would be wearing it? I think yer true love will look very pretty in pink."

"He's not wearing pink," Sorcha growled.

"Aye, a lovely pink gown with a lavender sash," Gwennore added with a grin.

"Nay, Gwennie." Maeve shook her head. "The lavender means he'll have lavender-blue eyes like you."

"Ah." Gwennore tucked a tendril of her white-blond hair behind a pointed ear. "Could be."

"Are ye kidding me?" Sorcha gave them an incredulous look. "How on Aerthlan would I ever meet an elf?"

"Ye met me," Gwennore said. "And apparently, in nine months, ye'll meet a tall and handsome elf in a pink gown." She and Maeve laughed, and Sorcha reluctantly grinned.

Brigitta turned to peer out the window once again. Over the years, the Telling Stones had proven to be an entertaining game. But then, a year ago, something strange had happened. Luciana's prediction for her own future had actually come to pass. She'd met and fallen in love with her tall and handsome stranger. And if that hadn't been glorious enough, she'd become the queen of Eberon.

Eager to experience something equally romantic, Brigitta had begged her oldest sister to predict a similar future for her.

A mistake. Brigitta frowned at the churning ocean.

Blue, gold, seven, and eight. Those had been the stones Luciana had selected. Blue and gold, she'd explained, signified the royal colors of the kingdom of Tourin. Seven meant there would be seven suitors to compete for her hand. And eight . . . in eight months, Brigitta would meet a tall and handsome stranger.

The eight months had now passed.

She pressed a hand against her roiling stomach.

When they'd boarded this morning, she'd quickly assessed the captain and his crew. None of them had struck her as particularly tall or handsome. Captain Shaw was portly, bald, and old enough to be her father.

As for the seven suitors vying for her hand, she had initially been thrilled, considering the idea wildly exciting. But when her sisters had likened it to her being a prize in a tourney, she'd had second thoughts.

Why would seven men compete for her? She had nothing special to offer. Even the gift she possessed for being

Embraced was hardly special. And did this contest mean she would have no choice but to marry whichever man won her? The more she'd thought about this competition, the more it had made her cringe.

So, five months ago, she'd played the game again, hoping to achieve different results. But to her shock, there had been four stones in her hand.

Blue, gold, seven, and five.

Had some sort of mysterious countdown gone into effect? Reluctant to believe that, she'd attempted the game again a month later. Blue, gold, seven, and *four*. Alarmed, she'd sworn never to play again.

But one month ago, Sorcha had dared her to play, taunting her for being *overly dramatic*. Those words never failed to irk Brigitta, so she'd accepted the dare. With a silent prayer to the moon goddesses, she'd reached into the bowl, swished the pebbles around, and grabbed a handful. And there, in her palm, four stones had stared up at her.

Blue, gold, seven, and one. A fate was shoving itself down her throat whether she liked it or not.

And she did not.

Brigitta had been raised on the Isle of Moon, where women were free to determine their own futures and everyone worshipped the moon goddesses, Luna and Lessa.

It was different on the mainland. Men were in charge there, and everyone worshipped a male god, the Light. Luciana had been fortunate to find a good man who respected her independent nature. As king and queen, they had declared it safe to worship the moon goddesses in Eberon.

But it was not that way elsewhere. In the other mainland kingdoms, Brigitta would be executed for making the sign of the moons as she prayed. Executed for being Embraced. So why did she keep picking the blue and gold colors of Tourin?

And why would seven suitors compete for *her*? She glanced at her sisters. Sorcha had always seemed the strongest with her fiery temperament that matched her fiery red hair. Gwennore had always been the smartest. Maeve, the youngest, had always been the sweetest. And Luciana had been their brave leader. Brigitta had never been quite sure where she fit in.

Gwennore, with her superior intellect, had always been the best at translating books into different languages. Maeve had excelled in penmanship, and Sorcha in artwork. Luciana had been good at everything.

But Brigitta . . . the nuns had despaired with her. When transcribing a book, she could never stay true to the text. A little embellishment here, a tweak there, and eventually, she would take a story so off course, it was no longer recognizable. This, of course, upset the nuns, for their male customers on the mainland were paying for an exact copy of an old tale, not the romantic fantasies of an *overly dramatic* young woman.

Whenever the nuns had fussed at her, her sisters had come to her defense, insisting that her story was much better than the original. And each time the nuns tried to use Brigitta's *overly dramatic* mistakes for kindling, her sisters always managed to rescue the pages and give them to her. They'd even begged her to finish her stories about dashing young heroes, so that they could read them.

Brigitta adored them for that. She'd do anything for her sisters, including this voyage to Eberon when she was so afraid it would activate the events she'd been dreading.

She shifted her gaze back to the rolling motions of the ocean, and her stomach churned. Did a person's destiny have to be set in stone, in this case, the Telling Stones? This was *her* story, so why couldn't it be one of her making?

Surely she didn't have to stick to a text that had already been written without her consent. Couldn't she be the author of her own destiny?

"Ye should watch the horizon, not the waves," Maeve said as she sat next to Brigitta on the window seat. " 'Tis a sure way to make yerself ill."

"Oh." Brigitta turned to her youngest sister. "I didn't realize . . ." Her stomach twisted with a sharp pain, and she winced.

Gwennore gave her a worried look. "Ye look pale. Would ye like some bread or wine?" She motioned toward the sideboard and the food that had been left for them.

Brigitta shook her head. Perhaps if she sat perfectly still for a few moments, the nausea would pass. "Did ye finish playing the Game of Stones?"

"Aye," Maeve answered. "Didn't ye hear us giggling?"

Brigitta groaned inwardly, not wanting to admit she'd been too engrossed in her own worries to pay her sisters any mind.

"My prediction was the best," Maeve continued. "In four years, I'll meet a tall and handsome stranger with green teeth, purple hair, and three feet."

Brigitta wrinkled her nose. "Ye call that handsome? How can he have three feet? Does he have a third leg?"

Maeve waved a dismissive hand. "We didn't bother to figure that part out. But he is taller than most."

"Aye." Sorcha snorted. "By a foot."

Maeve grinned. "As ye can see, the game is nonsense. Besides, I have no desire to meet any man, no matter how tall or handsome. I plan to live the rest of my life with all of ye at the convent."

"Aye," Sorcha agreed. "I'm not leaving my sisters for an elf in a pink gown. 'Tis naught but a silly game."

"Exactly." Gwennore gave Brigitta a pointed look. "So ye shouldn't believe anything the stones say."

They were doing their best to relieve her fear, Brigitta realized, and as her heart warmed, the ache in her stomach eased. "Thank you. What would I do without ye all?"

The ship lurched suddenly to the right, causing Brigitta and Maeve to fall against the padded wall of the window seat. The oranges rolled off the sideboard and plummeted to the wooden floor. Empty goblets fell onto the floor with a series of loud clunks.

Sorcha grabbed onto the table. "What was that?"

Loud shouts and the pounding of feet sounded on the deck overhead.

"Something is amiss," Gwennore said as she gazed up at the ceiling. "They're running about."

Maeve peered out the window. "I believe we made a sudden turn to the south."

"That would put us off course," Gwennore murmured.

The door slammed open, and they jumped in their seats.

Mother Ginessa gave them a stern look, while behind her, Sister Fallyn pressed the tips of her fingers against her thumbs, forming two small circles to represent the twin moons.

"May the goddesses protect us," Sister Fallyn whispered.

"Stay here," Mother Ginessa ordered, then shut the door.

"What the hell was that?" Sorcha muttered.

A pounding sound reverberated throughout the entire ship. *Thump . . . thump . . . thump.*

"Drums." Gwennore rose to her feet. "The sailors beat them to set the pace. They must be using the oars."

"Why?" Sorcha asked. "Is something wrong with the sails?"

Gwennore shrugged. "I suppose we need to go faster. Perhaps we're trying to outrun another ship, but there's no way to know unless we go up on deck."

Sorcha slapped the tabletop with her hand. "Why do we have to stay here? I hate being in the dark."

Brigitta clenched her fists, gathering handfuls of her skirt in her hands. The prediction was coming true, she knew it. Her stomach roiled again, and her heart thudded loud in her ears, keeping time with the drums.

Thump. Thump. Thump.

The drums pounded faster.

Beads of sweat dotted her brow, and she rubbed her aching stomach as she rose shakily to her feet. "The fate of the Telling Stones has begun."

"Don't say that." Gwennore shook her head. "Ye cannot be sure."

"I *am* sure!" Brigitta cried. She'd had eight months to consider this fate. Eight months to prepare herself. "'Tis happening now. And I will not remain hidden in this room, meekly accepting a future I do not want. I'm going on deck to face this."